AKATA WOMAN

BOOKS BY
Nnedi Okorafor

Zahrah the Windseeker

The Shadow Speaker

Long Juju Man

Akata Witch

Akata Warrior

Akata Woman

Ikenga

The Book of Phoenix

Lagoon

Kabu Kabu

Binti

Binti: Home

Binti: The Night Masquerade

Chicken in the Kitchen

The Girl with the Magic Hands

Remote Control

Noor

NNEDI OKORAFOR

AKATA WOMAN

Viking

VIKING

An imprint of Penguin Random House LLC, New York

First published in the United States of America by Viking,
an imprint of Penguin Random House LLC, 2022

Visit us online at penguinrandomhouse.com.

Library of Congress Cataloging-in-Publication Data is available.

Manufactured in Canada

ISBN 9780451480583

10   9   8   7   6   5   4   3   2   1

FRI

Design by Jim Hoover   Text set in LTC Kennerly

To my mother,

Dr. Helen Okorafor

In the beginning there was a river. The river became a road and the road branched out to the whole world. And because the road was once a river it was always hungry.

—Ben Okri, *The Famished Road*

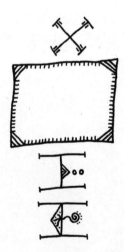

NSIBIDI FOR "LOOKING GLASS"

The road must eventually lead to the whole world.

—Jack Kerouac, *On the Road*

Even in palaces, there are spiders.

—Udide the Spider Artist,
Udide's Book of Shadows

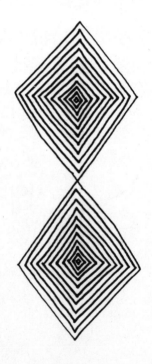

CONTENTS

NSIBIDI FOR "WELCOME"

ONYE NA-AGU EDEMEDE A MURU AKO:

LET THE READER BEWARE

Greetings from the Obi Library Collective of Leopard Knocks' Department of Responsibility. We are a busy organization, yet here we are again, on orders from the Head Librarian to alert you, to warn you, to help you be aware. Beware. Shine your eye. If you fear juju. If you are uncomfortable around powers that zip, buzz, creep, swell on this planet and beyond. If you don't want to know. If you don't want to listen. If you are afraid to go. If you aren't ready. If. If If. You are reading this. Good. This book is full of juju.

Juju is what we West Africans like to loosely call specific magic, manipulatable mysticism, or alluring allures. It is wild, alive, and enigmatic, and it is interested in you. Juju always defies definition. It certainly includes all uncomprehended tricksy forces wrung from the deepest reservoirs of nature and spirit. There is control, but never absolute control. Do not take juju lightly—unless you are looking for unexpected death.

Juju cartwheels between these pages like dust in a sandstorm, like a spider in the wind. We don't care if you are afraid. We don't care if someone told you not to read books like this. We don't care if you think this book will bring you good luck. We don't care if you are an outsider. We just care that you read this warning and are thus warned. This way, you have no one to blame but yourself if you enjoy this story.

There are places where you belong, where blood gives you access. However, they aren't always the best places to go. This book is about Sunny going where she belonged but maybe should have thought twice about going. It's about inherited debt, responsibility, and stepping up . . . when maybe you shouldn't. Common sense is a result of the truest education. Education is like wine. It takes time. It's a process. The young sometimes have to go through it . . . and sometimes they die trying.

Sincerely,

The Obi Library Collective of Leopard Knocks'
Department of Responsibility

1

HOLD ON

Sunny and Sugar Cream were walking again. Sugar Cream liked to walk. Today they were walking through the Dark Market, the shadiest part of Leopard Knocks where the shadiest dealings were known to be done. You could buy *chittim* with Lamb money here, though when Leopard currency was procured in this way, it acquired a telltale tarnish that lessened its value.

You could buy super-cheap marijuana here, though more potent, specialized marijuana could be bought at much higher prices in the general area. You could buy all kinds of dark, illegal juju powders, from "Liquid Jinn" to "Erasable Death Oils" to captive and trainable bush souls.

Sugar Cream and Sunny passed a woman selling night roses. One of the vicious thorny plants tried to swipe at Sunny, knocking her glasses off as she passed a bit too close. "Whoa!" she said, leaping out of its reach. "Geez!" She reached down and grabbed her glasses from the ground and inspected them for scratches. When she saw none, she put them back on, glaring at the plant.

"It's up to you to have your own back here, Sunny," Sugar Cream said, shaking her head. "Come on, student, don't embarrass me, *sha*."

"You're blaming *me* when *it* swiped at *me*," Sunny protested as they moved on.

"Blame is not of interest to me here. Pay attention. When you bleed, *you'll* feel the pain; the plant will feel nothing but satisfaction because it is unapologetically evil." She sighed. "Anyway, so people come to the Dark Market to bargain and deal," she said as they passed a man selling large black vultures with muscular wings. They stood on a thick branch and the one at the end watched Sunny pass as if it wanted her to die so it could eat her.

"When you need someone to do something for you that is not acceptable among most people, you come here," Sugar Cream continued. "Some of those requests aren't necessarily bad, evil, or illegal. I know a scholar who comes here because there was a man who sold an oil that left her hair smelling like flowers for months, even after she washed it. Couldn't find this oil anywhere else. I have my theories about where that oil came from. There's a reason it was so hard to find." She chuckled. "I like to walk through here once in a while to remind myself that all our faces are useful."

"Even that guy there, selling 'Six Million Ways to Die'?" Sunny asked.

The man had dreadlocks hanging to his ankles that were so neat and perfect they looked like cables. His large booth was packed with colorful bottles of various shapes and sizes; many had something undulating inside. No one was stopping to look at his wares . . . at the moment.

"In the grand scheme of things, yes," Sugar Cream said. "So, Sunny, you can glide fairly well now. It's useful, eh?"

"I wouldn't be able to sneak out of the house any other way." Sunny laughed. "I hear it's really hard juju to work." Gliding was one of her natural abilities, which meant unlike most, she didn't need juju powder to do it. To glide was to drop her spirit into the wilderness, shifting her physical body invisible. She'd make an agreement with both the wilderness (the spirit world) and the mundane (the physical world) and then zip through both as a swift-moving breeze.

"To glide as a natural is to die a little . . . and come back. And yes, it's *extremely* sophisticated juju to work for those who can't naturally do it. Since you've gotten so good at it, you can access something else. You already have . . . once."

Sunny stopped walking. Around them, people conducted

shady business, selling shady things, looking shadily at one another. The sunshine didn't even reach here because there was a tattered tarp shading the entire place. However, Sunny was focused on her mentor with every shred of her being. She'd been waiting over a year for this lesson. Ever since she'd done it once and been sent to the Obi Library basement because of it.

"It's called 'holding,'" Sugar Cream said.

And then all the activity around them stopped. Sunny's first instinct was to duck down. The lack of noise registered to her brain as the exact opposite of what it was. The silence and absence of motion was stunningly loud, jarring, terrifying. She looked around. The man with the vultures, the man selling poison, the women selling stacks and stacks of something that looked like blocks of cheese, all were . . . holding.

"Except you," Sugar Cream said.

"How are you doing this?"

"It is complicated and it is simple," Sugar Cream said. "I think it, want it, draw it to me. It's like grabbing a rushing river with both hands and *holding* it. It's like jumping on a road full of fast-moving cars and making all the people driving them see me at the same time *and* stop instantly. It is juju at its most intentional. It's not something I can use powder to achieve. It *must* be a gift."

Sunny didn't understand any of this, but she thought she could do it. That helped. She *had* already done it once. "Is that why you can breathe in this state? Because you have the gift? I nearly killed that Capo guy when I did it."

Sugar Cream nodded. "You can bring people with you into the rolling void you've created. However, if the person does not have the natural ability, it is like pulling the person into space. They will die within a minute. They cannot breathe; you have stopped all the molecules, their organs, everything."

"So I really *did* nearly kill him," she whispered.

"Yes," Sugar Cream said. "Thankfully, you didn't. Mastering holding is all about *control*, intent, and audacity. Stopping time takes a lot of nerve. If you are timid, you can *never* do it."

"If you have to focus like that, how long can you . . . hold?"

"I'm an old woman," she said. "I forget things, but my will is like iron." She made a fist with her bony hand. "I can hold for a *very* long time. It is not effort that maintains it— once you hold, it holds until you unhold. But to keep holding for more than a few minutes, you need to set down an object you keep. A talisman." She brought a white stone from her pocket. "It must be something very, very dear to you. I've had this stone since I was a baby. It's one of the few things I kept from the Idiok baboon village."

"You keep it with you?"

"At all times. If I wanted to hold for, let's say, the equivalent of three days, I just put this stone to the ground in a place no one would notice and make sure I know where to find it when I return."

"So you must come back to that spot when you return?"

"Yes. But holding for this long is not healthy."

"Why?"

"Oh, there's *always* a sacrifice," she said.

Sunny was about to ask what the sacrifice was, but something was coming. She instinctively moved closer to Sugar Cream. The noise was like an arriving train. When it passed by, everything continued. A soft breeze swept past them and Sunny smelled a wake of flowery perfume. She turned to Sugar Cream, grinning.

Sugar Cream laughed. "Stepping back into time is a breath of fresh air. And . . . it never gets old." She winked. "Are you ready to try it?"

Sunny nodded.

"Wait . . . your spirit face. Is she with you?" The pained look of concern on Sugar Cream's face made Sunny uncomfortable.

Sunny frowned, looking away. It was always so humiliating. Anyanwu left her often. So unlike a normal spirit face, Anyanwu spent more time going wherever she went than being with Sunny. A normal spirit face couldn't . . . *wouldn't* leave; it was one's . . . spirit. This was what it was to be doubled, a rare obscene condition for which Sunny had the terrible masquerade Ekwensu to blame. From the little Sunny could bring herself to read about doubling, most didn't even survive the trauma of the violent separation.

"Don't worry about it," Sugar Cream quickly said. "She may come when you glide. You can still hold without her, and remember, you have the advantage of having done it once already. Intuitively. That's good. Think back to that moment. Your anger. The Capo right there. How he led that confraternity to abuse, nearly *kill* your brother. Think about what you *wanted*." She paused. "It is the want. That is how you did it. Not the rage. The *want*. The power of it."

People were walking around them, and Sunny was distracted. However, she knew the look on Sugar Cream's face, too well. Excuses were irrelevant. You did it or you didn't do it. There was no in-between. She pushed away the distractions and let herself remember that night, that moment with the Capo. When she was so sure of what she wanted, and not knowing how she would get it didn't affect the clear fact that she would get it. In that moment, she wanted to isolate him from everyone and everything.

"Now *hold*," Sugar Cream said, looking hard at her.

With force pushed by the hot fury she'd felt from back then, Sunny thought the same word she'd thought that night, *Stop*. Unlike back then, this time she felt it. Then she felt Anyanwu fly into her. She stood up stronger, understanding exactly what Sugar Cream had meant by it being like grabbing a rushing river. It was less than a moment, but it was exhilarating and she *could* control it.

Everything stopped.

"Heeeeeey!" she exclaimed, grinning. "I did it!" A bunch of tiny gold *chittim* fell at her feet. *Anyanwu!* she thought, and she felt Anyanwu smile. It was a sweet feeling.

Sugar Cream chuckled. "Tiny *chittim* or humongous *chittim* mean pointed mastery. Well done. As you advance, I hope you're saving your *chittim*."

Sunny counted thirty-three. They were each the size of a fingernail and as light as one, too.

"The first time is the most difficult. This is your second," she said. "Now let it go."

Sunny imagined the river rushing forth with power and life, and there came the flowery gust of everything. She had the urge to try it again, and she did. Then she let it go.

"Don't play with this skill," Sugar Cream said, pointing a finger at her. "And keep it to yourself. Practice it, but alone. There is rarely a reason to use it. But when the time comes, you will. It's a powerful tool in your juju box."

Sunny smiled and said, "I know what I will use as my object." She touched the zyzzyx comb in her hair, the beautiful creation made by and gifted from her wasp artist Della. Not only was it dear to her, it was the most beautiful object she owned. The entire comb was made of tiny, shiny, multicolored zyzzyx crystal beads, even the teeth. It sparkled yellow-orange, but only when she turned her head a certain way; otherwise the many colored beads all together looked darker.

"Good choice. Your insect companion will be flattered."

Sunny laughed.

"Come," Sugar Cream said, linking her arm around Sunny's. "Why don't you buy me a bunch of those night roses with one of your teeny tiny *chittim*? My office spiders will like them, and they smell lovely at the stroke of midnight."

2
FOOT TO FOOT

After the day's lessons, Sunny needed to unwind. As soon as she got home, she changed her clothes and ran to the soccer field. Perfect timing; they were just starting. She'd been play-ing with these boys for two years, and they had an unspoken agreement that no one was to ask her why or how she could play in the sun. They were all Lamb and thus there was no way she'd ever be able to explain anyway.

All her life, because of her albinism, the sun had been her enemy. And then she'd gone through her initiation and all that had changed . . . magically. Some months ago, she'd asked Sugar Cream about it and she had responded to her question with a question: "Before you were initiated into Leopardom, before this mystical world opened to you, what was your greatest personal wish?"

Sunny didn't even have to think about it. "To play soccer out in the open like . . . like anyone else." Then she whispered to herself as she realized something, "I imagined I would be like a ballet dancer onstage. Dancing."

"Eh?" Sugar Cream asked.

Sunny only shook her head. "I . . . thought about it often."

"Sometimes things get caught up in the initiation," she said. "Especially when that thing is strong and deeply connected to what's being activated. There's a confusion, and within that confusion, yours became a gift."

She'd never been more thankful for a gift, accidental or not. Being able to run free in—and unburned by—the sun on the field fed her soul. There were times when she was so exuberant that tears came to her eyes. No one would ever know or understand. She wasn't supposed to be able to do this, but she was doing it. The boys around her would never know what they took for granted. And that was nice, too, in its own way.

Sunny was rushing by, dribbling the ball from foot to foot, dancing around the boys who tried to steal it with their fast feet. It was good to play . . . and not think about anything else. She bopped the ball again with the tip of her shoe and let it hit her heel. She smiled. Ah, there was the zone. It became a dance and the boys around her fell away. Distantly, she heard one of them laugh and say, "Damn, man, look at that! Wild."

Her breath was smooth and fast, everything around her was in harmony, every motion of her body a curl of water in an ocean. She could almost see the physics of her motion, especially as she felt Anyanwu come forward. Yes, Anyanwu was with her; she always joined in when Sunny played.

There was the goal. And there was her teammate Emeka. Her leg was a tool of physics on a cushion of mathematics. She sent the ball to Emeka, who grabbed it with his feet and shot it in the goal right past the goalie, who wasn't even on the side the ball flew through. "Damn it!" the goalie shouted, twisting and making a half-assed attempt to stop the ball already in the goal.

"Nice one!" she shouted as Emeka ran about, slapping hands with everyone. He slapped Sunny's hand and she laughed, turning to run the other way. As she did, a boy named Izuchukwu, who had recently joined their group, jogged past her and half slapped, half squeezed her backside. "Wish you were on my team," he said, leering. "I can think of better ways to play with you."

"What the—" She didn't think twice about it. During these games, there were no refs, just a general code of conduct agreed upon by everyone. And that code allowed for revenge when it was justified. She rushed Izuchukwu and, using her shoulder, knocked him to the ground.

She heard Anyanwu laugh in her mind. She stood looking down at him, waiting. He got up, glaring at her. The boys around her were quiet. She was glad he didn't try and come at her again. She'd already begun to feel guilty about knocking him down, and she knew in her heart that she'd have finished him if he tried her again.

They all continued as if nothing had happened. It was still a good game, though Sunny's shoulder was a bit sore.

At home, she spent much of the evening helping her mother prepare dinner in the kitchen. Today it was one of her and her father's favorites, ofe onugbu. Washing the bitter leaf was always Sunny's job and she hated doing it because it left a bitter residue on her hands that smelled funny. But it was always worth it; the ofe onugbu she and her mother made was flavorful every time. Robust with perfectly seasoned cocoa yam, crayfish, chunks of beef and goat, hot pepper, stockfish, the works!

As soon as dinner was ready, her brother and father appeared from wherever they were and gathered at the table. Sunny was always annoyed but also pleased. It was a funny feeling; she liked cooking and eating, but she liked that they liked eating what she cooked, too.

"Delicious," her father said as he scooped up more soup with a flattened ball of fufu. Her mother beamed. "Ugo," he said. "Have you finished your homework? What of your maths?"

"I hate calculus," he said, biting into a piece of goat meat.

"Only because it is mastering you," her father said. "*You* must master *it!*"

Ugonna shook his head. "No, I just don't see the point of it. I'm going to be an artist."

Her father kissed his teeth as he rolled a ball of fufu between his fingers. "Nonsense."

"Math is its own art, too," her mother said, taking more soup.

Ugonna groaned and Sunny laughed. They both had a point.

After dinner, Sunny retreated to her room and shut the door. She snuggled in her bed, her Nsibidi book in hand. She hadn't touched it for two weeks, at Sugar Cream's suggestion. Sunny could fluently read Nsibidi now, but she still couldn't control the toll it took on her. Sugar Cream's memoir, turned cookbook, turned sci-fi novella, turned Leopard history book, turned satire about the continent of Africa, turned memoir again was always an intoxicating read, no matter what it shape-shifted into. Sunny hadn't needed a "pleasure reading book" since she'd bought it.

"You should still take some time away from it," Sugar

Cream had said. "Read some Lamb books to give you and
Anyanwu a break."

And so over the last two weeks, Sunny had read two
novels. They were thought-provoking and immersive enough,
but neither had juju in them. And ever since coming into her
Leopardom, worlds without juju were worlds she wasn't very
interested in. Anyanwu especially found these books boring.
"They're not the *real* world," Anyanwu said.

Sunny opened the slim Nsibidi book and gazed at the first
page. The symbols cartwheeled, twisted, stretched, spun,
and wiggled around. Then they settled, quivering gently,
holding their positions. Today, the book had decided to be
Sugar Cream's memoir. Sunny smiled and flipped to the last
third of the book.

She always remembered where she'd left off, no matter
what narrative the book shifted into. Sugar Cream said that
one of the jobs of Nsibidi was to exercise and strengthen one's
memory. Sunny settled into her mentor's time as a student so
long ago. She felt joy every time the Nsibidi took her. This
was nice. But even as she read, a part of her mind lingered on
her friend Chichi.

Sunny and Chichi had both recently gone through some
things. And they'd each been there when the other had hit
that moment of strangeness. Chichi had been with Sunny on
that rainy day when a nearby car had backed over the shaggy
cat's tail. They'd been running to Chichi's hut during a

sudden heavy deluge when Sunny somehow heard it. Maybe it was because this large tabby cat had a low, almost human sounding meow that resonated over the noise of the rain, or maybe it was because Sunny liked cats and she didn't see many of them in Nigeria that were loved. Whatever it was, the cat's cries caught her attention.

"Wait!" she shouted, stopping. Both she and Chichi were soaked to the bone and she had to keep wiping her face to even see in front of her.

Chichi ran a few more steps and then turned. "What?"

They were standing beside the road and every time a car drove by, they were splashed. At this point, it didn't matter, though.

"Listen!" Sunny said.

They both did. And there it was again. Close.

"*Meow!*"

Sunny turned to the road to see a parked car with its hazard lights flashing. By its back tire was a tabby cat, soaked and miserable. The tire was on its tail. They rushed up to the car, Sunny going right to the driver's side window. Her concern for the poor cat was so strong that she didn't even fret about the cars speeding by so close behind her.

"Where's the car owner?" Chichi shouted.

"Dunno," Sunny said, cupping her hands and looking inside the car. No keys.

They both looked around for the driver. And on and

on the cat yowled and yowled. Minutes passed and Sunny couldn't take it anymore. She rushed to where the cat was and squatted down for a look. The cat hissed at her, tried to run away, and then continued yowling.

"We have to leave it!" Chichi said.

"No!" Sunny shouted back.

Chichi stared at her, not moving. "Yeah, we can't," she said, and began removing her T-shirt. "Maybe I can wrap it in my shirt and we—"

"No," Sunny said. "Let me try." She looked around again, this time to make sure no one was watching.

"Don't!" Chichi said. "If anyone sees, the council will—"

"I'm not," Sunny said. She threw down her soaked backpack and grabbed the side of the car. It was instinct and desperation. Certainly not realistic expectation. She set her jaw, took several breaths, then she pulled. And pulled. AND PULLED. Her shoulders flexed and tightened, her lower back clenched, her forearms constricted. She strained, nearing the end of her strength. Then she felt the car . . . *lift*. Her eyes shot open just in time to see the cat shoot off.

"You did it!" Chichi shouted. The cat paused a few feet away, staring at her in the pouring rain as if it, too, was shocked by what Sunny had just done. Was *still* doing. Sunny looked at her hands grasping the edge of the car. Its tire was inches off the ground. "What the hell," she whispered. She let go and the car bounced softly to the mud.

"What are you doing to my car?" a woman yelled from nearby. Sunny and Chichi turned and ran off.

In Chichi's hut, Sunny had fretted and fretted, pressing her hands to her cheeks. "What was that? How'd I DO that? I picked up a *car*! Oh my God, oh my God! A *car*, Chichi! And I haven't shown you . . . I just started really noticing. LOOK AT MY ARMS! Why?!"

She pulled up the sleeve of her T-shirt and flexed. Her biceps were slim but magnificent and rock hard. Chichi pinched the left one. "*Kai!* Na bodybuilda!" Chichi exclaimed with a laugh. "Sunny, you're a Nimm warrior," she said. "How many times do I need to remind you? That's what *happens*."

"But I just picked up a *car*," Sunny repeated. "For a *cat*."

"And the cat thanks you . . . Well, it didn't thank you, but that doesn't matter."

Sunny sat on the floor and brought her knees to her chest. She could barely do it because her lean, muscular legs were so long. She was six feet tall now. She pressed her face to her legs and sighed. "Whenever I get the hang of something, something else even stronger comes along and shakes it all out of balance again. This isn't even about juju or being Leopard."

"Nope," Chichi said. "This is blood."

Mere days later, the roles reversed. Sunny was with her brothers Chukwu and Ugonna playing soccer. It was evening and the sun was almost gone, and Sunny had been having fun . . . until the girls came. Sunny didn't even know their names. With her brothers, different girls came and went every week or two, following her brother Chukwu all the way from the university on the weekends he visited home. As if they couldn't bear to be away from him even for a few days. And they always brought a friend for Ugonna, which was pathetic since he hadn't even graduated from high school yet.

Sunny was watching them all walk toward Chukwu's Jeep when she heard a *pssst!* She frowned and then turned to the bushes on the far side of the soccer pitch. Was Anyanwu playing tricks on her again? She liked to do this at twilight when everything seemed strange. "Who's there?" Sunny asked.

"Me," a voice replied.

Sunny glanced back at her brothers and the two girls, then rushed to the bushes.

"Hey, where you going?" she heard Chukwu yell.

"I think I see an old soccer ball in the bushes," Sunny said.

She slowed when she reached them, chancing one more look back. When she turned to the bushes and trees, her temples immediately started throbbing. "What's . . ." Everything before her pulsed, soft and deep in the twilight. She shook her head and blinked. She squinted. Someone was crouching in there. "Chichi?"

Everything pulsed again, this time accompanied by a soft red glow that flared and then disappeared. Sunny felt it in her throat and at the bottoms of her feet. Chichi was curled up tightly, her legs to her chest, her head pressed to her knees. She wore a long red dress and, as usual, no shoes.

"Are you all right?" Sunny asked, stepping closer. "Chi-chi?"

Everything pulsed again and now Sunny could hear something in the distance . . . a flute? Sunny stiffened and stepped back. "Ah-ah! What is that?"

"Don't worry," Chichi whispered. "They're not close. I don't think."

"Who's not close?" Sunny asked, kneeling before her.

The leaves of the trees shivered, but there was no breeze. Chichi moaned and pressed her face to her knees again. "Do you have your mobile phone?" she asked.

"Yeah."

"Please, play some of my father's music."

Sunny paused, feeling hot around her neck. Chichi's father was a rich and famous Afrobeat singer, but he never sent anything to Chichi's mother and all Chichi had of his was an old DVD he'd given her. Chichi rarely spoke of him, but Sunny's father loved his music and had gotten Sunny into it.

"Oh, stop it," Chichi said. "I know you have his music on your phone. I've heard you playing it."

Sunny brought out her phone and played his song "Rebel with Five Causes." The song had a deep hip-hop influence and listed the five ways to cause trouble for Nigeria's government. Sunny loved the song not only because it was a great song, but because it had pissed off the government so intensely that it was banned in Nigeria last year. As the music played, it drowned out the distant native flute. The weird pulsing that kept happening synced up perfectly with the music, making the phenomenon more tolerable.

"Sunny?" Chichi whispered.

"Yeah?"

"I passed."

"Huh? Passed?"

"The second level. I passed *Mbawkwa*."

"Oooooh!" Sunny said, delighted. "Wow!" There were four levels of Leopardom. *Ekpiri* was the first and lowest, more initiation than anything else. Everyone went through this around five or six years old. Free agents, Leopard People who came from Lamb families and thus learned they were Leopard much later in life, went through it when they were older (as Sunny had). The second level was *Mbawkwa*, and those who were going to pass it typically did so around the age of sixteen or seventeen. Sunny had just turned fifteen, but Chichi . . . to this day, Sunny didn't know exactly how old (or young) she was.

"Chichi, how old are you?" Sunny asked.

Chichi only kissed her teeth.

"I was just—"

"It's not important," Chichi snapped.

They stared at each other for a moment. "What was it like?" Sunny asked.

"Not the same for everyone," Chichi said, pressing her fingers to her temples as things around them pulsed so hard that they could hear it over the music. "I . . . I . . ." She looked away from Sunny.

"You what?" Sunny insisted. "Come on, tell me. It might make you feel better."

"Will it? You'll think I'm—"

"Sunny!" her brother Chukwu called. "Who is that?"

Chichi looked at her and shook her head.

"Can you . . . pull it in?" Sunny asked. "Make it stop? At least until we get to your house?"

Chichi shut her eyes tightly and was quiet for a moment as a pulse thumped. She took a deep breath and let it out through her mouth. And gradually, the weirdness subsided. "Yes," she said, opening her eyes. But she was out of breath and looked more tired.

"C-can you walk?"

"Is that Chukwu?" Chichi asked.

"Yeah. Can you walk?"

"Ugh, yeah."

Sunny stood up. "It's Chichi! We're coming."

"Damn it," Chichi said, slowly getting up. She wavered on her feet.

"You need me to—"

"No."

They started walking toward the group. Sunny paused. "What happened during your level pass?"

Chichi paused and then said, "I talked to a masquerade. Why do they always come for me?"

Masquerades were spirits and ancestors who dwelled and danced everywhere, from the wilderness to the mundane world. Monstrous, beautiful, stoic, massive, minuscule, mad, genius, wild, each was its own universe, but all masquerades had one thing in common: They were powerful. Always. For Leopard People, they could privilege, curse, test, endow. If they chose to. They existed beyond time and space and life and death and could dance in all of it, too. Even in her short time as a Leopard Person, Sunny had encountered several masquerades. And she was *never* the same after each one.

"They always come for you, Chichi, because you've always come for them!" Sunny blurted. She pressed her hand to her mouth. "Sorry."

But Chichi chuckled. "It's true. I don't know what it is. I just want to always *bother* them. Poke at them. Irritate them. My mother says my grandfather was the same way."

After a few steps, Sunny asked, "What . . . did it say?"

Chichi chuckled and then said, "It's not what it said that's caused all this, it's what it did."

"What'd it do?"

"I don't know. But the moment it did, all this started happening, and all night last night whatever I touched, I could hear its . . . history. I touched my chair and I saw the tree sprout, heard it grow, felt it root, lived its life. It was *mind-blowing*! Thank GOD it's slowing."

They'd nearly reached her brother and the others when Sunny's heart suddenly flipped. She'd been so focused on Chichi that something more immediate had slipped her mind: the passive-aggressions that remained from well over a year and a half ago between Chukwu and Chichi since her friend had dumped him. *Wait a minute! This is gonna be weird*, she thought. They reached Chukwu, Ugonna, and the two college girls. "How far, Chichi?" Ugonna said. He took her hand and shook-slapped it. Chichi smiled, looking like absolutely nothing was wrong. Sunny marveled at the change in her.

"Ugonna, o, looking sharp," Chichi drawled. She turned to Chukwu, not acknowledging the presence of the girls at all.

Chukwu just stood there frozen, staring at Chichi.

"Hi," Chichi loudly said. "Are you all right? You look like you're seeing a ghost. I'm alive and well, *sha*."

Chukwu looked so uncomfortable that Sunny giggled. "Eh, yeah, Chichi, hi, what are you doing here?" He cleared his throat and stood up straighter. "Are you stalking me or something?"

Chichi rolled her eyes. "It's good to see you." She pulled

Sunny along. "Your sister is walking me home. Is that okay?" She moved on without waiting for an answer. "Have a nice evening." She waved over her shoulder. "Good to see you all."

"Slow down," Sunny said, laughing.

"If I slow down, I will fall over and this whole place will ripple and thump like a giant's heart," Chichi said.

Sunny strode along with Chichi on her long legs. "Ah, okay, you don't have to say it twice," she said.

"You still going on that date with Orlu?"

Sunny smirked and rolled her eyes. "I hope so," she said.

"Your parents are too strict."

"It's more my dad," Sunny said. "He doesn't trust Orlu."

Chichi snickered. "Nonsense ingredient."

"Totally," Sunny said.

The walk took only a few minutes and when they arrived at Chichi's hut, Sunny helped her spread out the bedroll she slept on between stacks of books. The room pulsed and Chichi sighed with the relief that came from not holding back the energy pushing through her.

"Where's your mom?" Sunny asked.

"She'll be back soon. She was at my initiation. She knows my . . . condition. She went to Leopard Knocks to get me something to relieve it."

"You were supposed to be lying down, weren't you?"

"It just got too weird and I had to find you. Sasha . . . I didn't want to burden him with this. He'll be too clingy."

"I'm not that nice," Sunny said, smiling.

"That's what I'm counting on." Once she had changed out of the strange red dress and was wearing her night wrapper, Chichi told Sunny to go home. "I'm fine now and my mum will be back soon."

"You sure?"

"Positive."

But Sunny stayed with her until Chichi's mother came home. In that time, the two girls sat side by side on the large bedroll reading. Sunny from a book called *The Book of Edans*, and Chichi from *Rain Queen Soft Juju*, both books that Anatov had assigned them to read for next week.

Throughout, Sunny kept glancing at Chichi. She hadn't said anything about it, and Sunny wasn't about to mention it until Chichi did. It was just below her neck, and it looked like a line that tripped into a loop and split into a cross, one half sweeping into a tightening coil. The coil tightened and released and wiggled as Sunny looked at it. It was still fresh, a raw and slightly swollen red, as if the markings had been put there in the last twenty-four hours. And no matter how hard she stared at them, they wouldn't come into focus. Did the masquerade give the coil to Chichi? When Chichi's mother came home, she looked over Chichi yet said nothing about the markings. Maybe it really wasn't that big of a deal.

Three days later, when she saw Chichi and the world

around her friend was stable again, Sunny noticed the markings had darkened to a rich black. And now she could read them clearly. They were Nsibidi and they said *Because the leopard does not speak, the moment it speaks, it becomes a woman.*

3

IT'S A DATE

Sunny had been looking forward to her date with Orlu for a week. She deserved some fun and she deserved to have it with Orlu. She really, really liked him. She'd never tell, but she kept three photos of him on her phone in a secret album. One she'd taken of him while they were eating lunch at school. Another was a selfie he'd taken of himself and Sasha when they were at Mama Put's Putting Place. And the third was a photo she'd secretly taken of him grinning at a large frog he'd caught in the rain. That one was her favorite. Orlu was a kind soul who understood so much about her and didn't judge the things about her he didn't understand . . . like being doubled.

"Please, please, please," Sunny had said last week to her frowning parents. They knew about her and Orlu, but that didn't mean they were open to it. "It's *just* dinner. Nowhere else."

"No," her father said.

"We'll discuss it," her mother said, glancing at her father.

"No," her father repeated.

They'd then called Orlu's parents. Orlu's parents had then warned Orlu. Her parents, mainly her father, had then warned her. And now here Orlu and Sunny were on their way to Mama Put's Putting Place, ignoring the fact that there were so many restrictions on their "date" that they barely had enough time for the actual dinner. Sunny was wearing her favorite yellow dress and Orlu was wearing jeans that Sunny had never seen before, a green flannel shirt, and white sneakers Sunny was sure he didn't want to scuff up.

Neither Sunny nor Orlu knew what the street celebration was all about, but neither of them complained. All Sunny knew was that it was the coolest thing she'd ever seen . . . even if she was about to be covered in dust.

"Let's go to the street party! We can go to Mama Put's Putting Place next time," Sunny said.

"Agreed," Orlu said. "But remember, we have to keep track of time. We mess this up and we'll never get to go out again . . . without trouble."

The dust started just after they'd crossed the Leopard

Knocks bridge. It billowed at them on a warm breeze as they walked up the path. "Whoa," Sunny said. Her dress went below her knees so she didn't have to worry about it flying up, but she did worry about it getting ruined. She tried to fan the dust away, but it only thickened.

"This isn't normal dust," Orlu said. "I can breathe it and it's not making me cough."

"Listen. You hear it?"

As they both stood there, they looked up the hill toward the Leopard Knocks shops and restaurants. Music was playing, live music. And there were lights shining. However, there was so much dust up ahead that they could only see a dome of hazy, colorful light.

All of Leopard Knocks seemed enveloped in a great cloud of music and breathable dust. They looked at each other, grinned, and ran into it. It smelled of honeysuckle. Dust devils swirled around them, blasting dust into the faces of those who stared too hard, and it did indeed dirty their clothes. Neither Orlu nor Sunny cared anymore. It was just too fun. It was indeed some kind of celebration—of what, Sunny and Orlu didn't bother asking.

Leopard People of all ages danced, sang, laughed, and ate in the swirls of dust. There was an energetic mosh pit near the band that was playing some sort of Afrobeat, hip-hop, and heavy metal fusion. Sunny jumped in and pushed around it three times.

There was one dark moment, though. The music was thumping and Sunny was reveling with all the other revelers. She had her hands in the air and she was laughing as she bounced in a circle with a group of teens. Then something caught her eye, some trees outside the party space, just beyond the lights and dust. She could see them because she was momentarily on the edge of the crowd. She stopped and moved away from everyone so she could get a better look. The music was thumping, a heartbeat rhythm that amplified the distant dread she felt.

The dust swirled and the music called her back. But . . . something was behind the trees. Something huge, hulking. The dust swirled thicker, hiding it. When it cleared, whatever had been there was gone. *Something that big couldn't have been there at all if it is gone that quickly*, she thought. But she knew. The thing had been the size of a small house. And maybe even had breath that smelled like burned houses. However, now it was gone. Sunny raised her hands and got back to dancing. Denial was always easier.

Eventually, Sunny returned to Orlu, who was sitting on a folding chair and eating corn on the cob. "Come and dance!" she said, grinning.

"No thanks, go ahead," he said, handing her a napkin to wipe the sweat from her brow.

There was a tent outside the bookstore that served wonderful party food, and Sunny sampled a bit of everything, including akara, roasted corn, puff puff, grasscutter and chicken suya, thirty styles of jollof rice, tainted pepper soup in bowls made of yam, and the sweetest pineapple slices Sunny had ever tasted. Orlu had offered to pay, but Sunny bought him another ear of corn instead. "You can pay next time," she said, biting into a hot, greasy, delicious puff puff. "Oh man. SO GOOOOOD!"

Orlu took the second of the fried, sweet spheres of dough from Sunny's napkin. He bit into it, grinned, and nodded. "I approve." He took the last one in the napkin.

What Sunny still couldn't process was seeing Sugar Cream dancing with some Igbo women in a circle, getting so low that it looked like she was threshing rice. Sunny had stood to the side with Orlu, grinning so huge that her cheeks ached. "Heeeeey, that's my mentor," she shouted, and Sugar Cream looked up at her, smiled, and danced harder.

By the time Sunny and Orlu emerged from the celebration she couldn't name, three hours later, they had full bellies and full hearts. All the stresses they'd still been trying to process the last two years, even from the last few days, seemed a thousand miles away. They were sweaty and covered in dust, and now that they'd left the festivities, they could see the moon high in the sky lighting the night.

As they walked back down the path, they found themselves alone, the celebration behind them. "Told you it would be worth all that trouble," Orlu said.

Sunny laughed. "You did, Orlu, you did."

"You had fun?" He took her hand.

"Yes!" she said.

They stopped walking and turned to each other.

"I still feel like I'm flying," Sunny whispered.

The breeze blew dust over them. Orlu glanced down at his extremely dusty shoes, and Sunny snickered and shrugged. She leaned forward and Orlu met her halfway. His lips were soft and his mouth was cool and warm. He smelled of dust, cologne. She ran her hand over the back of his neck as he pulled her closer. Were there leaves blowing in the dusty breeze? Was time passing? When the kiss ended, Sunny was sure there were shooting stars in the sky, even if there was too much dust to see them. She could feel them. A large copper *chittim* fell between them with a *thunk*. They picked it up and then stood looking at each other. Not for the first time, Sunny wondered where *chittim* came from and who decided when to drop it.

"You want to keep it?"

He shrugged. "It's both of ours."

"I know." She gave it to him. "Let's go home."

Crossing the bridge was effortless. Neither she nor Anyanwu gave the river beast who lived there more than a passing thought.

When she arrived home, she said goodbye to Orlu, something that took ten minutes and left her ears ringing and

clothes ruffled. When he was gone, she turned to the front
door. "Okay," she said. She shook herself. It was like waking
up from a dream . . . or coming back to Earth from soaring in
outer space. Everything settled right back onto her shoulders.
She had to hurry up.

"Okay," she said again, bringing out her juju knife. She
did a quick flourish and said, "Dust to dust." She shook herself and the dust on her dress, skin, and hair fell heavily to
the ground. She went inside. Her brother Ugonna was on the
family room couch watching TV.

"Sunny, you like to flirt with disaster," he said, laughing.
"Five minutes."

Sunny rolled her eyes and plopped on the couch beside
him. "On time is on time," she said. "What are you watching?"

"This animated film called *The Painting*," he said. "Ani-
mation and graphic novels from France are the *best*." He had
his sketchbook in hand, and his ink-stained fingers also held
his favorite pen. Sunny didn't look at what he was drawing.
These days he creeped her out so often with his unconscious
images of the Leopard world that it was better not to look.

"*The Rabbi's Cat* was really good," she agreed, sitting
back to watch.

"You should probably let Mommy and Daddy know
you're home."

"As if they didn't hear the door open and close."

He shrugged. "True, but it's all about respect."

Sunny nodded, getting up. "Fine."

"Yep."

She found her parents sitting at the dinner table, both eating bowls of ugba. Despite her full stomach, Sunny's mouth watered. She loved the spicy dish made from shredded oil beans. It wasn't easy to make, and her mother rarely did. Of course the day Sunny was out on a date was when her mother chose to do so.

"Hi," she said. "I'm home."

Her father looked her over and grunted. "Good."

"How was it?" her mother asked.

"It was good."

"Where did he take you?" her father asked.

"This . . . nice place," she said. "I ate more than I should have . . . but is there any ugba left?"

Her parents both laughed and so did Sunny.

"You snooze, you lose," her mother said. Her father chuckled some more and Sunny frowned. She turned to leave.

"Stop sulking," her father said, smiling. "We set a large bowl aside for you. You're just lucky you came home on time."

"Thanks, Dad," she said, grinning.

Once in her room, she flipped on the light. She glanced at Della's nest on the far side of her room near the ceiling. "Hey, Della," she said. "I'm home." She didn't expect a response. The wasp artist was usually asleep at this time, choosing to do its greatest work just before sunrise. Sunny had been up a few times when Della was in the throes of creating. During these times, Della didn't even acknowledge her presence.

She sprawled out on her bed and sighed contentedly, staring at the ceiling. "What a night," she whispered. She laughed to herself. She really, really liked Orlu.

NSIBIDI FOR "GOOD HEART"

4

REMEMBRANCE

Sunny looked around and walked faster. "This is so creepy," she muttered. She hadn't planned to come out today at all, *but* Chichi's mother only made Afang soup once in a while, and she wanted some while it was fresh. She stopped for a moment to look in her Tupperware container of soup. She sniffed it and grinned. So rich in perfectly chopped and cooked water leaves, shrimp, and hot spices. Chichi's mother still used palm oil, unlike her mother, who'd replaced it with healthier, less tasty olive oil. She closed the container, coming back to herself, remembering it wasn't a good time to be outside. She rushed on.

It was the middle of the day, yet the streets were empty.

The markets, banks, and schools were all closed. There was a big pro-Biafra demonstration today, highlighting the day the Igbo people declared the region its own country, the Republic of Biafra, remembering Biafran soldiers and civilians who died during the resulting civil war and protesting the fact that discrimination against Igbo people was still happening decades later. There were large pro-Biafra secessionist gatherings in the town square. Local authorities had warned against street violence, and security forces were on patrol.

Before entering her gate, Sunny turned to look at the quiet street one more time. There was not a soul outside, not a vehicle on the road. "So apocalyptic," she said. She squinted at a shadowy alley between two houses across the street. For a moment, she thought she saw something in the shadows. She shuddered and quickly went inside. When she opened the door, her mother peeked from the living room, her phone in hand. "Oh, thank *God* you're back. Did you see your father out there?"

"No. Why is—"

"Did you hear anything?"

"It's a ghost town out there, Mom," Sunny said. "Not even cars on the road."

"That's not what I'm seeing on Twitter," her mother said, looking at her phone and scrolling.

Sunny wasn't on Twitter much. She had an account, but she barely had any followers, and she only followed an account that liked to post about masquerades, a few media sources, Chichi's father, her parents, and the singer Rihanna. Being a Leopard Person put social media to such shame; there was just no contest between a virtual world of smoke and mirrors and working real juju, encountering actual spirits, exploring a world bigger than . . . the *world*! Sunny barely cared about anything she saw online anymore. Still, social media had its uses, like keeping her up to date on what was happening around the Lamb world and at home.

"It's getting scary," her mother said, going back into the living room, where the TV blared. Sunny followed her in.

"Today's peaceful demonstrations seem to have deteriorated into riots," the newscaster was saying. She was a safe distance away, but even from there you could hear the chaos and the crackle of gunfire.

"Oh my God, where is your father?" Sunny's mother shouted, throwing her phone on the couch. Sunny looked at her own phone, suddenly very anxious. She clicked onto her Instagram account. She'd never posted there, but it was good for quietly stalking her brother Chukwu. All he'd posted today was a video of himself bouncing his huge pectoral muscles as he smirked into the camera and drawled "Thug Life."

"Ugonna didn't go, right?" Sunny asked.

"No, he's in his room with his friends playing video games," her mother said. She sat on the couch, staring at the TV. Sunny sat beside her, stiff and worried, too.

When the front door opened a half hour later, they both jumped up. Her father and his brother Chibuzo were covered in dust and smelled like smoke. "Lock it!" her father shouted. "Lock it!" Chibuzo fumbled with the door as her father sat right there on the hallway floor, coughing and coughing. Her brother came rushing out of his bedroom with his friends and they stood there staring.

"Ugonna, get us some beer!" her father said. When he looked up, Sunny gasped. His still-tearing eyes were so bloodshot they looked as if they were bleeding. "They threw tear gas!"

Uncle Chibuzo sat down beside him, also coughing. He rubbed his hands over his hair and dust and dirt flew everywhere, pebbles clattering on the tiles. He looked at Sunny's mother. "I don't know who gave the order or when, just—" He coughed and hacked. "Everything, chaos. *Kai!*" Cough. "Beating, kicking, men, women, their feet found whomever they could reach." Cough. "They don't *treat* us like citizens, why fight so hard to *keep* us as citizens?" He hacked loudly, pounding on his chest.

"Here, here!" her mother said, taking the beer and towels from Ugonna and handing them to her father.

He opened the beer bottle with his teeth and drank deeply. Uncle Chibuzo was wildly wiping his face, his eyes flooded with tears. "Nnaemeka! They shot and beat him, o! And they shot three other men! They didn't even *care*! Like we were animals!"

"Nnaemeka?" Sunny said. "Orlu's uncle?"

Her father glanced at Sunny. He looked at her mother, who said nothing. "Yes," he said, coughing. "He's dead."

Sunny felt dizzy. Orlu had told her he was going with his father, too. "Was . . . was Orlu—"

"Sunny, go and soak two washcloths in milk," her mother quickly said. "They need to get this poison out of their eyes *now*." She pushed Sunny up the hallway. Sunny stumbled, but reluctantly rushed to the closet to get the towels. By the time she returned with the milk-soaked washcloths, four more of her father's friends had entered the house, and there was no chance to ask her question again. Sunny felt she would go mad with worry. By sundown, the house was packed with her father's friends and their wives and girlfriends who had been at the demonstrations, too. Sunny slipped out the back of the house, skirted around all the parked cars in the driveway, through the compound gate, and up the street. She moved swiftly, not giving even a glance to the alley across the street or anywhere else someone might hide or be waiting for her.

"Oh, thank goodness!" she gasped, rushing to Orlu. He was where she'd hoped with all her heart he'd be, on the steps of the front door of his house. And his eyes were red, too.

"Sunny," he said. "What are you doing here?"

"Are you okay?" she asked, slowly sitting beside him. He smelled like smoke.

He shook his head and stared blankly at the ground. She put an arm around him and they sat like that for a while.

"Today is a bad, bad, *bad* day," he finally said. "It was a good day on May thirtieth, 1967." He looked at Sunny and waited.

"I know," she said. "May thirtieth, 1967, was the day General Ojukwu declared the Republic of Biafra. The Igbo people had their own country, were free of Nigeria . . . for a little while. I know my history, too."

Satisfied, Orlu gave a small smile and shrugged. "Can't blame me for wondering how much you knew."

"Nigerian Americans have Nigerian parents and grand-parents who talk about the Biafran Civil War," she said. "I read up on it all myself because I got sick of not understand-ing the context of stuff."

Orlu nodded. Then the smile dropped from his face and he sighed. "Today it was bad."

"What . . . what happened?"

"I was there," he said.

"I know." He'd told her he was going. Orlu's grandfather and several of his granduncles and aunts on his Lamb side of the family had died in the Biafran Civil War. Igbo people had suffered discrimination in Nigeria since. It was a phenome-non that permeated the very political, social, and economic systems of the country. Over the last year, Orlu had grown more and more into a supporter of the pro-Biafran movement.

"My father had me work a protective juju around me. I was annoyed at the time; you can't really feel part of the crowd that way, you know?"

Sunny nodded. Protective jujus kept people a foot away at all times. It must have felt weird to Orlu, standing in the crowd.

"We were chanting 'The zoo must fall!' and 'No Biafra, no peace!' We all felt so *strong* and confident." He paused, frowning, clenching his fist. "The police were there, but they couldn't do anything. We faced them, *shouted* at them. There was a woman I see all the time; she sells pure water on the street, so quiet. *She* was even shouting!" He smiled, remembering. "Then . . . then I don't know what happened or who started it. There was pushing first. People bouncing off me like they'd hit a wall. I stood my ground. Then the tear gas and then *shooting*! No one could see who was doing what; that's why they could shoot! I . . . saw my uncle Nnaemeka, he was right in front of me. He had a handkerchief and he used it to pick up a smoking can of tear gas and throw it back at the—" He gasped, wringing his hands. He got up and started pacing. Then he stopped and looked at Sunny, his red eyes wide.

"They shot him," Sunny whispered.

Orlu nodded. "And rushed him and started beating him when he fell. They dragged him off like a sack of garbage . . ."

His uncle hadn't just been shot and dragged off; his uncle was dead. Her father had said so. Sunny wasn't about to tell Orlu. He would find out soon enough, let him have these last few minutes of not knowing. Orlu hit a fist to his leg. "It's wrong! The way they treat us is *wrong*. The ways they've *been* treating us. There is a Leopard faction of IPOB and my uncles are part of it."

Sunny grimaced. "Oh no." The IPOB, Indigenous People of Biafra, was the political group leading the protests. It was very active and very aggressive. Sunny appreciated their movement, but they often pushed to violence.

"Oh yes," Orlu said, a dark look on his face. "Leopard Igbos can do a lot to obtain the Biafra we all seek."

"Secession from Nigeria would turn so much upside down," Sunny said.

Orlu sighed, deflated and tired. "I know," he said. "I'm not *all* for it. I just . . . like the thought. It's *doing* something, *saying* something, not just sitting in the pit as if all this is okay."

"It'll lead to more trouble."

"There's trouble already," he said.

Sunny looked at him, worried. This was exactly the kind of thinking and feeling that led down a dark, dark, blood-soaked path.

He sat back down beside her. "Tear gas feels like acid and smells like vinegar. Taiwo calls it the devil's perfume."

"Taiwo was here?"

"He was at the riot," Orlu said. "Until he wasn't. Came to my house later."

Sunny wondered how much worse the riots would have

been if Leopard People hadn't been there. But then again, some of the police may have been Leopard People, too.

"You know what doesn't smell like vinegar?" she asked. She brought out her juju knife, did a flourish, and *paff!* a minty, fresh, yet smoky herbal smell burst around them. "Lavender." Orlu's favorite scent.

They both sat sniffing the lovely smell of flowers, and for a time, Sunny hoped Orlu forgot the smell of tear gas, politics, and death.

5

ALL THINGS CONSIDERED

The dark was warm and cozy and good. She had studying to do, but not right now. She and Chichi had to do what Udide asked, but not right now. She'd been dragged into the water by the river and lake monsters, but she didn't have to think about that now. She still had flashbacks of Ekwensu, but not right now. She had broken kola nut with the supreme deity Chukwu itself and she'd told no one about it afterward, but she didn't have to carry that heavy secret right now. And things between her and Anyanwu were . . . weird, but right now, she didn't worry about it. She sighed, relaxing more into the moment.

"Sunny! Sunny!"

The darkness was warm and cozy and good. Recharging. Sunny rolled over in her bed, the blanket a welcome weight over her head.

"Sunny!"

Her eyes flew open. "Chichi? What?" Before she knew what she was doing, she was on her feet and stumbling to the window. She was sure of it. It was time. Udide had come to demand they go and find what had been stolen from her. "Damn it," she muttered. She looked down at Chichi. "Is it—"

"Come outside!" Chichi said.

She felt dizzy with foreboding as she put on some jean shorts, a long sleeve T-shirt, and gym shoes. "Not ready, not ready, not ready," she muttered to herself. But at the same time, she felt a bit relieved. At least the wait was over. Avoiding the scary thing is often just as disturbing as facing it. But, man, she did NOT want to see that giant spider with the breath that smelled like burning houses . . . who wasn't really a spider. She sprayed herself with mosquito repellent because she was too stressed to remember the juju. She put her juju knife in her pocket, walked back to the window, and looked down. Chichi looked up at her and Sunny couldn't quite make out her face in the dim light from the side of the house. Were her cheeks wet?

"You all right?"

"Hurry down. It's important."

Sunny turned and glided through the keyhole of the front door. When she emerged outside, she was already running to the back of the house.

"What is it?" she asked, her heart slamming in her chest. They were standing near the large tree that grew beside her window.

"Sorry," Chichi whispered. She wiped her face with a handkerchief she brought from her pocket. "He's fine now. It was just . . . weird."

Sunny blinked. "Huh? Who?"

Chichi blew her nose, and when she looked up at Sunny, she was more composed. "Sasha."

"Ooooh," Sunny said, understanding flooding her mind. This wasn't about Udide at all. And this was something . . . good. "Sasha passed *Mbawkwa*?" Sunny looked back at her house. She hadn't checked her mobile phone, but she knew it was at least past two A.M. "Where is he?"

"At Orlu's place."

"Let's go."

It was a hot evening, and all the night creatures were excited by the heat. The crickets, katydids, mosquitos, frogs, and night birds were too loud, something was shaking a nearby bush, and an owl screamed from the treetops. They leapt over a gutter and moved quickly down the street. Just before they reached the gate in front of Orlu's house, Chichi stopped Sunny and said, "He disappeared. For five minutes, Anatov said. Completely. *Poof*, gone."

"What does that mean??" Sunny asked.

"During the test, there's a moment where you call out, and someone responds. For me, it wasn't the one Anatov expected to respond, and, well, it wasn't for Sasha, either."

"You mean a masquerade responded?" Sunny asked. Immediately, she felt anxious. She remembered what happened with Chichi, and it took days for the effect to stop. Chichi couldn't cross into Leopard Knocks until her mother was sure she was no longer experiencing it.

"No. Not a masquerade like I had. Let him tell you. He asked me to come get you."

They knocked on the door and Orlu immediately answered, looking worried. "Good," he said, when he saw Sunny. "Come in."

The house was dark and quiet. Orlu's parents were sitting on the couch in a dark living room with Chichi's mother. "Sorry, Sunny," Orlu's mother said.

"It's fine," Sunny said. "He's in there?"

They nodded.

"Did they call his parents?" Sunny asked Chichi.

"They'll be here in a few hours."

Sasha's parents were coming from Chicago, and Sunny wanted to ask exactly how Leopard People traveled internationally if not by plane. However, she was already stepping into the room where Sasha was staying and everything suddenly began throbbing.

It was as it had been with Chichi, and Sunny wasn't sure

how long she could stand it. Being indoors when it was happening seemed to make everything worse. "Why don't we go outside?" Sunny asked.

"No," Sasha breathed. He was sitting on a wicker chair, his arms on the armrests, looking casual as could be . . . except for his face. His eyes were squeezed shut, his lips pressed together, his nostrils flared, his brow deeply furrowed. "Being outside makes everything seem too . . . vast." He didn't have an Nsibidi sign below his neck as Chichi did.

Orlu sat on the bed and Chichi was on the stool beside Sasha. Sunny dropped to the floor in front of Sasha with her long legs to her chest.

"Anatov was here," Chichi said, "and he agreed that Sasha should stay indoors for the next few hours. It should get better. Sasha, ask Sunny what you wanted to ask her."

He squeezed his face tighter as if something was causing him fresh pain, and everything in the room pulsed again. Chichi grunted, Orlu pressed his face with the palms of his hands, and Sunny pressed her chest. She could feel the vibration roll down the center of her bones.

"Shit . . ." Sasha hissed. "Shit's out of control."

"It'll get better," Chichi said.

Sunny took his hand. "What do you need to tell me?"

"Don't try to pass *Mbawkwa* until you're actually sixteen," he said.

They all laughed, even Sasha.

"I'm telling you, this shit makes passing *Ekpiri* easy like passing kindergarten. First level is nothing, man." He paused. "So Anatov said I disappeared. I was in his hut, facing the flames, and then I felt funny, and I remember saying, 'Oh man' . . . then I was gone. Anatov said I was gone for five minutes. When you . . . when you slipped into the wilderness . . ."

"You couldn't have done that," Chichi said. "You'd be dead."

"I know," he said. He cracked open his eyes. The room throbbed. "But I went *somewhere* and . . . Udide was there."

"Eh?" Orlu exclaimed.

Sunny's belly dropped. "No," she whispered. She glanced at Chichi, but she was staring at Sasha.

"Have you ever seen Udide in the wilderness?" Sasha asked.

Sunny slowly shook her head and rubbed her face. *Oh man*, she thought, feeling the inevitable. *Oh man.* Because Sunny knew. It lived in the back of her mind. It lingered like a large spider in the corner, observing, expecting, biding. Udide's request when she'd met Sunny and Chichi behind that restaurant they'd stopped at on their return drive from Lagos over a year ago: *Written as a ghazal on a tablet-shaped Möbius band made of the same material as your juju knife, albino girl of Nimm, so you will recognize it. It will call to you. It cannot be broken. It is mine. One of my greatest masterpieces.*

It belongs to me. Go there, get it, and bring it back to me.

Sunny had looked up what a ghazal was; it was a type of poetry. And a Möbius band was a sort of infinity-shaped thing. Why did Udide suddenly need the thing if it had been stolen back in the nineties? And . . . if they failed to find the object, what would Udide do to them? Chichi knew more, but Sunny just didn't want to talk about it. To talk about it made it real, solid, *soon.*

All things considered, the fact was demands like that didn't just go away. Not when they were made by Udide. But one could be in denial and hope they would, no matter how many hints there were that the opposite was true. And so, though Sunny certainly hadn't forgotten the request, she'd hoped Udide had forgotten about her . . . and Chichi . . . and whatever stolen object Udide expected the two of them to retrieve from God knew where. And yet here Udide was, telling Sasha things during his *Mbawkwa* test.

Sunny didn't want to ask, but she knew she had to. "What'd she tell you?" Everything in the room pulsed and she shivered, a strong sense of foreboding cooling her skin. She held her breath.

He shook his head. "She . . . It doesn't matter. Not right now." He held his head in his hands for a moment and shut his eyes. He took a deep breath as everything throbbed again. It was such a resonant sensation that Sunny felt it in the pit of her belly. He opened his eyes and looked so intensely at her that she almost recoiled. "Sunny!" he said.

"What?" she asked, her voice higher than she wanted it to be.

"Anatov told me you would be able to do something for me."

"Okay."

"Bring me a blade of that grass you always see in the wilderness," he said.

"Why?" Orlu asked.

"Ah, it'll absorb the wilderness dust," Chichi said.

Sasha nodded. "The wilderness dust is like metal and the blade of grass will be like a powerful magnet. I'll have to . . . eat it."

"I don't know," Sunny said, looking skeptical. "That grass isn't really . . . grass."

"I know," Sasha moaned. "But Anatov said this would work. I'll do anything that works." Everything pulsed again and he sat back, closing his eyes.

"Shit," he whispered. "Come on, Sunny. Come ooooooon."

"Right now?"

"Yeeeeesssss," he groaned.

She looked at Orlu and Chichi, who both shrugged. It wasn't unsafe for her to go there. It was easy. But could she bring the grass from the wilderness? She was about to find out. She turned away from them all.

"Okay," she said. "Be right back."

She glided right into the field she always went to when she glided just to glide. It was the field Ekwensu had pulled her to and tried to make her face Death. She'd first returned to this place months after the incident upon Sugar Cream's insistence. "Anyone who's been through what you've been through will suffer some form of PTSD," Sugar Cream said, "even if you feel fine." Sunny had had nightmares of the incident ever since, so she couldn't argue. "If you feel ready, revisit that place where you faced Ekwensu. When you didn't turn around to look it in the face."

She'd gone there expecting the experience to bombard her with bad memories. Instead, she'd found an empty, vast field of tall, swaying grass beneath a light purple sky. And so she'd begun going there when she needed to think. There was rarely anything there except the occasional energy that would pop up from the grass like grasshoppers. And that was exactly how it was now. She stood in the field for a moment, savoring the quiet, the only sound that of the grass waving this way and that. No chest-vibrating thumping that felt and sounded like the beginning of cardiac arrest.

"Okay," she said, putting her hands on her hips. She looked around again, hoping to see Anyanwu. Nope. No-where in sight. "Always wherever she must be. Which is too often not with me. Like I don't matter." She grunted, looking down at the grass. Under her gaze it seemed to wave slower, as if it wanted her to stop noticing it. She knelt down.

Up close it looked just like grass, except . . . tougher. And softer. Like it would stretch if she tried to pull it out. She grabbed a small handful and pulled. And it did stretch. Not much. But enough. And it didn't break or uproot. She pulled harder. It wouldn't come up. "Hmm," she said.

She brought out her juju knife. When she took her knife's green, glass-like blade to the grass she held, she felt an electric-like zap rush up her wrist, and the smell of crushed leaves permeated the air. She sneezed and fanned the smell away. She held up the two blades of grass. They swayed in her grasp. "You better not have worked some kind of juju on me," she said. She sneezed again, feeling her nose filling with snot. "Oh, come on." She glided back.

Everyone was exactly where they'd been when she left. Except Sasha, who was pacing the room, pounding his head with the heels of his hands. "Make it stop, make it stop, make it stop!" *THOOM!* This time the room pulsed so hard that the entire house shook, a book falling from the shelf.

"I'm here," Sunny said, rushing to him.

"Do you need anything?" Orlu's father called from outside the room.

"No, Papa," Orlu said, "we're fine."

"Okay, o," his father said. "Sasha, your parents will be here soon."

Sunny gave him the blades of grass. They'd turned a dark green and become limp like seaweed. "Ugh," Sasha said. "Couldn't you get some that was . . . fresh?"

"It *was* fresh when I grabbed it. I'm just glad that I was able to bring it with me."

"Just eat it," Chichi said, "before you shake down the whole house."

"Think of it like eating spinach," Orlu said. "You ever seen that old cartoon *Popeye*?"

This made Sasha laugh hard and the whole house shook again.

"Eat it!" the three of them shouted.

He ate it. And grimaced immediately. "Blah! It's bitter."

"Of course it is," Orlu said.

They watched him chew and then swallow. "Whoa," he said. "Dizzy . . . but I think . . ." The house rumbled, but that was better than shaking. "I think it's working."

They all stood and waited. They could hear the door downstairs open and then the adults all talking at the same time. "Your parents are here," Chichi said.

But Sasha was already asleep. They tucked him in and left the room. Not once did anything pulse or vibrate.

"He's right," Chichi said to Sunny. "Wait until you're sixteen."

Sunny nodded. "I might even wait until I'm twenty."

"What do you think . . . Udide said to him?"

Sunny shrugged. They stared at each other, neither of them wanting to bring it up. Then they turned away from each other in silence.

6

CREATOR OF MMANWU

The moon was full and it lit everything. Sunny was glad. Sasha hadn't told them *what* Udide had said to him, but the fact that she'd singled him out and spoken to him at such a crucial time made her uneasy. Sunny had worked hard to put the giant spider out of her mind since everything that had happened nearly two years ago, despite the fact that she knew she was just in denial. But she'd tried . . . and mostly succeeded until today. She shivered, walking faster. Each step she took seemed to bring her closer and closer. Her phone buzzed and she shrieked. She brought it from her pocket and glanced at the time. It was 5:12 A.M. She took a deep breath and answered it.

"H-hi, Mom."

"Sunny . . . ?"

"I'm almost home," Sunny said into her phone, putting it on speaker as she walked. She leapt over a gutter and followed the concrete walkway. "I'm okay."

There was a long pause and then her mother simply said, "Hurry up."

"I will." She shut her eyes and took another deep breath. Her mother wouldn't tell her father that she was out at this late hour, and her mother wouldn't ask Sunny any more questions. But her mother knew. Not that Sunny was a Leopard Person, not specifically, but on some level she *knew*. Her mother had seen the same behavior with her own mother . . . who'd died so mysteriously. Back then, because Sunny's mother was a Lamb, Sunny's grandmother could never be open about being a Leopard Person to her, and now neither could Sunny. It must have felt so isolating to her mother dealing with such secrecy from her mother and then her daughter.

Sunny took another deep breath. Her mother was trying her best, and she would always be who she was. It wasn't an easy thing. She shoved her phone in her pocket as she passed the abandoned office building. She glanced at it. Always so creepy, especially at this hour. It was a building that was fully occupied during what her mother called the "dot-com boom," but all her life it had been slowly crumbling back into the ground, never occupied again. Something behind one of the broken windows moved and Sunny took that as her cue to move faster.

"Just a rat or lizard," she muttered. "Whatever, not my problem."

She arrived at the compound entrance and used her key to open the small door beside the gate. When she closed the door behind her, she breathed a sigh of relief. She'd felt as if something was creeping after her, and now that she was home she finally could admit this to herself. Sunny walked that way all the time, sometimes even late at night when she was returning from the funky train. And she could work some pretty powerful protective jujus these days, like the one that smoothly kept everyone four feet away from her at all times or just good old gliding away if something made her uncomfortable. However, the feeling she was having got past all that. And now, standing in the compound, she was sure something was solidly off.

She looked up at the moon. Such a clear and warm night. Not good for Sasha. Moonlight always made juju, no matter what kind, stronger. He would go through it tonight. Was his effect reaching all the way here? Nothing was pulsing, but something was . . . *wrong*.

"Anyanwu?" she whispered. No answer. Sunny frowned. "Ugh, where are you when I need you?" At least the moon-light lit everything up around her now. She turned around and looked toward the entrance of her home; she couldn't see it.

A spider the size of a house was standing in front of it.

Sunny's mouth fell open. How had she not realized all the night creatures had gone silent? Even the warm breeze had stopped. Her mother wouldn't see her if she looked out the window. Her mother wouldn't even *look* out the window. Not at this moment. Sunny knew what she was feeling now. Udide had held time. And in the moment, without looking toward the yellow glowing light beside her, she knew that Anyanwu had finally come back to her.

"Sunny Anyanwu Nwazue Nimmmmmmmm," Udide said. Her voice vibrated into Sunny's brain, electrical and gravelly.

"*O-O-Oga* Udide *Okwanka*, the Great Spider Artist, She who . . ." Sunny struggled to remember it all. In trying to avoid the inevitable, she'd studied up on Udide over the last year. Plus, the subject of Udide constantly came up while re-searching and learning Nsibidi. And in doing so, she'd become well versed in just *who* Udide was. "She who is the supreme artist who moves freely underground and through the wilderness. Creator of *mmanwu* from raffia straw. Spider the Artist."

The hairs on Udide's body vibrated pleasure as Sunny spoke her various names. With each vibration, Sunny shiv-ered. She still remembered Orlu's words from when they'd first met Udide, "Do *not* faint." To faint would be a show of weakness Udide would find insulting.

"I greet you," Sunny finished.

"Do you remember?" Udide asked.

Sunny shut her eyes and let out a great sigh. Here it was. Udide's request. It was time. Finally. Sunny nodded, accepting that it was time to face the great spider and what she expected. "But why are you coming to *me* about this?" she asked. "It's Chichi who—"

"You are Nimm, are you not? A warrior member of the clan."

Sunny opened and then closed her mouth. She was still getting used to the idea. Nonetheless, it was Chichi who had known that the Nimm women had stolen the ghazal from Udide, not Sunny.

"Everyone is connected to something. Connection brings you benefits, but it also makes you responsible. You, your Chichi, Asuquo, Omni, Gao, Ndom, all Nimm women. The offspring of Asuquo will bear that responsibility . . . and so will you. Get it back for me. *It is mine.*"

She crept closer to Sunny, all of her legs moving with the harmony of water. Black, the hairs gray. Her body was poetry and nightmare. Sunny held still. As always, Udide's breath smelled of burning houses and she blew it in Sunny's face, her mandibles working, her many black eyes focused on Sunny.

"I must have it back in seven days," Udide said. "There is something that is already here; I want all my tools available." She moved closer. "It was stolen by your Chichi's mother; they killed many of my children when it was taken. You and

Chichi will get it back for me or you will regret it. All of humanity will. And then I will make you regret it more, for I have reason for such revenge. I will write a story you do not want to read. I will start with your Nimm Village, but I won't stop there."

Sunny gasped, "W-wipe out a whole village? But . . . but that's genocide!"

"The highest stakes are not always death," Udide said. "Of all people, you should know that. How many times have you died? And yet here you are."

"Why all these threats?" Sunny whispered. She felt light-headed. "You just said humanity depends on it. Isn't that enough?"

Udide raised a leg and then brought it down. The tremor felt horrid and Sunny twitched. She could see them now. Tiny spiders. They skittered and scuttled, behind her eyes, in her veins. Tiny like nanobots. She shuddered some more, rubbing her forearms. She'd never liked spiders. Not at all.

"My venom runs through you, Sunny Anyanwu Nwa-zue," Udide said.

"But not through *me*," Anyanwu replied. Even in her fear, Sunny couldn't help smirking.

"Arrogant as always, Anyanwu," Udide said. "Challenge *me*? Very well."

Sunny was looking into Udide's eyes when she heard it, and for a moment she thought that Udide had decided to dry

up and shed her skin. But it wasn't something Sunny was seeing, it was what she was *hearing*. Something was crinkling,
crumbling, cracking. Then she realized it wasn't coming from
the spider, it was coming from behind the house.

"You have seven days," Udide repeated, working her
mandibles. "For your own sake and everyone else's . . . do
not fail." She raised her head, twisted her backside, and shot
a web into the sky. She scuttled up the web at an incredible
speed. When she was high in the sky, the strand extending so
high Sunny couldn't see what it attached to, Udide *jumped*!
She descended with all eight legs stretched out.

"What the—" The spider was falling right toward her.
Sunny ran. When she reached the door, she turned around
just in time to see Udide slam into the concrete on the driveway. The impact shook everything, knocking Sunny to the
ground. She curled herself into a protective ball as chips of
rock and dust pelted her. When she looked back, she saw a
giant hole in the driveway, its edge barely three feet from her
sandals. She slowly crept up and looked into it. Udide was
disappearing down the tunnel.

Then the hole began to fall in on itself. Falling and filling,
then slabs of the driveway's concrete refitted. Within minutes, the night was quiet and the driveway was intact, as if
one of the most impactful beings on Earth hadn't been there
speaking to her, reminding her, assigning her . . .

Threatening her.

Sunny looked at the moon and her anxiety was so intense that it seemed to be waning right before her eyes. Time was slipping away. Until what? What was Udide going to do? Anyanwu stood where Udide had been; she did a spunky jig.

"It's not funny," Sunny said.

"Sometimes it is a good thing to laugh."

Sunny quickly went inside. She'd had enough. She rushed to her room. She peeked into Ugonna's room as she passed. He was a lump in his bed, his laptop open and playing rap music. She never understood how he could sleep with that playing.

She shut her bedroom door behind her, dumped her backpack on the floor, and fell facedown onto her bed. She felt Della buzzing beside her ear. "Give me a second," she said. Then she heard it. Crinkling. She sat up immediately. The sound of dried leaves against dried leaves. Her heartbeat suddenly pounding in her chest, she turned toward the window where the sound was coming from.

"No, no, no, no!" she said, as she rushed to her window. It was open as always. She'd worked a permanent juju to keep mosquitos and anything that bit or carried venom outside. She blinked, feeling dizzy. That sound. Ekwensu. Sunny was suddenly back in Osisi, horrified with the realization that she and her friends were in the giant home of a most powerful masquerade. She was hanging from Ekwensu's dried, packed leaves for dear life. She was hearing the dry crackle-crinkle of Ekwensu's leaves. She was hearing it *right now*.

She grasped the window's pane and looked outside, sure of what, *who* she'd see. She stared. And now she was dizzy with a blend of relief *and* deep, deep foreboding. This was not Ekwensu, but this was not better. This was at her home, and this was a strong warning. The high palm tree that grew right outside her window, just beyond the compound's wall . . . it was not only dead, it looked as if it had been dead for a *decade*. Even in the moonlight, she could see this clearly. Its trunk was petrified, and its once green, leafy crown and rich red kernels were all a dead, dry brown. As the breeze blew, the dead tree made that crispy masquerade sound. Sunny shivered as she gazed at it. Udide had done this with a mere rise and fall of one of her legs.

Della flew beside her and buzzed harshly in her ear. She nodded and turned from her window. She smiled as she saw Della's latest creation, and for a moment, she didn't think about the dried-up, dead palm tree right outside her window that looked like some sort of masquerade waiting and waiting and waiting—and who wouldn't wait for long. The wasp artist had created an abstract piece tonight. Placed right at the edge of her dresser, it looked like a tennis ball-sized infinity symbol made from hundreds of tiny white flower petals.

Sunny looked at it closely. The moment she was an inch from it, she was hit with its sweet, sweet scent. "Oooh!" She grinned, sniffing. The scent was so beautiful that for several minutes, it was all that filled her mind. She turned to Della, who sat at the edge of her dresser, waiting. "Della! Beautiful! Oh, my room . . . I'll sleep so well tonight."

Pleased, Della zipped around her head and zoomed into its nest, where it was quiet for the rest of the night.

7

THIS ONE IS OURS

"This is a mistake, Chichi," Sunny said.

"I know," Chichi said. She wiped tears away, but she didn't stop walking. Nor did Sunny.

"Didn't you say they'll kill us?" Sunny asked.

Chichi's face squeezed as panic started hitting her again. "Yes."

"Then this is suicide."

"Yes . . . maybe . . . but we . . . we *have* to sneak in and see my auntie. All we need to find out is *where* it is."

They walked in silence. Sunny felt like jumping out of her skin. Her hands shook and her legs felt like noodles. The only way she was still walking was because for once

Anyanwu was with her, aligned as she used to be, holding her up. Anyanwu knew this was the only way, too. What a horrid feeling.

"Let's stop," Sunny said.

They both stopped. They stared at each other. They grasped each other's hands and both let their tears fall freely. Sunny was chilled down to her bones. She'd done a little research on the women of Nimm over the last year, and all she'd found were references to violence, cruelty, and wildly powerful juju that only Nimm women could understand.

Even Sugar Cream had once said, "I can understand you being a Nimm warrior. You're gifted and strong . . . I just don't wish it upon you. I'm glad you grew up outside their circle."

Sunny had spent most of the night packing as conservatively as she could. Chichi didn't need to tell, insist, or remind her. Sunny knew it was time. Since last night when Udide had come to her house . . . which turned out to be about twenty-four hours before Udide appeared at Chichi's house to give her a similar warning.

"Damn it," Sunny said, hoisting up her backpack.

"I know."

"Let's run away. Or hide in the Obi Library. Sugar Cream could definitely—"

"That won't protect the Nimm Village, our families, or . . . anything."

"If the Nimm will kill us for going there, why should we even *care* if Udide wipes them out?" Sunny asked. But she knew the answer. This was on them. If harm came to others, it was on *them*.

"This one is ours," was all Chichi said. Sunny sighed, grasping Chichi's hands tighter. She nodded. A *chittim* fell beside them both and neither of them bothered to pick it up. They just continued on their way.

They crossed the soccer field where Sunny had perfected her soccer skills in the early evenings with her brothers way back when her albinism kept her from playing in the sun. Walking through it at night was easy; she'd run around this place so many times after sundown when her brothers left. She looked up at the still full moon and frowned, thinking about what waited for her at home by now. Sunny had left a note. Her mother was going to stress out so badly, but what could she do?

"How far is it?"

"No idea."

"Then how do you know where it is?"

"Even *you* know where it is. Anyone with Nimm blood knows," Chichi said.

"My God, my . . . my father is going to really lose it," Sunny said. "The last few months, I think he's been starting to come around. He'd been—"

"Your father will *never* 'come around' until he truly accepts *you* for *you* and stops trying to force you in a damn box," Chichi snapped.

"Hey!" Sunny shouted. "Don't talk about my father like that."

Chichi ignored her, wiping sweat from her brow. "Also he needs to get over his patriarchal Igbo man bullshit. Girls are as good as—and a lot of times better than—boys at things."

"Ahhh, enough, enough, let's focus on where we're going."

"Eh heh," Chichi nodded. "Because you know I'm right."

Sunny gnashed her teeth, fighting the urge to turn and walk right back home. Why not? It was better than almost certainly dying at the hands of some wild women she was supposedly related to. Chichi laughed, knowing she'd gotten to her.

"Ey!" someone called.

"Oh, come *on!*" Chichi shouted. They both whirled around. Sasha *and* Orlu were rushing up the soccer pitch. Both of them carried backpacks.

Chichi narrowed her eyes at Sunny. "Did you say anything?"

"When would I have had time?" Sunny asked.

"You're not going without us," Sasha said.

"You're barely recovered from your initiation," Chichi said.

"Do you hear anything booming?" Sasha snapped. "I'm fine." They all paused, listening. Indeed, nothing boomed or vibrated. "Yeah, that wilderness grass tasted like poison, but it worked."

"Well, you're not Nimm," Chichi said. "They'll kill you."

"Don't matter," Sasha said. "They're going to kill you both, too. We're an *Oha* coven. We go on suicide missions together, man."

"Ugh, it's not a suicide mission," Sunny said, rolling her eyes.

Sasha laughed loudly. "Without us it is. You really think you can sneak into a village of crazy women without our help?"

Chichi paused, pursed her lips, and then blurted, "Yes." She put her arms across her chest and sighed.

Sasha scoffed. "We're coming."

Chichi shot a look at Sunny and Sunny shrugged.

"Did you explain the entire situation to your wasp artist?" Orlu asked Sunny.

Sunny bit her lip. What could she say? Plus, this morning, long before Chichi had arrived at her bedroom window, she'd known that it was time to address this problem because of what Della had done. Had *had* to do. Right there on her dresser stood her wasp artist, and next to it was a most peculiar and disturbing sight.

It had created what looked like a rendition of a swirling galaxy out of chewed-up mud, and at its center was the corpse of a large spider. It was curled up and on its back in typical dead spider fashion.

"Did it try to attack you?" Sunny had asked Della, and the insect had buzzed loudly. It flew around her head and then flew at the spider corpse with its stinger pointed like a sword and stopped a millimeter over the corpse. So Udide had sent one of her minions to remind Sunny of her . . . obligations by trying to kill her wasp artist. This had infuriated and terrified Sunny so much that she'd burst into tears. Then she'd taken the insect in the cup of her hands, sat on her bed, and told Della everything. Including the fact that she had to go somewhere for . . . a while.

Orlu nodded. "See? You explained *everything* to it before you left so it won't do anything rash if you don't come back soon. You *know* this is a dangerous journey."

Sunny touched the zyzzyx glass comb in her Afro that Della had made for her two years ago. She wore her Afro big these days, reveling in the comfort and boldness of it. No one she knew rocked it like this, and the fact that her hair grew so thick and yellow-white—she loved it and dared anyone to say anything.

Together, the four of them began to walk.

NSIBIDI FOR "WHEN THEY START THE JOURNEY"

8

BRING THE FUNK

"I left a letter that said *I'll be back*," Sunny said.

"Who are you—the Terminator?" Sasha asked.

Sunny shrugged. "Come on, what could I really say? I'm tired of trying to explain something I can't explain. And I think my parents are, too."

"True," he said. "They'll be all right."

"Can you two be quiet?" Chichi said. "I'm trying to think."

"How hard is it to call a funky train?" Sasha asked. "Draw the *vévé* with some juju powder, stab it with your juju knife, say the words." They were standing at the side of the road near a cluster of trees. Orlu was looking up the road. He knelt down and touched the concrete.

"I *know* how to call a funky train, Mr. Mansplainer," Chichi snapped. "I just . . . I don't know what to tell it about our destination. I've always known where I was going . . . on some level."

"Just send the request with a *no sabi*," Orlu said. "It'll take longer to arrive, but at least you won't have to deal with an angry driver."

"Hmm, true," Chichi said. "Good idea."

Sunny cocked her head. "You've had experience with this, eh?"

"When I was little," Orlu said, laughing.

An uncomfortable hour passed. They hadn't realized how close they were to a creek and all four of them had to work and rework the "Mosquito Killer," a juju that they'd created one evening while hanging out in Chichi's hut when a swarm of mosquitos had blown inside. They'd named it after an annoying Naija rap song Orlu had sung over and over some years ago.

"I dey kill mosquito well well!" Sasha shouted as he did one more flourish to rework the juju yet again. The moment his juju knife touched the dirt (the last part of the juju), the attacking mosquitos popped away from him like reverse shooting stars, and there was a blast of lemon scent. They'd made the juju to be not only effective, but dramatic. Of course, Sunny wished they could have made it also last longer than about ten minutes at a time and give warning when it wore off, but once a juju was made, it could not be edited. And making a juju was no small feat in itself. It had taken hours and energy from all four of them that left them tired for days. It was worth it, though.

"I see it," Orlu said, pointing up the road. Within a moment, they all did, for the vehicle was coming toward them at breakneck speed and seeming to float on a cloud of electric blue luminescence. Its lithium headlights pierced the darkness, and for a moment Sunny could see she and her friends were standing in a thick cloud of mosquitos and midges. Their "Mosquito Killer" juju was protecting them better than she'd thought.

A brilliant orange with a dented exterior and the phrases NO TIME TO CHECK TIME! and COOL BOY! printed on the side, the funky train pulled up and the door opened. An ancient, bony woman who looked even taller than Sunny sat in the driver's seat. "Three A.M., standing in a swarm of bloodsucking insects and no idea where you're going, na be life, o!" she said, laughing.

They rushed in and she quickly shut the door. The funky train was completely empty . . . at least of human beings. However, when it came to insects, that was another story. Ghost hoppers galore! One sat on every seat and even more stuck to the walls and a few on the ceiling. They were hearty, the size of an American football, and a bright red with huge, golden, compound eyes.

"Better than mosquitos and midges," Sunny said. Sasha sat across the aisle from Chichi, and Orlu gently picked up a ghost hopper from directly beside him so Sunny could sit there. He placed it on the head of the chair, where it crawl-hopped away. When Sunny sneezed loudly, it flew off and landed on the ceiling. If a grasshopper-like creature could glare, it did so at Sunny now. Sunny brought out her tissues as another sneeze began to tickle her nose.

"Ugh," she muttered. "This annoying allergy. I hate it so much." Orlu patted her on the shoulder.

"Driver, you have an infestation problem," Chichi said.

"Eh, they're just passing through," the driver said. "It's ghost hopper migration season."

They all looked at each other. Orlu was clearly ready to start in with his thousands of questions. Sunny elbowed him. Now wasn't the time.

"They'll fly off at dawn," the driver said. "So are you four joyriding or what?"

"We need to get somewhere, but we don't know where it is," Chichi said.

"Ah, and what is the place?"

"The Nimm Village," Chichi said.

The driver responded, but none of them heard what she said because a ghost hopper beside Chichi suddenly began to sing its wavery song, softly swaying side to side. Chichi glared at it and it sang louder. One jumped onto

Sasha's head and began singing, too, synchronizing its wa-very song with the one beside Chichi. Sunny took the mo-ment to turn toward the window and sneeze loudly and blow her nose.

"Sorry," Chichi shouted. "We can't . . ."

The driver got up and came to them. She really *was* tall, maybe around six foot three. "You two got anything to be stressed about? Ghost hoppers sing to people who are stressed out, but you've got to have it really strongly for them to sing when migrating."

Chichi sighed, annoyed. "No."

"I'm cool," Sasha said.

The driver picked the ghost hopper off his head and it sang softer. The one beside Chichi followed its cue and soon the five of them could hear each other speak. "Nimm, eh?" The driver eyed Chichi and Sunny. "Ah, those women."

"Do you know the way?" Chichi asked.

"I don't."

"Don't funky train drivers know *all* ways?" Sasha asked.

"The Nimm Village is not 'all ways,'" the driver said. "And Nimm women usually travel their own ways."

"I . . . we haven't learned that yet," Sunny said.

"You two are Nimm?"

Chichi and Sunny nodded. Sunny still felt strange about claiming it, but one mere flex of her powerful muscles was all she needed. And the memory of her grandmother.

"Okay," the driver said, returning to her seat. "I know *some* of the way."

"I knew it," Sasha said.

"But there's a certain point where *you'll* have to guide us."

"We'll sort that out when we arrive," Chichi said.

"Okay, o. Hopefully you will have time to do that."

9

V. HOYTEMA & C.

The ghost hoppers were singing again. Two more had landed on the back of Chichi's seat, and their combined singing was so loud that Sunny could feel the vibration in the backs of her teeth. Sasha didn't seem to mind, for he'd laid himself out on his seat and was fast asleep. Also unbothered by the noise, Orlu had brought a book out of his backpack and was reading it despite the swerving motion of the funky train. Chichi had scooted to the side of the seat closest to the window. She pressed her forehead to the glass and sighed.

"Chichi, you okay?"

She nodded but didn't say anything.

Sunny got up and slid into her seat. "You scared?"

Chichi shrugged.

"Well, I'm terrified," Sunny said. She paused. "But I think I'm more terrified of Udide."

Chichi perked up at this. "What kind of world is it where something like her even exists?"

They stared at each other and then both burst out laughing. "Like, like, the size of a HOUSE! And that's only what she lets us SEE! I think if I run into her in the wilderness, I'll go *mad* . . . and that's only because I can't *die* there!"

"Why . . ." Chichi was laughing so hard that she could barely breathe. "Why do we even say 'she'? She's everything! God, goddess, deity, spirit, ghost; she is too much for human language."

The ghost hoppers must have sensed the change in Chichi's emotion, for they stopped singing and suddenly Sunny could hear herself. Sobering up a bit, Sunny said, "Honestly, though, we should be honored. We've been sent on a dangerous mission, yeah, but, um, Udide makes personal calls to us."

"Sometimes I'd rather be boring and common," Chichi said.

"Where do you think the driver is taking us?"

"The Cross River National Park entrance in Oban Division," the driver said, looking at them in the rearview mirror. "The funky train book claims that the Nimm Village can be accessed from in there. Where? I don't know."

"Wait," Chichi said, standing up, so she could see the driver better. "The national park is HUGE! If you just drop us at the entrance, how are we to find it?"

"You'll have to figure that part out," she said with a shrug.

Chichi sat back down, looking thoughtful.

"It's night," Sunny said.

"And I'm not a big nature person," Chichi muttered.

"I've heard things about the national park," Orlu said, still looking at his book. "It's one of the world's top biodiversity hotspots and it's got a *huge* butterfly diversity . . . but there are other things, too."

None of them asked for details.

Orlu leaned back in his seat, getting more comfortable. "We've probably got about a half hour more of driving. Focus on how we can locate the village."

"So you don't visit there?" Sunny asked.

"No," Chichi said.

"Ever?"

"No."

"What about your mom?"

"Of course not!"

"Relatives?"

Chichi kissed her teeth. "My mom is forbidden from returning." She paused, frowning. "It's a long story. But she says that every Nimm woman knows the way. I just never asked my mom what that way was because, well, why? Do I know how to reach my father? No. What for? But blood memory is blood memory."

"Blood," Sunny said, thinking of Udide and her spider venom. It was in her and Chichi's blood, which meant Udide could find either of them at all times. "DNA, chemicals, blood cells, antibodies . . . the answer is in there."

Chichi nodded.

They were still wracking their brains when the funky train finally stopped. The road ended in a circle with a life-size, dark gray elephant statue at the center, its trunk raised in perpetual salute. In front of them was a gateway check-point. Trees and a blue sky were painted across the archway top with the words CROSS RIVER NATIONAL PARK in big green letters. And in smaller letters near the center it said OBAN DIVISION, EROKUT PARK ENTRY GATE.

"Wow," Sunny said. "We've come far." Though she doubted that the funky train traveled strictly by the laws of physics, time, and space. So maybe they hadn't traveled as far as they'd actually come.

"There are trails and paths in there," the driver said. "It's up to you."

The dirt road leading into the park became dark yards from the entrance point's lights. Sunny had looked at the park on her phone. It was over two thousand square miles wide. If the Nimm Village entrance was "somewhere in the Cross River Park," it would be impossible to find.

"Will you wait here for us just in case we can't find it?" Sunny asked.

The driver frowned and thought for a moment. "You are children, so I will wait for a half hour," she said. "Then I will take my leave."

They looked at each other. A half hour was nothing if they had to look in there. Plus, it was the middle of the night. Sunny shivered, despite the heat. "We're really going in there?" she asked.

"Do you have any better ideas?" Chichi snapped.

"Man, something is going to kill our asses in there, for sure," Sasha said doubtfully.

"I know some things," Orlu said. "They won't get us easily."

"Oh, that's cool," Sasha said. "At least I know that I'll be killed with difficulty instead of with ease. Great."

"Come on," Chichi said, walking toward the entrance. "We're wasting time."

They started walking. They hadn't taken ten steps before they heard it: a loud, sharp roaring, growing in volume.

"Motorcycles?" Sunny asked.

A group of bikers was coming up the road. There were five of them; their bikes were robust and shiny and each carried a bundle. One of them was blasting Afrobeat music. They rode around the circle, past the funky train, and then came right toward them.

"Do you think they could see the funky train?" Orlu asked, frantic.

"Couldn't tell!" Chichi said. "Probably? Lambs out here at this hour would be weird."

"Leopard or Lamb, we'll deal with them," Sasha growled. "I know exactly what I'm going to do."

"Don't do *anything*," Orlu said. "Not yet."

They brought out their juju knives, keeping them close to their legs. Sunny fought the urge to hold her hands over her ears. All the bikes were noisy but one of them was excessively loud. Its horrible chugging sent some birds in a nearby tree flying off squawking. Sunny felt around for Anyanwu. If they were about to get attacked by armed robbers, she needed Anyanwu with her.

"Shit," she muttered when Anyanwu was nowhere to be found.

The one playing the music cut it off. Sunny tried to figure out which one had the noisy bike, but now she couldn't. The woman in the front removed her helmet. The waning light from the entranceway barely allowed them to see her face. She was tall, strongly built, and looked a little younger than Sunny's father. She wore jeans and a black leather jacket embroidered with red beads on the shoulders. "What are you people up to?" she asked.

"None of your business," Sasha said.

The bikers laughed, each taking off their helmets.

"You have no idea what you are doing," a woman behind her said. Dressed from head to toe in sky-blue leather, her bike and braids also a light blue, she was so dark-skinned Sunny could barely see her face. "Turn around and get back on the funky train. This is no place for children, alone and at night."

Sunny relaxed . . . but not much. At least these were Leopard People. But then again, these were Leopard People. "Where are you going?" Chichi asked. "It can't be much safer for adults."

One of the bikers kissed his teeth. "Come on, let's leave them, Iroko. We're wasting time."

"You've never had a conscience," the woman in blue named Iroko said, shaking her head. She looked at Sunny. "We've got a long way to go, but my own conscience won't be clear unless I know why there are four kids walking into the park in the middle of the night. Talk."

Sunny was about to open her mouth when she felt Anyanwu sweep into her. When she spoke, her voice was steady and cool. "Tell us your names first. Why *you* are here."

Iroko paused and looked at the others. Then she climbed off her shiny blue bike, rested it on its kickstand, and stepped up to Sunny. Up close, Sunny could see her face better. She was much older than her mother and so short that Sunny looked down at her. But her tiny stature didn't hide her strong presence.

"Okay, o," she said. "I am Iroko." She pointed to the woman who had first spoken to them. "That is Tungwa Storm." She pointed to a tall, heavyset woman who wore all yellow leather; she was the one with speakers on her bike. "That's Tune." She pointed to a brown-skinned man with coily black hair. "Bami Bami. And that's Mba." Of all of them, Mba looked the most like her father . . . except for his long salt-and-pepper dreadlocks tied in a tight bun on top of his head. "We're the Lizard Biker Club. We're researchers documenting Nigeria. You cannot learn about your country without learning about the people, the culture, and the terrain. So we ride. Now, who are you?"

Sunny glanced at the others. Orlu nodded. "I'm Sunny, these are Orlu, Sasha, and Chichi." She paused. Anyanwu was gone again. "We're . . . we're on our way to the Nimm Village."

Iroko laughed and looked back at the others.

"On foot?" the woman named Tune asked. "Tonight?"

"What do you mean?" Sunny asked.

"Yeah," Chichi said, rushing up to Sunny. "What do you mean?"

"You can't get into the Nimm Village just by walking into the park. You have to go in, but then you have to know what to do, and you only know it when you're there."

"How far in?" Chichi asked.

"I've never been, of course," Tune said. "But I once drove a friend who went. She didn't allow me to stay when she went in, but I drove her about five minutes up this path and then she walked into the forest."

"On your bike?" Orlu asked.

"Yes, so a much longer walk. These bikes are fast."

"Well, if you're going in, can you take us?" Sasha said.

"We will," Mba said. It was the first thing he'd spoken to them. The others nodded.

After all of them exchanged a look, Tungwa Storm said, "But you'll have to walk back yourselves, if you cannot find it."

Chichi shrugged. "What else can we do?"

"It's dangerous," Orlu said.

"But we're running out of time," Sunny added.

Sasha raised his voice. "Fair enough. We'll figure it out once we get there."

Chichi rode with Iroko, Sunny with Tungwa Storm, and Orlu with Bami Bami. Sasha rode with Tune, not surprisingly, and the two laughed and blasted a blend of Afrobeat and rap music the entire way. Mba led the way, the quietest of the group, but the one who knew the national park best.

"He didn't say it, but he's been to the Nimm Village," Tungwa Storm told Sunny as they rode.

"Why didn't he say anything??" Sunny asked.

"He said you won't find it here."

"How would he know?"

"His ability is solid foresight. He also knows when people need to do something; you need to go in there anyway."

They used no juju to light the way, only the powerful

lights of their bikes, and it was enough. The red dirt road was wide and the terrain was flat. The sides of the road were flanked with lush, dense forest. It was Iroko's bike that chugged the loudest, but even over its jaw-rattling power, Sunny could hear the creatures of the forest make their clicks, grunts, squawks, hoots, and shrieks.

"Hang on," she said, and Sunny grasped her more tightly just in time. They shot off at impossible speed, the motorcycle hugging the curve as if a magnetic force was keeping it from flying into the bushes. Sunny shut her eyes and was dismayed to find that this didn't help at all. Instead of seeing the road crashing toward her, the darkness of her eyes showed her a tunnel, and she was flying through it. She opened her eyes.

"You okay?" Tungwa Storm shouted.

"No."

Tungwa Storm laughed. And didn't slow down. "Almost there."

"How do you know?"

"Tune is slowing down."

When Iroko's bike stopped, the silence that met Sunny was utterly creepy. The forest wasn't quiet at all, but compared to the machine noise of Iroko's bike, the contrast in intensity was jarring. "Well?" Tungwa Storm said when Sunny didn't move. "Off you go."

"Oh," Sunny said. She climbed off, her legs feeling a bit like jelly from squeezing the seat so hard. "Thank you."

Tungwa Storm nodded. "You sure you want to go there? To the Nimm Village?"

Sunny nodded. "We are."

Tungwa Storm chuckled. "You Nimm women are never afraid of death. Good luck!"

She rode off before Sunny could say anything more. Sunny joined the others, watching the other bikers leave. Then the four of them just stared at each other, clearly thinking the same thing: *Holy shit! Why are we out here?*

They waited for the bikers to be completely gone before using their knives to call the fireflies to bring light. They each worked the same juju, and within moments they were bathed in the vibrant light of firefly butts. In the middle of the rain forest on a very hot night, it was as if a galaxy surrounded them.

"Thank you," Orlu told the fireflies.

Sunny quickly followed suit. A grateful firefly was a bright and long-staying friend. "Yes, thanks!"

"*Dalu,*" Chichi said.

"What they all said," Sasha added.

"I've always wanted to come out here," Orlu said. "This rain forest houses one of the largest diversities of butterflies in the *world*, Africa's most endangered gorillas, not to mention that the Idiok baboons who created Nsibidi came from here. We're standing in one of the most magical places on Earth."

"Literally," Chichi said. "There's a reason why the Nimm

built their village in this place. I heard this is where *tungwa* were first seen."

Sasha suddenly dropped his backpack, frowning. He unzipped it and began rummaging inside. He brought out a bottle made of green glass with square sides, the type that was so thick that if you dropped it on concrete, it might chip, but it wouldn't shatter. Sunny could see that on the side of the bottle, molded in thick letters was v HOYTEMA & C. Sasha put it at his feet beside his backpack and stared at it as if it would burst into flames at any moment.

"When I was home, I took this from my parents' bookcase," he said. He was breathing hard. He crossed his arms over his chest. "It's one of my mother's most prized possessions, though I don't know why the hell it would be." He paused, glaring angrily at it.

"What is it, Sasha?" Chichi asked, stepping over to him and touching his shoulder.

"And why do you have it with you?" Sunny asked.

"Well, so . . . during my initiation, Udide told me where my ancestors were taken. She said I have all this white people blood—Irish, British, Dutch—but I'm mostly from *here*. She knew I took this and said I should bring it . . . here." He pointed at the ground.

"Like, *here* here?" Sunny asked.

"Yeah, like the Cross River Park," Sasha said. "Specifically! I didn't know we were coming here, but I brought it just in case. The moment we arrived here and I saw that sign . . . Yo, I've been kind of freaking out. It couldn't be a coincidence. Then those bikers showed up. Wasn't about to say anything until they were gone."

Chichi and Sunny pressed together, both of them looking at the bush all around them. Sunny shuddered when, for a moment, she was sure she saw Udide standing stoic and silent in the bush. Thankfully, it was just a network of trees oddly illuminated by the fireflies.

Orlu was wiping his face, annoyed. "We're here trying to find the Nimm Village with no clue of where to start and now you say this? Feels—"

"Yeah," Sunny interrupted. "Tungwa Storm, she said that Mba, the one who led the way, says we won't find it here, but we should *be* here. He can see the future or some-thing. This is too strange."

Sasha looked at all of them intensely. "Ever since I came to Nigeria . . . man, I love this place. It's been good for me. I came here not really knowing or *feeling* where I was from. I'm African, but what's that even mean? Africa was only Africa when white guys said it was. And . . . yeah, so I love it here, but I *carry* something." He touched his chest and looked at Sunny, and she nodded. "And since I've been here, I don't . . . I don't feel *seen*. Like . . . like . . . you all don't really acknowl-edge me. I'm American because I'm a descendant of slaves. And no one here talks about that. No one wants to. No big museums, no dedications, nothing.

"This is a gin bottle. I don't know how my mother got

it. There was juju performed on it and they know what it is, where it came from, its ghosts. It's the bottle of gin that was used to buy my ancestors. *The exact bottle.* That object is . . . death and torture and hate and destruction."

"Oh," Sunny whispered. Orlu and Chichi just stared at Sasha.

"My mom won't drink any alcohol because of this. My . . . my dad, he doesn't care about the past. He's never asked for or sought details. *That's* his revenge. He *knows* what he is and who he brings with him, but the rest can kick rocks. But my mother and this bottle . . . So I stole it. I wanted to bring it back to the place where it was exchanged. Return the purchase. Udide gave me the details. It was exchanged *here.*"

He put his backpack on and picked up the bottle. He shook it angrily. "Where?" he asked it. And suddenly, the bottle began to glow as if there was a dying flame inside it.

He looked around, holding out the gin bottle. The red-orange glow dripped from it, oozing in front of Sasha and pooling around him. "There," he said.

Sunny looked in the direction he was pointing. The foliage was dense, but sure enough, there was a very narrow, very dark path that led into it. The ground was clear of roots, vines, grass, all living things. Old. Dead. Sasha walked to it, Chichi following him.

"Hurry up, Sunny," Orlu said, following them onto the narrow path.

"Shouldn't we talk about this first?" Sunny asked. She glanced behind her as she followed Orlu. She shuddered again. The blackness of the forest enveloped everything as the fireflies moved on. Only a few remained around her now. It seemed they, too, wanted to see where Sasha was going. Sunny rushed after her friends, juju knife at the ready.

The path was narrow—red moist dirt with not a single plant growing on it, even as they moved deeper and deeper into the forest. Sunny stayed as close to Orlu as possible, working hard not to look back. She knew if she did, she'd only see darkness . . . and darkness in this kind of forest did not mean nothing was there. It more likely meant something *was* there. And whatever it was would get her first. In horror movies the worst place to be was at the back of the line.

"Orlu, what kinds of things live in this place?" Sunny asked.

"Buffalo, elephants, chimpanzees, gorillas, baboons, antelopes, Miri Birds, bush souls . . ."

"Okay," Sunny said. "Why did I ask . . ."

"Sasha?" Chichi asked. When he didn't answer and only kept marching up the path, she grabbed his arm. "Sasha!"

He stopped and turned to her, a wild look in his eye. "What?" The bottle in his hands was glowing even more brightly.

Sunny cocked her head as she looked at it. The light

inside sloshed around like liquid. *Don't some people call hard liquor like gin "fire water"?* she wondered.

"Where're we going?" Chichi asked. "We've been walking for fifteen minutes. The path doesn't look like it leads anywhere."

"When my ancestors were taken, they had no idea where they were going, Chichi. The way was dark and mysterious." Sasha turned around and just started walking and they all followed. It was a dark night, so seeing above the canopy of trees overhead was impossible. But you could feel it. Especially in the dark. The trees and bushes were creeping, crowding closer. The air grew heavier, warmer. Sunny began to feel claustrophobic and lost. How would they ever get out of here?

Sasha stopped. Where he stood looked no different from where they'd been walking for nearly an hour—a patch of path, darkness in front of and behind them. "Here," he said. He was sweating and his bushy Afro drooped in the humidity. There was a large iroko tree growing here, and Sasha stepped off the path to stand on its base. He tipped the bottle and what was glowing inside it poured out red orange, splashing onto the exposed parts of the roots like the blood of something burning. It hissed and spattered, some of it hitting Sasha's dirty Jordans.

The moment the last drop left the bottle, something began moving around in the bushes just outside the light of the fireflies. Not something, some *things.* All around them—

chop, sssss, shack! Large, huge! The friends crowded together, looking around. Several of the fireflies zipped away and their area of sight shrunk as the sound of whatever was rushing around them increased. Then the movement slowed and there were whispers. Closer. Humans.

"They're speaking Igbo," Orlu said. "But I can't quite understand."

"Old Igbo," Chichi said.

There was only one phrase Sunny caught. "Our son."

Sasha must have heard this, too. He stood up straight. Then he took the bottle and dashed it against the tree, where it burst into a thousand pieces like something made of thin, melting ice. There was a brilliant flash of rainbow-colored light and it washed over Sasha. He glowed like something else, something from the wilderness.

Sasha gasped, his eyes growing wide. Sunny couldn't hear it, but they were definitely speaking to him. Tears began spilling from Sasha's eyes and he dropped to one knee, his head to his chest. He nodded and whispered, "I understand." His breath caught in his throat. "I . . . I will." Sunny looked at Orlu and Chichi and then she got to one knee, too. Her knee ground in the soft, mulchy, red soil, and suddenly she could hear them all around her, too. She had shifted. It was something Sugar Cream had taught her recently. It was like doing a little scoot that took you into the wilderness, which was always near. She slowly looked around.

"Woooow," she whispered. They stood all around Sasha. There were ten of them—tall, humanoid, and glowing a brilliant gold. *Sasha's ancestors.* Their spirit faces were so multifarious that Sunny wasn't sure where to focus—they reminded her of those super complex and detailed ceilings of mosques in Iraq. Kaleidoscopic fractals that were constantly folding and unfolding. Sunny froze. Then she looked behind her. Blue, red, orange, and gold hexagon shapes were unfolding and multiplying into the shape of two eyes and a smiling mouth.

"Who are you?" they asked.

"Sunny Nwazue," she said.

"You are his friend?"

She nodded.

"Good."

Sunny heard *chittim* falling around her. She looked down. Gold *chittim* the size of her fingernail. When she looked up, the being was striding back to Sasha to join the others surrounding him. To her left, she noticed Orlu and Chichi, who had also taken a knee. Orlu had his hands held before him as he looked around frantically. One of Sasha's people was curiously touching his hands, and he had no clue. Another of the beings had her hands on Chichi's head as she looked hard at Sasha. Sunny turned back to Sasha and shifted out of the wilderness. And even then, though she could no longer see Sasha's ancestors, it was still like standing in the wind of exploding fireworks.

And then it all faded away. The colors flew off. The whispers stopped. The forest calmed. Everything settled. And all that was left were the four of them and the few remaining fireflies who'd have a most amazing story to tell the others.

Breathing hard, they stood there looking at one another for several seconds. Then Sasha bent down, grabbed a shard of the broken glass, put it in his pocket, and said, "Okay. Let's go." He took Chichi's hand and they headed back up the path.

Orlu and Sunny followed.

10
K. O.

The walk all the way back to the park's entrance took them an hour and a half. They'd each used their mosquito-repelling juju so many times that they'd lost count. Sunny could practically do the juju in her sleep . . . a few times, she *had*. To their shock, the funky train was still parked where they'd left it when they went off with the bikers. They broke into a run the moment they saw it.

"Oh, thank goodness!" Sunny laughed.

"I know," Chichi said. She grabbed Sunny's arm before they got on board. Orlu and Sasha sprinted past them. "Wait, Sunny," Chichi said. "I want to talk to you for a second."

"Yeah?"

Chichi tugged her off to the side. "We've got a problem."

"What?"

"Well, okay, so . . ." She looked up at the sky, and after a few moments Sunny looked with her. "The sun isn't going to be up for hours. Let's say we figure out the way . . . we can't be that far. We'll probably get there before sunrise."

"So?"

"They don't allow men or boys there before sunrise."

Sunny blinked. "Um, what?"

Orlu poked his head out the funky train door. "Hey, Sunny, Chichi, I think you need to see this." He disappeared back inside. Sunny and Chichi rushed into the bus, and what they saw left Sunny feeling dizzy.

"Oh my God!" Sunny screeched.

"What happened?!" Chichi asked.

"She's okay," Sasha quickly said, putting his hands up. He was kneeling beside the driver, who was sprawled out on the funky train's red floor. Her eyes were closed and her nostrils were flared as if she smelled something horrible.

"Knockout charm," he said.

"The ghost hoppers are gone, too!" Sunny said.

"Someone was here, then," Chichi said, looking around.

"Not anymore," Orlu said. "I had to undo five jujus. They even wrapped one of them around the whole funky train! My hands are actually tingling right now." He rubbed his fingers together as if he had crumbs on them.

"I think I know who," Chichi said, pushing past Sunny to get on the bus. "We must be close. They must have even been watching when we went into the forest!" She stood over the driver. Sunny stepped closer and saw that not only did the knocked-out driver give off the strong smell of peppermint, but there were tiny blue sparks popping off her like fleas. "The Eperi triplets . . . my cousins," Chichi continued. "Those blue sparks, that's their trademark."

"Oh, hell no. Them?" Sasha said. "You fought the oldest one when you were little, right? At some Nimm gathering in Leopard Knocks."

"*Beat*. Not fought. She tried to make me bow at her feet and I made her sorry for it. The triplets are my mom's sister's kids, Soon, Far, and Now. The oldest is Now."

"I'm confused," Sunny said. "If they're triplets—"

"They didn't come out at the same time," Chichi snapped. "Anyway, I think . . ." She nodded. "Yeah, let's get the driver up first."

They managed to wake her up, but no matter what they did she remained groggy, snickering and giggling and going limp whenever they tried to get her to her feet. Eventually, they got her into one of the seats. "She needs sunlight," Chichi says. "Once that hits her, the knockout will wear off."

"That's hours from now," Sunny said.

"We need to drive this thing to Nimm," Sasha said.

"Two problems," Orlu said. "We don't know the way, and none of us can drive a funky train."

"When I was in Chicago, I got to drive my friend's dad's Tesla."

"A Tesla is *not* a juju-driven car," Sunny said, rolling her eyes.

"I dunno," Sasha said. "Electricity can bring someone back to life. Hell, it brought Frankenstein's monster *to* life. Plus, how hard can a funky train be to drive?"

The funky train didn't have two pedals for driving. It had five, plus a lever on the left side for goodness knew what. On top of this, to sit in the driver's seat was to step into a web of what Sasha called "kind juju," juju that was meant for whoever sat in the driver's seat. "I can feel it," Sasha said. "It's a soft vibration on my skin. And when I touch the steering wheel, it feels like my hands are supposed to be there."

Chichi was standing beside him, looking at the other controls with a frown, and soon Sasha was frowning, too. Though Sasha felt the juju's presence, nothing would budge— not the pedals, the wheel, or the key in the ignition. "Feels like it's petrified," he said.

"Of course," Chichi muttered, kissing her teeth and sitting in one of the seats behind the wheel. "Nothing tonight is easy."

"Whatever they put on this funky train is still here," Orlu said. He gasped with surprise as his hands rose before him and his fingers wriggled and flexed as he undid yet another juju. There was a loud *POW!* as he raised his left hand and seemed to smack something away. They all jumped.

"That one just tried to knock us all out!" he said.

Sasha, who had his foot up as if to fend off an attack, said, "Your cousins are evil, Chichi."

"Yep," Chichi said, getting up from the floor. "Truly."

"The sound is probably what sent all the ghost hoppers flying off," Orlu said. "I think it'll start now. But it'll need a little push first."

The three of them looked at Sunny, who still stood in the same place. The sound had startled her, but something in her had also been prepared to meet whatever was attacking. She lowered her fists.

"What?"

"You're the strongest of all of us, anyway," Chichi said, with a smirk. "Nimm warrior."

"I think I could beat you in wrestling," Sasha said.

"Mmm, no," Orlu said, cutting his eyes at Sasha.

Sunny sighed and climbed off the bus. As she stepped out, she took a quick look at the dark forest around them. The night creatures screeched and croaked and sang. Occupied with themselves . . . for now . . . hopefully. "Okay," she whispered, moving faster. "Ah, when did it all come to this?" She flexed her arms and lifted her knees up as she walked to the back of the funky train.

She remembered how they'd done it last time. The men had all stood at the back of the funky train and grasped the edge. She looked at her hands. Her long fingers were still slender, albeit more veined. She'd gotten so much more toned in the last year. Her parents didn't ask much about it, but she knew they noticed, too. And wondered. Her brothers simply assumed it was a combination of all the soccer she played and genetics. They were kind of right. However, they didn't know the extent of it.

"You okay?" Orlu asked.

She looked up. He was at the back window. She nodded, glancing at the edge of the funky train. "Get ready. I'm going to push now. Tell Sasha to make sure it's in neutral, *if* there's a neutral."

I'm going to push an entire bus-like vehicle with my bare hands, she thought. She bit her lip. If she couldn't do it, then what? Maybe work a moving juju like the one Sasha and Orlu had worked last year when they'd traveled to Lagos. Or something. Who knew what a whole funky train required? "I'll try," she muttered. "Gotta at least try."

She grasped the bumper. She began to push. And push. And puuuuuushhh. The funky train was huge. Impossibly heavy. How in the world could one girl move something so huge? It was a silly thing to try, and she was glad for the dark solitude of the park entrance. Only the frogs, insects, owls, and monkeys would see this absurdity. Her muscles strained and her feet dug into the concrete. She felt pressure all over her body.

She grunted and gave up. It was so painful. But in giving up, she kept pushing. And that was when she reached the tipping point: right when she stopped straining but kept pushing anyway. It was as if her muscles took a breath and thus got a second wind—everything in her exhaled, and she found that she had more to give on top of what she was already giving. She leaned into this feeling and pushed harder. Was this what tearing muscles, overdoing it, or pushing too far felt like? If so, it felt *fantastic*.

The funky train moved. It-was-moving. She was doing it. "I am!" she hissed, breathless. A large bronze *chittim* fell beside her. She pushed harder, moving past the *chittim*, and within seconds the vehicle was rolling. Rolling fast enough to roll on its own. She stopped pushing, her muscles screaming to rest as the vehicle rolled on. "I did it!" She heard Sasha, Chichi, and Orlu whooping with surprise and joy. Sunny even saw Orlu rush to the back of the funky train, laughing and waving at her. "YOU DID IT! WOW! SUNNY! YOU'RE AMAZING!"

Bzzzt! The funky train popped as an electric blue current shot from its back to its front. It let out a puff of . . . not smoke, but something that smelled like incense and looked like mist, and then the entire vehicle shivered. It rolled to a stop and stayed there, silent. "Come on, Sunny! You can't hear it, but it's on!'" Sasha yelled. Sunny ran back, grabbed the *chittim*, and then raced to the funky train and climbed inside. She sat down hard on the seat, laughing and out of breath. She looked at the *chittim* in her hand as Orlu patted her on the shoulder and Sasha and Chichi showered her with praise from the driver's seat.

Sasha and Chichi clumsily turned the funky train around and off they drove, away from the national park toward the main road.

No one said anything for several minutes. According to the GPS on Sunny's phone, they were driving right through the Cross River National Park. The trees on their left and right were dense. No paths or trails here. This road was for transporting goods, not sightseeing. But where were they going? And how would they find the Nimm Village?

"Ooooh," Sunny said, grasping her head and squeezing it. She looked up. "Okay, seriously, guys, where are we going?"

"No idea," Chichi said, keeping her eye on the road.

"And so far, no one seems to see us, but how the hell are we staying invisible?" Sasha asked, laughing. "I don't know where we are going, but at least now I know where I'm from!" He hit the horn and the whole funky train vibrated with a nasal honk that sounded like a man screaming "SHHHHMAAAAAAAAHHH!!" Sasha and Chichi both laughed harder.

"Okay, pull over!" Orlu said. "Pull over!"

Slowly, they brought the vehicle to a pause at the side of the road. Orlu looked at the driver lying on the seat in the center of the train and then turned to the three of them. "We can't just keep driving without a destination and expect to get where we are going."

"Why not?" Chichi asked, still giggling.

"And who says we don't know where we're going?" Sasha said. "We're going to the Nimm Village."

Orlu rolled his eyes.

Sunny stood up. "You guys, stop. It's late. I'm tired. We need a plan."

"I'm not tired at all," Sasha said. "I could run a hundred miles. *Thousands.*"

"What about a dousing juju? Like the one we use to get to Night Runner Forest? It'll probably have to be a LOT stronger, but same idea."

Kaaaaaaaaaaaackaaaaah! They all jumped at the horrible noise. Orlu's hands went up. The driver turned over on her seat, closing her mouth and smacking her lips loudly. She snuggled down, muttered something, and was quiet again. They all stared at her for a moment, waiting for her to start snoring again. When she didn't, Chichi said, "Okay, let's try it." She put the funky train in park and pushed the lever to open the door. "You stay, Sasha. Don't turn it off." She climbed over him.

"No way. If we turn this thing off, turning it on will be like rolling the dice again. I'm staying right here."

Sunny and Chichi hopped off the funky train. The side of the road was dusty, and the forest was just beyond. Chichi bent down and rubbed her hand in the dry dirt to create a uniform area. "Okay," she said. "We need to make a *vévé*."

"I assumed," Sunny said. "But of *what*?" *Vévé* were complex symbols already; whatever symbolized the Nimm Village would be even more complicated.

"The Nimm Village won't have one," Chichi said, frowning at the dirt. "Nimm is too secretive to have a specific *vévé*. We have to create one." She looked sharply at Sunny and lowered her voice. "If this works, we can't share this with *anyone*. Not even . . ." She motioned her head toward the funky train.

"We won't look," Sasha called.

Chichi rolled her eyes. Sunny giggled.

Sasha scoffed. "As if you can keep anything from me."

"I'm serious!" Chichi shouted back.

"So am I!"

"You don't know Nimm women."

"I know one and I know her very, very well."

Chichi loudly kissed her teeth and looked away.

"Just figure it out," Orlu said. "We don't have all night. We'll close the door and move to the back of the funky train."

"What of the driver?"

"We'll use a muffle juju," Orlu said.

Sasha laughed hard, "As if I can't get you to tell—" His voice was cut off as if someone had hit mute; only the sounds of the occasional vehicle passing by and the night creatures were left. Orlu had worked the muffling juju quickly.

Chichi smiled. "Good."

"Use Nsibidi," Sunny said.

"Okay."

"But I don't know anything about Nimm, not more than the fact that the Nimm Village is old, only women and girls are allowed—"

Chichi nodded. "The men and boys can only return at sunrise. They have to leave at sunset."

"I'm Nimm," Sunny continued. "Because my grand-mother was Nimm. I'm a Nimm warrior and you're a Nimm princess, and Nimm women don't marry. That's about it."

"Oh, there's a lot more," Chichi said. "My mother and I should have been teaching you, I guess. We've all just gotten carried away with our own lives."

"It's all right," Sunny said. "We're here now."

"True. How has it . . . how's it been with all that muscle and the strength—has that been weird?"

"Yes." Sunny knew Chichi wanted her to share more, but she didn't want to. Not right now.

"So, Nimm is a lot of things. But if you need to really sim-plify it: Nimm women are an old, old, *old* bloodline of women fully, completely, utterly dedicated to the pursuit of knowl-edge, to peeling and peeling it like an onion, to going out and exploring to find more, to staying home and exploring to find more. We're *devoted*. We are a sharp point of Leopardom, so sharp we have to stay on the perimeter, and the Obi Library Council will come to Nimm when they need something big. Mostly they leave us alone. You want to know how white people viewed us when they came to the 'Dark Continent'?"

Sunny kissed her teeth. "I don't even care."

"Oh, it's too good. You've got to hear this. I've even mem-orized it. It's from *In the Shadow of the Bush*. She stood up and struck an exaggerated superhero pose. When she spoke, it was with a very bad and vigorous British accent. "'Nimm—the terrible—who is always ready, at the call of her women worshippers, to send up her servants, the beasts that flock down to drink and bathe in her stream, to destroy the farms of those who have offended. Nimm is, above, all, the object of the women's devotion. She manifests herself sometimes as a huge snake, sometimes as a crocodile. Her priestesses have more power than those of any other cult, and the society which bears her name is strong enough to hold its own. It is during the rainy season that she is most to be feared.'"

She paused and continued, "'A land full of mystery and terror, of magic plants, of rivers of good and ill fortune, of trees and rocks, ever lowering to engulf unwary wayfarers; where the terror of witchcraft stalks abroad, and where, against this dread, the most devoted love of faithful service counts as naught.'"

By the time Chichi finished, Sunny was holding her cramping belly because she was laughing so hard. "That's . . . that's . . ." Deep breath. "In a . . . book?!" She wiped tears.

"Verbatim, *sha*," Chichi said, laughing, too.

Sunny turned to the forest as her laughter finally subsided. There was nothing she could take from the white explorer's interpretation of Nimm, but that was nothing new. "Women," she whispered. "Interested. Innovative. Focused. Obsessed. Village. Men, but their own space, too." She smirked. "And knowledge by any means necessary. Who'd steal from Udide?" As she thought it all through, she could almost see the Nsibidi wriggling and quivering as it swirled and twitched into a shape, a representation.

She turned around.

"You got it?" Chichi asked.

Sunny nodded. "I think so. Let me do it." She knelt down and brought a small bag from her pocket. Only a few years ago she wouldn't have been carrying this powder, she wouldn't have known what to do with it, and she certainly wouldn't have even *imagined* what she was about to do. Now that she could read Nsibidi fluently and she'd read what equated to about fifteen books of it in Sugar Cream's one book, she'd considered trying to write it herself. However, the thought of it was intimidating. Merely reading Nsibidi leeched her energy; people who read the most advanced versions of it when they weren't ready often wasted away and died. What was *writing* it like?

But she had it in her mind, the Nsibidi for the Nimm Village. If she wrote it in the white juju powder and then invoked it with her juju knife, what was going to happen? "Anyanwu?" she asked. No response. Anyanwu was elsewhere again. She bristled with annoyance. Sunny knew that at some point she and Anyanwu would have to have a reckoning. For now she pushed this uncomfortable thought away.

She reached into the sack and touched the powder with the tips of her fingers. She held the Nsibidi image firmly in her mind and then turned the image over. She turned it to the side. She flipped it over. All this took a lot of concentration, but she'd practiced it enough times while reading Nsibidi. To read it was not just to look at and interpret each representation as one does when reading letters or symbols. To read Nsibidi was to see, feel, hear, experience it. It was a sharp, deep juju that few could endure. She flipped the image in her mind to be in the orientation that she knew it should be in, which was inverted.

She pushed up her glasses and brought out her hand, a pinch of the powder between her fingers, and blew it over the space in the dirt that was her canvas. Then she turned the pouch just enough to let some sift out.

"Do you know how you're going to—"

The powder hit the dust and that was all she heard Chichi say. Fine grains of powder on rugged grains of dust blended for a moment, and then the white powder began to dominate. She was drawing as she was drawn in. Chichi beside her, Sasha, Orlu, and the driver, the entire funky train, the trees, the night creatures, the sky. Everyone and everything leaned in. Because as long as she was writing Nsibidi, she was controlling. Controlling it all. She let out a breath and felt herself shift. She kept her eye on what she was writing.

Loops, swirls, curled lines, spikes, spirals. The powder fell, stacked, and pooled. "I love this," she whispered, and to speak felt like swimming through packed dirt. She stopped drawing and closed her juju powder bag. *Thunk!* A very large bronze *chittim* felt to the dirt beside her.

"*Kai!*" Chichi shouted. "Look at that!"

Sunny blinked, coming back to herself. She felt as if she were soaking wet, her mind slow, her skin tingling. Her ears were itchy. She touched the left lobe, and when she looked at her fingers, she saw that they were wet with blood. There were tears in her eyes, and when she wiped them away, she saw that her eyes were bleeding, too. She touched her nose and was glad to find no blood.

"Okay," she breathed. "Orlu, Sasha! I think we're ready to go," she called. The world looked hazy and it was hard to focus. She looked at the first Nsibidi she'd ever written herself. She blinked as her eyes focused on it, pushing her glasses up again.

"It's the biggest *chittim* I've ever seen!" Chichi said.

"Look at that!" Sasha said, opening the door and spotting the *chittim*.

"I'll help you bring it inside," Orlu said. "That kind of thing, certain people have a nose for it."

"I've heard of that," Sasha said. "*Chittim* sniffers were all over Chicago and especially Tar Nation in the South."

"They're wherever big knowledge earners are," Orlu said.

"It's so ridiculous, because it's not just the big ones that are super valuable, but the tiny, tiny ones, too," Chichi said.

"There was an old Navajo lady in Santa Fe who had a microscopic *chittim*," Sasha said. "My mom met her once." The three of them stared at Sasha, totally distracted.

"Anyway, yeah, fine," Chichi said. "Just don't look at the symbol."

Orlu slowly climbed out, making sure not to look at the Nsibidi. "Oh my God, it's so heavy." He grunted as he strained to pick up the large *chittim*.

Sunny nodded. She didn't care. All she could do was stare at what she'd drawn. It reminded her of the spirit faces of Sasha's people. Maybe seeing them had even helped inspire her to create this. She took her juju knife and touched it firmly to the center of the fractal-like pattern. She inhaled a deep breath and, ignoring the ache in her throat, said, "Nimm Village, come."

There was a soft hissing sound. The pattern changed from white to a dull yellow and seemed to harden, and then the whole thing started to rotate, scraping the dirt as it turned. When it stopped, the end with the loop and square at the tip turned to face the forest beside the road. When the wind started blowing and the trees started beating at themselves and then doing something more, Sunny turned and stumbled up into the funky train.

"What's happening?" Chichi was saying as she watched the Nsibidi's effects.

"Look at that huge *chittim*!" Sasha said as Orlu brought it in. "I've only seen that with the big, big brains purposely trying to make it happen! Sunny's rich!"

"Figure it out," Sunny said. "Have to . . . lie down."

"Are you all right?" Orlu said, dumping the *chittim* on a seat. "Sunny?"

But his voice was far away and Sunny was falling. She was still falling as she fell onto the long seat in the back of the funky train. The stinging in her ears and the corners of her eyes, a shadowy figure so heavy she was sure she had shifted into the wilderness, and there was music too, the haunted flute of a masquerade.

"Did it," she muttered. She felt like she'd accomplished the world. And then, before she remembered nothing more for a while, "I hope I wake up before they try to kill us."

❤ ❤ ❤ ❤

The bump of the funky train woke her, and for a moment she listened hard. It sounded like branches were hitting the windows. *Anyanwu*, she thought. Where the hell was her spirit face? *Where have you gone?* No response.

"Then we'll just walk," Sasha was saying. "It's probably better to go on foot from here, anyway."

"If Sunny doesn't wake up, we don't go," Orlu said.

"That's not an option," Chichi said. "Sunny *has* to wake up. She's supposed to be my bodyguard, my woman show. That's what Udide said."

"Udide just wants her damn scroll back," Sasha said.

"Sunny *has* to come with," Chichi said.

When she felt them all looking at her, she opened her eyes. "I'm going. I'm fine." She sat up and sniffed. Her nose was so stuffed. Her world swirled and her forehead throbbed deeply. "Oh man." Her voice was so nasally, it was almost cartoonish. She had to open her mouth to breathe. "Wow. Writing Nsibidi is . . ."

"But you did it, Sunny. And it worked!"

"It did?" She paused as Orlu handed her a tissue from her backpack. She blew her nose hard, filling the tissue. Orlu handed her two more. "Great . . . I guess." She sneezed.

"Look out the window," Chichi said. "Can you get up?"

She did, and she felt a little better. Behind them was a flat dirt road flanked by forest so dense and dark, the night sky looked brighter. She blew her nose one more time, her allergies calming down. "Hand me my backpack," she said. Sasha gave it to her and she opened it and brought out a bag of plantain chips and bottle of water. With each crunch, chomp, and sip, Sunny felt more like herself. She stared out the front window.

"Whoa, is that . . . Nimm?" she said. She opened the window and stuck her head out for a better look.

"Yeah," Chichi said.

"Are we safe being this close??"

"The train's on stealth mode," Sasha said. "Figured that one out an hour ago."

"But can they still detect us?"

"Feels quiet," Orlu said. He was standing at the front, with his hands up.

Sunny rose, stretched her back, and moved to the front of the funky train. One more time, she called to Anyanwu. This time there was a response, but not as a voice or a thought in her head. An image. She saw the image as she looked upon the Nimm Village ahead of her. And in this way, Sunny saw Nimm in two ways at the same time, from the village square far up the road where Anyanwu was and from where she stood on the funky train.

Sunny's first impression of the great Nimm Village was embodied in one word: "chaos." It was more scattered, strange, and nonsensical than even Leopard Knocks. Huts, but like no hut Sunny had ever seen or even imagined. Some were made of brick, others of adobe, most were made of red mud, most were partially covered with solar panels, one was lit by a hanging street lamp, engulfed in a thin layer of smoke and surrounded by hovering *tungwas*. There were palm trees that grew too high, a baobab tree right in the center of the village square that took up the space of several of the huts, and lots of other trees. The flat, red dirt road wound through the village, branching off in many directions from the town square.

However, in the chaos was a joyful brilliance, and Sunny was able to notice this because she saw through Anyanwu. There were flowers on bushes, fruits on trees, and night butterflies and moths with blue bioluminescent wings fluttered about, among what could have been bats or birds, their flight around the swaths of street and groups of huts light and quick. Nothing was cluttered or overlapped. There was an order if you unfocused your eyes and thought with a different part of your brain. And the place smelled . . . fresh. Anyanwu inhaled the scent—it was spicy, woody, peppery, and sweet. *African nutmeg,* Anyanwu said. *A spice that agrees with the wilderness. These women want to make this place full, though few of them have the ability to move through it.*

Sunny took a large gulp of water and finished her plantain chips. As she walked to the front of the bus, she took one more look at the driver. She was sprawled on her back, her mouth open wide as she snored. Sunny looked at her watch. It was nearly five A.M., about an hour until sunrise. She tapped the driver's chin to close her mouth and helped her turn to the side.

"So how does this work?" Sasha asked. "We just sneak into the village and then you have an . . . aggressive home-coming with your auntie?"

"Something like that," Chichi said. "Sunny, you have the best chance of gliding in. Get to the baobab tree in the center. It's named Never Fall for a reason. It's the village's heart."

Sunny nodded, squinting up ahead. "I see it."

"Anyanwu is already there?" Chichi asked.

Sunny nodded again.

"Good," Chichi said. "It's late. Anyanwu is Nimm, but they won't expect her because they don't know you. Few will see her, and if they do, they won't immediately understand."

"So we're the distraction," Orlu said.

"Um . . . yes. Sunny is."

"Against a whole village?"

Chichi paused. "Yes. They will . . . want to speak to me. As they do, Sunny, you speak to my auntie."

"How?" Sunny asked.

"Just go inside, trust me," Chichi said. "Inside the tree while in the wilderness."

Sunny paused and widened her eyes at Chichi. When could they tell them?

Chichi glared at her.

"Yes," Sunny hissed. "Now. When else?" She turned to Orlu, but when she tried to speak, nothing came out.

Orlu frowned. "What is wrong with you two?" He rubbed his hands together. "What aren't you telling us? What's wrong?"

Sunny glanced at Chichi again. Chichi looked like she was straining, like something was biting at her, pulling at her. Sasha made for the door of the bus and opened it.

"Sasha!" Chichi was finally able to say. "Wait!"

"Nah, man," he said, stepping in front of the bus. "I'm not a fool." He crept near the trees, keeping out of sight.

"What are you doing?" Orlu whispered from the funky train door. "You're exposed now!"

"It's the only way," Sasha said. "Just stay there and watch."

"What's he doing?" Sunny said, leaning out beside Orlu.

"No idea," Orlu said.

Sasha moved up the path, staying close to the trees. He stopped. "Ouch!" Sasha shouted, jumping back. He looked at his hand, flexing his fingers. He touched his face. Then he swayed on his feet and dropped to his knees.

"What's happening?" Sunny screeched.

Orlu raised his hands.

Chichi leapt out of the bus, saying to Sunny and Orlu, "Don't follow!"

"Wait! Don't come here," Sasha said, holding a hand up.

He pointed at them. "Orlu, put your hands down or you'll alert them."

Orlu lowered his hands.

"What the fuck!" Sasha slowly got up, stumbling. Then he seemed to be struggling with something. "Ow! Shit!"

"Sasha," Chichi started.

"Shut up!" he shouted.

"Fighting it is not going to help."

"You knew! And you said *nothing*. All this time."

"I *couldn't*," Chichi said. "Literally! That's how it works! It's old Nimm juju that makes you unable to talk about it until you figure it out while *with* a Nimm girl or woman! If people could just discuss it with whomever, they'd scheme to get around it."

"Nimm women. No wonder—"

"Don't," Chichi warned, helping him up and back to the funky train.

Sasha kissed his teeth as he leaned on her and they hobbled back. "Whatever."

"Ah, okay, so it's a Nimm-level trust knot," Orlu said.

"Yes!" Chichi said. "I'm so glad we can finally discuss it!"

"I could never undo something like that," Orlu said, more to himself. "Might kill me first."

"You will both just have to wait until sunrise. It's not long from now. But if we're to get to my auntie, we have to go *now*. Once the sun's up, the Nimm Village is awake and ready. My . . . people are diurnal. My mother calls them 'solar people.' The sun makes them strong, the night makes them rest. The juju guarding the village is not something one can speak of until the person being spoken to *knows* it's there. That's why I couldn't tell you."

"So this village is shut to males," Sasha said, falling into one of the seats just in front of the sleeping driver.

"Male humans," Chichi said sheepishly. "Until sunrise. That's when all the men and boys, from sons to lovers to friends to fathers to people on business, return. They sleep in a village about a mile away." Chichi smiled to herself, and Sunny wished she wouldn't.

"You think this is funny?" Sasha asked.

"Kind of." This time she actually giggled. Sasha gave her a glare full of daggers and guns.

"You should be relieved," she said. "At least you won't die tonight. I can't say the same."

"Enough of that talk," Sunny snapped. Tears were welling in her eyes again. She took a breath and strengthened herself. "Time's wasting. Chichi, just . . . try and stay hidden while I go in. We've only got an hour left."

Chichi nodded.

"Here," Sasha grunted, his lips pursed with anger. He had his juju knife out and he did a complex flourish over his hand. When he opened it, there was a piece of wood on his palm. It glowed weakly and looked greasy. It smelled of palm oil.

"A 'Seven,'" Chichi said. She looked at Sasha. "Those are so expensive."

"I know. Just . . . just use it."

Chichi took the piece of wood and put it in her pocket. "Fine." She turned to Sunny. "Okay . . . Sunny, I'm going to use a 'Seven' juju; I'll put it on the trees."

"A 'Seven' juju?" Sunny asked.

"Don't worry about it," Sasha said. "Until you have to."

"Just get to the village square," Chichi said, pushing the door open. "Anyanwu has seen it; get there and go inside." She paused, looking up the road, Sunny close behind her. "Stay close to the nutmeg trees, but *don't* touch them." She turned to Sasha and Orlu. "Come . . . as soon as you can."

They nodded. Sasha held out a shaky hand and Chichi took it.

"We'll see you in an hour," Orlu said. He smiled. "We'll guard your giant mega *chittim* for you."

Chichi and Sunny took out their juju knives as they crept toward the town near, but not too near, the trees.

11

THE SECRET OF NIMM

"What was happening to Sasha?" Sunny asked as they approached. She slowed her walk.

"He'll be numb for a while," Chichi said. "Lambs just won't see the village. But the border is meanest to non-Nimm Leopards, especially when boys or men try to enter the village at night. Don't worry."

"Are you sure?" They were almost to where Sasha had felt something so painful he'd fallen to his knees.

Chichi linked her arm with Sunny's and they walked faster. Around them was forest, and something in the treetops flew off. Sunny was more aware of the sweet, nutmeg-like smell in the air and the light, warm breeze. She shut her eyes when they reached the part of the narrow dirt road where Sasha had been, tensing for the jolt of pain then numbness.

She felt it after the first two steps. A resistance. Her only assurance that she was Nimm had been the letter from her grandmother. Until now. She knew the precise moment she crossed into the Nimm Village. It wasn't painful at all. She felt the allowance deep in her heart. How she could feel so accepted in a place that had tried to kill Chichi's mother and would most certainly try to kill Chichi was beyond her. She heard something exhale warm and close to her ears. It pressed at her cheeks and then her shoulders. Then something shoved her, but where Sasha had stumbled backward, she stumbled forward, breaking from Chichi's grasp. Something flew low over her head and she ducked.

"It's the welcome," Chichi ominously said.

Whatever had flown at Sunny did it again. "What is it . . . exactly?"

Then she saw for herself because it landed in the dirt in front of her. A barn owl.

"That's Nkolika," Chichi said. "They will all know we are here now."

The white-faced owl placed something on the ground and after a moment, Sunny stepped forward and picked it up. It was a bright red orchid-like flower, and it smelled spicy.

"It's a nutmeg flower," Chichi said. "The species around here is the only type in the world."

Sunny sniffed at it and the smell blossomed in her mind like an actual flower. "Oooh!" she said. The bird flew off.

Sunny had to pause there a moment. She was still a little weak from writing Nsibidi and this awakened senses she didn't even know she had. Everything around her grew clearer. It was like going through a second initiation. "What is . . . that?"

Chichi shrugged. "I've heard people describe it as suddenly being able to see a color you've never seen before. It's called 'homecoming.' Only those who are 'lost' remember it."

"Lost?"

"You just learned you're a Nimm warrior. You're almost sixteen years old. That's lost and now found."

"Well, I wouldn't exactly describe myself as—"

"Shh," Chichi suddenly said.

Sunny looked back at the funky train in the bushes.

"Don't look back," Chichi whispered. "Focus on what's ahead."

Sunny nodded. "When will they—"

"Whenever they do," Chichi snapped. She squinted. "At least we have the moonlight on our side. When we get to the first house, glide for Never Fall, the tree," she said.

"And you?"

"Don't worry about me. There are women here who can read minds, even from far away. They'll know I'm here. Best you don't know what I'm going to do."

They'd nearly reached the first hut, where they could either step fully into the bushes or onto the path. Directly ahead, but several huts away, was the baobab tree.

"Chichi Nimm," a voice said. It was so loud that it sounded as if it were coming from everywhere at once. Chichi and Sunny froze. "Our daughter's daughter, welcome. *Kai!*" Laughter.

"Sunny," Chichi said, looking earnestly at her. "Go!" Then she ran for the bushes.

Sunny didn't wait, either. She ran, dove the way Sugar Cream had shown her, and glided into the wilderness. She felt it surround her, slippery and airy as it always was. She realized something, but she didn't slow down. The wilderness was also the *physical world*. It was as if she was flying up the road, except everything was also overgrown with waving green and yellow plants and the village huts were giant ghost trees that reached impossibly high into the sky. Was this a full place, a place that was both wilderness and physical world? How had she not felt this? World overlapping world.

Women and girls were coming out of their huts. Two were looking right at her. But they could do nothing. She was gliding too fast. She was nearly there when she zoomed past a plump woman in nothing but a wrapper. The woman yelled something, jumped on the dirt road, and started running in the direction Sunny had come from. For a moment

Sunny worried for her friend, and then she did what Chichi said to do: she focused on what was ahead.

She was almost there, and she had just one moment to process two things. The first was that there was a huge *tungwa* floating right at the base of the tree. The second was that Never Fall still looked like a tree in the wilderness. Then *PAFF!* She smashed through the huge *tungwa* and glided right into the tree.

It was reminiscent of her initiation when she'd been dragged through the dirt; she could feel the tree's flesh biting and pulling at her as she passed through it as nothing but spirit. She kept going. She didn't know how long she burrowed, and more than once the fear of getting stuck inside the solid flesh of a tree crossed her mind. Then she heard the cracking and splitting of wood and she slowed down.

When she tumbled onto the smooth surface of the tree's wooden floor, she was Anyanwu and Anyanwu was her. They moved together and they felt confident in their motion. The rays of sunshine that glowed from her spirit face lit the entire room. She looked around. Smooth yellow wood, as if it had been shaped and then polished by a most meticulous hand. The large space was round like the inside of a nut and vast like the inside of a whale.

"Hello!" Anyanwu said in her rich, husky smoker's voice.

How great it was to be one with Anyanwu again. Her voice echoed. She took a few steps, slowly. "My friend says your name is Abeng, but I know I should call you Auntie Nimm." She took more steps and muttered, "She watches us." Sunny could feel it, too. A strong prickly feeling on their neck.

When she turned around, she was facing Auntie Nimm, who sat on the floor quietly, watching. She could not have been there a moment ago. Not with a spirit face like that. Sunny frowned. The last time anyone had openly shown a spirit face to her had been over two years ago when Chichi had given her a glimpse. To show one's spirit face was like parading around naked and doing a wiggle and a twirl. It was a bold, all-exposing act. Even Chichi had only shown hers for a brief moment.

This woman sat in the middle of the vast space that had no door, her legs crossed. Her spirit face was so huge it practically reached the incredibly high ceiling. In the center, where the face would have been, was a circle of blackness surrounded by a thick golden border. From the circle branched gold and red spirals, each ending in a large orange puff that blew in the room's inexplicable breeze. And at the top of the giant mask was what looked like a mirrored cube. The cube caught the light from Sunny's spirit face and reflected it all around the smooth room like a kaleidoscope. She wore a long sea-green dress, and the palms of her hands were colored red-orange and covered with dark blue *uli* designs.

"Sit." Her voice was smooth and kind, but Sunny remained on edge. Anyanwu made her sit.

"Who are you?" the woman asked.

Anyanwu let her speak and Sunny was glad. "Who are you?" Sunny asked.

"Abeng Nimm," she said. "She Who Lives in the Tree."

"Why do you live in a tree?"

"Because it's a good tree. Who are you?"

"Sunny Anyanwu Nwazue."

Auntie Nimm leaned forward. The blackness of her spirit face was so deep that Sunny shivered looking into it. It was like an abyss. Sunny felt nauseous. "You're a Nimm warrior, but . . ." She leaned closer. Sunny was so struck by the blackness that for a moment, she was sure she was falling into it. "What has happened to you, child?"

"I'm doubled."

"And you are all right?"

"We are." Sunny could hear both her and Anyanwu's voices layered over each other, individuals but smooth and fluid. One.

"How?"

"It's a long story," Sunny said.

Abeng shuddered with disgust, something Sunny had seen even Orlu do. She let it go with a sigh; to be doubled was deeply disturbing to Leopard People, so much so that it was horrifying. Like walking around with a bloody head wound that showed exposed skull. Abeng rested her hands on the surface of the ground. Her nails were long and painted silver and they scraped against the wood.

Even Sunny could feel the vibrations of whatever was happening outside. Whatever the "Seven" juju was, Chichi had set it off. However, time was strong in full places; was it already sunrise? Or had no time gone by at all?

"Ah," Abeng said. "I know who you are . . . at least who one of your friends is. Do you know who she is? Who her mother is?"

"I know she's—"

"What are you here for?"

Sunny felt another strong vibration shudder through the space they sat in, almost as if something had hit the tree directly. "We're . . . we're not here to stay."

"We would never let the daughter of . . . that woman stay."

"We just need something that you . . . took."

"The women of Nimm are not thieves."

Sunny shook her head. "I didn't—"

"I know what you seek."

"Where is it? Please."

"Let me tell you about the mother of the friend you'd risk your spirit for."

"Please, I don't think there is time," Sunny said, getting up.

"Oh, there is *always* time in the wilderness," Abeng said. She reached into her dress pocket and brought out a juju knife that looked as if it were made of glass. It was almost exactly like Sunny's knife, except Sunny's was tinted green and hers was not. She did a quick flourish, caught the juju pouch in her hand with a wet slap, and then threw it to the ground before her. There was a resonant *PAFF!* and the room filled with what looked like white smoke. The plants of the wilderness rose from the ground around Sunny, sprouting from the curve of the walls and the ceiling.

"They will kill Chichi for coming here," Abeng said.

Sunny felt a tightness in her chest and she retreated from Anyanwu. She cowered and inside she began to cry. What if Chichi was already dead? Orlu and Sasha were going to come rushing into the village the moment the sun rose and they would be killed, too.

"Tell us what you must tell us," Anyanwu said.

"Your friend's mother was a *murderer*," Abeng said. "She killed two Nimm queens in cold blood. With her bare hands. We here do not just run our people out of the village because they dissatisfy us. We are a complex people, so it takes a *lot* more to reject one of our own." She paused. "Those girls were her best friends . . . they were *my* friends, too. If I were you, I would watch my back. A girl with a mother like that is doomed to repeat her mother's sins."

"Is this—"

"I was there when they found them," Abeng said. "All covered in blood."

Sunny felt even more ill.

"Where is the scroll?" Anyanwu asked. "If we do not return it to Udide, she will erase this place."

"It's not here."

"Where then?"

"Somewhere along The Road."

"What?"

"It changes. Every moment. Like a river. So you cannot find it by looking."

"Like Nsibidi?"

"You can read Nsibidi?" Abeng asked.

"I can," Sunny responded.

Quickly, Abeng dug a palm-sized piece of wood from the floor. She whispered something and her juju knife began to glow orange red, though it did not burn her hand. The room grew foggy with the smoke. The smell of it as she etched the Nsibidi into the wood was not as strong as Sunny expected. Then Abeng was putting the wood into Sunny's hands and pushing her toward the wall. "Time has begun again. Go, go, go," she said. "That is the way. Read it and follow and you will find . . . eventually."

"You can't tell me more? We only have a few days!" Sunny cried, her sandals straining on the curve of the wall. She went to slip the piece of wood in her back jean pocket, but it didn't seem all that secure. She shoved it in her bra, as she did with her mobile phone when she had to use a dirty public restroom.

"Then get to it," Abeng snapped. "Glide!" She shoved Sunny so hard at the wall that Sunny nearly forgot to glide. Confused, the only reason she glided in the direction that she did was because it had been the one from which she came in. Sunny tumbled out of the tree and the wilderness at the same time, rolling in the dust. Coughing, she leapt to her feet, immediately becoming aware of the air's heavy heat and the spicy smell of nutmeg. She coughed harder, putting her hands to her knees. When she looked up, she nearly screamed. The same plump woman she'd seen before was holding her wrapper up and running right at her at full speed, eyes bulging. "They're coming! They're coming!"

Sunny crouched down as the woman leapt over her as if she were nothing more than a large stone. "Stay away from the trees!" the woman shouted over her shoulder as she kept running. But who could? All over, the trees with the red flowers had come to life, flinging their branches this way and that. And then Sunny saw one do it. It brought a branch back and *whipped* it forward and PHOOM! There was a great explosion of red dust. The dawning sun began to light the sky, and in this way Sunny could see that the once quiet Nimm Village had turned into what looked like a war zone. Women and girls ran here and there. A man even raced by. So the men had returned to the village, too. Red dust was everywhere.

"Chichi!" Sunny shouted. She spotted her just in time to see that she was being held by two girls and being punched in the gut by a third. All three looked the exact same: tall, with long black braids, each wearing flowing orange nightgowns. These had to be her cousins, the triplets Soon, Far, and Now, who'd knocked out the funky train driver. Chichi's nose was already bloody, but still she was laughing. "Thunder will find you, Now!" Chichi shouted.

Sunny didn't think before she did it. It was a move she'd done only once in soccer. To that uncouth boy Izu. She rushed at the girl standing over Chichi and rammed her as hard as she could with her shoulder. She used the momentum to whirl on her toes and throw a fist into the other girl's side. The third girl stumbled back. Sunny grabbed Chichi and took off.

It was all a blur. And what was even stranger was how she knew which direction to run without thinking about it. For several seconds she ran, and then she realized Chichi was shouting. "Okay, Sunny! Okay! You can put me down!" And then Sunny became aware of how much her lungs burned, how her arms were screaming, how her left bicep was cramped up like a stone, and how *heavy* Chichi was. She nearly dropped her. Thankfully, Chichi caught herself just before she did.

"You all right?" Sunny asked.

"Are you?" Chichi asked, wiping her still-bleeding nose. She slapped the blood to the dirt and then pinched her nose.

They both looked back. The trees were still throwing their exploding flowers. Women and men were throwing

"Stun" juju at the trees. One tree burst into flames . . . and then it started throwing flaming flowers. Red dust enveloped the village, but standing about two houses away were Chi-chi's three cousins.

"You should have let us kill her!" one of the girls shouted.

"Ask her what her mother did!" another added.

"Why don't you ask *why* your father was foolish enough to fuck your mother?" Chichi shouted back.

Sunny could see the insult hit the girls even from far away. Who needed juju when you had Chichi's mouth? Sunny brought up her juju knife, ready to defend herself. Then Queen Abeng appeared beside the three girls, and the girls swallowed whatever they were about to say. She slowly raised a hand. Sunny hesitated and then raised a hand in re-sponse. The place was in chaos, occupying the attention of the Nimm women, yet the queen had her eyes on both Sunny and Chichi. She could have easily killed both of them, but instead she was letting them go.

"Come on!" Sunny said. "I got what we needed."

Chichi was already stumbling away.

"What's a 'Seven'?" Sunny asked Chichi, catching up with her.

Chichi turned to the side and spit out bloody saliva. She wiped her nose again, glancing back as she staggered off the path toward the trees. "It's what you want to do, times seven." She coughed, rubbing her chest. "It's bad juju in the wrong hands, but I threw it with my right." She laughed at her own strange joke and coughed again.

When they arrived at the place where they'd left the funky train, it was gone. Sasha and Orlu leapt out of the bushes and came running up the path. "Oh, THANK GOODNESS!" Sasha called. "The funky train driver just woke up and drove off! Didn't even ask what the hell was going on!" He looked closer at them, his voice cracking. "Chichi!" He made to grab her and then froze. "Are you okay? What happened?"

"I met up with my cousins . . . and it had been a while," she muttered. Slowly, she moved into his arms and Sasha hugged her.

Sunny met Orlu's eyes and nodded. She was okay, too.

He nodded back, handing over her backpack.

"What the hell did you two do over there?!" Sasha asked Sunny. "We could hear it from here, but the barrier wouldn't allow us to come into the village. You should have seen what happened to Orlu when we got close to it." He flung his arms all over like a wild man.

Orlu kissed his teeth, taking Sasha's hands and pushing them down. "Stop. It wasn't that—"

"Yes, it was," Sasha said. "You looked like that Neo guy in *The Matrix* when he dodged bullets."

"I thought the sun had risen, but we should have waited just a bit longer," Orlu muttered.

"Looks like you guys made yourself known," Sasha said, grinning.

"You're the one who gave her the 'Seven,'" Sunny said. "Come on, let's at least get in the bushes."

"O-ho," Sasha laughed. "Chichi, what'd you make it do?"

"The African nutmeg trees," Chichi said. "My mother used to talk about them a lot. And the moment we entered the village, they smelled so strong, they were all I could think about. So I said seven times stronger and angrier. The aura of the village did the rest." She chuckled tiredly. "A *lot* of anger in that place."

They walked to where Orlu and Sasha had kept Sunny's giant bronze *chittim*. "How am I going to carry that?" Sunny asked.

"We can take turns," Sasha said.

"Me?" Chichi said, cocking her head. "I can't carry that."

Sasha laughed nervously and then admitted, "Neither can I."

"Me neither," Orlu added.

Sunny bent down and touched it. It was warm, and when she looked closely, she realized that it had symbols etched into it. She touched the piece of wood in her bra, thinking of the Nsibidi etched into it. The symbols on the *chittim* weren't Nsibidi, but they were something. She couldn't leave it. She took off her backpack and opened it. She took everything in it out and then picked up and placed the *chittim* inside. The backpack was sturdy. It would hold as long as *she* could hold it.

"Orlu, can you carry my things in your backpack?"

He nodded and packed them in his bag.

"Here, I'll take the bottle of water," Sasha said.

Sunny put the straps over her arms, took a breath, and lifted with her strong legs. "Oof!" she said, feeling a bit unstable. "Okay, I can do it."

"Nimm warrior," Chichi said, clapping.

"After today, I don't think I want to be Nimm anything."

Chichi nodded agreement. "If only it were a choice."

They walked for a while, staying close to the trees. Once she got into the rhythm of it, carrying the giant *chittim* wasn't nearly as difficult as she'd thought it would be. She sweated and was definitely getting a workout, but she could handle it. It kept surprising her, her Nimm warriorhood. She said nothing about it to the others, however. Only Anyanwu, whom she saw was walking about fifty feet ahead. They spoke mentally.

Soon I'll be able to fly, Sunny said to her.

I can already do that.

Gliding isn't flying.

It is.

Sunny smiled. *At least I don't look like a bodybuilder. I don't really want to.*

Not yet, at least.

Will I eventually?

I don't think so.

Good. But man, I can't believe I can carry this thing.

It is yours to carry. So why not?

True.

The road was narrow and overgrown with plants from lack of use. As it was morning and they were walking away from the village, the likelihood of them running into anyone grew slimmer. Especially when they turned onto an even narrower path. Occasionally they stopped and drew a *vévé* on the dirt to call a funky train, but none came, and so they walked on.

As they walked, all glad to just have a moment of quiet, Sunny told them about her talk with Abeng. Then she brought out the piece of wood from her bra. The swirling Nsibidi was so sharp that Sunny felt dizzy and tired just looking at it. She'd built up a strong tolerance for the mystical script, so it must have been extremely potent. The others only saw blurry swirls, arches, lines, the image of what could have been a man or a woman, crosses, and more swirls.

"I need to sit with it," Sunny said. "But I know I *can* read it and it won't take me long." What she didn't say was that she didn't know what consequence it would have on her. More and more strength was required of her in whatever she wanted to do now. Physical strength, internal strength—it was always exhausting, it always *took* from her. Nonetheless, they were alive and had directions to where they would go next.

The Road.

"We go home, regroup *fast*, and take it from there," Orlu said. They all agreed.

"Cool," Sasha said. "But we're going to be stuck out here for a while."

"Why?" Chichi asked. "We'll eventually get to a place where a funky train will catch our ride request."

"That driver we had has clearly put the word out about us," Orlu said. "When she woke up, she was seriously spooked."

"My cousins are wicked," Chichi said sheepishly.

Sasha laughed. "She threw our bags out, nearly broke the stairs rolling the *chittim* out, then drove off faster than I've ever seen a funky train go. I mean, she used disappear mode. I've only seen a funky train do that once in Chicago, when some friends and I had one drop us off in a shady part of the South Side at night. She was scared, but she was *pissed*, too."

"Yeah, no one's coming out here until tomorrow, most likely," Orlu said.

Sunny groaned. Another day gone, and they were currently stuck in the Cross River Forest. At least she'd packed her bottled water and snacks.

❤ ❤ ❤ ❤

They walked for hours. They rested once beside a tree for two hours and then walked again until the sun began to set. They stopped, and right there in the middle of the dirt road, Orlu drew the *vévé* for Leopard Knocks—a leopard paw knocking an edge. It shimmered with the usual orange glow. However, yet again, no funky train answered the *vévé's* call.

"This should be illegal!" Chichi shouted. "They can't just refuse to pick us up!" She sat down in the middle of the path, exasperated. They all did. In all the hours they'd walked the forest-flanked path they'd seen neither person nor vehicle.

"Someone will come eventually," Orlu said.

"Someone should have come hours ago," Chichi said. "I'm so hungry."

"And gassy," Sasha said, rubbing his belly. "Eating a ton of mangos from some random tree really isn't the best idea during times like this."

"Better than nothing," Sunny said. She took off her backpack and let it drop heavily to the ground. She sighed and stretched her back. "I feel like I'm going to pass out," she groaned, twisting this way and that. "Your horrid farts are the least of my worries right now."

"Let's see what you'll say in an hour," Sasha said, rolling onto his back with his head on his backpack.

As Chichi gathered firewood for a small fire in the middle of the path, Sasha worked the mosquito-repelling juju, and Orlu stepped to the forest to listen for anything lurking. There was a quiet agreement between all of them to let Sunny rest and she was *so* glad. She sat, took a deep breath, and then checked the messages on her mobile phone. There was only one. It was from her mother. **Please text me when you can**, it said.

Nothing even from her brother Ugonna. "At least there's service here," Sunny muttered. She texted her mother, **I'm okay. Back tomorrow.** Then she turned her mobile phone off. Her battery was still at seventy percent, but if her mother called, it was the best way to avoid the obligation of answering.

With the fire going, the mosquitoes kept at bay, and the knowledge that nothing nefarious was lurking nearby, Sunny found their spot calming. For the first time since they'd entered the Cross River Forest, she felt herself relax. Her mind cleared, and soon she was thinking about all that had happened in the Nimm Village. The home of her grandmother. And Chichi.

Ask what her mother did, Anyanwu said.

Sunny shivered and bit her lip, no longer so relaxed. She looked at Chichi and found Chichi was looking at her, too, as if she knew what she was thinking. Ah, Chichi, with her mind so fast she was practically psychic. Then Sunny realized she must have been putting out some strong energy because Sasha and Orlu had stopped playing cards and were waiting almost expectantly for Chichi to say something. The bond between the four of them was so strong.

"Sunny, I know what my mother did."

"Okay," Sunny said carefully.

Chichi looked at her, then Orlu and then Sasha.

Sunny shook her head. "You don't have to tell us if—"

"I will tell you," she blurted. She frowned, fighting back tears.

Sasha put his arms around her and the tears came faster.

Sunny took her hand and Orlu took the other.

"My mother is more than a mother to me," Chichi said. "She told me everything when I was ten, and then she told me again just last year. She said she had a feeling she should. She always has these feelings, and she always acts on them." She wiped her tears. "Yeah, my mother tells me everything. She's not your typical mother."

"Definitely not," Sasha said.

"Shh!" Sunny said.

"Hope you didn't interrupt her the way we interrupt you," Orlu muttered.

Chichi laughed, wiping away more tears. "I did. I always have questions and I always ask them." She remembered verbatim both times her mother told her this story, because she was Chichi. She took a deep breath and then she told her mother's story using parts from when her mother had told it to her both the first and second time, though more the second.

12

HERSTORY

You keep asking me about this as if you don't know. What, child, you think I will change my story just because it has been a few years since I told it? I miss a few facts and you will go through them like mistakes in a mathematical equation. Memory isn't math, Chichi. But fine, fine, I'll tell it again. And I'll tell it again in a few years when you ask me yet again. This will never be something I forget. Who can forget being chased off by the people, the community who you love? These people raised me; I am who I am because of them. Nimm. To tell this again is to relive it.

So let me relive it.

They ran me out of the village because I was pregnant with you. But it goes a lot further back than that. It started in the nineties. *That animal of a dictator General Sani Abacha was destroying Nigeria, yes. And a military doctor was giving him access to all sorts of bad and mostly false juju. At the general's villa in Abuja, there were hooves of rams, black pots, candles of every color, small guards, a miniature coffin, all kinds of nonsense. And General Abacha was sacrificing humans more than Black Hat Otokoto. He was feeding people to crocodiles in a river near his home in Abuja.*

He almost always wore sunglasses. Look at the photos of him. The sunglasses were to hide his eyes, dry and red from the juju powder they kept blowing in his face to give him the ability to see his victories. But these charlatans, including that military doctor to whom he was paying millions of naira, were not Leopard People. They were people who had somehow gotten their hands on those things they could never understand. So he saw delusions solidly fixed in reality, but could not see his fast approaching death.

At the time, I was twenty-one and studying to pass Ndibu. To prepare for this is not to read books or "study," though these were things I was always doing, as you do. Ndibu is the third level, the PhD of Leopardom. Few ever come near it. To prepare for Ndibu is to pursue and practice your passions. My passion was holding conversation with masquerades, as you know. This was dangerous for anyone, but my mentor had taught me, was still teaching me well. And with my ghost ear, I was a powerful listener, of course.

I had many conversations with an Ojionu masquerade

about General Abacha. It had many opinions and wanted to know many things from me about my ideas. I wanted to join the protests. I wanted to do something. Those conversations kept me balanced.

It was while I was talking to the Ojionu that my mentor tapped me on the shoulder. I opened my eyes and there were three Nimm warriors there to ask me to the palace. There I learned that Nimm had its own problems. More immediate ones than a vile Lamb dictator playing with dangerous juju he would never understand. I remember standing in the main room of the palace, looking around. The only time I'd ever been in there was on the moonlit night I was born and my mother offered me to the Nimm goddess, as every girl child there is offered. My mother is the youngest sister to the queen, so the palace wasn't where she grew up.

All the staircases and the Nsibidi—I was so distracted when I entered. You know my natural ability. I've had my ghost ear since I was born, probably even before that. I've never felt like one who is deaf in one ear because of it. It's why I can remember being born in that palace. I could hear when I came out. The sucking sound, the pressure, the rush of air, the sound of my own cries, the hooting owl outside in the night, the crickets, and always the song of the masquerades.

So I remembered this place. It hadn't changed much. One of my younger cousins led me in. "Any idea what this is about?" I asked her.

"No," she said. She walked faster. I remember that. She wanted to get her little job over with and be away from me as fast as she could. So I didn't ask her anything else. And this gave me a chance to look around and really take it all in.

The Nimm Palace was full of books. From the outside, it was always the biggest hut I'd ever seen, but from the inside, you really understood why. And you also understood how different it was from the way most women in the Nimm Village lived. Where the baobab tree was the soul of the village, the palace was its heart, the inner machinations of what we were. Anarchic, mystical, complete. It was a hut the size of three houses and just as spacious inside. There were sleeping and cooking and bathing spaces, all separated by piles of strategically grouped books. It was the chaos of Nimm organized into one large space. You could walk through the open entranceway and see across the huge palace. My way was blocked by a great stack of vertically organized books.

I stepped up to the wall and looked at the first book that caught my eye. I still remember what it was—a wide old tome with the title The Treasures of Ogbanje Demystified scrawled across the spine in white chalk. I'd heard of and always wanted to read this book but had never been able to find it. I reached for the book and a sparkly red print bloomed where my finger touched.

Books, books, books in the palace. At rest. In hands. The hut's walls may have been made from mud and solar panels, but its insides were mostly books. They were crowded under beds, packed against walls, used to make walls, piled under tables, gathered around showers and bathtubs. The hut's ceiling was a hundred feet high, and on the sides of the hut were mud spiral staircases that went to mud platforms at the top of the hut where book stacks were embedded in the walls.

Almost everyone in the palace was staring at me as we passed. I knew a few of the girls from around. Older princesses, warriors, and librarians of high rank and knowledge. It was hard for me to focus on faces, so I stuck close to my cousin. I followed her up one of these staircases. There was no banister, so I had to walk deliberately. When we reached the top, there was a door. My cousin knocked and said, "I have her."

The door opened and we went in. When I smelled the strong incense flood the room, I started feeling less excited and more nervous. This type of incense burned into a cloaking smoke and was used when a conversation was going to happen that needed to be private. I started wondering about all the women standing around in groups talking quietly as we walked to the palace. I wondered if the storm clouds coming in and darkening the sky weren't just storm clouds. I'd been in conversation with a masquerade for several hours. Something had happened in that time that I had missed. I was still numb and detached from my time with the masquerade, so it was all hard to grasp.

There were three women there waiting, and my cousin rushed off, leaving me with them. Two of my older and . . . wildest cousins, Omni and Ndom, and the Nimm Queen Eka-Eka, a kind woman whose age no one knew.

"Took you long enough," Omni said, giving me that smirk that always made people uncomfortable with her. Ndom only glared at me with her feral eyes. Both were powerful young women, the most powerful of my generation. And among the Nimm, where skill always runs strong, this is saying a lot. They were both shape-shifters. Omni had brittle bones and was always breaking them when she was younger. Now she could change into many things, and she loved a man who could do the same. The two were known for running wild with panthers, lizards, and hawks, and writing books about it. Ndom could "become" whatever she understood, from a fly to a truck to a meteorite that falls into the forest. Ndom was always a healthy person, except when she suffered bouts of depression.

"I was . . . doing something that was hard to get away from," I said to the queen. "I apologize. I came as fast as I could. Please, what is this about?"

All three of us turned to the queen. Waiting.

"The Egbo Clan is coming," she said. "We have about three nights before they come."

"Gao has seen it, then," I said. Gao was a mentor known for her ability to see exactly three days into the future.

"Yes."

"They will wipe us off the face of this Earth," Ndom said, her wild eyes wide. "Unless we wipe them first."

"We are not a warlike people," the queen said.

"Excuse my forwardness, but speak for yourself, my queen," Omni said. Her face hardened, panther hairs already sprouting at her temple, her brown eyes turning gold. "Nimm has defenses. We have warriors. What else are we for?"

And then I understood. Me, Omni, and Ndom. It made sense if it was to work. "You want us to steal Udide's story, the ghazal." She nodded. "It will have juju we can use to stop the Egbo Clan without bloodshed."

"I knew you'd know of it," the queen said, nodding. "The council knew you would, too." She looked to Ndom and Omni. "And you two may prefer battle, but I think you'll like this plan more."

They sent the three of us alone. Me because I'd specialized in researching juju books and my cousins Omni and Ndom because both of them were vicious and loved the idea of sneaking into a deity's lair and stealing one of her most precious items. We used an edan to get there quickly. This one looked like a bronze woman carrying an astrolabe. My mother had cast it only days ago as part of a series of modern edans and ikengas. It was actually quite beautiful. This was my first time touching one, and I wasn't ready for the kick it gave. Omni and Ndom had not only used an edan before, but they were shape-shifters, so they were used to that feeling of being outside of self. I, however . . . wasn't ready.

Omni actually had to leap into the ether and pull me back

as we moved. We were in Lagos within seconds. As we walked through the market on our way to find Udide's cave, I was limping and stumbling like a drunkard. It's difficult to shake off journey by edan. I kept feeling like I was losing myself. I remember that clearly because when we arrived at her cave, the feeling of going in there was heightened by the edan-lag I was struggling to shake.

Chichi, daughter, you now know what it is to descend uninvited into a cavern dug by millions of spiders. You have met and faced the Great Udide in her house. That still amazes me. When I was there, both Omni and Ndom changed into spiders, so they blended in easily. I could only make myself ignorable, but as I moved through the place in the dark, they were definitely aware of us. Millions of spiders darting this way and that, scrambling down from the ceiling on their webs. Trying to find me. It felt like we were never going to get out of there alive.

But Udide wasn't there. This day was a very, very important day. I learned later that the queen knew this. There are few days when Udide is preoccupied, when she is too busy to pay attention to the infinity of unfolding stories of her favorite city of Lagos. There was the Great Crab who lives deep in the Atlantic Ocean. Udide loves this crab and goes to see it once every millennium. This was that day, Chichi. I don't know how this would have gone if she had been there. But she wasn't. She was on a date!

And that's how we were able to look and then find her treasures in that cavern. There was a space in there full of things. I won't tell you the many things in there beside her various books, but the one we sought was in there. I was the one who could hear it, so I was the one who took it. It looked like a football-sized strip of clear, green glass that had been coiled into a circle. It was a Möbius band, so if an ant crawled all the way around it, the ant would return to its starting point having traveled both sides of the band without ever crossing an edge. The Nsibidi etched into it was tiny, but you could read it if you squinted or used a magnifying glass. I'd find out later that the writing was quadrupled, so you could read around the band four times and still read something new. Spider physics is the most complex in the world.

I grabbed the ghazal, went ignorable, and we all took off. By this time, the spiders had seen me, and they attacked. It's a sight I never want to see again, and I'm ashamed of how many Ndom and Omni killed to protect me. A copious number, millions, gallons, the caves had begun to smell of the stench of crushed spider viscera. Acidic, dusty, a brown smell that was like soil blended with iron. It is a smell I'll remember forever; it was the smell of death so I could live. Ndom and Omni enjoyed killing the spiders and were good at it. I think when you shapeshift into predatory animals and live as them very often, there is a taste for killing you acquire. They crushed, caught, dismembered, and flung Udide's children like rotten fruit. Keeping them off me, from beneath me, from falling on me, from attacking me, from stinging me. It was the only way I got out of there.

When we escaped and rejoined the market, they were laughing like hyenas. I felt like sobbing. We all smelled like dead spiders; Ndom even had burned spider parts stuck in her long braids, Omni's short Afro was covered in ash, I was wet with spider innards, and people were looking at us strangely. None of us cared. We had the book. After a few minutes, I was laughing, too. It was exhilarating, I admit. Triumphant. We were going to use this to save the Nimm Village.

I remember the weight of it in my hand as we walked. For such a small item, it was so heavy. And so smooth, even with the etched writing on each side of the band. The letters were white in the green glass-like material. But what was most amazing was that I could hear it. Like the scrape of leaves, the legs of spiders, the scratching of pen to paper, the wisps of smoke in the air. But underneath was something so powerful I would have happily thrown it in the ocean if I could. If I were a fool.

I held it because I could hear it. And I think Ndom and Omni sensed there was consequence to holding it for too long. Actually, now I am sure of it. Let me tell you why. We stopped at a roadside restaurant to eat a little something. I used napkins to wipe myself off as best I could. No one would sit next to us and we didn't care. Our world was still strange, and the Lamb world was never a place that really interested any of us. The sun was going down by this time.

When we took the edan-influenced steps home, it was the dead of night. We went from the frantic, festive energy of Friday night in the Lagos streets to the soft symphony of night creatures of the forest and the red dirt path. The air smelled different; it was warmer. I remember a group of moths fluttered by.

"Bring light," I said. And the fireflies came right away. They fluttered around me and I smiled. We were home, the village a few minutes' walk down the road. We still had days before the Egbo Clan would attack. Plenty of time to interpret what we needed from the ghazal, create that necessary juju, work it, and wait.

I was still looking at the fireflies when Ndom suddenly changed into a panther. Her juju knife hit the dirt, landing with the handle up. Her clothes tore, then ripped, fell. She shook off her sandals. I was watching her when Omni must have changed into a leopard. Her juju knife fell to the dirt in the same way. If I had tried to grab either knife, I'd have been stung by something or been unable to remove it from the dirt or I'd instantly die . . . something. One does not touch the juju knife of another without permission, but that is especially true of a shape-shifter's knife after they have shifted.

Both Ndom and Omni were bigger than lions. Ndom raised her black head and opened her mouth wide, almost like a yawn. Omni growled low and guttural, pacing around me.

"What are you doing?" I whispered. I could feel all the

blood draining from my cheeks. My heart began to race. I held on tightly to the ghazal. And I brought out my juju knife. They only growled back. Both were pacing around me now. "Why?" I asked. And I heard Ndom speak, even though she was a panther. It was a thin voice, as if spoken through a deflating balloon. "Give us the ghazal," Ndom said.

Omni's voice was rough, low, and full of violence. "Or we'll tear you apart."

"Wh-why?! This is to save—"

"Cut the shit, just hand it over," Ndom said.

"But why?!" I shouted. "Just steal it after we use it!"

"He wants it this night," Ndom said.

"Who?"

Growling. They were edging closer.

"You have chosen to die," Omni said. And I knew she was not exaggerating or trying to scare me. I held the ghazal and my knife more tightly.

"Okay," I said. "But let me die understanding what you are trying to do."

"Or you can join us," Ndom said.

"No," Omni snapped. "I won't share any of my half of the money."

"Money?" I asked. "Not chittim?"

"Money makes the world go round," Ndom said. "Not chittim."

I spat to the side. Angry. Oh, I was getting very, very angry.

And if she said what I was thinking she was going to say, I was ready to die trying not to let it happen. "Who?" I asked again.

They came closer. I worked a protective juju and caught the juju bag in my hand.

"That will not help you," Omni said.

"You don't know what it is," I said.

"It won't help you," Omni repeated.

I knew they'd both passed Ndibu, and shape-shifters who passed this could hold and work juju in their mouths, coat it on their teeth. It was how they'd killed all those spiders while masquerading as spiders themselves.

"Damn it," I muttered.

"I will offer General Sani Abacha your head along with the ghazal," Omni said. "He'll appreciate that."

I had my answer and it was what I suspected. I learned these details much later: While our village was threatened with extinction from a terrible outside threat, these two saw an opportunity. Ndom and Omni were the ones who'd agitated the Egbo Clan to attack the Nimm Village; they'd secure high positions in the opposing clan once the Nimm Village was wiped out. Tricking their own people into giving them an edan, and then me into helping them get the ghazal to sell to Nigeria's dictator, had been a plan on top of their plan. Sani Abacha himself had offered them a billion naira for the ghazal, and he planned to use it to assure his eternal life and ability to rule Nigeria. Treacherous traitors.

My village was in my hands. And I reacted as if it was. They came at me, ready to tear my throat out. But that is not how it went, my daughter. I had learned this juju from my mentor. She had taught me this juju only two days ago. I'd frowned because it was not the type of thing she usually taught me. She called it mfebede. She said it was good for slicing plantain just right when you are in a hurry. She was always teaching me cooking jujus because she believed every woman should know how to cook delicious meals. "It's the best way to keep yourself sane. The act of the cooking and the act of eating well."

This juju had been a lot of fun. You threw the plantain in the air and threw the juju at it, slicing it up in twenty perfect slivers. Always exactly twenty, no matter the size of the plantain. My mentor could see three days into the future, and she can explore the landscape of the vision to see from whatever angle she needs to see. She was an old, old quiet woman, having lived her entire life in the village, never traveling anywhere. She had only mentored two women before me. Most of her life she'd lived in Nimm—tending to everyone, cooking for everyone, her man living in the nearby village. But my mentor always, always, always knew when to use her ability to strike. And this was the one and only time in her life where she did.

As my cousins came at me, I understood many things. And I accepted those things, too. And that's how I was able to do it. They came at me at the same time, so I threw the juju one after the other, like . . . knives.

I could hear the juju divide the air. Into twenty pieces. Exact. When they hit Omni, she screamed, and then the scream became a gurgle as she fell on me into exactly twenty bleeding pieces. Then Ndom. She was quiet, maybe shocked. They'd both been mid-pounce, so their remains hit me hard enough to knock me down. Blood, entrails, fluids, hair. It was worse than the biggest tungwa explosion. It was the quivering warm flesh of my cousins. Dizzy, the world around me fuzzy and fading, I heard, "Ah! What did you DO!" I tried to explain, to push words from my mouth. But everything grew too heavy. There were warm, still quivering hunks of flesh weighing me down. My head felt as if it weighed fifty pounds. There were drums pounding inside it, and I could still hear the ghazal I held, telling me, talking to me, asking me. I coughed as I saw some people coming to me. No words.

I passed out.

Yes, there'd been three people who'd been coming up the road. And they saw the aftermath, not the attack. They saw me lying blood-soaked and unconscious in the dirt of the road beneath the sliced-up bodies of panther and leopard, Ndom and Omni. They dragged me to the palace, and that was how I came to—on my back, choking from the dust billowing around me, the back of my head raw. It seemed everyone in the village was surrounding me; there were so many bodies pressing in. Warriors guarded me, keeping women from kicking me in the head. It was just before sunrise and I was lucky, for if there had been men in the village, they would have surely killed me.

By this time everyone knew about the Egbo Clan coming and our mission to get the ghazal. And everyone knew I'd killed Ndom and Omni. But no one knew why, except my mentor, who stayed quiet. I'm glad she did. They'd have killed her if she tried to defend me. My mother was arrested, my sisters, too. And even they thought I was a murderer who sought to betray the village by stealing the ghazal. It didn't matter to anyone that this didn't make any sense. When you are afraid of annihilation and someone gets in the way of you stopping it, you will see that which is not there.

I was dragged to my feet and brought into the palace. My left eye was so caked with blood that I could barely see out of it, my body ached, and oh, my head hurt. With every step, it felt like something in my brain was coming loose. I was nauseous, but somehow I didn't vomit.

I was still holding the ghazal when they shoved me into the central room. The room I had stood in only twenty-four hours earlier, a different person. I stood before the queen, shivering at this point from shock. The warriors continued standing around me. No one comforted me. No one asked me questions. No one spoke to me. The queen sneered at me and then reached forward and pried the ghazal from my hands. She had to work for it because even in my state, I wasn't ready to let go of it.

"No," I said, low and guttural.

The warriors descended on me. Punching, slapping, curs-

ing, calling me "murderer." I don't remember it all. They threw me in the Night Runner Forest, where I would have died if an Obi Library graduate student named Anatov had not found me and listened to my story of how I got there. He brought me to Sugar Cream, and she introduced me to many others who listened to me. I recovered. I healed.

I learned through channels that the Nimm Village had succeeded in defeating the Egbo Clan using amazing jujus no one had ever seen before. The ghazal had been useful. I briefly wondered if they'd returned it, but in my heart I doubted it. Giving back that level of knowledge has never been the Nimm way. I didn't care. Let Udide descend on them; I wouldn't be there for it.

I went on, met your irresponsible genius father, and had you, Chichi. But the hurt from all that never leaves. I was cut off from the Nimm Village. For five years, I had no family, no link to where I grew up, what I identified with, who I was. Everyone knew I was Nimm; people called me Nimm, but I could not set foot there. If word traveled to them about me, no word traveled back.

Yes, so I had you. Oh, Chichi, I was so proud. Your father loves you, even if he doesn't know the first thing about being a father. I was happy studying at the Obi Library. Learning so much. Coming to understand what had happened and why. I even had the chance to work with the women who eventually brought down the dictator Sani Abacha. You know what happened to that man, right? The international and local news reported that he had a heart attack, but it was the prostitute women from India who really did away with him. They fed him a poisoned apple, like some twisted version of Snow White. Oh, learning about it made me smile.

But you know what is never reported in the Lamb world? The fact that those women were Leopard Women, and a team of local Leopard People helped them enact the assassination and then escape. Abacha had false and true juju worked around his home and in his body, and I was part of a group who studied how to undo it all and instruct the women on what to do. I never told any of my colleagues about my cousins and how they'd tried to get him some of the most powerful juju in the world.

I don't know what possessed me to do the unthinkable. My pregnancy with you had been easy. I felt great. You were a dream, sleeping when I slept, eating when I ate. I began to bring you to the library with me to study. You even studied when I studied. I was growing. I had more chittim than I had ever imagined. I was learning so much. I'd earn chittim and I'd rush right to the bookstore to buy the strangest books I could— the ones the Obi Library refused to carry. I was happy. I was good. Maybe that's why I felt it was time to take you there. How could you become if you didn't know what you were?

I was such a fool. For all my knowledge, I was such a fool. I took a funky train to the village. I brought you with me. You were two and a half, but you could run so fast and climb so high. It was sunny, and by the time we arrived it was raining. And thundering. And the path was mud by the time we walked into the village . . .

13

BUTTERFLIES

Chichi stopped talking and looked at the three of them, her eyes wide.

"Well?" Sasha said.

Sunny touched Chichi's shoulder.

"You remember," Orlu said. "Don't you."

Chichi nodded. A tear squeezed from her wide eyes.

"You don't have to . . ."

"We . . . we got there," Chichi continued. "It was raining so hard. I don't know if it was something, some juju to alert if my mother ever returned. There were mudslides all around us. Trying to block the road." She closed her eyes and took a deep breath. "They came up the road. I don't know who was who." She stood up and started pacing. "Ah, let me say this, let me say this." She wrung her hands. "Someone tried to hit me with a knockout juju. My mother *blocked* it. My mother is a badass." Chichi was shaking. "Then she grabbed me and ran *at* one of the mudslides. *AT IT.* And that's how we escaped. She skied up that falling wall of mud like white Americans ski down slopes of snow on those TV shows. I remember the wind and the mud slapping all over us both—it felt so good. Like life." She sat down and stared off into space.

Sunny stood up and walked up the road a bit. She needed to move around, stretch her legs, shake it off. Behind her, she heard Sasha talking quietly to Chichi. Orlu, too. She swung her arms out and then gave herself a tight hug as she stepped up to the forest and looked up at it.

"Damn it," she muttered, bringing out her juju knife. A mosquito was already trying to bite her; she'd stepped too far away from the charm guarding their small camp. She worked the juju again and the mosquito buzzing near her ear was gone. She looked back at the forest and sighed, trying to process the story of Chichi's mother's exile. The image of her sliced-up dead cousins falling on Chichi's mother flashed through her mind, and Sunny suddenly felt ill. *What else could she have done, though?* Sunny thought. But still she shuddered, fighting nausea.

At first, she thought the wind had picked up. Then she thought she was just seeing things. If there was a time to question what was right before her eyes, it was now. Then she wished she were more scatterbrained than she was because before her, in the darkness—yes, even in the darkness, where the firelight just barely reached—were giant, glistening black eyes. Eight of them. How Udide could stand silently and easily in the dense forest was the least of Sunny's worries. The fact that Udide was staring right at her was the greatest.

Sunny stared back. She could hear the others, yards away, talking softly. Chichi chuckled, but it sounded as if it came through the thickness of tears. The longer Sunny watched Udide, the more clearly she could see her eyes, head, enormous black legs, the soft white hairs on those legs that caught the firelight just so. Udide was standing among the trees all around her. Would she knock down all of them to get to Sunny? She could.

"Huuuuuuuaaagh!" Udide exhaled, and her breath rolled over Sunny like a warm breeze . . . that was on fire. Burning houses. And then the image burst in Sunny's mind, and as it did she felt Anyanwu jump into her lightning fast. Fast enough to catch Sunny and shield her from the weight of. . .

Tearing . . . then stitch, stitch, click, stitch. The threads of silk were story. Shiny silver, thin and strong and then they were . . . stitch, stitch, the baobab tree. The queen was inside. Sitting. Cracking, like the crash and crush of lightning. The smooth round walls imploded and collapsed and splintered. Dry and brittle. Then like ash. And a plume of dust and the splintering fell in on itself. On the queen. You could not glide away. You were a trapped insect in the tree called Never Fall as it fell, stitch, stitch . . .

Sunny was sitting on the road, staring into the forest. Anyanwu was gone again. Udide was gone. But her friends were around her now. "Udide," Sunny said simply.

"We smelled her," Chichi said, helping Sunny up.

"You all right?" Orlu said, putting an arm around her waist.

"She's done something," Sunny said. "I *saw* it. She's done something back at the Nimm Village."

Chichi kissed her teeth, rubbed her sore belly, and muttered, "Good."

"It's not good," Sunny snapped. "What she does to them, she will do to your mother, my family, anyone we love, tenfold. It's bigger than us."

"What did she do?" Orlu said.

"I think she just killed the Nimm queen!" Sunny said. "That baobab tree fell in on her!"

"Never Fall?" Chichi asked. "That's impossible!"

"She knocked it down?" Orlu said.

Sunny shook her head. "She just . . . she made it so. Like weaving a web . . . or . . . retelling a story, just differently."

"Oh," Chichi whispered, looking worried.

"Yeah," Sunny said. "Glad you get it now."

"Udide!" Sasha yelled. The three of them whirled around.

Sunny almost fell over; thankfully Orlu caught her. Sasha was in front of the trees, standing precisely in front of where Sunny had seen Udide.

"Sasha!" she shouted. "What are you doing?!"

"Why don't you come out and face us, like a REAL GOD!" he shouted. "Why lure my friend away from us before you scared the shit out of her! Come out and fight like a spider!"

Chichi grabbed his arm. "Stop it. Not now!"

Sasha stumbled with her. "I'm not afraid of her!"

"You should be," Chichi said. "And you really don't want to fight anything that fights like a spider."

For the rest of the night, Sunny stayed close to her friends. She looked at the clear, starry sky directly above and fought hard not to think about what the Nimm Village was going through with the death of their leader. It was the tip of the iceberg of what Udide was capable of. *Breathe*, she thought. She thought about calling Anyanwu, but then decided against it. When she finally drifted off to sleep, she slept deeply. And somehow, the dreams she had were free of spiders, crushed queens, sliced-up cousins, and all other nightmarish things.

In the early morning, Sunny, Chichi, and Sasha stood on the side of the dirt road as Orlu drew the funky train *vévé*. Sunny felt grimy, her muscles ached, and her clothes were dusty.

"If this doesn't work, it's time to riot," Sasha said, annoyed.

A gorgeous blue butterfly fluttered by, landing in one of the trees. Sunny blinked. The tree was full of them. "That's pretty," she muttered. Then she saw Anyanwu standing under the tree, looking up into it. Sunny smiled as Anyanwu did exactly what she'd have wanted to do; she touched one of the blue butterflies resting on the tree's trunk. It fluttered gently into the air, bothered but unafraid of Anyanwu. It landed on Anyanwu's head and Sunny grinned.

"What are you looking at?" Chichi asked.

"Anyanwu, she's over there," Sunny said. "Playing with—" The pained look on Chichi's face was enough. "Ah . . . it's nothing."

The sound of the horn sent some birds flying from a nearby tree. Sunny shrieked, startled.

"Finally!" Sasha shouted.

The funky train that pulled up to them was completely empty, the phrase GO AND SIN NO MORE drawn over the side in huge, colorful, swooping letters. It was shiny and clean as if it had just been washed. The driver who opened the door to look at them was a lanky, light-skinned man in his thirties who wore long white pants and a brown caftan with white lace embroidered around the collar. Around his neck was a thick gold chain, and on each finger was a gold ring. When he grinned at them, the gold tooth in his mouth glinted. He spoke to them in a language Sunny didn't recognize. Thankfully, Sasha and Chichi did. After they talked to the man, he nodded, looked at Orlu and Sunny, and switched to English.

"It's early."

"We know," Orlu said.

"What you doing out here? You come from Nimm Village?"

Sunny and Orlu looked at each other.

"It's fine," Chichi said. "Tell him."

"Yes," Sunny said. Better to say as little as possible when you're unsure. She'd learned that from her mother.

"I heard about your *wahala*," the driver said, narrowing his eyes at them. He pointed a stubby finger at them. "You no go bring am for my train?" he asked.

The four of them shook their heads.

"Okay, o," the driver said. He motioned for them to enter. "Come."

"Your Efik is getting better," Chichi said, smirking at Sasha as they got on. She leaned forward and gave him a kiss.

"Just get on," Sunny said, pushing Sasha. "Let's get out of here!"

"No sense of when that's appropriate," Orlu muttered.

The driver, who insisted on being called Buddy, being an entrepreneur-type, made the ride home more than pleasant. His funky train was clean, it smelled like perfume, and the seats were super plush. Once they were comfortable, they were happy to buy the bags of plantain chips, pure water, and orange Fanta that Buddy offered them. But though he played soft church music and the open windows let in a pleasant cool breeze during the four-hour drive, none of them were able to sleep. When things are quiet and one is comfortable, only then does the magnitude of one's most pressing problem become clear.

They had only five days left to get Udide's ghazal back to her.

14

LIKE ELECTRICITY

Sunny unlocked the gate and gently pushed it open. She glanced up at the shining midday sun. She'd been gone for nearly twenty-four hours, and everything was wet from what had probably been a rain- or thunderstorm. She stepped over a puddle, noting all the leaves scattered around the driveway. "Must have been windy, too," she muttered. It was Sunday, so everyone was not only up, they were home. Both her parents' cars were in the driveway, and her brother Ugonna's motorbike was there, too. She turned her phone back on as she walked to the house. She'd had it off since last night when she'd checked it. No new messages. Had they called, though? Her phone wouldn't tell her that unless they'd left a message.

"I am weary of all this sneaking around," she heard Any-anwu say.

Something about Anyanwu's tone really rubbed Sunny the wrong way. "Well, I'm sorry that I'm a teenage free agent," she said aloud.

Anyanwu said nothing to this and walked to the back of the house and paused, looking at the dead and dried-up, but currently dripping palm tree. "We are more," Anyanwu said, also aloud.

Sunny sighed and nodded. "I know." There were days where Sunny wondered if she and Anyanwu had been some sort of mistake. A wrong pairing. Anyanwu was epic; she'd done amazing things over millennia, traveled far, experienced much. How was she supposed to be the spirit face of a free agent like Sunny? And now that they were doubled and Anyanwu was even freer to just be, the bond seemed even more fraught. But she loved Anyanwu; Anyanwu was her.

She felt Anyanwu move within her in a way that Sunny understood was a hug. Sunny smiled. Despite being epic and knowing it, Anyanwu loved her, too. Sunny opened her backpack, dug a hole in the soft, muddy dirt, and dropped the *chittim* in the hole. Then she pushed the dirt back over it and stuck a stick in it to mark her spot. "Okay, that's done. Now the hard part," she muttered. She was glad when Any-anwu made no remark. She used the faucet at the back of the house to wash her dirty hands, put on her backpack, and went to the front of the house.

Her legs felt like jelly as she stepped up to the door, clutching the strap of her backpack. She opened the door with her key. As she pushed the door open, she was pulled forward by the strength of the door opening farther. There stood her father. He wore his Sunday clothes, a blue caftan and blue pants.

Sunny looked up at him, her heart fluttering. "I . . . Dad, I'm sorry, I can explain. Well, no, I can't . . . but I—"

The slap was electric. She felt the inside of her cheek catch on her closing teeth as her head whipped to the right. Behind her eyes, she saw a great burst of sunshine yellow, and then it retreated and disappeared like a flame descending into a deep pool of water. Sunny stumbled back, holding her burning cheek. Tears of shock and pain stung her eyes as her mouth filled with blood. She stared at her father. He still had his hand up. His eyes glistened, but his lips were pressed together so tightly that no words escaped them.

"Dad!" Sunny said, shakily. She sobbed, glaring at him.

From right behind her, she heard Anyanwu, angry, outraged. What she spoke was firm and simple: "No." Then Sunny felt her go. Then she, too, turned and ran from her parents' home. As she ran across the driveway, she stamped down hard in the puddle, splashing water on her sandals and jeans. Her father did not call her back.

Sunny ran and ran. When she finally slowed to a walk, she was shuddering so hard that she had to stop. Two cars and a truck passed close to her as she stood on the side of the road, but she didn't even care. She put her hands to her knees, head to her chest. She felt she would fall. Anyanwu had fled. To where, Sunny didn't know. She wiped her face with her shirt and straightened up. A man standing at a bus stop was looking at her.

"God will carry you," he said kindly.

She smiled at him, nodded, and walked on. She walked all the way to Chichi's hut. She found Chichi outside, leaning against the hut and smoking a Banga herbal cigarette. The right side of her face was still swollen from the beating she took at the hands of her cousins in the Nimm Village.

"Sunny," she said, blowing out smoke and smiling. Then the smile dropped from her face and she rushed over. "Oh, what happened now?"

"My father."

Chichi took Sunny's hand and pulled her inside. "Sit," Chichi said.

Sunny stiffly sat on the large, soft, leather-bound book she usually sat on. It was bigger than she was and too heavy to move around, which was why it was always in the same spot. Chichi's mother was in the corner, sitting on a stool, reading a large dusty red book. She looked up as Sunny walked in.

"Good afternoon, Mama Nimm," Sunny said.

Chichi knelt beside Sunny, looking into her face. "Your eye," she said.

"What?" Sunny asked. "Yeah, my dad slapped me."

"Hard enough to burst a blood vessel in your eye. Be right back," she said, rushing off. Sunny brought out her phone and used the camera to look at herself. She gasped. There was a circular splotch in the left side of her eye. She blinked a few times. It didn't go away.

"Subconjunctival hemorrhage," Chichi's mother said. "I had those dotting both of my eyes once. Not from eye trauma, but from giving birth to Chichi. The one you have is small-small. Give it a week or two." She closed her book, put it down, and came over to Sunny. She sat on a stack of books across from her. "Are you all right?"

"Y . . ." Sunny sighed. She shook her head. "No."

"Family will not always understand," she said. "Especially the families of free agents."

"I think it goes further back than that," Chichi said, returning with a cup of tea. She handed it to Sunny. Sunny took it and sipped. Sweet and strong, no cream. She took another sip. "Sunny's dad is a traditional Igbo man and she was born a girl—"

"An 'ugly' one," Sunny added, side-eyeing.

"Oh, don't say that," Chichi's mother said.

"I'm only repeating what I once heard my dad tell his best friend when I was little, when I used to sneak and listen." Tears filled her eyes as she felt her father's slap again. " 'I have two sons, so a daughter's okay . . . but couldn't she *not* look like a forest spirit?' Then laughter and more Guinness beer. That was a long time ago. What will he say now that I'm tall and lean like a guy?' "

"You *don't* look like a guy," Chichi laughed. "You look like a runway model who decided to go for runs instead of starve herself."

"And you are beautiful," her mother said. "Anyanwu, sun goddess. You have albinism, yes, *embrace* it, *see* it. And stop sulking." She cocked her head to the side. "You think you were the first one to be thrown out of her home because of a misunderstanding?"

Sunny was so shocked by her words that she just stared at Chichi's mother, her mouth hanging open.

Chichi's mother grinned. "Ah, now you forget sadness. I did it. Yay!" She got up. "Drink your tea. Stay here tonight. Use your, ah, phone to tell them you are here." She took her book and went out the back of the hut. "And take some time and figure out the Nsibidi on that piece of wood."

Sunny sipped her tea as she brought the wood out from her bra. She put it back in. Not yet. When Chichi lay on the floor beside her, Sunny asked, "How are *you* doing?"

"Sore," she said, rubbing her side.

She lowered her voice. "You tell your mom everything?"

Chichi nodded.

"And? What did she say??"

"She said, 'What did you expect?'"

"She wasn't mad?"

"Oh, she was mad as hell," Chichi said.

"At least she didn't slap you."

Chichi shrugged. "There are many ways to slap some-one . . . but yeah, she didn't slap me. But she was super angry. Sunny, that really *was* a suicide mission. She said they'd have happily killed me . . . and you. If Queen Abeng didn't think that returning that ghazal was so important, she'd have had both of our heads." She paused. "And they *like* taking people's heads there, my mom said . . . if you're the enemy. They to-tally *annihilated* the Egbo Clan."

"Using juju from the ghazal?"

"Udide is the finest juju maker in the universe. Her juju is relentless, thorough, and merciless."

While Chichi's mother prepared dinner, Chichi and Sunny went out in front to enjoy the cool night air. For once, Chichi wasn't annoyed when Sunny brought out her mobile phone because Sunny played all sorts of Afrobeat tracks. Together they danced and danced themselves sweaty, and the joy of motion and music brought them up from the darkness that neither of the girls realized they had descended into.

Then Chichi showed Sunny the makeshift shower in the

back of the hut, a mud cove with a hose run through a hole at the top of the wall. The water was cold, but in the warmth of the night it felt great. And as she stood in the narrow stream of water, Sunny felt another layer of darkness slough off. Wearing one of Chichi's cheap yellow wrappers and an old T-shirt with someone named Joan Jett on the front, she sat beside Chichi as her mother served them huge bowls of hearty edikaikong soup with pieces of roasted goat meat, dried fish, and plump shrimp, and soft, smooth balls of fufu on the side. Sunny's favorite!

"Oh man," Sunny said, barely able to contain her delight.

"I love you, Mama," Chichi sang, resting a head lovingly against her mother's arm.

Her mother laughed, pouring them both glasses of weak palm wine. "I know."

An hour later, Sunny fought to keep her eyes open as she cleaned her teeth with the chewing stick Chichi gave her. She quickly sent a text to her mother to let her know where she was and then turned off her phone. By the time she'd chosen a spot on the floor to unroll her mat and place her pillow at its head, she was groggy with fatigue. Chichi had set up her space a few feet away. Sunny suspected Chichi's mother was either in the front or back of the hut smoking, because she could smell the cigarettes. She detested smoking, but tonight she found it comforting.

"Your mom, does she miss home?" Sunny asked, closing her eyes.

"Yeah. It's weird. I wouldn't miss that place. She says the Obi Library is her home now, but home will always be home, I guess."

"Yeah . . ." She was drifting off. "Chichi?"

"Yeah?"

"I'm sorry."

"For what?"

"Everything your mom went through back then, everything you went through today; it's not fair."

"The world isn't fair . . . but thanks, Sunny."

She heard it land right between her and Chichi and she smiled, turning over onto her side. The ghost hopper's sweet melancholy singing lulled her into the warmth of yet another unusually pleasant night's sleep.

15

"NSIBIDI" IN NSIBIDI

Sunny woke up early. She touched the side of her face. Still tender. The cut in her cheek stung, but it didn't feel as raw. She felt good. Rested. She turned on her mobile phone. It was seven A.M. She'd slept for ten hours. There were two text messages.

One was from her mother: Okay. Glad to know where you are. Come home.

And one from Ugonna: wtf is going on?

She responded to her brother first: I'm fine. Coming home later today. Just a fight with dad.

Then her mother: Okay. Later today. ❤

She considered texting her father but instead decided to

look at her eye using her phone's camera. It looked just as bad as it did yesterday. No, she wasn't going to text him. *He* could text *her* . . . if he could ever bring himself to do so. She slipped into her jeans and put her bra on under her T-shirt. She looked at the T-shirt with the guitar-carrying, spiky-haired white woman on the front. She had no idea who Joan Jett was, but she looked cool . . . and strong.

"Chichi probably stole it anyway," she said, smiling to herself. "Might as well continue with the tradition."

She took one more look at the still sleeping Chichi, slipped on her shoes, grabbed her backpack, and headed out. Chichi's mother always went to the library in the early morning and Chichi would probably be asleep for another two hours. Even during the school year Chichi slept in, since the only school she went to were sessions with Anatov and the reading she did on her own.

Outside, the sky was blue and the sun was climbing. Everything was still a bit wet, but at least it didn't seem as if it had rained since they'd returned. She waited for a few cars to pass before rushing across the street. As she walked with a few people on their way to wherever they were going, she began to feel kind of normal despite everything. School still wasn't for another month, so there weren't many kids her age out and about. She was glad.

"Sunny! Good morning." It was her math teacher, Mr. Edochi.

"Good morning, sir," she said, thankful that he was across the street and going in the opposite direction. Sunny quickened her pace. She reached the gate to her house and carefully let herself in, her heart beating hard in her chest. Her father's car was gone but her mother's was in the driveway. She'd barely taken three steps down the hallway when her mother came rushing from the dining room. She was dressed for work.

"Oh, honey, I'm so glad you're back!" Before Sunny could respond, her mother swept her into a tight hug. She smelled of her fruity perfume, and her long, gray-brown braids crept down Sunny's back. After several moments, Sunny relaxed and hugged her mother right back. They stayed like that for a while.

"Are you all right?" her mother asked when she finally let go of Sunny.

Sunny nodded. "I'm sorry."

Her mother shook her head. "It's okay. There is food in the fridge."

"Thank you, Mom."

"You won't be going away again—"

"Mom, I—"

"—tonight?" her mother quickly finished. "Not tonight."

They stared into each other's eyes, the unspoken so, so strong between them. "Not tonight, Mom," Sunny softly said.

Her mother nodded. "Good. I have to go."

"A lot of patients to see today?"

"Five appointments just this morning," she said, looking at her mobile phone. "Okay, Sunny, I have to run." She grabbed her car keys and made for the door. "Your father . . . we will deal with it tonight."

On her way to her room, Sunny peeked into her brother's room. His music was blaring, so he didn't hear her open his door wider. He was hunched at his desk drawing something, Coca-Cola bottles and plantain chip bags scattered around him. He looked like a mad scientist so deep in the zone that he'd forgotten the world around him still existed. She grinned. "Ugo!" she shouted. He started and then turned around. He touched his phone and the music stopped.

"Where the hell were you?!"

"I . . . I was just with Chichi, Sasha, and Orlu."

"For over a *day*? Who are you, man?"

Sunny rolled her eyes. "You don't even *have* a curfew."

"I don't have a curfew because I'm responsible. If I did, I wouldn't disappear for two *days*!"

"You've never had a curfew, and you and Chukwu used to stay out until three A.M. doing God knows what. *I* have a curfew because I'm a girl and our parents have swallowed the patriarchy."

"Now you sound like Chichi."

She rolled her eyes. What was the use?

He got up and went to his bed. He reached for something on the far side of the window. It was a large sheet of drawing paper. "Here," he said. "I drew this the night before last, when Daddy was clomping around in a rage because you weren't home." He handed it to Sunny. When she looked at it, she gasped. The energy in it was stunning.

Her brother had become so good at drawing that he'd been selling his work in the market and actually making a decent amount of money. There was even a professor from the University of Nigeria, Nsukka, who'd come to their house to talk to his parents about Ugonna studying art there next year. Sunny thought she was the smartest professor on Earth. There was no way her parents would have ever considered letting Ugo go into the arts unless an actual PhD-wielding professor came to their house and spoke on Ugo's behalf without him even knowing about it.

The painting her brother handed Sunny now did the thing that she was coming to know her brother for: it amazed her. It was a shock of motion, energy, and mystery. How did he do it?

"Did you see the fog last night?" he asked as she stood looking at it.

Sunny nodded, lost in the painting. Last night she was hours away in a forest.

"It was so thick. I went outside," he said. "It's the kind of night where witches and thieves lurk—"

Sunny looked up. "What? What do you mean?"

"—and people die on the road." He shrugged. "I saw on the news there were ten car accidents in Aba. People never know when to just stay inside." He eyed her. "Anyway, I drew this. Thought you might like it."

"I do," Sunny said. "It gives me the creeps."

He grinned, sitting back down at his desk. "Glad to be of service," he said.

She giggled, leaving his room. "Man," she muttered, looking at the painting. "He's getting good."

The moment she opened her bedroom door, Della was buzzing around her head. "I know, I know," she said, putting her backpack beside her bed and striding to the window. She poked her head out and looked down where she'd buried the *chittim*. Between the bush's leaves, she could see the stick. She looked up at the dried palm tree in the distance. From her bedroom window it looked like some kind of guard watching, waiting. Della landed between her eyes and buzzed its wings. "Okay, okay, where is it?"

Della zippity-zipped around her and then headed toward her dresser where it hovered above its latest work of art.

Sunny rushed over to see. "Ooh!" She bent closer for a better look. Such *detail*! Della had created the dead palm tree from gnawed, dry raffia, probably from the tree itself. Della had sculpted every part of the tree with such precision that the smooth trunk was actually smooth and the crown of leaves like a spider. Della flew down and flapped its wings hard near the tree until it gently toppled.

"You don't think it'll fall, do you?" she asked Della. The wasp flew around her head and zipped back into its nest and was quiet. Sunny stood the tree back up. She was glad when it didn't fall again. She plopped onto the bed and then—and only then—did she bring out the piece of wood from her backpack and look at it. "All right," she breathed. She took off her glasses and threw them on the bed.

The chunk of wood was smooth and gray, the texture soft, almost spongy. When she was little, Sunny had gone through a time when she was obsessed with photographs of baobab trees. What kid wouldn't love a tree that looked like it was growing upside down? How annoying it had been to finally see one in person and barely get the chance to look at it from the outside before having to glide *inside* the tree. One fact that Sunny remembered was that baobab trees were known for holding water. Baobab tree wood was fire resistant, too. Whatever Abeng had used to burn the Nsibidi into it would not have incinerated the whole piece of wood. If Della had wanted to sculpt something with it, it wouldn't have a very hard time doing so. She sniffed it; it smelled light, a bit nutty, almost floral. She pressed it to her nose and inhaled.

Then she held it close to her face and started reading. Nothing. Then she saw it. She grinned. Her brother was getting good at drawing, and she was getting good at reading. Abeng had written the Nsibidi to be read not from left to right or right to left. It was meant to be read in a counterclockwise spiral. Sunny's head ached from the effort she made. She'd been used to reading Sugar Cream's inside-out style where she had to read from the center of the page to the outside. Sugar Cream said that every master of Nsibidi had a style. "It varies depending on how a person sees," she said. Sugar Cream would be proud of how quickly Sunny was able to understand this Nsibidi. She put it on her lap, sat up straighter, and read.

It took everything in her power to not look away with fear when she heard a deep, throaty chuckle and then a voice. "Foolish girl. Come . . ." With her peripheral vision, she was vaguely aware that the sun was setting. Her room was darkening.

"Sugar Cream will be proud," she whispered to herself. And she felt Anyanwu come and settle inside her.

Where have you been? Sunny asked.

Went for a walk in the wilderness. Your father—

Our *father*, Sunny corrected.

Your father is cruel. He does not know who I am. None of you do.

Anyanwu, I'm only fifteen years old, almost sixteen. I'm human. You're—

If I truly showed you everything I am, which is everything you are, your mind would break.

Yeah, but—

We are one, but we are doubled. I am no longer just your "spirit face." We are something else now. There is no definition. There is no word. It's not something to be understood or controlled. But what I know is that I will no longer be unappreciated. I will not make myself small. Your father cannot, WILL NOT treat me like a child. HE is a child to ME, a very, very young one.

Okay, Sunny said.

It is not.

Sunny wanted to step away from Anyanwu. When Anyanwu got like this, Sunny could physically *feel* Anyanwu's magnificence. It was like being too close to an electrical charge. Any closer and the powerful feeling would become pain. And Anyanwu was so angry she was probably hoping for Sunny to "get closer." Sunny really didn't understand how she was supposed to relate to Anyanwu now. They'd been tiptoeing around it for months. However, for now, there were more urgent matters. Anyanwu seemed to agree because the electrical charge feeling calmed down, allowing Sunny to relax a bit.

There will come a time, Anyanwu warned.

I know.

After a moment, they focused on the Nsibidi . . .

Two steps forward. Nine steps back. Slip to the side. No turning back. Two steps forward. Nine steps back. Slip to the side. You will know. You . . .

Sunny was in the dark and her mouth was wide open.

Her lips were so dry that they were cracking. She needed water. Someone was shaking her and she snapped out of it. Then she felt Anyanwu leave her in a whisper. "Ugh, whatever, Anyanwu," she muttered. "See you later then."

Distantly, she heard Anyanwu respond, *Later*.

Sunny slowly moved her neck. She was still in the exact same position, looking down at the piece of wood. It glowed a soft red. She tucked her chin to her chest and flexed her shoulders. She glanced out her window. It was dark outside. She sat there remembering. She'd only taken one step onto that damn Road and it felt like her head was going to explode. "I can't read the rest," she whispered. "I don't have the . . ." Her brain couldn't take it. Or she didn't know how to read it. Or something. All she knew was that if she had taken even a second step onto that Road . . . she was never coming back. It was the wilderness, and she was used to being in the wilderness. To glide in and out of it had become second nature to her over the last year. However, *that* place, that Road, was a part of the wilderness she'd never witnessed. Maybe *beyond* it, if that were possible.

"So potent," she whispered.

Four days left.

She had to go see Sugar Cream.

16

HERB, STONE, AND METAL

Lessons with Anatov had been moved to the daytime until school started. With all the tension at home, Sunny was relieved. Less sneaking out. At least for that reason. Nonetheless, they'd certainly be sneaking out soon enough to find Udide's ghazal. Chichi begged Sunny, Sasha, and Orlu not to tell Anatov about what had happened and what they had to do.

"My mother keeps that side of her life private," Chichi said. "Anatov took her in when she came to the Obi Library, so he knows most of it. But he doesn't know *that* part of it. She's never told him the details. She won't." She paused. "You get it, right?"

Sunny shrugged. "This is really urgent, but I guess I understand. That whole 'keeping up appearances' thing that adults do."

Chichi nodded.

"But word might travel," Orlu said.

"If it does, let it not travel from *us*," Chichi said.

"I have to tell Sugar Cream, though," Sunny added. She'd have insisted they tell Anatov if this weren't the case.

"I know," Chichi said.

"Sugar Cream is . . . Sugar Cream."

They all nodded. Sugar Cream was Sugar Cream. If anyone could help, it would be her. But first, they had to get through Anatov's lessons.

"'*Njomm*' juju is too elusive for a definition to ever capture," Anatov said.

All four of them were restless, but Sunny was having the hardest time hiding it. How they were going to get through this when the Udide problem was hanging over their heads—with the clock ticking as they sat here—was beyond her. Orlu, Sasha, and Chichi all agreed on this: even if the end of the world was possible, school was still important. Sunny thought this was total nonsense, but it was her one to their three, so here she was, fidgeting and barely able to listen.

Anatov paused, glaring at Sunny. She sat up straighter and raised her chin, and he nodded, satisfied. He continued, "However, every juju includes all uncomprehended, mysterious forces of nature. Elementals, like herb, stone, and metal. The word also includes deep secrets of humans and others. Do you know why I am called the Defender of Frogs and All Things Natural?"

The question caught Sunny's elusive attention, and for the first time since sitting down on the hut floor, she stopped glancing at the exit. She raised her hand, and Chichi, Sasha, and Orlu all frowned at her. "Mr. Mohammed at Bola's Store for Books once told me, when I mentioned you were my teacher," she said. "When you first came to Leopard Knocks from America—"

"Atlanta, to be exact."

"Didn't know that," Sunny admitted. She continued, "When you first came from Atlanta, Georgia, you were super vocal about your views on eating meat."

"Yes, you shouldn't eat it," he said. "Embrace beans and veggies; your bodies and souls will thank you for it."

". . . And you were especially vocal about frogs being the thermometers of the Earth."

"Correct. Human beings are *notorious* for ignoring the fact that Earth's other creatures are workers of the finest ju-jus," he said. "I won't let that happen to any of my students, not on my watch. People here started calling me the Defender of Frogs and All Things Natural, expecting it to piss me off. I embraced it. If I used business cards, I'd put it on there, too."

They all laughed.

"So," he continued. "Today we are going to learn '*Njomm*' juju from wall geckos, more commonly known as 'suns of the morning.'"

"What's a silly wall gecko going to teach us, Prof?" Chichi asked.

"Those things eat spiders and such, which is a big plus in this country," Sasha said.

"Better than any insect repellant," Orlu added.

"Yes, yes," Anatov said, waving a dismissive hand. "But there is something deeper you can learn from a wall gecko if you give it your truest attention. I call it 'the scoot'; there is no word for it here in Nigeria because you people don't take animals as seriously as you should." He kissed his teeth. "Watch."

He held up a gecko for them all to see. "We see them every day," he said as the delicate pink reptile scurried to the tip of his hand. "In corners, on walls, at night watching the moths and mosquitos near the light. Now you see her . . ." And then right before their eyes, the gecko disappeared.

Sunny felt her nostrils tingle. She brought out a tissue to blow her nose.

"What the hell?" Sasha said.

Orlu was smiling. Chichi was frowning.

". . . And now you don't," Anatov said with a grin. He reached into his chest pocket and brought out the wall gecko. "They are experts at finding hidden places, an ability we all could use."

"They just move fast," Chichi said. "How is that juju?"

"Did you see it move to my pocket or does your theory just make you feel better?" he asked. "Again, not only human beings are Leopard People."

"So all geckos are . . ."

"Did I say 'all'?" he asked. He tapped his ear. "Listen and don't be blinded by your philosophical resistance, assumptions, and beliefs." He held up the gecko again, and this time Sunny paid as close attention as she could. It scurried up his arm and paused, looking at them all sitting on Anatov's hut floor. It licked its beady eye with its tongue, and Sunny could have sworn that it grinned wider before flat-out disappearing right before their eyes.

This time both Sasha and Chichi exclaimed, "Shit!" Orlu's eyes shot side to side. Sunny looked in her own pockets. That gecko was not to be trusted.

It was from Chichi's pocket that it scurried, and it disappeared again before she could screech and slap at it. She jumped up, wiggling and exclaiming, "Yeeeeeek!"

"Stop it," Anatov snapped. "It's just a gecko, not a scorpion. What will it do to you?"

"Tell me what person wants a lizard in her pocket, *abeg*," Chichi snapped back, still standing.

He held his hand up and opened it, and there was the gecko. "Many thanks," he said to her as he stepped outside the hut. He came back in, looking at them skeptically. "Leopard Geckos don't use juju powder," he said. "They produce juju agents in their skin and then use cells of shed skin. See Stella Balankang's research, 'Gecko Mischief and Other Jujus of the Reptilia Class.' She doesn't mention scooting in there, but she discusses several larger things. Now, what can we learn from the scoot? We learn that there is always a place to hide. So let's try it."

The lesson was about paying attention, finding the spot, and then using juju powder to help you scoot into it. For the moment, all four of them were deeply focused and it was good. Sunny was delighted to discover how many places there were to hide just in and around her. Behind Anatov's box of incense. A space in the dirt near the far side of his hut. She used her powder to spirit herself into his garden. The juju set her there, but also cloaked her from being found for the next thirty seconds.

As she crouched, giggling because she was sure no one would find her there, she glimpsed a pepper bug. It was on a pepper, hanging way too close to her face. She leapt out of the garden just as Anatov came out of the hut looking for her. Better to lose the game than end up getting hit with a puff of pepper bug fumes. Her sneezy, runny nose from her juju powder allergy was more than enough to deal with.

It was one of the wildest lessons yet, and it was all learned from a tiny wall gecko. As they left his hut three hours later, exhausted and oddly pleased—they'd learned a lot—Sunny spotted the gecko creeping up the side of the hut. The moment she did, it looked at her and disappeared.

"Leopard Knocks?" Orlu asked.

The three of them nodded. It was time.

Crossing the bridge was a joy. Anyanwu had been absent all day until the moment Sunny stepped onto it. These days, Sunny didn't worry about her absence when stepping on the bridge. She always came, even if it was seconds before, like now. Still, it was nice to be back with Anyanwu after what had happened with her father. The Leopard Knocks bridge was a place where Sunny and Anyanwu always saw eye to eye. They danced along the balance-beam-narrow stretch of wood, taking their time. They did leaps, chaîné turns, pas de bourrées, and near the end, a nice deep plié. All the while, the river beast watched and kept its distance.

However, even in the joy, Anyanwu and Sunny didn't joke with the river beast. They didn't even speak. And when they finished the deep plié, Anyanwu leapt out of Sunny, dancing up the path into Leopard Knocks.

"See you there," Sunny muttered. She glanced at her friends. They could never understand what it was to be doubled. To be here and there and unaligned with yourself. As they excitedly walked past the two leaf-shedding iroko trees into Leopard Knocks, Sunny noticed the leaf pile guards turn and watch her pass . . . as they always did when she entered Leopard Knocks, since she'd been doubled. As if they sensed that though she belonged here, she was off somehow.

She left Orlu, Chichi, and Sasha as they were shopping in Sweet Plumes, the juju powder shop. "Meet you at Mama Put's in about two hours," she said. She looked back at the shop as she walked up the road. It was two red huts stacked on top of each other, sloppily so, like the person who built them relied more on juju to hold them up than physics . . . which was probably the case. The red exterior was painted with thousands and thousands of tiny white circles, making it look almost like a sleeping dragon coiled around itself. It even smelled sulfuric inside. The silver cloth that covered the round, doorless entrance blew in and out like the building was breathing. Inside was always hot, too—the owner said it kept the juju powders fresh. But Sunny thought there was something suspicious about the building.

As she walked through Leopard Knocks' main stretch, listening to the haggling and conversations, passing the various shops and local trees, she smiled. She was all right. Despite everything. Despite being doubled. Despite facing Ekwensu. Despite her father never understanding. There was darkness, but she was okay. For the next few days, at least. The clock was ticking, and even if they did find the ghazal to bring to Udide, what if the damn thing itself was radioactive or something? Chichi's mother had held it, and look what it did to her life. An object that was beloved to Udide had the power to change everything it touched or spoke to . . . and according to Chichi's mother, it definitely spoke because she had been able to *hear* it.

The pleasant smile dropped from Sunny's lips and she walked faster. She sensed a great spider creeping up the back of her neck.

When Sunny finished talking, Sugar Cream continued gazing at her with such intensity that Sunny considered scooting. "Let me see it," she said. Sunny handed her the piece of wood, and Sugar Cream sat back in her chair, turning the piece of wood over in her long, thin fingers. She brought it to her nose and sniffed it. "Eh-heh, I know the tree this came from."

"You've been to Nimm?"

"Long ago, yes. As a guest." She held the Nsibidi side close to her eyes. "Be quiet."

"I wasn't—"

"Shh."

As Sunny waited, she sensed movement to her left. She was sitting on Sugar Cream's office floor, and it was only a matter of time. Ever since Sunny had been stung by Udide's minions a while ago, the curious red spiders who lived in this office had become even *more* curious about her. They scrambled right to her now, some trying to land on her from above—twice succeeding! Sugar Cream assured Sunny that the spiders wouldn't harm her, but this fact never helped.

The good thing was that dealing with them so often had

forced her to somewhat confront her phobia. Never in a million years would she have touched one of these types of spiders before. Now, however, she looked at the one about to climb on her jeans and then flicked it away with a finger.

Sugar Cream suddenly twitched. She put the wood piece on her table and glared at it. She kissed her teeth and looked at Sunny. "How much of that could you read?"

"Only the first part."

"And you are all right?"

"It took my entire afternoon and part of my evening," she said. "It was not dark when I started—"

"That blood splotch in your eye, is it—"

"No . . . my . . . my father, when I came home, he . . . slapped me."

"Free agent problems."

Sunny nodded.

"Do you need—"

"I can handle it."

Sugar Cream paused, cocking her head.

"I can."

She pursed her lips. "You haven't been seeing or hearing things?"

"No."

"When you walk on the road, it stays . . . the road?"

Sunny thought about this. Here was mention of The Road again. "Yeah," she said. "It just stays the road. I walked along it to catch the funky train to get here."

"Good." She sat back on her chair, her twisted back making her look always uncomfortable. "Good. I'm thankful."

"Why?"

She picked up the piece of wood and held it up. "*This* is an invocation, Sunny. I had to stop reading before I began calling. To read it is to *call*."

"Call what?"

"The Road."

Sunny felt chills creep up her spine. "Do . . . do you mean—"

"Uzo Mmuo, the Spirit Highway, the Great River, Chukwu's Edan, Chineke's Vein and Artery, it has infinite names all over the world, wilderness, and elsewhere," she said. "To step onto it, you have to be *very* deliberate. Do not join The Road by accident. It is easy to get lost on The Road and even easier to lose yourself on it."

Sunny shivered. "But it will not come for me on its own."

"No."

"I have to invoke it. Call it."

"Yes. The Road is trouble you have to choose to seek," Sugar Cream said, holding out the piece of wood. "Come and get your map."

Sunny got up and stepped to her mentor's desk. As she took it, Sugar Cream held on for a moment. "If you choose to read this, you will see things."

Sunny let go of it and stepped back. "Like what?"

"Only you will know," Sugar Cream said. She reached

forward and took Sunny's hand. "Anyanwu got here before you arrived." She chuckled and shook her head. "Ah, Sunny, your . . . condition is something I am still trying to get used to. Your Anyanwu, she is on the fourth floor right now. She said there was someone she needed to see. Human or spirit, I don't know. There are many scholars who read the books there. But, Sunny, listen to me: Anyanwu will be drawn to The Road and she may have a hard time leaving it. Stay close to her."

"That's easier said than done," Sunny muttered.

"Doesn't change what I said."

"The ghazal is there, isn't it?"

"Yes."

"And we have to find it."

"Yes. Udide is brilliant and magnificent, but she can be wicked. You *have* to do this; she's not giving you a choice."

"How do I stay close to Anyanwu when I can't even keep up with her, when she is . . . *more* than me?"

"I don't know. Anyanwu will at some point have to come down to your level for you both to coexist. That's just a fact." She held the wood to Sunny. "Take it."

"I . . . I'm scared," she said.

"You should be." She held Sunny's gaze, and when she said nothing else, Sunny took the wood. "Sunny, the first time I went into the wilderness was when I was barely seven years old. And I was not ready. I was with two of my classmates when I came upon . . . this man. To this day, I don't know who he was. He was standing in the broad daylight, but his face remained shaded. At first I thought he was just a very dark-skinned man. Nothing unusual. He was dressed in Hausa clothes. He stood over me, looking down at me. My friends were afraid, so they moved away. But I wanted to understand his face." She paused, looking at her hands. Sunny didn't want to hear the rest. There was an unusual look of fear on Sugar Cream's face.

"The man *killed* me. He . . . he put his hand up like this." She raised her right hand and thrust it forward like she was throwing and releasing something heavy. She spread her fingers wide. "He put his hand right in my face. And he said, 'Go.' My friends say that I just crumpled to the ground and lay there. For me, it felt like he'd grabbed me by both shoulders and violently shoved me backward. But I didn't fall. I *slipped*. From here to there. I was standing in the wilderness, though I didn't know it. And he was there, too. And he looked the exact same. We were in a field of swaying grass."

Sunny nodded. "I know it."

"Of course you do. I looked around and I began to cry. Then he did it again. And that's when I found myself on the precipice of The Road. Sunny, you think you are afraid now, try being a child who had none of your skill standing before a chaos of spirits. I was there for mere seconds, but that was enough to leave me hearing things for months. The place was *powerful*, so much movement, energy, it could tear you apart in an instant if you step onto it unready, unprotected, too young." Now Sugar Cream shivered. She rubbed her hands over her arms to warm up. "Thankfully, I would not see that place again for another five decades."

"How did you get back, when you were seven?"

"Eze, the woman who would be my mentor ten years later, happened to be coming out of a shop feet away when it happened. She came and pulled me back, first from The Road, then from the wilderness. At the time, because I had no other point of reference, I thought she was Jesus Christ."

At that, Sunny started giggling, and soon both she and Sugar Cream were laughing. There was a knock. An Obi Library student stood at the door, looking at Sunny and Sugar Cream, perplexed. "Professor," she said. "The scholars from Saudi Arabia and Oman will be here in thirty minutes. I have your outfit ready."

"Ah, yes, duty calls," Sugar Cream said, slowly getting up. "Been looking forward to this. I have questions." She pushed the piece of wood into Sunny's hands. "Our lessons are on hold. This is urgent. I would recommend a book to you, but there are no books that will make what you must do clearer. There are times where you have all the tools you need and all there is to do is to do it. I can't help you read an invocation. What I will say is read it *only* when you are ready. And read it *soon*."

She stood before Sunny, looking up at her. "When did you get so tall?" she asked.

"A few months ago," Sunny said. "Plus, *you* don't exactly grow upward, Professor."

Sugar Cream laughed. "Oh, Sunny, I enjoy your company. You've come such a long way." She paused. "I was scared when I was seven and dead. I wasn't ready, I wasn't prepared, it didn't make sense. I didn't even know The Road existed . . . but it didn't break me. Don't let it break you. You can do this, Sunny. Don't fear. *Shine.*" She walked to the doorway and looked back at Sunny. "And give my regards to Anyanwu."

Sunny watched her leave. "What's she meeting with Leopard People from Saudi Arabia and Oman for?" she asked herself, then chuckled. "I'd rather go with her to find out than do this crap." A movement beside her caught her eye. When she turned, one of the red spiders was hovering less than a foot from her face. She twitched and stumbled back. "Come on, leave me alone." One of the masks on the wall snickered and blew raspberries at her. The one with the chubby cheeks, as always.

"Oh, shut up," Sunny snapped at it. "Always quiet until Sugar Cream leaves." The mask puckered its thick lips at her and blew a kiss. The other masks giggled, all of them.

She put the wood piece in her backpack and left her mentor's office.

17

INVOCATION

Mama Put's Putting Place was busy when Sunny stepped into it. Mama Put had expanded the dining area, and ever since, the place was packed at every time of the day except early morning. Sunny looked around. There they were— Sasha was just tucking into a large bowl of rice with stewed chicken and Chichi was rolling a ball of egba to scoop up her okra soup. Sunny's stomach grumbled, but this wasn't the time.

"Where's Orlu?"

Sasha grinned and Chichi rolled her eyes.

"What?" Sunny asked.

"He had to go," Sasha said. "It was pretty awesome. Grashcoatah *and* Taiwo's Miri Bird came for him. I think they were both sent and they found him at the same time. Everyone came rushing to see Grashcoatah. Some of the kids were hugging and petting him. Probably felt like hugging a furry wall. Some girl even had a brush! Why?! They climbed on his huge back, massaged his cheeks. Of course, he *loved* it all. People were throwing him their groceries, which he ate like candy. Someone even threw him a whole bundle of sweet grass."

"It was ridiculous," Chichi added.

"You're just jealous," Sasha said, putting an arm around her and pulling her close. "I'll give you some attention if you need it."

"Give me, then," Chichi said, smirking.

Sunny rolled her eyes. "What about . . ." She lowered her voice. "Getting the thing for Udide?"

"You still have to read the piece of wood, right?" Chichi said.

Sunny frowned. "Yeah . . . yeah, I do, but—"

"He'll be back by the time you do," Sasha said.

"Where'd he have to go, though?"

"I dunno," Sasha said. "Taiwo just wanted to see him."

Sugar Cream had called on her a few times for various things. Once she'd called on Sunny right after school by sending a bird messenger. When Sunny had arrived at her office, Sugar Cream introduced Sunny to her best friend for over forty years, an old man from the Caribbean island of St. Vincent who had the ability to see hundreds of colors humans normally couldn't see. But Sugar Cream's calls were never so urgent. "I hope he's okay."

"With those two looking after him, I'm sure he's fine," Chichi said, touching her arm. "Did Sugar Cream have any answers?"

"She said it's an invocation," Sunny said.

Chichi leaned forward. "The Nsibidi itself?" she asked.

"You read it and it summons," Sasha said, pinching his chin. He looked at Sunny with wide excited eyes. "What does it summon? Oh man, did she summon whatever it was?!"

"No, no, she stopped reading before it could."

"So what does it call?" Chichi asked.

Sunny looked around. The place was pretty full today, a group of teens sitting behind them and a table of what looked like scholars to their right. She caught the eye of a tall man wearing a red and white Igbo cap leaning against the order pickup counter. She quickly looked away. "Let's talk about it later."

Sasha got up. "I'll get containers for our food." He rushed off.

"We need Orlu here for this," Sunny said.

"Tonight," Chichi said. "And if not, we'll go and find him."

Sunny groaned when they found that Chichi's mother wasn't home. Sunny had hoped she could answer some questions.

"Don't know where she is," Chichi said, rubbing her healing face. "Damn, maybe she's back at Leopard Knocks."

"Whatever, tell us what's up," Sasha said, throwing his backpack on the floor and sitting among a pile of books. Chichi sat down, too.

"Okay, so it's an invocation," Sunny said. "For The Road."

Both of them just stared at her.

When they continued staring, she grew irritated. "What? Why are you looking at me like that?"

Both of them stared for a few more seconds and then Sasha finally said, "What's 'The Road'?"

Sunny blinked. And then she grinned. She jumped up. "Ha!" She stretched out her arms dramatically. "Hoooold up! This is not a drill! Hahaha! It's happening!" She danced around the hut, laughing. Now it was their turn to look annoyed and this made Sunny laugh even more.

Chichi kissed her teeth. "Neither of us ever said we knew *everything*."

"Yeah, but I've never seen it happen!" Sunny said, sitting back down. She chuckled. She wished Anyanwu were with her to laugh with. "The Road . . . I don't know what it is, either. But Sugar Cream said it's where the ghazal probably is. It's a road of spirits or something. The way she spoke. It was like you had to glide to be there or something."

"Then how can . . . Does she think you have to go looking for it alone?" Chichi asked.

"Nah, man, no way, not happening," Sasha said.

"The way she made it sound, it would sweep me away." Sunny shivered.

"Don't worry, Sunny. We're not going to let you do that," Chichi said. "Not alone."

Sasha was looking at a pile of books. "Meantime, we need to find some info about this Road."

"She called it some other names, but I can't remember them."

"We'll find something if there's something to find." Sasha picked up a book and smirked. "I say we go to the Obi Library and ask them to get us into the fourth floor. We have the perfect reason!"

"Oh, heck yes!" Chichi said, slapping hands with Sasha. "Us on the fourth floor of the Obi Library?! That's one step away from third level!"

"Udide said seven days, and that was days ago," Sunny said. "Don't you have to go through all these channels if you're not an Obi Library student there? There's no time!"

"Your mentor is Sugar Cream, you can get anything," Chichi said. "Just ask."

Sunny shook her head. "You don't know her."

"Ugh," Chichi groaned, rolling her eyes.

"Fine . . . so you read it," Sasha said. "And when you do, we'd better be ready for whatever comes next."

"Don't look at that thing again for now," Chichi warned.

"But how do I learn to read it? It takes a while to inter-pret, to *read* Nsibidi. It's not like picking up a book and you read. You have to . . . I dunno. And it's really heavy Nsibidi."

"Hmm," Sasha said. "We'll cross that bridge when we get to it."

They agreed that they'd each go home, rest, shower, eat, and then meet back at Orlu's house at midnight because by then he'd surely be home. Then . . . then they'd see what the invocation invoked.

When Sunny got home, she saw her father's brother Uncle Chibuzo's black Mercedes in the driveway. "Great," she muttered, quietly pushing the door open. "Hopefully he's been here awhile; I'm not breaking any damn kola today." She could already hear them laughing inside. They were in the living room, and she was able to slip by in the hallway with-out being noticed. But something gave her pause. She backed up and peeked in.

Her father and uncle sat on the couch, a bottle of Star Beer in hand, a bowl of shelled groundnuts and a pile of shells on the coffee table in front of them, and a soccer game on the TV. Yeah, her uncle had been here a while. She was about to move on when her father, in mid-laugh, glanced her way and caught her eye. Sunny caught her breath. She and her father hadn't spoken since the slap two days ago. The smile faltered on her father's face. Then he quickly looked away. He kept chuckling, but it now sounded fake.

"So who made you believe that counterattacking is bad? Look at the evidence that you are wrong!" her uncle said.

"Ah, you're talking rubbish," her father replied.

Sunny quickly moved on down the hall, blinking back the sting of tears. In the kitchen, she found her mother sitting at the dinner table. She was talking on the phone with her sister in Chicago. Her mother reached out and took Sunny's hand.

"Hi, Mom," Sunny whispered, not wanting to interrupt her conversation. Her mother nodded a hello and continued listening to whatever story her sister was telling her. Sunny took three oranges from the sack on the counter and a bag of *chin chin*. She went on her way. Her brother's door was open and she could hear that he also had company, his new girlfriend, Amarachi. His computer screen was streaming a movie, and as Sunny passed by, she could see them both sitting on the floor in front of it, looking at their phones.

"No football. I like this movie," Amarachi said.

"Why don't most girls like sports?"

She kissed her teeth. "I like watching tennis as much as you like watching football. Do you know who Naomi Osaka is?"

Sunny laughed. *Good comeback*, she thought. Once in her room, she shut her door. She threw aside the Leopard newspaper on her bed that she rarely read these days and plopped down. She ate one of the oranges and then decided to take a short nap. When she awoke, it was nearly dark outside and her door was open. She looked at her phone—she'd slept five hours! "Oh, no!" She jumped up and rushed to take a long, hot shower.

"Della," she said when she was dressed. She heard the buzz of wings, but the wasp didn't emerge from its nest. Sunny felt badly about waking it up. "Sorry, but I need to tell you something. Come out. Please?" After a moment, Della peeked its metallic blue head from the hole in the bottom of the mud nest. It buzzed its wings.

"I'm . . . going to Orlu's house tonight. I don't . . ." She sighed, the weight of everything starting to push down on her. What *was* going to happen if . . . *when* she read the Nsibidi? "I don't know what will happen. If . . . I might have to go somewhere soon. Be gone for a while. Just understand."

Della zipped out of its nest and landed on her head. More specifically on the zyzzyx comb she always wore in her Afro. She turned to her mirror and nodded. "Of course I'm bringing it with me. I always wear it."

Della zipped back into its nest and was quiet.

"Okay," Sunny said. "Good. At least I've taken care of that."

She quickly packed the two remaining oranges and bag of *chin chin*, a packet of tissues, an extra juju powder pouch, her mobile phone and charger, lip gloss, some silver and two bronze *chittim*, and a few other small items in her backpack.

Essentials, but not too heavy. She put on some jeans, the Joan Jett T-shirt which she'd come to really like, fresh socks, and gym shoes. She stood there for a moment, looking over her room.

She glanced out the window. Even in the dark she could see the dead palm tree with its dry trunk and brown leaves. In the evening breeze, she could even hear the leaves scrape against and tap each other like the bones of a skeleton. She tapped the juju powder pouch in her back pocket and her juju knife inside her jeans against her hip. Last but not least, she touched the piece of wood with the Nsibidi on it in her front pocket. She held on to her backpack tightly and turned to the closed door. Then she glided through the keyhole.

When she arrived at Orlu's house, Chichi and Sasha were already sitting outside on the front doorstep waiting for her. "He's not back yet," Chichi said.

"Why?"

Sasha shrugged.

"His parents don't know?"

"I think they know something," Sasha said.

"I say we go to Taiwo's hut and—"

"He's coming," Sunny said, pointing at the sky. Sasha and Chichi got up. As Grashcoatah landed, Sunny knew something was wrong with Orlu. It wasn't as much what she saw, for she couldn't see him on Grashcoatah's broad back from where she stood. It was what she *felt*. Where it had been hot and humid, there was suddenly a cool breeze. The dust in the driveway swirled around them and she turned away, protecting her eyes.

"Shit! Orlu!" Sasha shouted, rushing to Grashcoatah regardless of the dust. He coughed as he grabbed Grashcoatah's fur and climbed up. Slowly, Sunny walked up to the flying grasscutter as Chichi followed Sasha up. She touched Grashcoatah's soft, silky fur and looked up his side, listening.

"Oh, damn," Sasha said. "Why didn't you—"

She heard Chichi gasp. "Oh! Uh . . ."

"Come on. How old are you?" Sasha snapped.

"I just—"

"Where's Sunny?" Orlu said. His voice sounded so hoarse.

"I'm down here," she called up. She was about to start climbing onto Grashcoatah when everything seemed to vibrate. *Thoom!* She let go, stumbling back and looking around. *Thoom!* "What's happening?" she shouted, holding her head. All her mind kept telling her was one name, Ekwensu. Had Orlu called the terrible masquerade back? What did that mean? "WHAT IS HAPPENING?!"

Sasha jumped down from Grashcoatah. He grabbed Sunny and hugged her. "It's not Ekwensu, relax. It's okay."

She was shuddering so hard that she could barely think. "It's not?" she whispered. She hugged Sasha, tears streaming from her eyes. What was happening to her? "Then what's wrong with Orlu?"

Chichi was climbing down now. "He's coming down," she said. "Just . . . prepare yourself."

Sunny frowned, grasping Sasha. "Prepare . . . ? For what?"

Then over Sasha's shoulder, she *saw* Orlu. *Thoom!* Everything vibrated again as he jumped down and landed like something so solid and stable that it weighed a thousand pounds. He stood tall, and when he spoke, his voice was the voice of an ancient spirit. "I passed *Mbawkwa!*" he proclaimed. "And I don't know what the actual fuck is happening."

Sunny's mouth fell open as she let go of Sasha, then she started laughing. *Never* in all the time she knew Orlu had she ever heard him drop the f-bomb, and of all times, *this* was the time to do it. Sunny had only seen his spirit face once, very briefly during a car ride into Leopard Knocks. And he hadn't known she'd seen him. This now? Oh, this was something else entirely. She stared at him. They all did. One's spirit face was more private than one's naked body, but how could they not look at their friend?

His face was like a window-sized rectangle of bright green wood carved with thousands of tiny, wiggling Nsibidi symbols. Sunny wanted to step closer and read them, but just looking at him was impolite. Sitting there and reading him would have been downright rude.

"Taiwo said I'll be okay in a few hours, but *this . . . is . . . bizarre,*" he said.

"It's different for everyone," Chichi said.

Grashcoatah sniffed at Orlu and Orlu turned to him. "Cut it out, you know it's me." But Grashcoatah continued sniffing at him. "My name is Oku," he proclaimed. Grashcoatah grunted, satisfied, gently licking him and then stepping back and resting on his haunches.

"Let's go inside," Sunny said, looking at her feet as she took Orlu's hand.

Thoom! It made her jump, but she held steady, thinking to herself, *It's not Ekwensu, it's not Ekwensu.*

"Grashcoatah," Orlu weakly said, leaning his huge head on his great hide. "Thank you." Grashcoatah grunted. Orlu took something from the pocket of his jeans. "Can you fly this back to Taiwo? Doesn't seem right to keep it past sunrise."

Grashcoatah took whatever it was into his mouth. Then he flew into the air and was gone, leaving them in another swirl of dust.

"What was that you gave him?" Sunny asked.

"A night guard," he said. "When you come out of *Mbawkwa*, you're more vulnerable than normal to the creatures in Night Runner Forest. Some of them will be attracted to you. Now that I am out of the forest, though, they'll go back to where I came through looking for remnants."

"Damn, I hope Taiwo's not battling bush souls or armies of other íhẹ́ ndi dị́ ńdụ̀ right now," Sasha said.

"It's Taiwo," Orlu said. "He can handle it. But still, that's why I sent it back, *sha*."

Inside, Orlu's parents hugged and congratulated him after a very awkward moment when they looked at Sunny, Sasha, and Chichi.

Orlu's mother rushed to the kitchen to warm up the meal she'd made for Orlu. "Do you mind if I call Sasha's parents?" she asked from the kitchen. "They've been calling all day to see if he is all right."

Orlu had grunted an okay. "Just don't tell them about . . . this." He motioned to his exposed spirit face.

"Okuuuuu!" his father sang. "My great son is power-ful, o."

This made Orlu look up, and his spirit face didn't smile, but it got brighter, and Sunny was sure she even saw sparkles.

The four of them sat in the kitchen, while Orlu ate like he'd never eaten before. Granted, the meal of spicy *egusi* soup, heavy with roasted goat meat and chicken, a large por-tion of *egba* on the side, probably was delicious, but Orlu ate the equivalent of what three grown men would eat. Sunny watched him eat, in awe of what a spirit face shoveling food into its wooden face looked like.

When he finished, they went outside. The house's gen-erator vibrated nearby, but that was the only other noise out here. They sat on the steps in front of the door. Sasha brought out a pack of Bangas. He shook one out and began smoking it.

He passed it to Chichi. Sunny brought out her juju knife and worked a juju she'd grown used to doing. The smoke from the cigarettes swirled straight up, the air around Sunny remaining fresh.

She glanced at Orlu and quickly looked away. This was too weird.

"So . . . who'd you speak to?" Sasha asked.

"Give me some time on that," he said.

Sasha nodded.

"But you feel better?" Sunny asked. As if her question caused it, everything shook with a deep *thoom!* "How come that didn't happen as much when we were inside with your parents?"

Orlu shrugged. "Taiwo gave me wilderness grass and it didn't work at all, either."

"It's different with everyone," Chichi repeated. "I keep saying it because it's true."

Orlu nodded. "The Nsibidi, did you ask Sugar Cream?"

"Yeah," Sunny said. While Sasha and Chichi smoked another Banga each, Sunny told him everything. By the time she finished, she'd started to feel a bit tired. She yawned.

"Well?"

"Well, what?" she asked.

Thoom!

"Have fun getting sleep with that goddamn noise shaking you every few minutes," Chichi muttered.

Sasha laughed. "I'm more worried how he's going to sleep with a head the size of Texas."

Chichi snorted with laughter and soon both of them were snickering. Sunny covered her mouth with her hand.

"Read it," Orlu said, still serious. "Let's see what happens. You have it with you, right?"

"Yeah," she whispered. "But . . . I'm kind of tired. Tomorrow might be better. What if I can't—"

"Orlu, we don't know what will happen," Sasha said. "We can wait for—"

"No time." He turned to Sunny. "Read it. You know you can."

"Wait!" Chichi said. She ran inside. A second later, Sasha said, "Good idea, Chichi." Then he ran in, too. Sunny wanted to look at Orlu again, but she didn't. There was another *thoom!* They both giggled nervously. After a minute, Chichi emerged carrying a purse and Sunny's backpack and Sasha came out with his and Orlu's.

Sunny frowned. "You really think—"

"Yup," Sasha said.

"Always good to be prepared," Chichi added.

Sunny sighed. "Okay." She was ready. She'd already snuck out. This was what she was here for. *So I'm here for it,* she thought. "Okay," she said again. She brought the wood from her pocket and held it in her hands.

The world vibrated again and Orlu groaned. "Oh, make it stop," he said.

Chichi patted his shoulder and Sasha nodded at Sunny. "You can do it."

She looked at the Nsibidi and it did nothing. *Relax*, she thought, but it was difficult. There was no time to fail. *But what if I can't do it?* She tried to read it again. Still nothing. She blinked her drying eyes and took a deep breath. When she looked up, the three of them were leaning toward her. Waiting.

"It's not working," she whispered. "I can't . . ." One of the loops on the edge of a symbol started coiling tighter. Just a tiny bit. She focused on it, and as she did, she remembered. She could read Nsibidi and she could read it well. Sugar Cream had taught her, and she had spent hours and hours working at it. And then more hours reading, being, playing it. The dot behind the coil began to spin. A line stretched. A symbol that was a tree cartwheeled to the side.

She sighed as it all came to life, flipping, tumbling, twirling, squeezing, stretching about like tiny spirits. If she asked Sasha, Chichi, or even Orlu if they saw this happening, they'd say no. Only Nsibidi readers could see this phenomenon . . . and read it. So she read it aloud, but the words that came from her mouth didn't sound like her own. "When the day ends and the night falls, two steps forward. Nine steps back. Then slip to the side. No turning back. Two steps forward. Nine steps back. Then slip to the side. You will know. Do this correctly and you will venture out and return with more plantains."

She stopped talking and looked up the driveway. Another of Orlu's vibrations shook everything, and that seemed to heighten what she saw. Anyanwu stood there, bright and ethereal as ever.

"I . . . I see her," she heard Orlu say, but Sunny was barely listening. She was hearing something else. The music of a haunted flute. And then she was standing up. She reached into her pocket and brought out her juju knife. She tried to stop her hand, but to do so would be wrong, so she allowed it. Her eyes returned to the piece of wood she held. She looked. The Nsibidi, still quivering the slightest bit, froze in place and even seemed to burn deeper into the wood for emphasis.

Right into the driveway, Sunny drew the Nsibidi, her juju knife sparking as it scraped. She heard Chichi say, "I've heard of this. The invocation is doing it. Don't touch her until she's done."

And indeed, Sunny couldn't stop if she wanted to, but she didn't want to stop. This was it. So she pushed on by looking at the Nsibidi as her hand drew it. When she was nearly finished, it began to glow an electric blue, the flute growing louder, Orlu's vibrations oddly growing right along with it. Sunny stepped back from what she'd done.

"I don't feel tired," she said. Why this worried her, she didn't know. But boy, did it worry her. And so did the fact that the trees around them were shaking. The palm trees actually looked like they were beating themselves at their crowns as they swayed. The bushes seemed to be trying to spin. There was no breeze. When the Nsibidi began to rotate counterclockwise, Sunny understood what was happening.

"It's going to take us!" she shouted.

Not for the first time, she was glad that Sasha and Chichi were so intuitively quick minded. There was no time to explain.

"You can't go!" Chichi said.

"Not alone!" Sasha added.

But they hadn't completely understood. This powerful juju Abeng had given her was not only going to take her . . . it was going to take all four of them. That had been what she wanted, before she understood that to get to The Road, one had to travel into the wilderness. To be in the wilderness was to die. She could die and live because this was her natural ability. But her friends were simply going to die.

The Nsibidi she'd drawn was slowing down. Already, she could see that the trees were no longer trees, they were more than trees, trees with leaves that swayed when there was no breeze, trees that had *never* been alive. She looked up and met the face of herself, Anyanwu. A glory of wooden sun, her wooden rays stretching out as she shined. Sunny looked into her hollow, round eyes.

"Oh man, please let this work," Sunny said. "PLEASE." Then with all her focus, she shut her eyes and . . . she *held*.

She waited. She could feel it, other, elsewhere, she was in the wilderness. But she didn't open her eyes.

Anyanwu? she said.

I am here.

Don't leave me here.

No. I will stay close. Though you will not die if I leave.

You're still angry.

We will not discuss that here.

Sunny focused on her surroundings. She could still hear the trees slapping their leaves about, but she felt no breeze. Nor did she hear the car engine sound of the house generator anymore. All her friends had gone quiet. Slowly, she opened her eyes. And she understood why Sasha, Chichi, and Orlu were so quiet. Thankfully, it wasn't because they were dead. Sasha's spirit face was the wooden head of a fierce-looking, stunningly red parrot with a powerful yellow beak, and it was about twice the size of Orlu's spirit face.

Finally, Sasha spoke. "Why . . . why does my head feel so big here?" he asked Chichi. His voice sounded like two voices, one female and one male.

Chichi was still staring at him, oblivious to the fact that her spirit face had come forth, too. Rectangular and a marble-like periwinkle substance with white lines painted down each eye and a large, black, grinning mouth. Her two eyes were square indentations colored in with what looked like blue paint, and they blinked at Sasha.

Orlu's spirit face was still showing, too, but his vibrations seemed to have stopped. Or maybe such things didn't need to happen in the wilderness. He was staring at Sunny and Sunny felt an embarrassment so deep, she didn't know she was capable of it. He looked down at the wriggling grass at their feet and asked, "Are we all—"

"Yeah," Sunny said. "We're in the wilderness . . . I knew you'd all be brought here and die, so I—" She froze, looking into the field. A yellow line of Nsibidi symbols stretched through the field. Three things at once: a ghost, a spirit, a path. "Oh," she whispered.

"Aw hell naw, you *stopped time*! You HELD?!" Sasha exclaimed. He looked and sounded weird with his parrot head and two voices . . . but in a way, he didn't.

She tore her eyes from Sasha and looked around. She stepped to the tree that looked the most like the tree at Orlu's house. Digging the soil away felt weird. Though a rich red, it felt dry and airy. Just as Sugar Cream had instructed her to do with her special holding object, she dropped her zyzzyx comb into the hole and pushed the dirt over it.

"Okay," Sunny said, looking at the path. "Can any of you see that?"

"See what?" Chichi asked.

"The yellow line thing made of . . . Nsibidi. It's floating just above the grass." She took a step toward it and it seemed to move a few yards away.

They all shook their heads.

"Interesting. Well, I see it, and I think we follow it. I can't even see where it ends." When none of them said anything, clearly preoccupied with their spirit faces, Sunny shrugged. "Okay, so this is happening. We . . . I don't know how long I can hold this, and then after we return to the world, we'll *still* have about a day, so let's just take a moment and, uh, get used to this or whatever."

They all slowly approached each other.

"I'm okay . . . with it," Sunny said. "St-st-stare all you want right now . . . and then, that's it."

She did the same, taking in all their spirit faces. Every single detail, unflinchingly. She started to read the Nsibidi on Orlu's face, but then stopped herself. She'd only do that with his permission.

"Pointy," Chichi said.

"Oh, stop," Sunny said.

"At least she looks like what she is," Sasha said. "I don't even like parrots. A giant macaw once bit the hell out of me when I was little."

"Doesn't your mother have an African gray as a pet?" Chichi asked.

Sasha scoffed and rolled his eyes.

"What's your name, Sasha?" Sunny asked.

"Njem," Chichi said.

"And Chichi's name is Igri," Sasha said.

Sunny glanced at Orlu and bit her lip. She rarely asked him anything about his spirit face.

"I'm Oku," Orlu said to her.

"I know," Sunny said, smiling. The name meant "light" in Igbo. And *anyanwu* meant "eye of the sun." She gazed at him a few moments longer. She giggled to herself and turned to the others. "Okay. Can we move on now?" She held a hand up, a thought popping into her mind. "Wait, one more thing . . . and when I show you, *none* of you are allowed to talk about it. Don't even mention it."

They waited.

But she made no move.

Chichi grew impatient. "Fine. We all agree, right?"

Sasha and Orlu agreed.

"Okay," Sunny said. She stepped to the side, leaving Anyanwu standing there. She touched her face; it was the one she was born knowing. She looked at the three of them as she stood beside Anyanwu and felt instantly annoyed. She'd always known it, but this was still solid evidence: none of them really truly understood what it was to be doubled. And they were still disturbed by the very concept despite the four of them being so close. All this she could tell by the looks on their spirit faces and their silence. Even Orlu's.

But she knew to wait. It wasn't easy for them. She understood. She was a free agent, which meant this life, this state of *being* wasn't something she'd lived with all *her* life. It had only been her last three years. So it wasn't as ingrained into her as it was for them. They'd been born knowing the close-ness of their spirit faces, and to be doubled was like being a Lamb born with a brain that could live perfectly fine outside one's body. It was unnatural. And here in the wilderness, she'd just shown them this on the most literal level she could.

Orlu sat down in the wiggling grass, his hands on his knees. He lowered his head, as if in meditation. Chichi just stared at Sunny and then Anyanwu and then back at Sunny. Sasha stepped forward. Neither Sunny nor Anyanwu moved. Now it was Sunny's turn to be shocked. He took Anyanwu in his arms and hugged her. Sunny stared at this, her mouth hanging open. She was kind of surprised Anyanwu even al-lowed it. Then the rush of tears was so intense that she was sobbing before she understood what was happening.

"I can hug you anytime," Sasha said, looking at Sunny.

Sunny wiped her eyes and laughed. She walked to Orlu and sat on the ground in front of him. He looked up at her and she gazed into his spirit face. "You are truly amazing," he said.

She smiled and took his hand, helping him to his feet. "I am," she proudly said.

"Do you ever get confused?" Chichi asked.

"Not at all. Never."

"Ah-ah, you're truly an *akata* witch," Chichi said, smirking.

"My God, I hate that phrase," Sunny said, flaring her nostrils.

"*Akata* bitch, then? How's that?"

Sasha and Sunny glared at Chichi, and Chichi raised both of her hands. "Okay, okay, I'll never say the word again."

Sunny cocked her head, thinking. The word had a life of its own already, that's for sure. "Or maybe only Sasha and I can use it."

He nodded. "That's fair."

The Nsibidi path led them through the field of wavery grass for what felt like hours. There was a strange, erratic breeze that Sunny thought felt warm, but could you *feel* in the wilderness, really? Regardless, it was warm and kind of pleasant, even if it did keep starting and stopping almost at random. For a long time, three tiny glowing lights followed them. Specifically Sunny. The interesting thing was that she'd seen these before in the wilderness. Always three of them. They'd fly beside and often above her. Always a steady, soft yellow. In her mind, she began to call them "fireflies," and for some reason, they didn't bother her. Their presence actually felt nice, like she had friends here in the wilderness. There was nothing threatening or sinister about them at all, as could often be the case here. The others didn't seem to notice them, or if they did, were unbothered, too.

Up ahead was what looked like miles and miles of more wilderness grass. Orlu had tried to pull some out. After much effort, it had broken free from the ground with a haunted *ooooo* sound. None of them had wanted to try it again.

Sunny had never spent so long in the wilderness . . . but was it really that long? No time had passed, technically. She wasn't hungry, nor did she have to go to the bathroom. Anyanwu walked ahead, standoffish as ever.

"Are we even getting anywhere?" Chichi asked.

"The trees aren't in view anymore," Orlu said. "So we are moving through 'space,' at least."

"But where are we going, man?" Sasha groaned.

"We're following the juju path from the Nsibidi," Sunny said.

"To where, though?"

She shrugged. "We'll see. For once, time's on our side."

"Thanks to you," Chichi added.

"You know," Sasha said. "We're all technically dead."

Sunny rolled her eyes. "Pfff, big deal. I die all the time."

None of them realized they were walking on an incline until they reached the top of the hill and came upon what Sunny could only call a village of roots. It loomed before them, a huge tangle that reached for the ethereal, star-filled blue sky. And Sunny could hear the place cracking and snapping long before they got close enough to see that there were . . . people walking about through the town's arching root tunnels, around its tangles, and into its knotted branches.

When they joined a path through the grasses that led right into the town, the fireflies finally left Sunny. Maybe they didn't like the piney scent that was so strong it smelled almost false. Or maybe it was the people here who looked to Sunny like stick versions of Ents from *Lord of the Rings*. Frail, but somehow still sturdy and surprisingly dexterous as they moved about, some on two stick legs, most on three or four. The Nsibidi path led right into the village.

"Hopefully they're nice," Chichi said.

"We'll see," Sunny said. If they weren't, she wasn't sure what they'd do. She could glide out of the wilderness easily enough, but she wouldn't be able to find this place the juju had sent them to. And what would happen to Sasha, Orlu, and Chichi if she weren't here to maintain the "hold"? Come to think of it, if something happened to her here, would they . . . die? She shook off the worry but wasn't able to do so completely. *I have to be careful*, she thought.

It was only when they reached the village itself and one of the people walked by without a glance their way that they realized these root people were walking backward. They had faces, but they were so embedded in the wood that you had to stare hard to see them. And the fact that the face was on what looked like the *back* of the head, as opposed to the front, made the realization take even longer.

One of the people came to a bunch of roots, stopped, and

blended with it, its body joining the collective, its three legs sinking into the rich red soil, its body bending, hardening, snapping, cracking, and looping with the other roots. They were all doing that, walking here to there, however far, then rejoining bunches of roots.

When they'd gotten halfway through the village, Chichi said, "Should we *say* something? Sunny, is this how wilderlings normally act?"

"Normally?" Sunny said. "There is no 'normal' in the wilderness. Remember Osisi with all the people, creatures, beasts, whatever? It's like that, only weirder. Things shift, disappear, appear, without warning. And danger isn't danger in the same way here. We're not alive. As long as nothing is trying to consume your essence, then you just exist." She frowned, remembering the jinni who'd tried to do exactly that to her in the wilderness during her punishment in the Obi Library basement over a year ago.

"In that case then . . ." Sasha went right up to a large root person with four legs and said, "Hey, 'sup, mah nigga, your roots looking fine as wine; mind if I ask you where the hell we are? 'Cuz we ain't from here, and, you know, we're trying to get somewhere important."

"Oh my God," Sunny muttered.

Chichi giggled. "I love him."

Orlu brought his hands up.

The root person turned around so that the face on the

back of its head could look at Sasha. Its four legs, rooted right there in the path's dirt, churned the soil softly. All the business of the village immediately stopped as they all turned to Sasha. Sasha glanced at Sunny.

Sunny held up her hands. She had no idea what to do next.

"Hey, 'sup, mah nigga . . . Hey, 'sup, mah nigga . . . Hey, 'sup, mah nigga . . ." Sasha's voice and words echoed off the root person, the sound traveling down its stationary body. Sunny could hear it traveling into the ground.

"Ooookay, well, yeah, it's been great talking to you," Sasha said, a perplexed look on his face as he stepped around the root person to rejoin the others. When he did, the root person uprooted and continued on its way, walking backward with more purpose than ever. All of them seemed to move faster, stepping around Sunny and her friends, politely, but clearly ignoring them. Minutes later, they emerged from the other side of the village.

"I wonder who they were talking to," Orlu said.

"What do you mean?" Sasha asked.

"Trees always listen," Orlu said. "Those roots were probably ears. Someone knows we're here now."

Now they were walking a path that went through another field of wavery grass. Anyanwu was several steps ahead again. "I feel like a character in *The Wizard of Oz*," Sunny said.

"Is Anyanwu always like that?" Orlu asked.

Chichi nodded. "Was going to ask the same thing."

"She can hear you, you know," Sunny said.

Orlu shrugged. "I assumed."

Sunny looked at her feet as she walked. "Not always . . ."

"So what's wrong?" Chichi gently asked.

Sunny stopped, and she noted that Anyanwu kept right on going. "Something." She frowned and then pushed the words out. "My dad . . . when I came home that night, after the Nimm Village, my dad s-slapped me. Anyanwu fled. I don't blame her, but I think she kind of blames *me* . . . or something."

"So you two aren't talking?" Orlu asked.

"We are . . . I'm here, but we're just kind of weird with each other. I don't know what to do."

"I'm sorry, Sunny," Chichi said. "I can't even imagine it. Give it some time."

Sunny nodded.

"Sunny," she heard in her ear. Aloud, not in her mind. She looked up and Anyanwu was looking right at her. "Get ready."

"Huh?"

"Get ready!"

"What do you—" She turned to the others. "Something's about to happen." She tried to see up ahead, but Anyanwu was suddenly so far up the path that she couldn't quite see her.

"Whoa," Orlu said, rubbing his hands together. "I feel something."

"Juju?"

"No, not juju," he said. His hands twitched. "Just something . . . it's powerful . . . in a scary way."

"What is that?" Sunny whispered. Then the breeze that had been stuttering and starting became a wind. It was so strong that it pushed them forward. A particularly hard gust even knocked Chichi to the ground. Then the fog came, rolling at them over the field like the breath of a spirit. Sasha helped Chichi up just as it blasted over them. It was cold and smelled like crushed leaves.

"Hold on!" Sunny said, and they all linked arms. In this way they followed the Nsibidi path slowly toward where Anyanwu stood, unmoved by the wind and glowing like a tiny sun. When they reached her, the fog began to roll away.

"Sunny," Anyanwu said. Sunny felt Anyanwu join with her, her spirit face coming forth. Though the fog left things chilly, she felt warmed. *I am old, but never have I met this one. We must be careful.*

The fog cleared, and about a half mile ahead the dirt path ended, the Nsibidi path either ending or leading *into* it: the jungle stretched so high that several of the treetops would have been lost in the clouds . . . if there were clouds. It stretched so wide that it covered the expansive horizon in an entirety Sunny would never have thought possible until now.

And standing at the end of the path was . . . someone.

"Who the hell is that?" Sasha asked as they approached the figure.

Orlu let go of Sunny's hand to shake out his hands. "Makes them itch," Orlu said. "Never felt it so . . . ugh!" He rubbed them together. "What is this? What is *it*?!" The Nsibidi on his spirit face began to spin.

"Whatever it is, it's mighty," Sunny said.

"Read up plenty on Osisi and other full places, but I never gave enough attention to the wilderness," Chichi said. "I don't even really understand the part of it we're in now."

"Me neither," Sasha added. "Figured I'd never really see it until I was dead, so why bother."

"I . . . I don't think that's part of the wilderness, though," Orlu said. The Nsibidi on his spirit face was spinning madly now. He looked like he was having an allergic reaction . . . if a spirit face could have one. "My undoing skill is going haywire. The laws of that place are not of the wilderness or our living world!"

I cannot let anything happen to me, Sunny thought. So whatever it wanted, there would be no fight. Sunny shivered. "Is this damn ghazal worth all this?"

"No, but we're here," Sasha said. "No turning back now." Sunny, Sasha, and Chichi brought out their juju knives. As Sunny grasped hers, it felt curiously like something inside it was humming. It felt surer in her hand, and this was oddly comforting, even if she didn't know why.

"I'll aim for above it," Chichi said.

"I'll aim below," Sasha said.

"Don't aim *anywhere*," Orlu snapped, still rubbing his hands. "We can't beat it that way."

About a fourth of a mile away, the path went from dirt to sand, and whatever it was began to move toward them. They froze, and Sunny felt a lightning bolt of terror shoot from her feet to her spirit face. It was . . . dancing. Was that . . . the electric slide?

Sunny squinted. "A man?" she asked.

"Looks like it," Chichi said.

"No spirit face," Sasha said.

"That's not a man," Orlu said, bending down and scooping up dirt and scrubbing his hands.

The figure danced and danced toward them, kicking up cascades of sand, and even though he utterly creeped her out, Sunny found herself feeling profoundly annoyed. He couldn't have been taller than four and a half feet, his arms both muscled and chunky. He whisked back the sleeves of his red caftan; the sleeves were so long they dragged dramatically in the dirt.

He had dreadlocks that were thick like snakes, and they were so long that they reached the sand. They grew around his head, covering his face. His large potbelly pushed through his curtain of dreadlocks. When he reached them, he put his hands on his hips and shook them unnaturally fast as he moved in a circle.

"The fuck is this?" Sasha muttered.

The man stopped, pointing a toe out.

Sunny kissed her teeth, now so annoyed she was angry. She hated the way he was pointing his toe. His feet were strange, alien somehow. They looked like the feet of a man who spent most of his time lying around. His toenails were perfectly manicured, even polished with clear gloss, despite the sand on them.

He stood before them, his hands on his hips. Sunny tried to see his face, but his dreadlocks covered it so perfectly that any move he made gave her nothing. He must have had the coarsest of African hair because his locs were solid, locked tightly all the way to his scalp like tree roots. The tips were encrusted with sand.

"The princess, the American, the dyslexic, and the albino have arrived at my front door," he said. "Dyslexic, what is wrong with you?"

"What *are* you?" Orlu breathed, rubbing dirt on his hands.

"What is that place?" Chichi asked.

"Why are you so annoying?" Sasha muttered.

"Are we supposed to go in there?" Sunny asked.

"Are you supposed to go anywhere?" he asked, dancing in a circle, reveling in the music of their annoyance. He stopped and waited. However, the four of them had learned over the years. They waited, too. Quiet. Respectful.

Then Sunny said, "We're here. When you're ready."

He nodded and sat down on the path, his dreadlocks perfectly pooling around him in the dirt. They did the same. When you met an elder and that elder sat before you, you sat down, too. Sunny hoped this elder wasn't an asshole.

"Oh, I'm definitely an asshole," he said, chuckling.

They all looked at each other and Sunny tried not to laugh. Had all of them been thinking the exact same thing?

"I am the Desert Magician," he said. He leaned forward and his voice dropped to something that vibrated in Sunny's mind; it reminded her of how Anyanwu often spoke to her. She wished she could see his face, it would make her so much more comfortable. "Udide and I have written screenplays together. I have told masquerades what to do. I tripped an officer in Nkpor Agu when they invaded that church. I stood with the protesting African students in Nanjing. I helped loot that Target store during riots in Minneapolis. Princess, I know your father well. His music slaps when I join him on the drum machine. I am always here. At the crossroads." He paused. "So . . . why must you find and bring back this thing?"

"The ghazal?" Sunny asked.

"You know where it is?" Chichi asked anxiously.

"Who asked a question first, *jhor*?" he snapped.

Sunny held up her hands. "Oh, sorry, please, sir, I . . ."

"I am no 'sir.'"

"*Oga?*" Chichi asked.

"Desert Magician."

"Okay . . . Desert Magician, yes, we need to get it," Chi-chi said. "Udide will . . ."

"Oh, I know what she can do. Udide will wipe out your *ancestors*. She will rewrite your future. Edit your present. And she'll do it in a few days. How many are left? Three? Two? And you ain't even close!" He laughed with glee. "I have seen her do it. And I know what that object can do. You don't. You have no idea." He cocked his dreadlock-covered head. "But what if you fail?" He pointed at Sunny. "Maybe Udide will rewrite you a life where you are not doubled any-more." To Orlu, he said, "Maybe Udide will make it so that you are a Biafran and you Igbo people finally get all that you deserve." To Sasha, "Maybe Udide will write it so that you never had to be sent back to dark Africaaaaah." He laughed at this one. "Maybe humanity needs a good cleanse."

"Cleanse?" Sunny asked, frowning. But the magician pushed on.

"Now, Chichi, well, I don't think Udide will be so kind to you, no matter what you do. You are no free agent, and you are a direct blood descendant of one of those who went into her home and stole from her." He nodded. His accent thickened to very Igbo. "*You* need to get that ghazal for your personal problem."

"We want to find it," Sunny said. "See how far we've come."

"Many have traveled far for reasons they learned were foolish," he replied.

"If you are the one to let us pass," Chichi said firmly, "then let us pass!"

"Oh, I see I have touched someone's nerve," he said.

"You've touched all of our nerves," Chichi shot back.

The magician stood up and they stayed sitting. "Eh heh, good," he said, pleased. He held up his left index finger. The nail was also perfectly manicured. "All roads lead to death. *But* some roads lead to things which can never be finished. I know where you are going, and it is my choice to let you go where you must go." He looked behind him at the wild jungle. He turned back. "You are sure?"

"Yes!" they all said.

"Then welcome to Ginen. What you hear, you heard, what you say is said." He raised his hands and Sunny saw that he now carried a long, gnarled walking stick in his left hand and a very basic-looking dagger in his right. "Sunny," he said. "You can rest from holding. But remember, when you return here, *if* you return with your friends, you will need to return to that same place to bring them back to the living."

She nodded.

"Don't forget."

"I . . . I won't," she said.

"Your friends will die if you do."

She nodded.

He stabbed the walking stick into the sand, and immediately water began to bubble from the spot. The sand around it darkened under the gush of water, and the Desert Magician laughed. "I am the Desert Magician. I bring water where there is none."

"Oh my God," Sunny whispered. Either something huge was coming through the jungle of foliage, or the foliage itself was that something huge. The trees swayed, the bushes undulated, each one to its own rhythm, some slowly, others as if they were being electrified. One palm tree even appeared to be spinning. To see an entire jungle that stretched across the horizon do this was like standing in the shadow of a great, great beast's foot right before it came down on you. It was hopeless to run. It consumed your common sense. There was nothing but the moment.

The smell blew at them like something's breath; the smell of solid leaves, trees, bushes, stems, and flowers, warm and thick, smothering. Sunny pressed her hands to her chest and coughed, feeling Anyanwu right beside her. They looked at each other, and it seemed Anyanwu involuntarily slid away from her as if on a conveyer belt.

Sunny turned to Orlu, who was still rubbing dirt on his hands, the Nsibidi symbols still spinning on his spirit face. "You ready?" she asked. Speaking felt like talking through molasses.

"Yeah," he said breathlessly. "Anything to get away from this guy." Sunny held out a hand to pull him up. Before he could reach for it, something hot zoomed past her cheek and slapped Orlu's hand away. "Ah!" he exclaimed. And then he was fighting with it. Whatever it was. Sunny could see nothing, but she heard him grappling with and slapping at it. "Hey! Hey! No!" He looked at Sunny with wild eyes. "My hands!" Then he was making all kinds of motions. Sunny had seen Orlu undo many times, but never had she seen his hands move so quickly. They were a blur.

"Hurry," the Desert Magician said. "This is not a door that will stay open."

"Orlu, what's happening?" Sunny screeched. "What can I do?!"

"Something's attacking him," Chichi said, running up with Sasha. "Let it hit you, Orlu. Stick your hands in the mud!" She had her knife out.

"No!" Orlu said, still fighting with it. "Don't . . . do . . . anything . . . too strong!"

"Time's a-wasting," the magician sang.

"Can't you see what's happening?" Sunny snapped.

"Seeing is not the same as caring," the magician replied. "You're American; you should understand that more than anyone."

Orlu was losing the battle, his hands slowing down. He made fists with both hands, and then opened them wide, a final motion. Then whatever it was pressed him to the ground, grinding his hands into the dirt.

"Make it stop!" Sunny screamed at the magician.

"I'm not doing anything," he said casually, checking his annoying manicured nails. "Entry sometimes requires a challenge met."

"Fuck this," Sasha said, bringing out his juju knife. "Chichi."

Chichi nodded. "Sunny, get back." They moved in perfect unison, their juju knives parallel as they swirled them and then held them upright. "Back!" Sasha shouted at the same time as Chichi did the same in Efik. There was a meaty sound as whatever was holding Orlu down was knocked back. Orlu tried to get up, but the invisible attacker jumped right back on him, pinning him down again. Orlu started screaming, his spirit face stretching horribly, the Nsibidi glowing a hot yellow, and Sunny saw it as she heard it. *CRACK!* His arm, right at the midpoint between his elbow and his wrist, buckled.

Sunny gagged. Chichi gasped. Sasha leapt at Orlu, slapping at whatever was there. Sunny heard him hit something. "Get away!" he was screaming, his voice cracking. "GET OFF HIM!"

"Orlu!" Sunny screamed, dropping beside him. Chichi stood over her, working some sort of protective juju. Sunny stared at his arm, afraid to touch it.

"You children are wasting my time, o," the Desert Magician said, bored.

"Shut up!" Sunny, Chichi, and Sasha shouted at him. He chuckled but said nothing.

Orlu's face was squeezed in a cringe of pain. "Sasha," he hissed. "Chichi. Do . . . some . . . thing!"

Chichi hesitated. "I've protected us . . . as much as I can in the wilderness."

Sasha nodded. "I have an idea, but, yeah, how will this place affect it?"

"Just do it!" Sunny shouted. The sight of Orlu's broken arm and the pain she knew he was in was making her nauseous. She clutched his leg and he grabbed her arm with his other hand.

Sasha jumped up and turned toward where they'd come from, brought out his sack of juju powder, reached in, and, as he cut the air with his knife, blew a pinch of it from between his fingers. He knelt down and sliced the air with his knife again. "Ha!" he shouted. Immediately, something came up the hill they'd just scaled. It hit the path, kicking up a burst of dirt, then it was flying again, tumbling through the air on its own wind. Sunny had a moment to register that it was some sort of stick, maybe from the village of stick people. Then Sasha was yelling, "It's coming! Get out of the way!" as he dove next to Orlu.

Sunny had just enough time to roll to the side. Behind her, she heard another *crack!* and she heard Orlu yelp. When she turned around, he was sitting up, looking at his arm.

"What the hell is that?!" Sunny cried. "*What is that?!*"

Sasha stood over Orlu, a half-smug, half-worried look on his face. "Damn," he said. "It worked! I think."

"That's . . . it's one of those people," Chichi said, looking closely at it. She touched it and it chittered. But it stayed right where it was, grasping Orlu's arm.

"You worked a call," Chichi said, looking at Sasha with admiration. " 'Call and Help Will Come.' Those are tough to get right."

"And if you're too desperate, things can go wrong," Sasha added.

"I think you were lucky you spoke to them back there the way you did."

"Yeah," he said. "The thing that comes is called a *papa*, no matter what form it takes. It heals."

"Will *Orlu* heal?" Sunny asked.

Sasha nodded. "It's like a cast."

But it wasn't like a cast at all. Not to Sunny. It was like a foot-long stick creature that had attached itself to Orlu's arm like some sort of stick baby. Sunny poked at its hard skin, and it chittered again, pressing what could only have been its "head" to Orlu's arm, protectively. "Weird."

"Well, if you all are too busy," the Desert Magician said. "I'll just be on my way."

"No!" Orlu said. "Sunny, help me up."

"You sure?"

They both looked at his arm *papa* and it looked back at them. "Yeah," he said. "It doesn't hurt that much anymore. Just a dull throb. We're in the wilderness, anyway. Maybe

I'm not . . ." He trailed off. The wilderness and the physical world were connected. "It's fine now . . . or will be."

They made their way toward the jungle. "I'll go ahead," Sasha said. Then he took off at a jog. He paused at the Desert Magician. The magician nodded, and Sasha continued on.

"Don't get too close until we're with you," Orlu said, cradling his arm.

"You sure you're okay?"

"Yeah," he said, walking faster toward the jungle.

"Sunny?" Chichi said when Orlu was a few steps ahead.

"What?"

"Don't keep bringing his attention to it," she said. "It works better if he gets his mind off it."

"Okay," she said. But that was easier said than done with the sound of his screaming still echoing in her mind.

"See the opening!" Sasha shouted from up ahead, point-ing. "That's a hell of a way to enter a jungle." Where the jungle had been a dense wall of foliage that stretched hundreds of feet into the strange starry sky, it was now a wall of *battling* foliage, leaves and branches shuddering, smacking, twisting, and writhing. And directly ahead of them was a dark tunnel into it, created by an arch of bent trees. The Nsibidi path led right through it, the only thing that remained bright.

Sunny, Orlu, and Chichi joined him, the magician behind them. "Are my eyes playing tricks on me or is that tunnel . . . moving?" Chichi asked.

Sunny could see it, too. It was as if the bent trees were making an effort to bend, and that effort wasn't easy. Maybe it was even painful. Trees didn't normally bend . . . and certainly not into an arch shape.

"We should hurry up," Orlu said.

"Indeed, you should," the magician said. He was leaning on his walking stick, water pooling around his feet.

"What about you?" Sasha asked. "Will you be here to let us out when we come back?"

"*If* you come back," he corrected. "And what makes you think so linearly? You go there, then you come back here? What if here is not here, and there is here, and the only way is nowhere?"

"Come on, Sasha," Sunny said in irritation. "Let's just go. We'll figure it out." She grabbed Sasha's arm before he could respond. Thankfully he came along.

"I'll be where I'll be when I go where I go," the magician said, doing a dance around his walking stick, which didn't fall when he let go of it. He kicked up a splash of sandy water and stamped his feet in it. "The doors are open; the lion may sleep tonight, but the lioness rears her head. There's more, more, more!"

Sunny was glad to leave him behind. Aside from the fact that beneath his veneer of playfulness, she could sense something so powerful it was terrifying, he was possibly the most annoying person she'd ever met.

When they reached the arch, they could see that the trees were putting in more than a little effort. A few of them had even begun to straighten back up. The jungle was loud with the calls, the songs, and the chatter of creatures. Something large and green jumped from the top of one of the trees and bounced on the ground, tumbling and then *running* into the bushes.

"This is Night Runner Forest times a thousand!" Sasha said. "Let me lead the way. I'm more used to this kind of place than you all." Sasha spent most of his time with his mentor, Kehinde, in Night Runner Forest, so this was mostly true. Mostly.

"Oh, please," Orlu said. "I just spent a *whole* summer in forests wilder than Night Runner, sleeping out in the open with a Miri Bird and Grashcoatah." He stepped in front of Sasha, his hands up.

Sasha grinned and shrugged. "No lies told. Sorry, I forgot."

Orlu smirked. "So you *can* forget things."

"Blame it on that guy?" Sasha said, motioning to the magician, who stood behind them, still watching. "He's got a weird effect."

But I'm the one who can see the way, Sunny thought. *I probably should be first.* Nevertheless, it was Orlu and then Sasha, but all four of them were pressed so closely together that it didn't really matter. Sunny felt the moment they crossed. First there was a whooshing sound close to her ears. *Anyanwu!* she called in her mind. But Anyanwu didn't answer. Then the pressing, like the warm hands of something huge clasping her. "You guys feel that?" she asked. None of them answered, but she knew they did because they all had stopped. Right past the line where the sand became soil and the bent trees began.

She heard Chichi say, "Why do you sound like that?" Then the pressing she felt reversed, and Sunny was expanding, tripping, pouring over everything! Green, green, green was all around her, and the others were in it but far away. She felt herself fall to her knees, but at the same time, she was falling . . . over *everything*. She fell over the lush world of trees, stems, flowers, roots, leaves. As she fell, she *saw*, and, oh, there was so much to see.

When she came back to herself, she had her mouth wide open as she inhaled as deeply as she could. She gazed into a clear, light-purple sky, with the sun shining down between the trees. So much sun! In fact, there were *two* suns: one there, and one there. "What the hell?" she whispered. With her mouth still open, the air's flavor suddenly registered on her tongue, and she shuddered with surprise. She smacked her tongue and flared her nostrils, loudly inhaling through her nose. She coughed.

Orlu was looking down at her. "Get up," he said, laughing, the *papa* still tightly clinging to his arm.

"We're okay?"

He nodded and helped her up. "Do you feel okay?"

"Where is your spirit face?"

"Where it usually is," he said.

"Your arm?" she asked before she could stop herself.

Orlu shook his head. "Just let it be. I'm all right."

"Anyanwu," she called.

I am here, Anyanwu answered in her mind. But she was far ahead.

Wait, then.

She felt Anyanwu's annoyance, but she waited. Then Sunny saw a flash of where she was. Anyanwu was up ahead on the path. The mental image disappeared. Anyanwu had never done that, cloak herself. So Sunny could feel her, but not her exact location. Sunny didn't like that. She coughed again. Sasha and Chichi were nearby, leaning against the trees. Both looked through their usual selves, their spirit faces hidden away again.

"This isn't the wilderness anymore," Sunny said.

"Nope."

"Then where are we?"

"Somewhere *else!*" Sasha said. "Check your cell phone. Does it have service?"

She brought her phone from her backpack and swiped it

awake. According to her phone, it was five P.M. Above, the suns sat in the middle of a purple sky. She frowned. "That's . . . interesting."

"No cell service?" Chichi asked.

"I have all four bars of service," Sunny said. "But I have no idea what 'OoniGin' is." She tested it by going to her Instagram feed and refreshing it. Her brother Chukwu had just posted yet another photo of himself flexing his muscles seconds ago. "It works." She glanced at her messages. There were twelve, seven from her mother, two each from her brothers, and one from her father. A notification popped onto her screen: GEKAO WOULD LIKE TO SHARE "WELCOME" WITH YOU. Before she could click anything, her phone vibrated and the document opened up.

"Come and look at this," Sunny said.

Her phone was hot in her hand, hemorrhaging a percentage of battery charge every minute. She shut off the cellular service and Wi-Fi to stop it. The others gathered around her and read the document on Sunny's phone. It was a strange read, indeed:

Field Guide Introduction:

Sunny Day, Pleasant Night.

This is an automatic alert doc sent to anyone who enters any part of the Greeny Jungle. Welcome. We are glad you have chosen to enlighten yourself about the world around you by entering it. Down with ignorance! If there is one thing we, the Great Explorers of Knowledge and Adventure Organization, cannot stand, it is the fact that the people of Ooni choose to remain ignorant of the world around them! The Forbidden Greeny Jungle is the world. How can a whole sophisticated, matured civilization with all its technology, plants, and gadgets choose to live in a span of a few hundred miles? It is primitive! It is preposterous! It is pathetic! You must wonder the same thing, otherwise why are you out here seeing for yourself?

This alert doc will give you basic information about the section of the Greeny Jungle you have stepped into. What's most important is what you may encounter. You are in the AJEGUNLE sector. You have entered the Ooni Kingdom.

Consume this information and let it grow within you like a seed, for that is why we did and continue to do it all. Again, welcome and happy exploring.

Personalized selections from
The Forbidden Greeny Jungle Field Guide
Gathered and compiled by the Great Explorers of Knowledge
and Adventure Organization

Purchase of the complete field guide is
strongly suggested if you plan to travel deeper.

Download is unavailable at this time.

"Yo, I think we're in a different *world*," Sasha said. He laughed loudly, grasping his head as he walked away. Then he walked back. "That's why we're not showing our spirit faces anymore."

"'Ginen'? In all my days, I have never heard of this place," Chichi said.

Sasha frowned at Chichi. "Say that again."

"In all my days . . ." She tapered off, staring at Sasha.

Sunny kept reading, ignoring them. And she wasn't surprised when Orlu did, too. The descriptions of the things that lived in the jungle were extraordinary. Tiny humanoid creatures called Abatwa who rode ants and lived in the mountains and hills of the jungle because they liked the idea of being above things. Bullion fish who were the color of the gold lake grasses they consumed. Burning bushes that glowed like small fires every ten years and vibrated loudly enough to be heard throughout entire towns. Large, wide-eyed rodents called bush cows who had hands like human beings and were known for their thievery.

Sunny stopped reading and rubbed her temples. It was all so much; she was finding it hard to concentrate. And there was something else, but she couldn't quite put her finger on it. Orlu took her phone, continuing to read, and she felt relieved. "Take it, take it," she said. She looked up and wished she hadn't. She swooned. There were suns in the clear sky, a sky that was . . . a light purple instead of sky blue. "Shit," she said.

"Hey, Sunny!" The sound of Sasha's voice made her feel even less in control, and she reached a hand to a tree trunk to steady herself.

"What?"

"Do you notice it?" Sasha said.

"Huh?" Sunny was growing annoyed. She needed to sit down and there was nowhere to sit. She looked at the ground thinking, *If I use the mosquito juju and lie down here, how quickly will something else bite me?*

"Say something," Chichi said.

"Something." Sunny frowned. She said it again. "Something. What the . . . what is happening?!" She wasn't hearing herself say those words. When she spoke the words, different sounds came out. And she was hearing the others speak a strange language, too. And she was understanding it. "What's hap—"

Something large snorted nearby and they all jumped. The sound of it walking away was so heavy that it shook the ground and a large white bird flew from a nearby tree.

"Everybody!" the bird squawked. It said it in English . . . from Earth.

Sunny rubbed her hands to her cheeks and squeezed her face. "Oh man."

"The Everybody Bird," Orlu said, reading from Sunny's phone. "No explorer has been able to catch one alive, and when they die, they are quickly consumed by any animal lucky enough to find this bird's corpse. Everybody seems to find the Everybody Bird tasty, even creatures that are normally herbivores. While alive, the Everybody Bird flies about happily singing a four-syllabled song, 'Everybody.'" He laughed. "At least we know it's accurate."

"Do you hear yourself?" Sunny asked.

Orlu shrugged. "I hear it. So? It's fine. We can probably talk to people here and understand them, too."

"But how?!"

"Some cosmic-scientific laws shifted when we crossed over," Sasha said.

"Quantum physics at its most jujufied," Chichi said.

"Does it really matter?" Orlu asked. He handed Sunny's phone back to her. "We have to be careful and get out of here before dark."

Sunny was only able to get moving because she knew Orlu was right. This was *not* the place to be when the suns went down . . . whenever that was. If they weren't on Earth, who knew how much time they had? But her head still ached from trying to process too much. The weird language thing. The knowledge deep in her being that she'd left Earth behind, and that where she was now was stranger than anything an astronaut would experience. What she'd seen when she'd crossed over.

Sunny reached out for Anyanwu and found her up the path, still waiting. Had she felt and seen what Sunny had seen? Not for the first time, Sunny wished she could really talk to Anyanwu like she used to. Before the doubling. As she followed her friends, last in line, not daring to look behind her, she let her mind touch what she'd seen. Not only had she glimpsed that this jungle went on and on, she'd seen a strange city. Not strange like Osisi, strange like Tokyo or New York if they were in Lagos and two hundred fifty years from now.

"Oh God, my brain is going to explode," she muttered, pushing her thoughts away.

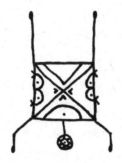

NSIBIDI FOR "THE DESERT MAGICIAN"

18
ZED

They walked for an hour before they arrived at the cliff with the view that blew all of their minds. After the first few minutes, it was clear that Sunny needed to lead because twice the path forked in three directions and only she knew the way. The bright yellow Nsibidi path was always solid.

"At least we know that Nsibidi works here," Sunny said. If anything, it was stronger here, the path allowing her to walk right up to it, even touch the glow. It was warm and insubstantial like incense smoke, but it always drifted back into place. She wondered how far they had before it led them to The Road.

"You think we should slow down?" she asked.

Chichi chuckled. "For what?"

Sunny only shrugged and grinned sheepishly.

"Better to get there sooner than later," Chichi said.

"You sure about that?"

The jungle to their left and right remained thick for the whole hour they walked. Though she didn't like how the shade muted everything, she was glad that at least she couldn't see what occasionally screeched, growled, or thrashed in the bushes and treetops. Also, juju worked here and that was only clear because of the Nsibidi path. But of course, the mosquitos were just as sneaky and itchy as back home, so they'd each worked their mosquito-repelling juju twice, and it had worked. But not before one of the mosquitos had bitten Sunny on the arm.

The insect had been transparent and marigold yellow, and Sunny had fretted for a half hour about its bite being poisonous in a way they'd never experienced. She relaxed when all she felt was the usual itching. Sasha had twice spotted what he described as a small black horse on the path behind them. Not long after this, the path had suddenly veered to the left, feeding onto a wide, flat road that made Sunny's heart feel like it was pounding in her throat.

However, after a few moments, Sunny concluded this wasn't The Road . . . it was just *a* road, a futuristic one. They stood looking in one direction to the other, and their tentativeness saved them because three super-fast, sleek vehicles swept by, right through the Nsibidi path. The four of them crept single-file down the road, cars zooming past them every few minutes. And they were indeed cars . . . colorful cars with flat wheels made for the road; one had slowed down just enough for the driver (an old woman with a large gray Afro) to get a good look at them.

To Sunny's relief, the path left the busy road and led back into the jungle. They soon arrived at a cliff with a breath-taking view. The cliff ran right along the path, the drop so deep that the sight of it made Sunny dizzy. The treetops of the dense forest below were so far away that the flock of red birds flying over them looked as small as pepper bugs. The jungle was a thousand shades of green, branches waving in the wind for miles and miles, clouds of mist hovering over some places. But this wasn't what was most stunning about the view. The skyline was.

"My God," Sunny said, rubbing her temples. "This is too much."

Sunny had been born and raised in New York City with its famous skyline until she was nine years old. But even to *her* eye, this otherworldly skyline was epic. It was miles away and they were high enough to see horizon to horizon, and still she couldn't see where the enormous city ended. And it wasn't just the size of the city, it was the height that it reached and how the buildings *looked*.

"Even the smaller skyscrapers make the Burj Khalifa in Dubai look amateur," Sasha said.

"And small," Orlu added.

"They look almost like . . . I dunno," Chichi said, squint-ing. "Look at the big one on the far left side. Doesn't that look like a giant flower?"

They were quiet for a moment, just gazing at the sight. The buildings were various shades of green and brown, a few bright blue and pink and even red. And they *did* look like plants, like giant blades of grass, stems, and roots.

"That's because they are," Sunny whispered to herself, shivering with awe.

Chichi stepped to the edge of the cliff, holding her arms out as a strong wind blew in. "Whoo!" she shouted, her voice carrying. A group of something down below replied to her with various octaves of "Whooooooo!" Chichi turned to Sunny with a grin of delight, but Sunny just wanted to move on before whatever responded came to see who was calling to them.

The path led away from the drop, and soon they were surrounded by jungle again. Then they came to a clearing of fallen trees that cut across the path and ended in an old airplane. By this time, the wind had picked up and the sound of the waving leaves around them was almost deafening . . . yet beautiful. It was mystical, like music. Sunny could have listened to it for hours. So when she saw the airplane, her first reaction wasn't fear or horror, it was wonder. All four of them stepped off the path and went to check it out.

"Looks like something from our world. How'd *this* get

here?" she asked, gingerly stepping through the short grass.

"Who knows?" Chichi said. "Looks like it's been here forever."

The fallen trees had rotted and collapsed into themselves and no new trees had grown in their places. The clearing was full of sunshine and only marred by patches of the short, tough grass . . . and the trail of dry dirt that led up to the airplane, as if plants didn't dare grow in the path of such a machine. The upper parts of the airplane were dark green, but something had eaten away at the paint on the lower half, exposing its gray-silver skeleton. The propeller that remained intact after the crash was slowly being torn apart by tree roots and rubbery vines. The nose pointed toward the sky, still carrying its original paint, though faded. Here was a face, a huge eye on each side of the plane and a wide toothy grin that extended from one side of the nose to the other. White teeth with red behind.

"That's an A-26 Invader," Orlu whispered.

Sunny looked at him, "Since when are you into war planes?"

He shrugged. "I know some."

"You notice how there are no planes in the sky here?" Chichi said. "Even when we saw the whole sky from the cliff. Doesn't look like the city would have an airport with the way it's embedded into the forest with no cleared areas."

"Yeah," Sasha said, looking up at the plane's big grin.

"Place seems like paradise; what reason would they have to fly away from it?"

Sunny wanted to tell him that he was right, but she didn't because he'd then ask why she thought this. And she didn't want to tell anyone that. Well, there was one she did want to tell, but that one was somewhere up ahead and more standoffish than ever. She wanted to tell Anyanwu. Especially because Anyanwu didn't know. Anyanwu hadn't been with her when it happened.

Sunny stood on the path and looked back into the forest. Back in the direction of where they'd crossed over. When *she'd* crossed, something had happened to her that hadn't happened to the others. If it had, one of them would have *said* something about it. Especially Sasha and Chichi. When Sunny had crossed the border, she'd fallen to the ground, but also . . . *upward*. She'd broken from her body and then spread over the forest, then even farther and farther and higher and higher. And in this way she'd seen, truly seen, where they were. She'd thought it had all been some sort of waking dream, a reflex of her brain to cope with the reality of stepping into another world.

The jungle she saw had been dense and expansive, and then she'd somehow seen the faraway city up close. It was like something out of the wildest science fiction novels. So futuristic that the city had gone not back, but *forward* to nature, nature being the greatest technology. It was like Osisi if

Osisi were built by humans in the future, using the finest and most environmentally conscious tech. And beyond that huge city was not an ounce of human anything. She'd seen a large lake and one wide, rushing river, but it was mostly dense jungle. Then she was zooming out so far that she could see that the entire *planet* was mostly jungle. How could a whole planet . . . but then again, Earth was mostly water. And then she'd been in *space*, floating there like some alien. All this she was shown in the seconds before falling back into her body. Why had the Nsibidi brought them here?

"Hello . . . sir, *Oga*," she heard Orlu say. His voice sounded startled.

Sunny whirled around.

There was a man standing before Orlu at the plane's nose. The man was very old, very dark brown skinned, very bald, very muscular, and carried what looked like roots with large flowers tied to their ends. These flowers glowed a bright blue in the shade of the trees. He wore green pants and a top that looked like it was made of green netting. Behind him stood a furry creature the size of a dog. It looked like a giant guinea pig except for its dexterous . . . front and back . . . hands?

"A bush cow," Sunny whispered, pleased to see something she'd read about in the field guide. She rushed to Sasha and Chichi, who stood closer to her. Slowly, the man put down his armful of plants.

"We're kind of lost," Orlu continued. "Just trying to find—"

"You have a *papa*," he said.

"Um . . . yes," Orlu said.

"Yet you're not from here," the man said. A statement, not a question.

Orlu looked back at his friends. He turned back to the man. "No."

"You're not from Ooni."

"No, we—"

The man cocked his head and moved toward Orlu so fast that Orlu had no time to bring his hands up.

"Hey!" Sunny shouted. Sasha grabbed her arm.

"Wait," Sasha told her.

"Shh!" Chichi said. "Guy doesn't seem the violent type, just weird. I think he lives out here."

They looked back. The man was staring Orlu down. Sniffing him.

"How do you know?" Sunny snapped.

"His body language," Sasha said.

"Decades," the man whispered, stepping back from Orlu. "I haven't smelled that smell in decades. Never thought I'd smell it again. Never wanted to . . . but I kind of did."

Orlu was more cautious than afraid now. "Are you from . . ."

"Biafra," the man said.

Orlu stared at him. "What?"

"How did you children get here?" the man asked.

Sunny slowly joined Orlu, pulling Chichi with her. Sasha

came, too. "The Desert Magician," Sunny said. "He opened the way—"

The old man stiffened, stepping back. "I have forgotten how to speak Igbo," he said. "It's like something in me is broken. I cannot curse in the way that I want to curse. You stay here long enough and you lose it. The Desert Magician." He kissed his teeth loudly. "That one changed my life without my permission."

"The A-26 Invader was your plane," Orlu said. "You crashed here."

He nodded. "In 1967. And could never go back."

"We're trying to get . . . somewhere," Orlu said. "But we're lost."

Sunny squinted at the man. Would he even understand *where* they were going? There was no way to tell if he was a Leopard Person . . . Did they even *have* Leopard People here? And if this man was a Lamb, how did he know about the *papa*? And would the council still *somehow* come for them if they revealed themselves to him?

"My name was Nnabuike, now I am just Zed because this is where my journey ended." He waited, and it was Orlu who realized he was waiting for them to introduce themselves. They each did so, and Zed looked very pleased. "I don't like strangers," he said. "And now you are not." The bush cow at his feet turned and started walking its bumbling walk back where they'd come from. "And that is Nnabuike. He's a bush cow, and bush cows like to steal. He stole my old name. But I am fine with that. Come to my home. It will be dark soon enough, and whether you come with me or not, wherever you think you're going, you won't get there today."

They followed him for twenty minutes, the bush cow leading the way, knowing which paths to turn onto. Orlu walked with Zed, talking to him about goodness knew what, and Sunny lagged behind with Sasha and Chichi.

"This jungle is wild, man," Sasha said. He ran a foot over a bunch of fern-like plants, and tiny red flowers opened up between the tiny leaves. "Seen plants that fold up when you touch them, but I don't think I've ever seen ones that open and basically say, 'Hey, what's up?'"

"I think I see something up there in the trees," Chichi said, pointing.

The three of them looked up, and, indeed, looking right back at them from the crown of a tall skinny palm tree was a fat, furry, gray blob about the size of a child with eyes so large Sunny could see them from where she stood.

"That wasn't in the field guide excerpt," Chichi said.

The thing in the tree twitched its face (for there was really no head) to turn and watch as they continued on. Sunny pressed her fingertips to her temples. She needed to rest, to stop moving so that she could digest all that had happened without missing anything. She felt dizzy, stumbling to the side a bit. Thankfully Chichi and Sasha were so preoccupied with spotting another of those fat, gray, furry mammals in the treetops that they didn't notice.

Sunny looked at her feet as she tried to reach out to Any-anwu. And that was how she saw Zed's home before she arrived there. *Did he build this himself?* Sunny asked. She smiled when Anyanwu responded to her.

Doubtful.

It looked like a baobab tree . . . It *was* a tree. Another one with a function that was more than just being a tree. It was a house, and who knew how long it had taken to become this. Anyanwu floated all around it, and Sunny found she had to concentrate extra hard on walking as she was paying such close attention to what Anyanwu was seeing. The front door was round like a hobbit's door, but it was part of the tree. It had been *grown* that way, not carved out or installed. She could only see that it was a door because it seemed logical due to the location of the two large, oblong windows to its left and right. The outline of the door was something Anyanwu had to look at very closely.

The glass in the windows was thick and smoothly em-bedded into the wood. There were other windows all around the building and another door in the back . . . Well, maybe the front was on the other side. She actually couldn't tell which side was the front. The whole house was surrounded by a sort of cleared area just like the baobab tree back in the Nimm Village. The jungle didn't encroach over this invisible perimeter, leaving the flattened red soil free of even a bud.

Then Anyanwu went up and over the tree, which was quite high. At its top lived another of those furry blob things. It reacted to Anyanwu's presence by trying to sniff her with its wide, flat, velvety nose. It even had its own tiny room that the tree seemed have grown for it up there. Anyanwu reached down and patted it.

When they arrived at the house, Sunny stayed quiet while the others walked around it and asked Zed a thousand questions. She could see Anyanwu standing near the front door, the blob thing with her, then she saw her disappear inside.

"Come in," Zed said, stepping to the door. "I'm sure you all could use a hot meal." He touched the door and it silently swung up, the bush cow quickly trotting in before him.

"Hell yeah," Sasha said, following Zed in.

"Thank you," Orlu said.

"What do you have?" Chichi asked. She turned back. "Sunny, hurry up."

Sunny was about to enter, then something caught her eye. She looked at the open door and then to her left. The path. It had changed to a more detailed cascade of lively Nsibidi, swirling lines and loops of it, but all still remaining within a line that was about two feet wide. Some of the symbols were the size of a tennis ball, others swept yards in length. Cartwheeling, wriggling, twirling, stretching, and shrinking into a path that began just beyond the house and went into the forest.

Sunny hesitated for a moment. She turned and started toward the path. "Oh," she whispered. It was almost as if it were aware that *she* was aware of it and thus decided to truly show itself. Now it stretched from her feet up the path. Up close, the symbols looked like insubstantial living things. *Protozoan ghosts*, she thought. She bent down and tried to touch the symbols, and her hand passed right through them. She brought her hand to her nose; it smelled floral and smoky, like incense. She moved closer. The Nsibidi ran from her feet, farther up along the path. "And this is the direction we'll continue in," she said to herself aloud. "Cool. Good to know."

"Sunny, what are you doing?" Chichi called from the doorway behind her. "Come on."

"Just looking at the way we're supposed to go. The path looks different now."

"I guess that's not all that surprising when you consider everything," Chichi said. "I'll bet it manifests a little differ-ently in every world. It's not going to disappear or anything, right?"

Sunny considered this possibility. "I hope not."

They both paused for a moment, the uncomfortable question of *What if it does?* hanging between them. Chichi shrugged. "Come and eat. He's got jollof rice, plantain, and some kind of roasted meat he says tastes better than chicken!"

∨ ∨ ∨ ∨

The meat was from a large mammal and it was *delicious.*
Everything was. "My God, this is the best food I've ever
eaten," Sasha said, sitting back in his chair and patting his
belly. He sat up and took another skewer of what Zed called
orb fish.

"Ginen food makes Earth food taste like sawdust," Zed
said. "Hopefully when you return home, you won't quite remember the taste. Otherwise, you're ruined for life. Nothing
will ever measure up."

It was all truly scrumptious, but between seeing the Nsibidi path extending from her to the closed door and the hyper-
futuristic quality of Zed's weird tree home, Sunny couldn't
fully focus on the food. She sat back and looked around yet
again. The inside of the house was far more spacious than it
looked from the outside, with a high ceiling and large main
room. But also, Zed had next to nothing cluttering up the place.

On one side was the dinner table and on the other side
a fireplace. There was nothing on the smooth walls, though
Zed said when places on the wall's surface were touched,
drawers and cabinets and even the inside of what he called
a "cool plant" would open up. And above the fireplace was
a bud that projected "Networks." All the lights in the home
were "glow lilies," and twice Sunny saw what Zed called
hush monkeys, monkeys that lived in his home. He said they
had an overly focused need to pick up any refuse on the

floor, and they even cleaned up after themselves.

The floors were soft and green with a type of moss Zed said was unaffected by foot traffic. Sunny took her shoes off, and the softness was a dream. Chichi had even gone to lie on it near the fireplace on the other side of the large space. Zed's bedroom was up a flight of stairs, a small room that was the only room upstairs. "For now," he said. "In another two years, a second room will grow. There's already a bud of one. I use it as a closet."

"Why won't your bedroom just get bigger?" Sasha asked.

Zed shrugged. "When a tree decides a room is done, it's done. This one decided about three years ago."

"Can we help you clear the table?" Orlu asked.

Zed waved a hand and the hush monkeys came out. Where they'd been hanging out all this time, Sunny didn't know. They were about the size of cats with long black tails, dark brown fur, and white furred manes around their black faces. One of them slapped at Sunny's ankles as it passed her, and she quickly moved aside. They sniffed at and ate the leftovers, took the plates, tidied up, and within minutes the table was clear.

Sunny, Sasha, and Orlu joined Chichi on the floor.

"I have an oil bath in the back that you can each use, and if you are fine with it, you can sleep here for the night. As long as you don't mind the hush monkeys joining you. They're very clean and won't mind being around you as long as you are clean, too."

"Oil bath?" Sunny asked.

"Oil cleans better than water," he said. "And it keeps you looking fresh, too. Would any of you like to take one?"

They all looked at each other. "Do you have a . . . normal shower?" Chichi asked. "With, uh, water?" she grinned sheepishly.

He shrugged. "If you like. I don't use it much, these days, but I do."

"Yes!" Chichi said.

Sunny bit her lip and spoke up. "I'd like to try the oil bath."

Sasha laughed loudly and Orlu frowned at her.

"Really?" Chichi asked.

"Yeah," Sunny said. She was curious.

Zed led Sunny to the far side of the house and opened a door. "Wait here," he said. "I'll get you a robe, some clothes, and a towel."

When he left, she looked around. Large glow lilies on the low ceiling gave the room a sunshiny feel, despite the fact that it was night. The walls were rounded at the corners, and they were polished so smooth they shone. However, the floor was rough with tiny ridges—and for good reason. In the center of the room was a wide tree stump with its insides carved out and filled to the brim with clear oil. The fragrant woody smell was probably from the oil.

"These should be okay," Zed said, reentering the room

with his arms full of clothes. "From the family stack. Plenty where those came from, don't worry. Keep what you need."

"Thank you," Sunny said. "You have family here?"

"After so many decades? You can't live here and not have family. Ooni people never forget their own, even if you've been gone a hundred generations."

"Oh, okay." She didn't understand what he meant, but it sounded cool.

"So the bath is ready . . . it always is," he said. "It looks like a tree stump, but it's alive. When you finish bathing, the oil will drain through an opening here." He pointed at the base of the stump that touched the wall. "It goes into the soil and feeds the house."

"A symbiotic relationship," Sunny said.

He nodded. "Take as long as you like. To come out, just touch the door." Then he left. Sunny waited until she heard the door click and seal itself. She looked at her clothes and grimaced. No amount of antiperspirant could freshen them. She looked around one more time and then undressed. When she got into the oil, she sighed. It was soft and warm and smelled wonderful—like the sage her auntie was always burning. The bath had a bench, and when she sat on it, she was submerged all the way to her shoulders.

"Oh man, this is so awesome," she whispered. She felt more buoyant in this oil than in water, so there was an odd sensation that she was floating. After a few minutes, her skin felt a little itchy, and when she rubbed it, a dirty layer sloughed off. It was both gross and satisfying. This was like the spa treatment her mother was always talking about.

Sunny scrubbed all over and the dead skin came off and sunk to the bottom of the bath. Then she took a breath and submerged her whole head under the oil, shaking out her hair and massaging her scalp. When she came up for air, her Afro was weighed down with the lovely nourishing oil, resting near her shoulders. She giggled and did it again and a third time. Then she sat back for a few minutes, feeling so relaxed that she even fell asleep for a moment.

She began thinking about the weird thing that had happened when she crossed into this world, but she pushed it away. "Nah," she said. "Just chill, Sunny. Be in the moment." She smiled. She was here. She was alive. She knew where she was going. Without realizing she was doing it, she called to Anyanwu. How could she not share this moment with herself? No answer. She called again. No answer.

Then she was thinking of Udide. And what Udide would do if they failed to bring back the ghazal. And those Nimm cousins punching Chichi. And how she was doubled . . . broken, unable to ever be fixed. She wasn't a triumph, she was a tragedy. Her eyes stung with tears. "Enough of this," she muttered, getting up.

The ridged floor was perfect for preventing slipping, even with all the oil that dripped from her body. As she stood there, she saw that there was something about the ridges that channeled the dripping oil to a hole near the base of the trunk. Whoever had created this place had thought of everything. There was a spiderweb in the window with a large black spider sitting in the center, and she could see why. There were gnat-like insects who hovered around the hole, landing on it and then flying away. "Just a normal spider," she muttered. "As long as you stay over there, we're cool."

She toweled off and put on the clothes Zed had given her, light green pants and a matching top made of a thin cloth. Very comfortable. She sat and braided her softened hair into three thick braids and then wrapped them with the cloth he'd left for her of the same material. There were no mirrors in the room, but she didn't need one to know that that bath left her skin and hair looking fantastic. She put her glasses on and rejoined the others.

They were already changed and lying down in the main room when she came out.

"Took you long enough," Sasha said.

She laughed, plopping down on the couch. "It was worth it."

"Told you," Zed said from upstairs. His bush cow, Nnabuike, stood beside him, munching on a thick stalk that ended in a yellow flower.

"It was *fantastic*!" Sunny said.

"Need anything else? I'm going to bed."

"Nothing else," Sunny said. "Thank you so much, Zed."

He nodded and went into his room, followed by Nna-buike, who'd finished his flower stalk.

"The man is too nice," Sasha said.

"His bush cow is sneaky," Orlu said. "Caught him rummaging in my backpack. Tried to steal my ChapStick!"

"Oh, that's nothing," Chichi said. "We're lucky to be in here. That jungle at night is probably so treacherous"

"Maybe that's why everyone here is so nice," Sasha said. "How else could anyone survive here? Everyone has to help everyone."

"We are definitely not on Earth anymore," Chichi said.

Sunny slept on the couch, Orlu on a mat on the floor beside her, Chichi and Sasha beside him. Sunny was just settling down when she felt one of the hush monkeys come, sniff her legs, and then stretch out on the couch with her. Five more came and nestled down among Sasha, Chichi, and Orlu, too. For about a minute, Sunny lay awake freaking out about the fact that a monkey was sleeping on her, and then she was fast asleep, too.

She was awakened by her cell phone. It wasn't buzzing or ringing. It was cool in her pocket, like a piece of ice. This was actually not unpleasant at all, since the room was a little warm. A soft light was shining through the windows; it must have been just after dawn. She brought her phone from her pant pocket. On the screen, in blue letters with a black background, it said COOL MODE ACTIVE. She held her phone to her cheek. *This place has done something to my phone*, she thought. *Phones don't air-condition*. She turned to show Orlu, but he wasn't there.

She sat up, looking around. Sasha and Chichi were both asleep on their mats. She heard Orlu's voice; it sounded like he was outside. She crept to the window on the side of the house opposite from where they'd entered and pressed her face to the glass. The window was cracked open, so she could hear them perfectly—Orlu, Zed, and whatever those *things* were.

"They have no official name here," Zed said. "I call them Gari. They are kind."

Two of the large gray blobs rolled to Orlu, leaning on him. Slowly, he reached a hand down and patted the top of one as Anyanwu had. It looked up at him with its huge eyes and he took his hand away. "You sure they're nice?" he asked, his voice shaky.

"Yes. And they're harmless," Zeb said.

The Gari leaned closer and pushed some of its blobby body under his hand. "Ooh," he said. "Warm."

"They saved me," Zed was saying. "When I crashed, the front window was smashed in. As the plane was slapping into the jungle, one of them jumped in and inflated like those fish in the ocean. That's the only reason I survived."

"Did you know you'd . . . crossed here?"

Zed frowned. "That magician appeared in my cockpit not long before my engine failed. I was flying over the jungle near Calabar. Then he disappeared." He paused. "The war was bad. We could not have won it. But we needed to." He shook his head. "I don't know."

They were quiet for a moment, Orlu kneeling down to let the Gari see his face up close. He laughed.

Another Gari rolled in a circle around Zed, though Zed seemed too deep in his thoughts to care. "The people here are a mostly kind, content people," he said. He sat down on the dusty dirt, the Gari still rolling circles around him. "The Ooni Kingdom is like Africa if it were never Africa, you know what I mean? Five thousand years from now! And they don't care for air travel. No need for it. So when I crashed, they knew I was an alien. But these Gari were what convinced them that I was human. You know the nickname they are given here? 'Little judges.' Ooni people don't pay them much mind, *but* they will listen to them when they judge a thing."

The Gari that had been inspecting Orlu rolled toward Sunny, and Orlu and Zed turned to her. She stepped back from the window as the Gari rolled right up the glass to the top of the house.

"Sunny," Orlu said.

Sunny smiled. "I didn't want to interrupt." Plus, she

didn't want one of those things pressing its weird *fufu* body to her.

"Sunny day," Zed said.

"It's a greeting," Orlu added, seeing her confusion.

"Oh," Sunny said. "Sunny day."

Zed smiled and nodded. "Are the others awake?"

"We are now," Sasha said, coming up behind Sunny.

"Are those breakfast?" Chichi asked, pointing at the Gari behind Orlu.

It muttered something that sounded almost like human language . . . *offended* human language, and then rolled to and up the side of the house.

The two women arrived just after Sunny and her friends had finished breakfast and were packing their things. They were muscular and wore the most beautiful dresses Sunny had ever seen. But she wondered how heavy the dresses were, since they were made entirely of tightly woven, tiny, colorful glass beads. The one who was tall like Sunny wore a close-fitting yellow dress over her lean frame. The other wore a red and white dress and had vines for bracelets on each wrist.

"They just need some company and direction," Zed told the women. He turned to the four of them. "This is Ogwu." He motioned to the tall one. "And this is Ten." He motioned to the one with the vines on her wrists. "Meet Sasha, Orlu, Chichi, and Sunny."

"Where are you going?" Ogwu asked the four of them.

After a moment, Sunny pointed in the direction she'd seen the Nsibidi path extend and then said, "That way."

Ogwu frowned, looking and rubbing the yellow beads of her dress. "Well, that's not—"

"The Gari suggest they go to the southwestern market," Zed said. He looked at Sunny. "It's in the same direction."

"How do they . . . How do you talk to them?" Sunny asked.

The two women laughed and Zed rolled his eyes. "I understand their language. It's in the way they move and grunt. Ooni people for some reason find this hilarious. But it doesn't keep them from seeking answers from me and the Gari for all kinds of things." He looked at Ten. "Like where husbands go after the Festival of Mirrors."

The smile immediately dropped from Ten's face.

"Anyway," Zed said, turning back to them. "The Gari think you should go to Gra Gra."

"Eh!" Ten said. "Why?" She looked at them and asked, "Is where you are going terrible? Gra Gra only sends people to terrible places."

"Who's Gra Gra?" Chichi asked, pulling Sunny to her as she frowned at the woman.

"These are just children," Ogwu snapped, then she

laughed. "But . . . that man will consume them, Zed. You sure that's a good idea?"

Now Ten was laughing, too. These two women seemed to have their own ideas of what was funny.

"He's a man who knows much," Zed said to Chichi. "Don't mind them. They enjoy exaggeration."

"Are you going to go with them, Zed?" Ogwu asked.

"No," he said. "These four can handle themselves better than you think."

Sasha sneezed. "Excuse me," he muttered.

"Hey," Ten said, pointing at Sasha.

"What?" he said.

"You see that?" she asked Ogwu.

"Yes."

"See what?" Sunny asked.

"I sneezed," Sasha said, frowning. "I don't have a cold or anything."

"What's cold? It's nice outside," Ogwu said.

"Ah, I see," Ten said. "They're Village People."

Ogwu nodded. "Been a while since I met Village People."

"I knew the moment I saw them. They'd just arrived and this one already had a *papa*," Zed said. He turned to Orlu. "Here, *papas* are common, but only those who, uh, know what they are doing can command them."

"Village People," Ogwu said.

"Oh," Orlu said.

Sunny frowned. Back home, the phrase "village people" was a very negative term for people and evil spirits who wished misfortune on you. Here, it was another way of saying Leopard Person.

"Fine, fine, we'll take them," Ogwu said. "Village People can handle Gra Gra. Maybe."

Zed walked with them up the path for a few minutes before turning onto a smaller one that led into a darker part of the jungle. Before he'd walked away, he'd taken Orlu to the side and they'd spoken for a few minutes.

When Sunny asked what that was about, Orlu said, "He doubts his family survived the war, but he wants me to check on them . . . when we get back . . . and some other things. And he gave me this." He held up his right wrist, on which he now wore a bracelet of pinkish coral beads. "It's the only thing he owned from Earth. He doesn't want them anymore."

"Why?"

Orlu shrugged. "He's left it all behind, mostly. The war wasn't good to him, Nigeria wasn't. Most of his immediate family was killed in the North in the Igbo massacres—five brothers, his parents, aunts, uncles. All he had left was a sister and his wife when he went off to fight."

"That's terrible," Sunny said, looking at her feet. Before the Igbo rebels declared the self-made country of Biafra, seceding from the country of Nigeria, the Hausa and Fulani people were killing Igbos in the North. Though most of Sunny's relatives were in the southeast, Sunny had relatives who never made it back, too. It was a dark time the elders would always talk about when they got together. She looked at Orlu. "Can I see it?"

He handed it to her, and she put it on. It was weighty. She took off her glasses and held it up close. The beads were rough, the holes through them narrow. "This is nice. These are the real thing."

"You can tell?"

"Yep. My mother loves coral," she said. "She's got this big chunky coral necklace from her wedding day. It's worth two million naira. And she's got this blue coral bracelet that looks like it belongs to Mami Wata. She taught me all she knows about how to tell the paste junk from the real thing."

"Can I have it back now?" Orlu asked.

"No."

He laughed and rolled his eyes.

Sunny glanced at the *papa* on his left arm, swallowing the question on her lips. *The less attention he pays to it, the sooner it'll heal*, she reminded herself.

The women showed them through a village of green houses that looked to be made of braided plants, and they were quickly surrounded by curious children around five to eight years old on their way to school. They wore uniforms of yellow pants and tops embroidered with red beads, and

Sunny noticed that almost all of them wore vines around their wrists.

"Sunny day," they said, their curiosity focusing most on Orlu.

"Did you name it?" one girl asked.

"What did you do?" another asked.

A boy tapped Orlu on the shoulder and asked, "Did it come in your sleep?"

"Where are you from?"

The path had widened, and twice they'd all had to squeeze to the side to let one of the sleek, flat vehicles pass, neither of which had distracted the kids one bit.

"A land far, far away," Orlu said to the kid closest to him.

"Give it this," a girl said, handing Orlu a palm leaf. When Orlu held it to the *papa*, it grabbed the leaf with its third arm and started to eat, gently working its insectile mandibles.

"Thank you!" Orlu said.

The girl laughed and walked off. A deep bell rang and the rest of the children ran off.

"Oh, thank goodness," Chichi said. She wore a new necklace of leaves.

"It's a school village," Ten said. "The children are always comfortable here. You don't want to know what would happen if any of those kids felt scared and called for help."

"I do," Sasha said. He was up front walking with Ogwu.

"See those trees next to the classrooms?"

"Those are classrooms?" he asked. "I thought they were houses."

"Everything in the village is the school," she said. "If you tried to harm one of the students, the Nchebe Ants would come down those trees and no one would recognize you if you lived."

"Like . . . *ant* ants?" Sasha asked. "The tiny black insects who always have things to do?"

"Busy insects, yes, but they are white and nearly as big as you," she said.

"Let's walk faster," Sasha said, doing exactly that.

19

GRA GRA

Ginen was more than Sunny could have ever imagined. Its buildings were plants that had "agreed" to house human beings, and thus downtown Ooni's skyscrapers reached higher than any of those on Earth—and they'd continue to reach even higher. These plants had been reaching for the skies long before human beings began to live in them, and they'd still be there when humans were gone. Sunny was kind of glad that they remained in the suburbs and only saw the skyscrapers from a distance; they looked so overwhelming. Even the skyscrapers in New York and Chicago made her feel dizzy, and the ones in Ginen were way higher.

Ginen's vehicles ran on electricity-producing plants and

only emitted fresh air. The roads were tightly packed dirt that ran between the natural paths the jungle's "consciousness" cleared. The vine armbands were actually wearable tech that did more than any mobile phone, the residents had computers that grew from seeds, and all their lighting was bioluminescent. It was overwhelming to process. And also somewhat depressing when compared to Earth with its environmental issues and inferior technology.

On a cosmic level, Ginen existed somewhere "beside" the Earth, yet somehow was nothing like it. Where the Earth was mostly a planet of water, Ginen was a planet of jungle. Sunny had seen this with her own eyes, but it was another thing to have two women explaining it to her so matter-of-factly. Sasha had asked how they knew the entire planet was jungle when the people of the Kingdom of Ooni didn't travel the planet by flight. The response was . . . a lot.

"We have birds who love to fly well beyond," Ten said. "The same birds who like to dive deep into the water. They come back and they zone trees, and that's how we get the downloads of what they see."

The four of them had glanced at each other, but none of them asked what the hell "zoning trees" was or how images from the minds of birds could be downloaded for human beings to see.

"Space traveling birds with Wi-Fi feet," Sasha said. "Oooookay . . . that's unexpected."

"What about people coming to Ginen from . . . from Earth?" Chichi asked.

"They don't come often, but often enough," Ten said, laughing. "You're not the first, second, or even fourth group I've met."

"Ten has a way of always being in the place at the time," Ogwu said. "Our uncle calls her 'magnet.'"

"I was already on my way to Zed's place just to wish him a sunny day before going to market when he met me on the road," Ten said. "Let's see, I've met people from Sahara, Mali, your Untied States—"

"United States?" Sunny asked.

She nodded. "From a great city called Nola."

Sasha laughed. "New Orleans." He narrowed his eyes, clearly thinking something. Then he asked, "Everyone's Black?"

"Black?" Ogwu said.

"Like . . . does everyone look like us? Thick lips, nappy hair, brown eyes, browner skin?"

"How is that black?" Ten asked.

"I don't understand," Ogwu said.

Sasha chuckled and nodded. "That's answer enough."

"Have you met the Desert Magician?" Orlu asked. He'd been quiet for most of the walk, feeding his *papa* leaves and looking into the jungle around them.

Ten and Ogwu stared at him a long time before responding.

"The Desert Man enjoys himself," Ten said, kissing her teeth and cutting her eyes. Ogwu said nothing.

"Do Ginen people ever . . . uh . . . leave?" Sunny asked.

Ogwu smiled. "Yes. And they always come back."

The two women laughed hard. This was clearly an inside joke, but not really. Even Sunny understood. Why leave Ginen for Earth? The one subject that the women refused to talk about was the very person they were going to meet, the one called Gra Gra. "Only Gra Gra can explain Gra Gra," was all Ten said.

When they finally arrived at the market, it was like any market in Nigeria—aside from the presence of Ginen tech and various Ginen creatures. There was laughter, bickering, dickering, and shouting. The smells of fruits, vegetables, perfume, meat, sweat, incense, oil, and wood. Children were everywhere, running errands, working, playing. Things were transported and dropped off. There were people who wore beaded clothing, long, flowing green pants, caftans, tight-fitting pants, and dresses that made them walk strangely. A man who wore a dress with a train that ran many feet behind him was able to move about with ease, his dress untrodden upon.

"What is he, some kind of royalty?"

Ten and Ogwu frowned and shook their heads. "People just respect his sense of style."

One booth made Sunny's jaw drop. It sold windows,

tables, stools, tea sets, plates, all kind of items . . . all made of a clear, green material. Just like what Sunny's juju knife was made of.

Chichi, Orlu, and Sasha had joined a small crowd to watch a man giving a puppet show with puppets made of leaves.

"I'll be right back," Sunny said.

"Don't go far, now," Chichi warned.

"Just going there," she said, pointing to the booth.

Chichi nodded, turning back to the puppet show and giggling.

Sunny walked straight to the booth and just stood there.

A tall, lanky young man in front of the booth said, "Sunny day."

"Sunny day," Sunny said, smiling sheepishly. "I . . . what . . . what's all this made of?" She cringed, smiling sheepishly at her question.

He laughed. "The question almost everyone asks," he said, making Sunny feel instantly better. "Come, I'll show you."

"I don't have any money," Sunny said. "I don't want to waste your time."

"You'll have money someday, though," he said.

Sunny followed him into the booth.

He handed her a cup made of the material. "Here, hold."

She took it and smiled. It felt so much like her juju knife, it was like family. Cool and solid.

"Nice?"

"Yes. Very."

He took the cup and dashed it against a concrete table. Sunny gasped. The cup didn't break. And even stranger, one of the sheets of glass and two of the plates had first flashed and then faded a moonlight green. He held the cup to her eyes. "It's called *engenakonakala*," he said. The way he spoke the word sounded strange to her ear, as if the word were not of this world. Literally. Maybe it wasn't.

"*Engeh . . .*"

"My mother taught me how to say it. It's an old word," he said, putting the cup down. "We usually call it kala glass. Look there," he said, pointing into a pen near the back of the booth.

Sunny went to look. "Oh!" she said when she saw the three beetles milling about there that were the size of small children. Their wings were mottled white and black.

"Kala beetles," he said. "When they grow to adulthood, they will be very big; they turn green, transparent, and very, very hard. When they molt, the exoskeleton they leave behind, particularly the part that covers their wings, is the kala glass."

"So this is all made from beetle wings?"

"Indeed. And it won't break, fade, or crack. Nothing will stick to it. You mold it by heating it extremely hot. It is an art. One cup made of kala glass will be passed on from generation to generation," he said proudly. "My family cares for the insects and sells the finest kala glass. Remember the name Nduka's Kala Glass."

"I will," Sunny said. "So . . . is it very expensive?"

"Of course. But you will grow to be someone very wealthy." He winked at her.

"Why did that other glass glow when you tried to break the cup?"

"Oh. Yes. That's what happens when you strike a kala glass object made by the same insect."

Sunny hesitated and then brought out her juju knife.

The man's eyes grew wide, his smile broader. "Are you from my family?" he asked. "What is your name? Nkduka? Aminu? Onwuegbuzia?"

Sunny shook her head. "I'm just passing through." She could see Chichi looking for her. "I have to go. Thanks for answering my questions!" She quickly shook his hand, ignoring the strange look he gave her at the gesture. "Bye!"

"Remember Nduka's Kala Glass!" he called after. "When you are ready!"

There was so much business being done. Sunny was reminded of the last time the four of them walked through a busy open-air market on a mission—when they were on their way to find Udide. This time, they were seeking a different shadowy figure. The encouraging thing was that the Nsibidi path extended before them the entire time. It was clear that to this Gra Gra was where they were meant to go.

"Gra Gra has his own section of the market," Ten said. They were passing the meat section, and the smell of blood was making Sunny nauseous. The sight of a giant booth that seemed to only sell intestines of various lengths, widths, and colors didn't help. It was run by four tall, beefy men with sharp cleaver-like tools, and the place was surrounded by excited customers raising their hands for service. Sunny swatted a fly out of her face and wished the place weren't so crowded. It seemed to take forever to get past this particular booth. When they did, everything seemed to change, includ-ing the smell, thankfully.

"Oooh," Chichi said, sniffing the air. "That's quality sage."

They swiftly went from meat being sold all around them to textiles, bundles of herbs and spices, shiny stones, and tiny trees for sale. The people who moved about here all wore beaded attire like Ogwu and Ten. The friends soon came to an area where a purple cloth was spread over the dirt and a yellow curtain surrounded the entire area.

"This is where we part ways," Ten said.

"Wait," Orlu said. "Aren't you going to introduce us?"

"He's right in there," Ten said. "It's not up to us to intro-duce you or explain."

"Only Gra Gra can explain Gra Gra," Ogwu said yet again.

The two women stood looking at the four of them for a second. Then Ten shook her head and said, "Go in. Ask for him and tell him that you are the Desert Magician's latest passengers."

They gave each of them a tight hug, wished them "sunnier days," and then Sunny, Chichi, Sasha, and Orlu were on their own in a market in the suburbs of a city in another world. Sunny tried to watch the women go, but they disappeared too quickly into the constantly shifting river of people.

"I'm uncomfortable," Orlu muttered. He glanced at the curtain they stood beside and then away.

"Whoever this guy is, he's not going to be worse than the Desert Magician," Sasha said.

"There's a lot between normal and that guy," Sunny said.

"I hate speculating when we know nothing about what we're speculating about," Chichi said. "What's the point?"

Sunny's eyes went to the Nsibidi path that ran right through the curtain. She called to Anyanwu, got no response, and sighed. "You're right," she said. "Come on." She stepped to the yellow curtain and pushed it open.

The image flashed in her mind and she thought, *Wait a min*— But then she stepped in, unable to stop her momentum. She balled her fists and flexed the muscles of her strong arms, the image of what Anyanwu had shown her sinking in. Anyanwu was already there. She'd already spoken with him. But how? The others ran into her back as she stopped, making her stumble closer to the man standing right there.

Gra Gra.

"I was beginning to think my day would go differently," he said. "Who stands outside the curtain for that long?"

Even to Sunny he was tall, possibly six foot seven, and like the Desert Magician, she could not see his face. But not because it was covered by thick, long dreadlocks; this man wore a purple-and-yellow-striped mask made completely of tiny beads. He wore a purple and yellow striped caftan and matching pants as well. Around each arm, from wrist to elbow over his sleeves, he wore bracelets made of green plants. The ones at his shoulders extended their stems into the air, ending in green flowers. But it wasn't only the sight of him that threw Sunny off. It was the fact that they seemed to have stepped into a small jungle of . . . marijuana plants? Well, not jungle; it wasn't dense like what they'd walked through to get here. People were walking among the plants, most of them with shopping bags packed with leaves.

"What?" was all Sunny could say.

"Whoa!" Sasha said, laughing. "Look at all this kush!"

"She said you were coming," the man said. "You're lucky she was telling the truth."

"Who said?"

"'Who said?'" he mocked. He laughed and then grew serious, stepping closer to Sunny. He smelled like the sage she'd smelled since they came into this section of the market. "What has gone wrong with you?"

Sunny felt her heart flutter. She stepped away from the tall man. "Anyanwu?" she whispered. Anyanwu was standing right beside him.

Gra Gra laughed. "She's still not sure," he said to Chichi. "Not really. Both of them are still trying to work it out."

"It's none of your business, anyway," Chichi snapped, looking him up and down as she protectively stepped in front of Sunny. Being very short, she had to look way up to meet the man's eyes. This didn't deter her at all.

The man stared down at her for more than a moment and then said, "You better mind yourself, o," as he pointed in her face.

"We've come too far for games," Chichi said.

"Indeed," he said. He stepped closer to Chichi and she took an uncharacteristic step back. "Children always suffer the sins of the mother."

"What?" Chichi exclaimed. "What do you know about—"

He pointed at her. "*You* have the most to lose if you don't go as far as you must. Not just your present and future, but your past, too. *She* has explained it all to me."

"You don't know a damn thing about me *or* my mother," Chichi shouted.

Gra Gra scoffed. "I see you. Listen, princess, you have seen the Ooni Tower. The one with the Great Bloom is said to communicate with beings in space, it is so powerful. I have a room in there, just as all royals do. The chief of Ooni is my brother. *But* I don't accept privilege from blood. Royalty is erasure. Build your own way." He stepped closer to Chichi, who was looking at him with wide, quivering eyes.

Sunny took her hand and Chichi grasped it.

When Gra Gra said, "Your cousins," the tears finally burst from Chichi's eyes. She put her chin to her chest, her shoulders shaking. For the first time, Sunny realized that Chichi hadn't gotten over the beating her cousins had given her in her mother's village. "Your cousins hurt you," Gra Gra said, his voice still firm. "Anyanwu told me that you still hide a fading bruise on your side, from when one of them punched you."

Chichi only nodded.

"They're violent because their mothers are violent. It is the same with my brother who killed two of my other brothers to be chief." When Chichi looked at him, he nodded. "Yes, this Ooni Kingdom is *not* a perfect place. My advice to you is to leave that history, that past, that hate behind. Let it die with them. Let it burn out. You don't have to go back, not for revenge. Leave it. Get this thing for the Udide. We know of her here, too. She is one whose wishes it is smart and good to honor."

"I'd only returned home," Chichi whispered. "And they *beat* me for it! I could have done things to them . . . oh, I should have . . ."

"But you didn't," Gra Gra said. "And now you progress." He stepped away from Chichi.

"Are . . . are you Gra Gra?" Orlu interrupted. "I mean, I assumed, but . . . it's good to make sure." He smiled sheepishly.

"I am," he said, turning around. "Follow me. Business is brisk at this hour; I have little time to spare." He led them to another section within his section.

Anyanwu returned to Sunny, standing beside her. Sunny was beyond relieved . . . though a little annoyed, too. What took her so long? This place had a stranger vibe than out there, more potent.

The cloth that he'd pushed aside this time was purple, and the space inside was carpeted with tall grass. The leafy plants grew all around them, like guards. A large grasshopper leapt up and flew from Sunny's descending foot. It clung to the cloth near the top, probably giving Sunny a dirty look.

"I have met only one person from your Nigeria," he said. "This woman had the loudest mouth I'd ever heard!"

Sasha, Orlu, and Sunny couldn't help bursting out laughing. Even Chichi giggled.

"Funmi was in a different world, yet within a week, she was running part of my business, and within a year, growing a bigger home than me." He nodded. "She fares well here. So, you see what it is I sell and grow: it is vegetable, it is spirit. On Ginen, these are the same." He went to one of the plants and plucked a leaf. "*Iriran* is vision."

"Of what?" Sasha asked.

"Maybe you should try and find out," he said, smirking.

"No, thanks," Sasha said.

"It would be wasted on you, anyway," Gra Gra said with a chuckle. He glanced at Anyanwu.

"How can you see her?" Sunny asked.

"Because I am Gra Gra," he said.

Sunny held Gra Gra's eyes.

He didn't look away.

"Can you help us?" she asked. She rubbed her face and heard Anyanwu say, in her buttery-smooth voice, "Relax. Nothing will come of helplessness."

"It's not up to me," he said.

"If he can't help, then let's go," Sasha said, taking Chichi's hand.

"Nothing but some kind of drug dealer," Orlu muttered.

Sunny stayed where she was as the others turned and walked, continuing to lock eyes with Gra Gra.

"Sunny," Chichi called. "Come on. We're wasting our time."

"The Nsibidi path ends right here," Sunny said, keeping her eyes on Gra Gra.

He grinned as he ate the leaf. "I don't really need it," Gra Gra said to her. "But they taste good and are good for the body."

"You can see it end?" Sasha asked, rejoining her.

"Maybe you have to work the Nsibidi juju again," Orlu said.

"Like the mosquito juju," Chichi said.

"If it's not up to you, then who is it up to?" Sunny asked Gra Gra, ignoring the others. No, it wasn't a matter of re-working the Nsibidi juju. She could feel it. It was still going. Just not here.

"It's always important to ask the right questions," Gra Gra said. "You are Village People. This is Village business."

"If you can see Anyanwu, then you're a Village Person, too," Sunny said.

"He can?" Sasha asked.

"I'm not," Gra Gra said. "I was just born able to see; that is part of why I left the palace. I saw my brother's . . . other face and it was monstrous. But that's a story for another day . . . I can see everyone's other face. Village People or otherwise. I see the faces in plants, too. People buy this *iriran* for this vision. Those who want to see, who don't have the ability to see, can." He paused. "Your Anyanwu told me where you need to go. There is a way. You are in the right place. You couldn't have come to a righter place. But what will you give me?"

"For what?" Sunny asked, frowning.

"For what must be done," he said.

Chichi scoffed and muttered, "There's always a price."

"Not always," Gra Gra said. "But today there is."

"We have nothing," Sunny said.

"Nothing of value to you, at least," Sasha said.

"Can't you just help us?" Chichi said.

He looked squarely at her. "I already have."

Chichi lowered her head.

"I think I have something," Orlu said, reaching into his pocket. "I was hoping to grow it myself . . . but I guess it rooting on Ginen of all places is best." He brought a large oval thing from his pocket. It was smooth and shiny gold with black squiggles all over it.

"What is that?" Sunny asked.

"Found it in one of the forests I stayed in with Grashcoatah," he said. "Taiwo says it's a 'clockwork seed.' It'll grow into a plant that's also a machine."

"Ah, of course the one with the *papa* will be the one with a thing like that," Gra Gra said. He took it and stared at it. He sniffed it and held it to his eyes. Then he grinned. "This pleases me." He looked at Orlu. "You have pleased Gra Gra."

Orlu nodded.

"Are you sure you're not from Ginen?"

"I'm sure," he said.

"A new type of seed from a different place is always welcome in Ginen," Gra Gra said. "Welcome," he said to the seed. He put it in his pocket and looked to them. "Stay here," he said. He left.

"You sure you should have given him that?" Sasha asked.

"Did you have anything to give?" Orlu said.

"Nope."

"If he grows that here, he'll introduce foreign vegetation to Ginen," Chichi said.

"Honestly," Sunny said, "I think he knows what he's doing on that front. And he doesn't seem like the type to cultivate things to destroy the world."

"What is it, again?" Sasha asked. "Plants aren't my expertise. A clockwork seed?"

"You know passionflowers?" Orlu asked.

Sasha nodded. Sunny knew them, too.

"You know how they look a bit like . . . like orreries? Those convoluted mechanical models of solar systems? Like something mechanical, but a plant?"

"Yeah," Sasha said.

"The clockwork seed looks even more like one," Orlu said. "I've seen the full-grown plant. They're really cool and behave a lot like sunflowers."

"Hmmm, so at least they're not perennials," Chichi said. "They won't keep coming back."

"Unless you want them to," Sasha said.

They whirled around as what looked like a bush of dried leaves was pushed though the curtain.

"Set it right in the middle," Gra Gra said from outside.

The four of them moved out of the way as a woman and a man in clothes like Gra Gra's, minus the cloth mask, pushed in a human-sized bunch of tightly packed and dried *iriani* leaves.

"Hi," Sunny said. "Uh, sunny day."

"Sunny day," the man said, looking at her with such sus-picion.

Sunny wondered what Gra Gra had told them.

They both left the area quickly, the woman averting her eyes from all four of them.

They were going to burn the whole bundle. And the four of them had to be in there as it happened. Even with the top open, Sunny was sure they were all going to die of smoke inhalation. "It's the only way to open up the way you seek," Gra Gra said. "The smoke is the bridge to the realm you're trying to get to." He pointed to the place farthest from the entrance. "Sit on the grass there."

As they did, the two people came back in, one of them with a burning stick and the other carrying a leaf as big as himself. They set the dried leaves on fire, which burned up faster than Sunny expected. The bushel became a giant roil-ing ball of smoke.

"Heeeeyah!" Gra Gra exclaimed with joy. "The spirit is always strong."

Sunny couldn't see the man or the woman through the smoke, only Gra Gra, who stood to the side.

"Fan it! Fan it!" Gra Gra said to the man holding the large leaf, and now the smoke was coming toward the four of them.

Sunny shut her eyes and held her breath. She could feel it rolling over her. Warm and soft. When she couldn't hold her breath any longer and she didn't hear the others coughing around her, she opened her eyes and inhaled as little of the smoke as she could. She pinched her nose . . . then she frowned. All around her was white smoke; she could just barely see Gra Gra standing there watching. "Why don't I . . . ?" She took another tentative breath. Nothing. Not even the smell of smoke. And the smoke didn't sting her eyes, either.

"Because you're not really here anymore," Gra Gra said. He'd stepped closer to her. "You're going." He looked toward the other side of the smoking leaves. "Fan it! Harder!"

Sunny looked for Orlu, Chichi, and Sasha, but all she saw was swirling smoke.

"Works so fast and effortlessly on your kind," Gra Gra said. "I'm envious."

"How do I—"

"Just relax, it will take you," Gra Gra said. "Tell your friend I thank him for the seed. I have not seen one of these since the pictures in the folktale e-books I used to read when I was a little boy. They have been on Ginen before, just long ago."

Sunny could see the path ahead now, through the burning leaves. She stood up.

"You've moved from living world to spirit world to new living world. Now you move another level deeper. Beware, traveler," Gra Gra said though the smoke. "If the bush does not kill you, The Road will."

Yet Sunny kept right on going. Into the burning leaves.

20
THE GHOST ROAD

Sunny felt it first. The feeling of being watched by many. It crept up her neck and pressed at her chest. She'd walked into the burning leaves and everything around her was gray and wispy, and then it was like walking on the path in a jungle. To her left and to her right was dense jungle. The Cross River Forest or Ginen, she couldn't tell. She found herself on Orlu's heels. And then she saw Sasha in front of him and Chichi.

"This is so wild," Sasha said. "If we make it back alive, I cannot wait to tell all this to Anatov."

"If?" Sunny echoed.

"We're passing through another border," Chichi said.

"Orlu?" Sunny asked.

"I'm fine . . . but . . . I thought I knew all the sides of my ability . . . This has . . . I never knew I could *sense* like this. This place is like . . . It's like . . . like one of the really electrical thunderstorms full of lighting, and I can feel all of the *strikes*. Does that make sense?"

"No," Sunny muttered.

The bush path emerged from the dense jungle into waver-ing spirit grass. They kept walking. Then the rich soil the grass grew in ended and became sand. And right on the border between the soil and sand stood a lizard. A hearty green-and-orange lizard, staring at them. They stopped. But not because of the lizard. They stopped because what was beyond it became glaringly visible. An illusion was whisked aside, and the reality behind it was even more unreal.

"Holy shit!" Sasha whispered.

"Shhhh!" Chichi said.

Sasha crouched down, staring at Chichi.

"They can't hear us," Orlu said, stepping past the lizard onto the sand. He walked straight up, unafraid. He raised his hands. The *papa* on his arm was vibrating so fast that Sunny could even hear the humming sound it made.

"How strong is whatever you're feeling?" Sunny asked.

"Oh, it's massive," he said.

The Nsibidi extended right toward it. "Oh man," she whispered. Then she saw Anyanwu and she nearly fell to her knees in terror. No, she didn't want to go on there. Not into *that*. The spirit road . . . The Road. "Anyanwu!" she shouted. Then she spoke with her mind, *What the hell are you doing?*

Sunny could feel her grin. *Testing the waters.*

Everything went silent as Sunny watched Anyanwu step onto The Road. There was a moment where she felt whisked away, though she stood right there. It passed through her, full of unknowable motion, like a solar wind. Then she heard Anyanwu laughing. *Come on in, the water is fine.*

Sunny nearly jumped out of her skin entirely when Orlu touched her arm. "Are you all right?"

"Are . . . are you?"

"No." He looked at the *papa* on his arm. "I think we've arrived at the end of the world."

Sunny wanted to disagree. The Nsibidi path led right onto and down The Road. "Anyanwu is standing right there," she said, pointing. "On the side." She let out a sigh. "Which might as well be on the other side."

"Whoa," he whispered.

"Yeah."

For a moment, they both stood there, facing it together. Sunny was reminded of Nsibidi . . . if Nsibidi turned into various masquerades two feet to ten stories tall, five inches to a hundred feet wide. If the symbols were both insubstantial and jostling. If they were made of raffia, cloth of every color, branches, soil, oil, water, fire, and stone. So many ran, rolled, danced, shuffled, floated, whirled. Giant rolling clouds reached a hundred feet high. An old, hunched woman kept changing shape as she slowly walked in the middle of the road. A yellow spirit with seven heads and eight arms held seven swords. A bush soul was guarded by a swarm of dragonflies. There were insubstantial mists, half there and half elsewhere. Figments of imagination, fragments of unreality.

Sunny had glided through the wilderness just to glide, and she'd seen all kinds of things so strange her mind was still processing them, but this . . . this was something that made her want to babble to herself. It made her just want to be done with holding on. It made her want to question existence. She put her hands on her knees and bent forward, suddenly feeling nauseous. She inhaled. "Geez," she muttered. "Every step, more and more. Why?"

"Better to grow than shrink," Chichi said, patting her back.

"How are you so cool with everything?"

"I'm not," Chichi laughed. "I'm just . . . open. I take it all in." She paused and then added, "That's what my mama has taught me since I was little. All Leopard Children are taught this, Sunny. You *move* with it. That's why I think *you* are so badass. You're a free agent Nimm warrior who's been doubled, come through a world from the wilderness, and have now gone all the way to the Road of Spirits that's so charged few of even the best scholars have ever seen it, and it's only *now* that I'm seeing you get nauseous. You are so *strong!*"

Sunny smiled and then a wave of nausea rolled over her and she gagged. She waited for a moment, her eyes closed. She breathed and felt herself settle. *I am here*, she thought. *In body and in mind. And in spirit. I can do this.* She waited, thinking about how things used to be . . . before all this. Before she'd made the trust knot with Chichi and Orlu. Before her world cracked open like an egg and an even bigger world danced out of it. When she'd just been the "albino girl" fighting Jibaku in the schoolyard. She giggled to herself as she remembered her fist connecting with Jibaku's face. Jibaku was *such* a jerk.

She let go of Chichi's hand and straightened up, her nausea passing. Before she could stop herself, she glanced toward The Road. "Ooh," she moaned. But instead of feeling nausea, she laughed. Anyanwu still stood on the edge of the organized chaos, and what looked like a house made of leaves blown by a tornado was tumbling up the road, knocking others out of the way. *There is dust here that will never settle*, Anyanwu said. So many were traveling. Two lanes. This way and that way. Vehicles, spirits, beasts, ghosts, deities, monsters, creatures, ancestors, maybe even some aliens. So many people. Like a rushing river.

All traveling, on the move, all heading somewhere. The sound of them was like the ocean, the wind, like fire burning, bees in their hives, like the highway on a warm, clear night. Individual, yet a uniform buzzing and howling and screeching and whispering that ebbed and flowed in a rhythm one had to be a part of to understand.

When Orlu tugged at her sleeve, it was like waking from a long dream. She'd been staring at a giant beetle-looking thing marching by, surrounded by what looked like thirty drones. It stopped, screeched, and then zipped away in a way that reminded her of a battleship in *Star Wars* jumping into hyperdrive.

"This is making me dizzy," Orlu said.

"Yeah. This is . . ." Sunny glanced at The Road and then looked back at Orlu. Yes, she very much preferred to look at his face. "The total opposite of logic."

"No, *this* is the next level," Sasha said, putting an arm on Sunny's shoulder.

"I'll bet only a handful of Leopard People have ever witnessed this," Chichi said, grinning.

"We have to . . . go on that?" Sunny asked. Even now, she could see the Nsibidi leading along The Road's shoulder.

"*You* tell *us*," Chichi said, laughing. She turned to The Road and the sheer joy Sunny saw on her face made her feel a little better. She wasn't having a good time, but at least someone was.

"Orlu, how's your *papa* doing?" Sasha asked.

"It's not shaking as much," he said, looking down at it and giving it a gentle stroke. "I guess it's going to stay." The *papa* looked up at him with more trust than Sunny had ever seen any insect give a human being.

"Brave little thing," Sasha said. He turned to Sunny. "We go on it, right? Is it going to kill us?"

"Not on it," she said. "Alongside." Anyanwu still stood before The Road, watching the spirits pass by. What looked like a shadow with five large, brown eyes passed her, every single one of its eyes staring at Anyanwu with hungry interest. "We . . . we should hold hands."

"I need my hands to be free," Orlu said. But he took Sunny's hand anyway.

Sunny looked down at the *papa*, and it looked up at her, its beady eyes full of worry, but still that trust, too. "Don't worry," she told it. "Just keep holding on."

Chichi took Orlu's other hand.

"This is the edge of yet another world," Chichi said. "Once we begin moving along The Road, we officially step out of Ginen. I think juju is the least of our worries here."

Sasha grabbed Chichi's hand.

They'd started to creep toward The Road when Orlu squeezed Sunny's hand and said, "Wait!"

Sunny was happy to wait. There was a transparent, liquidy sphere that looked like it was made of thousands of hand-sized green bubbles. Even greener balls floated inside it like beach balls. It had slowed to a stop right in front of them. "What do you think it is?" Sunny asked, staring at it.

A brown, erinaceous creature the size of a tennis ball

jumped on the giant sphere and the whole thing began to spin like a top.

Chichi shrugged.

"I think we need to fit in," Orlu said.

Sunny was having trouble concentrating on his words with that thing there.

Anyanwu still stood to the side of the road, feet away from it, laughing.

"We can't die here," Chichi said.

"I'm not willing to test that theory, though," Sasha said.

"There was a juju I learned while I was with Grashcoatah in the forest," Orlu said. "Taiwo taught us . . . for when we were observing night wolves."

Sunny glanced toward the road and she immediately felt ill. *Anyanwu, what is wrong with you?!* Sunny snapped.

Anyanwu made herself glow brighter and the thing spun faster. *Just curious,* she said. *Fear won't get you far here, Sunny.*

Sunny felt Orlu squeeze her hand and she turned back to him. "What?"

"Hold your breath," Orlu said. He turned to Chichi and Sasha. "Hold your breath."

She wanted to ask "Why?" but instead, on instinct, she held her breath. Then warmth spread all around her.

"Stay close," Orlu said. "It only works if we all stay close."

Sunny was looking at her hands as they changed. She'd have screamed if she weren't holding her breath. Her skin grew shiny and oily before it melted into a lush green. Then what looked like sharp blades of grass ridged and then extended from her skin. "What is this?" When she looked up at Orlu, all she saw was a quivering bright green bunch of lush leaves and his two eyes. "Whoa! What the—"

"You've made us *ewedu* wolves," she heard Chichi say. Her voice sounded as if she were speaking from beneath a forest of grass. From head to toe, the four of them were large wolves made of vegetation.

"*Only* if we remain close," he said again.

They were four but they were one, and as they crept toward the road, pressed together, Sunny felt like giggling. If her mother could only see her right at this exact moment. No, not her mother, her father. He wouldn't even understand what he was seeing. He would understand nothing.

They were almost there. The Nsibidi path was clear. "How long will it last?" Sunny asked.

"Honestly," he said, "I have no idea."

She heard Sasha laughing and Chichi exclaim something in Efik. Then Sunny's grassy paw stepped on The Road. The shiver whipped through all her leaves like an electrical current, and she grunted. Then what could have been a thousand images shot through her mind, so fast that she couldn't see what they were. Vibrant, sharp, charged images that she knew she would never forget even if she never remembered them. She stumbled, grasping Orlu's grassy hand, then she steadied herself, focusing on the Nsibidi. *We are here*, she thought, *for a reason. Follow reason. Follow reason. Follow reason.*

Because all around her was NOT reason. The spirits shuffled, screeched, scraped, and some leapt right over her. Then Orlu was yanking her to the side of The Road. "Oof!" she said, bumping into the *ewedu* wolf that was Orlu.

"You all right?"

"Yeah," she said. "I must have slipped."

It wanted a taste, Anyanwu said. She stood to the side.

You could have told me that was going to happen, Sunny snapped.

You're fine, Anyanwu said as she started to move up The Road in the direction of the Nsibidi path. And just like that, with the eyes of the spirits, ancestors, gods on them, they were on their way.

The Road's surface looked like fresh concrete. Black, rich, and thick. Like it would last forever. Sunny knew the texture intimately because staring at it was the only way she could keep going. If she looked up and saw the horrors that traveled The Road beside her, she would lose all her nerve. So, yes, The Road looked like a road, but she knew it was not. Nothing was like The Road. Nothing.

She glanced to the side. And met the eyes of a great beast with irises like emeralds and teeth like knives. She looked down again and focused on where her feet were supposed to be. She did not know how long they'd been creeping along, pressed together like a tiny field of grass. And none of them had said a word the entire time. Did time even exist here? The Nsibidi stretched on before them, and Anyanwu walked far ahead, following it.

In the time they'd walked, however, the traffic on the road decreased. Who knew why? They were still going in the right direction, so that was good. But less traffic highlighted those who *were* on the road. In some ways this made it even worse, for whatever Sunny saw always saw her right back.

Then just like that, *pop!* Her skin grew cold, as if she'd been doused with alcohol then blown by a moderate wind. She shivered as the blades of grass retreated into her flesh and she felt her body shift. She found herself crouching on the side of The Road, fully human, clothed, still carrying her backpack.

"Well, that lasted way longer than I thought it would," Sasha said, dusting himself off.

"At least we're safe," Chichi said, stretching her back. She shook out her hands. "Does anyone feel like their hands are waking up? All prickly?"

"Yeah," Sasha said.

"How long did that juju last?" Orlu asked. "Felt like we were shuffling along for miles." He was looking at the *papa* on his arm. It was still there and seemed calm.

"Maybe three hours?" Sasha said.

"More like one," Chichi said. "Wasn't that long."

"Oh, forget I asked," Orlu snapped, looking at the road as a small masquerade-looking creature leapt, dove, and cartwheeled by. "It got us here in one piece, didn't it?"

Chichi rolled her eyes. "Didn't say it wasn't a good idea."

Orlu sighed and asked, "Sunny, is the Nsibidi path still there?"

"Yeah. It follows The Road as long as I can see."

They started walking again.

"I wish we could 'drive' or whatever they all do," Sasha said. "Sunny, you probably could glide."

"I thought about that," she said. "I don't think this is the wilderness, exactly."

"Well, yeah, we wouldn't be here if it was. You're not holding for us," Chichi said. "We're going deeper and deeper. Wilderness, then Ginen—a whole other *world*, one that's more than Earth will ever be. And now . . . this place. It's a world that's a road that's a highway for powerful beings. A spirit vein. This could be how people travel to other planets and universes for all we know."

"Take The Road all the way to Jupiter," Sasha said.

Then he and Chichi were both silent as they stared at each other in a way Sunny was familiar with. Stephen Hawking would have reveled in their intellectual energy.

"It's too quiet," Sunny said.

"Look at the sky," Orlu said.

Sunny hadn't given the sky a single thought since they'd stepped onto The Road. Honestly, what was "the sky" here? They weren't really on a planet, per se, and that meant there was no atmosphere or . . . She shook her head. When she started really thinking about it, her mind started hurting from the lack of logic. However, she was pretty sure that "the sky" hadn't been swirling with lightning and rumbling with thunder. Did it rain here? "Something's coming," she muttered.

You have no idea, Anyanwu replied. She was standing in the middle of the now empty Road. *It was only a matter of time. The time being precisely when Orlu's ewedu wolf juju wore off, to be exact.*

Sunny twitched, about to step onto The Road. But could she survive it like Anyanwu? "Orlu, don't follow me," she said. "And don't let Sasha or Chichi, either."

"What are you—"

"Anyanwu. She's over there. I have to stop her." Then Sunny glided. The shift was small, but her movement was smoother than ever. She *could* travel fast on The Road. It lay right beside the wilderness like a deeper layer of skin. She was beside Anyanwu in no time. And standing in the middle of The Road was like looking down a wormhole. Brilliant, un-dulating, and glimmering for miles and miles and even more miles when she looked ahead and behind. She gasped. As she stared down The Road, the sight was so overwhelming that she felt she would fall into it. Not a soul interrupted her view. She felt Anyanwu grasp her arm.

Shut your eyes, she said.

Immediately, Sunny did so. The sensation stopped, but the view of The Road did not go away. She could see it behind her eyes, too. Because sight was something else here. She felt better, but at the same time she felt worse. The sensation of tunnel vision had lessened now, and the sky looked like nighttime as opposed to the otherworldly twilight. But what was The Road doing? The concrete of it looked like it was starting to heat up and buckle. Did she catch a scent of tar?

Now open your eyes and look to your friends, Anyanwu said.

Sunny did. They looked close enough to touch, but in her mind, she knew they might as well have been a world away. You had to really *be* on The Road to experience The Road. Still, the sight of them was comforting.

Hold on to your perspective, or you'll get lost.

Sunny was about to ask Anyanwu what the hell that even meant when something scurried over her foot. A large orange-and-dark-green lizard. She shrieked, jumping to the side. She always saw this exact type of lizard scurrying up walls and between buildings all over the place back home. What was it doing here? Another ran by near Anyanwu. Another stopped a few feet away and stared at her. It did push-ups and then dashed off.

What's happening? she asked Anyanwu.

Just get behind me. Do not run. Ignore the lizards. It always brings lizards.

It? There was a vibration beneath her feet. She knelt down and put her hands to the concrete, and it was warm. No, not warm . . . *hot.* Fevered. And it was twitching. Another green-and-orange lizard came and stared at her. She sniffed and wrinkled her nose. The stink of hot tar was stronger. Now she could smell car exhaust, too. And . . . burning. Not the burning-houses smell of Udide's breath, just . . . burning. Burning air? She looked up ahead and immediately wished she hadn't.

Possibly a mile away, The Road was undulating like warm black taffy. A ripple flapped up and rolled slowly toward them, and by the time it arrived, it was just a tremor. Then a section of The Road, closer now, rose up and folded in on itself with a loud *SLAP!* Chunks of it broke off and crumbled hotly to the side. It folded over and crumbled again. And again.

"Sunny!" she heard Chichi shout.

"Stay there!" Sunny shouted at them.

"Get off The Road!" Sasha shouted back. Orlu grabbed Sasha as he tried to come for her.

"Yes! Good, Orlu! Stay *there!*" she shouted again. "Don't step on The Road!"

Now the entire Road where they stood and the parts

that extended behind them were filled with waiting orange-and-green lizards. *Slap!* More concrete folded and crumbled, expelling acrid fumes. Some of the lizards fled, startled by the vibration of the slamming concrete. However, they quickly stopped, their attention recaptured. The great thing was roiling and steaming two hundred yards away now, a mound of hot concrete rising hundreds of feet high. Sunny coughed as a gray blast of fumes rolled over them. It was so strong that it stung her eyes. She heard Orlu, Chichi, and Sasha coughing, too. "Anyanwu, what is it?"

One whom I've met before. It is the Bone Collector.

"Who's that?!"

The stacks of Road were tumbling and breaking, making the most obnoxious racket Sunny had ever heard. She pressed the heels of her hands to her ears and then cursed because the stink was just as horrid. Bitter and vile. More slabs of Road fell and crumbled and piled into hot black stones. The black mound of melted asphalt was rising and expanding, and soon it was only yards away, the concrete and the sand beside it completely swallowed by the pile. There was a hiss and a blast of heat as some of the tar stones tumbled backward like something in reverse motion, some of them melting completely.

Then the mound of shiny black melted stone began to arrange itself, and finally Sunny's legs became too weak for her to stand. She withered to the ground as she watched, her hands on the warm concrete beneath her and Anyanwu.

An enormous shape soon emerged. First a thick body on two crouched legs, then a long, wide tail and short arms. The head, the size of two cars, was box-like with hollowed eyes and a wide O for a mouth.

There was a whispering sound as green vines crept from the bushes onto the remaining borders of sand, then across The Road and up the creature's body. Thick, ropy, dry vines that looked papery to the touch. They grabbed the giant, looming creature and wrapped around and onto it like veins. They tumbled past Sasha, Chichi, and Orlu, slapping the lizards out of the way, pooling around Sunny and Anyanwu.

A great beast made of The Road. But it was so much more than that. Sunny could sense it, and for this reason, after an initial glance up at it that left her feeling nauseous and dizzy, she focused her eyes on a staring lizard. But she still heard it speak, and it was a voice she would hear in her nightmares for many years to come.

Its voice was a deep, rumbling growl that made the filling in Sunny's back tooth vibrate. "You owe me a fight."

"I owe you nothing," Anyanwu replied as she went from being the wavering glow Sunny usually saw to glowing so brightly that Sunny had to turn away. "Don't look away, Sunny. For once, see who I am." Hearing Anyanwu's rich voice aloud as opposed to telepathically was jarring to Sunny. She'd certainly heard it before, but vary rarely.

Sunny peeked through her eyes just in time to see the

bright light squeezed and flattened to The Road. When the light dimmed, Anyanwu was the shape of some kind of in- sect. She flew at the Bone Collector like a shooting star and crept up the mound that was one of the beast's haunches and then—*zip*—she disappeared between two large stones beneath one of its short arms. The area glowed red and the beast roared, slapping at its side.

"Sunny!" Chichi shouted. "Come on!"

Sunny shook her head. "I can't . . . she's my—"

The ground shook as the Bone Collector began to twist and shudder. Sunny could see Anyanwu creeping up the side of its head, a tiny but bright yellow light. And she could hear Anyanwu proclaiming, "Who are you? Who am *I*!"

Sasha, Orlu, and Chichi rushed onto The Road. "Whoa!" Chichi said, looking behind them as she hung on to Sunny. "Is this why you couldn't move?"

"No," Sunny said. "It's that I will never abandon my . . . self."

The beast twisted again. Its tail rose and slapped hard at the side of its head, blasting into a spray of hot tar rocks. *PAFF!* Sasha and Orlu had their juju knives out before Sunny could finish her words. "Cover us!" they both screamed, Orlu in Igbo, Sasha in English, as they slashed the air and pointed their knives upward. The barrier above them hardened just in time to catch the hot rocks. They bounced and clattered all around them.

Sunny was too focused on what was happening to her spirit face to care. "My God, I'm about to become a zombie," she muttered, tears falling from her eyes. "Anyanwu, what the hell are you *doing?*"

"We need to get off The Road," Orlu said. "Feeling . . . ill."

"Yeah," Sasha breathed. He was bent forward, holding his belly. "Can't even look up anymore."

"It's vertigo," Chichi gasped.

"But . . . Anyanwu," Sunny said, pulling away from Chichi. "You can't see her; she's *fighting* it!"

Anyanwu zipped to the Bone Collector's head. She changed back to herself, standing tall like the lighted angel on top of a Christmas tree . . . if a Godzilla made of hot gravel and tar were the tree. Then . . . oh, then . . . then came the moment that shifted something deep inside Sunny that would never shift back. The Bone Collector's head flattened and spread right beneath Anyanwu, like a giant pan. Then *CLAP!*, it closed on her completely like a Venus flytrap.

Sunny saw Anyanwu crushed. Then she FELT it. She was doubled, which meant that she could go far without Anyanwu and Anyanwu could go far without her. Even as far as the wilderness for meetings with old friends. But they were still one. Not that it made any sense to Sunny. What made sense was the fact that everything around her was vanishing. She was falling. She was dissipating. It was like when she was first initiated and was pulled into the ground. But now she was pulled into The Road. Through a sinkhole of concrete. Chichi grabbed her arm and for a moment, she was looking up at Chichi's stunned face from the hole swallowing her.

"*Sunny!*"

Sunny's hand was slipping from Chichi's. Sunny was falling now. Sunny tried to scream, but a force was sucking her downward too fast. Pulling at her legs, dragging her, hot gravel and tar burning and crushing her, blocking her vision, filling her nose with its hot bitter stench, her mouth, her ears.

Blackness.

When she awoke, she remembered. And to remember made it physically difficult to raise her head. "Unnhh," she moaned, turning her head on the concrete. She felt gravel and rocks tumbling from her face and arms. When she opened her eyes, her friends were far away again. Yards. That meant that behind her was . . . She stayed where she was. Her head pounded more. So heavy. More rocks fell from her as she slowly sat up; they were warm on her skin and through her clothes. "Anyanwu," she whispered.

I'm here, came the voice from behind her.

"How? Why?" Sunny asked.

Because if we are going to exist, really exist, you need to get stronger.

Sunny could still see:

The people on the road in the village. They carried baskets, bundles of cloths on their heads. They looked tired and scared. They were falling and the road was rising. The road was swallowing them as some of them turned and ran, most making it into the bush. At least twenty were sinking into the road. The road.

"My husband is in there!" a woman screamed from the bush. "MY HUSBAND!"

Then Sunny saw a familiar light. And there were planes above. Planes like the one Zed crashed. But they couldn't help these people from all the way up there.

Too heavy.

M o r e   b l a c k n e s s.

Her father is crying. His shoulders are curled in. He is standing in the rain outside the hospital. When he exhales, his breath is a fog around him. It is cold. He doesn't care. Nothing could have prepared him for this. Everything had been fine. All these months. How could this have happened? He wonders not for the first time if they should go back home. Maybe his mother was right; maybe the cold winters really are like poison. When his brother speaks into his ear, he speaks in Igbo and Sunny's father listens. If his brother had spoken to him in English, he would not have listened at all.

"Come inside," his brother says.

"Why?"

"*Your wife needs you, your two sons, Chukwu and Ugonna, need you.*"

"*What of my son who has just* died?" *he asks, looking his brother in the eyes, water dripping from his lips and eyelashes.* "*What about him, eh? I was going to name him Anyanwu. That is the name my father chose for him after he had a dream.*"

"*He will come back to you,*" *his brother says.* "*When he is ready.*"

At this, her father bursts into more tears and the pouring rain seems to grow harder. His brother puts an arm around his shoulder and the two slowly go back inside, into the warmth.

Sunny was facing Anyanwu. The knowledge rushed in again as she became aware of herself and where she was. *The lights,* she thought, understanding so much. She opened her eyes. Beyond her, the impossible girth of a monster, looking right down at them both. The Bone Collector's head had formed back together. The Bone Collector could never die. Sunny knew that now. The Bone Collector was one of the souls of The Road, an ancestor reborn when the roads had been paved, and Anyanwu had known this for a very, very, very long time.

"You got your fight," Anyanwu said to it now. "You have consumed us both. Let us pass."

"That is not collecting."

"You will never collect us."

"What of those two there, the princess and the one from the land of roads? They are not broken like you, and I have already eaten the ancestors of the other one."

"No. Let us pass."

"Why?"

"We are here on behalf of Udide," Anyanwu said. "There is something along your Road that belongs to her."

The Bone Collector moved its head to the side to see around Anyanwu, and suddenly Sunny was looking in the face of an ancestor. For a moment, she gazed into its empty, black, cavernous eyes. *I have broken kola with Chukwu*, she thought. And the thought gave her some strength. She fell into the eyes of the Bone Collector and saw an infinity of ancestors. She looked away. Fast. It looked at her more closely, hot rocks falling around her but somehow not on her . . . except one that bounced off her jeans, leaving a burn mark.

"I may have broken this one for good," it said. "*Ogbanje*. A come and go."

Sunny shut her eyes. Then all that she now remembered rushed at her again and she opened her eyes. She looked toward the still roiling, gray-blue sky. She felt better. "I'm not broken," she breathed.

"You still see the Nsibidi."

She glanced behind her. The Nsibidi path still led up

The Road. She turned back, and keeping her eyes cast down, pushed herself to speak. "I do."

It looked at Anyanwu. "I will let you pass."

Sunny didn't look at the folding, melting, smoothing. She could hear it, smell it. She heard her friends come running. They were grabbing her, pulling her off The Road. Stumbling as they did so. But Sunny had to normalize first. Like the giant *chittim* she'd earned after they'd left the Nimm Village, she had to carry it.

Chichi was talking to her, saying something about how she'd finally heard Anyanwu's voice and that she sounded like a superhero or a goddess. Orlu was checking and even undoing some kind of juju he said was worked around her. Sasha was fanning her with a large leaf he'd picked up from somewhere.

Sunny just stared at the sky. *I'm an* ogbanje, *a come and go.* That's what the Bone Collector had told her. She shivered, letting the knowledge sink in like a large stone thrown into the ocean. An *ogbanje* was a spirit who came and went, always coaxed back to the spirit world by her spirit friends. She had been born to her parents a year before as a boy, and then she'd died. Back then, her father had wanted to name her Anyanwu, the name her grandfather had been given for her in a dream. When she was born again, she was a Leopard Person with the ability to glide. That ability had not come with her albinism, it had come with her being an *ogbanje.* Her spirit friends . . . they were the fireflies she'd been seeing in the wilderness.

Her spirit friends knew she'd always be close, so unlike those of most *ogbanje*, hers never pressured her to come back to them by dying. They knew she'd be back to the wilderness again and again. Years ago, when she had malaria and a warm light had watched over her . . . that had been one of these friends. She knew and understood all this now . . . and she now knew the seeds of her father's resentment of her. He'd actually *had* a son and he'd died at birth. Then she had come. This didn't make it better, but at least she knew the root was a trauma that was more than simple patriarchy. She squeezed her head and massaged her temples, thinking about how she'd felt when they'd crossed into Ginen, falling into the sky.

She couldn't settle with it all. And so she did what she did when she was overwhelmed with nerves on the soccer field. She took a deep breath and just stopped thinking. Stopped thinking completely and let her body take over. "Stop," she gently said to Sasha, putting a hand on his to stop him from fanning her. "I'm okay." They were in a patch of dry grass on the side of The Road now. She kept her eye on the sky, which was now clear and sunset indigo. As she got to her feet, carrying all she now carried, knowing all she now knew, she inhaled and then slowly exhaled.

She didn't touch any of it with her mind. She imagined kicking a soccer ball instead. She headbutted it and caught it with her foot. And she smiled. She felt better. Focused.

Her eyes fell on Anyanwu, who stood a yard away, near the edge of The Road. Watching her. Sunny could almost see a face on her now. Not a young or an old face. Not even a human face. It was the face of Anyanwu when she was only her spirit face. But Anyanwu would never be only her spirit face again.

I could have died, Sunny said to her. *For good.*

Now you know how I have been feeling all this time, Anyanwu said coolly. *It has been as if I were dead.*

Sunny's head ached. But Anyanwu was right; it didn't kill her. It just dragged her down with its weight. She stared at Anyanwu for a long, long time. It was the strangest thing, being angry to the point of almost hating that which was you, which was not, which was. There was so *much* Anyanwu had kept from her. Not anymore, though. She twitched when Orlu touched her shoulder.

"I wish we could see her," he said.

"Doesn't matter," Sunny said.

"We did for a bit, when she was fighting the Bone Collector," Chichi said. "She's beautiful."

"She's cruel," Sunny said, still staring at Anyanwu.

Chichi surprised her by laughing. "You are who you are."

Sunny kissed her teeth, looking past Anyanwu. The Nsibidi still led the way.

"Are you all right?" Sasha asked.

"No," Sunny muttered. "But let's get the hell out of here before that thing comes back."

It'll come back if it wants to, when it wants to. This is its road.

"Shut up, Anyanwu," Sunny snapped.

Both Sunny and Anyanwu led the way, Sunny with her friends, Anyanwu a few steps to her left. They walked on the side of The Road without disguises. The traffic wouldn't bother them here after the encounter with the Bone Collector. Sunny knew this as well as Anyanwu. Sunny now knew *everything* that Anyanwu knew. The knowledge of more than a thousand years on Earth. Sunny's mind now carried that knowledge, those memories, and then the timeless times in the wilderness. It was heavy duality.

"What the actual fuck," she muttered.

Orlu moved close to her as they walked down the center of the spirit road that was The Road. "So what . . . happened?" he asked.

"Gimme an hour," she said.

He nodded. Then he said, "My grandfather, during Biafra, he witnessed what the Bone Collector could do. On a road."

"Anyanwu was there," Sunny said. "It . . . ate people. While they were fleeing the North. On the road. It collects on the road. She showed me. I think it still eats people."

Orlu nodded. "Naija roads. My auntie Uju has always said

more than any road on Earth, they are the most haunted."

"She doesn't know the half of it," Sunny said, chuckling dryly. His auntie Uju was a Lamb who'd taken one look at her, noticed her albinism, and started screaming to Jesus Christ about hellfire. She looked all around them at the wild Road ahead and behind that could rise up into a giant road beast whenever it wanted. She'd thought the river and lake beasts were bad; they were *nothing* compared to the road beast known as the Bone Collector. She looked at her friends walking not far from her, to the side of it. She sighed. She was okay.

NSIBIDI FOR "THE BONE COLLECTOR"

21

SANCTUARIES AND SECRETS

Orlu, Sasha, and Chichi walked on the side of The Road, unable to stand the vertigo they felt when they walked too far onto it. It was different for Sunny. After a while, walking on it became more tolerable to her and she began to challenge herself. She wanted to do what Anyanwu could effortlessly do. Why shouldn't she be able to? She was an *ogbanje*, right? One born to die, one who could come and go. And so as they followed the Nsibidi path, she became familiar with The Road.

She and Anyanwu had to travel slowly for the sake of Chichi, Sasha, and Orlu, but that didn't stop Sunny from gliding far ahead and back. First, she wrestled down her fear of "falling" into The Road, coming to understand that part of gliding here was falling, letting go, letting it take her but knowing she couldn't *be* taken. Then she had to understand how to keep in step with her friends, to not lose them when she glided into the current of The Road. There were two currents, each going in opposite directions. But that wasn't the trick, it was holding on to their essence, which was almost like a smell, but not. She'd glided too far ahead once, and as she stood there panicking and looking around at the empty Road and the spirit forest on the left and right, Anyanwu had appeared beside her and said, "Are you trying to get lost?"

Sunny had just stared at Anyanwu. Never had she been so relieved. The lonely Road was not quiet. She could hear the breeze that was always blowing and weaving through the treetops. But that didn't change the fact that there was a silent stillness here that was like how it felt to be floating alone in space. And how did she know what floating out in space felt like? Because she'd done exactly that for a few moments when they'd crossed into Ginen. Sunny shivered, annoyed at how relieved she felt that Anyanwu had found her, because even if it wasn't for long, she *had* been utterly and completely lost.

"No," she said. "I . . . I think I just went too far too fast."

"Yes," Anyanwu said. "You are capable of going even faster." She paused. "But don't."

"Are we lost?"

"You are."

"You're not?"

"No."

"Then I'm not."

Anyanwu was silent. Sunny smirked. "So how?"

"It is a smell. But you will feel it in your chest," she said. "They are your best friends." She touched Sunny's chest and Sunny immediately felt more sure, stronger. Then she was turning back the way she'd come. "Oh, I see," she said. How had she ever doubted that she could find them? She glided right back to Sasha, Orlu, and Chichi. They hadn't even known she was gone. Sasha had been rapping "Rewind" by Nas as he marched backward, Chichi was laughing, and Orlu was feeding his *papa* a fresh leaf to keep it calm. Sunny walked with them for a while and then returned to "playing" in The Road, as Sasha had put it.

The final lesson of The Road that Sunny learned was that she could travel with the spirits and *enjoy* it. She glided with them as dolphins swim together in the ocean: in the same direction, carried by each other's momentum. She'd glided down The Road with a spirit that looked like a tornado made of straw. It had rolled and twirled around her as she flew. Then she glided with a ghostly woman made of smoke, a swarm of locusts, an oily mist that left her shiny and smelling of roses.

When they arrived at the break in the forest, Chichi shouted with relief. "Finally!" she said. "I thought we were going to be walking forever." Sunny looked at the sky. It was no longer the odd periwinkle, but a deeper purple, giving the place a feeling of twilight or dusk. Was there night here? But that didn't make sense.

"I think we *have* been walking forever," Sasha said.

"Which way does it go, Sunny?" Orlu asked. "You sure it goes off The Road?"

Sunny nodded. The Nsibidi led right into what looked like a wall of dried-up bushes that stood almost as tall as Sunny. She shivered. After Gra Gra, dried-up bushes would forever make her nervous. "Can you come close, Orlu?" she asked as they stepped onto the dry dirt and approached the bushes. Orlu rushed up to her, Sasha and Chichi close behind with their juju knives out.

"Do you sense anything?" Sunny asked him.

"No," Orlu said, his hands up.

"If anything comes at us, it won't touch us," Sasha said.

"And it'll be sorry for even trying," Chichi added.

Sunny relaxed a bit. There was juju protecting her, and Orlu was ready to undo any juju that came at them. And so she felt brave enough to approach the wall of dried bushes. She squinted at it and reached forward to part the leaves. They crumbled as she pushed them aside, the dried branches snapping and cracking. She reached farther. She couldn't see all the way through, but she saw that the Nsibidi path led through the wall and onward to a dark path into the dense forest. And it didn't just lead through it, it seemed to thicken and glow brighter. They had to go in there. "Why's it always a forest?" She stepped back and looked up. She knew she could scale it. She looked back and met Chichi's eyes.

"Oh, come on," Chichi said. "I'm not. Tearing through it is no good, either; it's probably full of thorns or toxins or something."

"But the Nsibidi leads *right* through it," Sunny said.

"It'll fall apart under us if we try to climb it," Chichi said. "And probably poison or possess or consume us in the process. No, climbing a dried bush in this place is a bad idea."

"We're close, though," Sunny said. She felt Anyanwu realize it at the exact same time as she did. She stepped back from the bush and then stepped back some more.

"What is it?" Orlu asked, raising his hands and looking around.

"Just wait. Hold on," Sunny said. She didn't want to talk about it. She had to do it. Explaining what she was doing wasn't important. She was over two yards away from the wall of dried bushes now. Steps away from the black concrete of The Road. She could feel The Road's energy, and she shut her eyes. She spent so much time distanced from Anyanwu that when they aligned it felt like the sun rising. She opened her eyes and looked at the Nsibidi path before her that went right into the dried wall of bushes. All the symbols were thicker, more alive, brighter than ever. Some of them planted themselves in the dirt and sprouted what looked like yellow leaves, some of them softly exploded and reappeared.

Her eye went to the Nsibidi glyph for "journey." It was the closest to her, coiling in deeper on itself. She stepped up to it. Usually, the Nsibidi moved with her, always remained a few feet out of touch. However, this time, it didn't move away as she approached. She reached down and plucked the tip of the "journey" and gently pulled it straight. It felt like pulling a coiled plant vine.

The wall of dried bushes shook menacingly and Sunny felt Anyanwu jump out of her to stand right beside her. "You guys, move away!" Sunny shouted. "Move away!" It took everything in her to stand her ground.

"No matter what," Anyanwu said. "Not even a step back. No fear."

The bushes were shaking so hard that many of the leaves were falling. Sunny heard someone clapping, and right in front of her where the Nsibidi disappeared into the wall, a spark ignited. It caught on fast, and soon flames were spreading across the wall of dried vegetation.

Sunny glanced at Orlu, but he only stood there with Sasha and Chichi, near The Road but not on it. His hands were at his sides.

"Did you do that?" Chichi asked.

"Just wait," Sunny said, turning her attention back to what was now a roaring wall of bright orange flames. The heat wafting from it was intense, even from where she stood, and the smoke had a sharp smell that tickled her throat.

"Don't cough," Anyanwu said. "That's an insult."

"I know," Sunny muttered.

"Why are we just standing here waiting?" Sasha said. "Something is obviously trying to come through."

"Sasha, don't!" she heard Chichi shout.

"If y'all too scared to, then I will!" Sasha said.

Sunny turned around just in time to see Sasha fly past, running fast, juju knife out. He made a slicing motion with his knife and held his other hand below it, catching the juju bag.

When Sunny opened her mouth, it was Anyanwu's voice that came out. "Sasha, do *not* do that!"

"I know what I'm doing!" he shouted back. He threw the juju, and Sunny saw it do something in midair. It was a light blue as it sailed toward the fire, then it flamed like a firework igniting. *PHOOM!* Then it stopped in midair and . . . zipped right back at Sasha. His eyes grew wide as the redirected juju flew at his hands and *SHHHHPAH!* The explosion sent a shock wave that knocked all of them off their feet. Sunny's teeth chattered. Smoke from the flames wafted over them and she couldn't see Sasha . . . but she could hear him. He was screaming. *"My hands! My hands!"*

Chichi was on her feet first, working a juju to blow the smoke in a different direction. Orlu was close behind her, his hands moving lightning fast as he undid other jujus that must have been thrown at Sasha. Sunny stood behind them, staring at Sasha as he writhed in Chichi's arms, the fire burning way too close.

"Stop," Chichi said. "Hold them up! Let me see!"

Orlu held Sasha's shoulders as Chichi caught his wrists. The palms of his hands were black with soot, smoke still rising from them. Gingerly, Chichi touched one with her index finger. Sasha hissed with pain. "What are you doing?"

"What were *you* doing?" she snapped. "Are you *trying* to die?!"

"I . . . needed . . . to provoke it," he said through gritted teeth.

"His juju knife," Orlu said, pointing. Sunny's mouth fell open. He couldn't be referring to that shiny puddle smoldering in the dirt?

"Forget that," Chichi said. "These burns look bad."

Straining with pain, Sasha shook his head. "They look worse than they are. I'll be okay. Just find a way in and get the damn thing." They helped get him away from the fire just in time. A moment later, the fire flared even hotter and brighter.

Chichi used some of Sunny's tissues and bottled water to clean the soot off Sasha's hands. He was right—the burns weren't terrible, though the flesh of both his palms was an angry red and painful to the touch. The wall raged for a bit, and then calmed, growing lower and lower. After a few minutes, Sunny stood up and walked to it. She squinted, trying to see what was beyond it now that so much of the leaves were burned away. Where before she'd seen a dark forest, now she saw a building . . . a house or shrine or obi. It wasn't close, but it wasn't far, the dense jungle making way for it. The Nsibidi led through smoke and dying flames, right to the structure less than a quarter of a mile away.

But first . . . the fire burned away almost all of the dried bush. Sunny and Anyanwu stood still, gazing at the smoke and taking in the moment. Sunny knew the being's name; she could sense it right on the tip of her tongue. But when she tried to reach for it in Anyanwu's memories, to think it, to be able to say it, she felt that horrible sensation of tripping on her feet and falling into the sky.

"Stop doing that," Anyanwu said.

"I want to know its name."

"Danafojura," Anyanwu said. And the sound of the word was a relief to Sunny's ears. No more need to risk falling into the sky. "Now stop trying to remember. It was a long, long time ago, even for me. Stand your ground. Focus. It'll know if you are not."

Knowing about something through Anyanwu's memories—which were older than she'd ever live as a human being—was one thing, but seeing and understanding it was something else entirely. "Do *not* move," Anyanwu said.

Smoke rose from the burned bushes, the breeze blowing it toward the structure beyond. And directly in front of her, in the path of the Nsibidi, something huge and black was emerging from the charred remains of the bushes. The black mound was the size of a car, ash puffing up and charred sticks tumbling. It rose slowly. Tall and lean as a wraith, a shadow of a tree. It might have been five feet tall. Then seven. Nine. Fifteen. It stopped growing.

"Eh," Orlu said. "A masquerade."

"See why throwing that water juju at it nearly got you killed?!" Chichi said.

"I was trying to stop a fire from—"

"Ugh, just silly," Chichi snapped.

"Whatever. Damn masquerades are unpredictable."

Sunny didn't dare turn to her friends. She didn't dare *move*. It was lean and tall, standing in a mound of ash, made of burlap-like stiff cloth that was black like soot, with long, long arms and no face.

"Open your eyes. See." Its voice reminded Sunny of cracking branches, and she could not tell what language it was speaking, only that she understood it. It stepped out of the ash much faster than Sunny expected. And before she knew it, the thing was standing before her and Anyanwu. No. Not Anyanwu. Her. Just her.

She quickly looked down, too afraid to look up. And in this way, she saw that its cloth was thick, maybe leather, the hem encrusted with cowry shells all the way around. It smelled of the smoke still rising from it. It did not move. It said nothing. Anyanwu said nothing. Her friends, steps away, said nothing. For a brief moment, she wondered if time had stopped, but she knew it hadn't. They weren't even in time, really. This was a place deeper than the wilderness. This was a place along the spirit road.

Slowly, she brought her eyes up. There were two parallel tracks of raffia woven into the cloth and threaded with a line of large brown cowry shells. Between the tracks, large seeds stuck to the cloth like giant coffee beans. She brought her eyes up more. The masquerade did not have hands, though its sleeves were filled with something that gave it arms. This thing could knock her head from her shoulders if it wanted to. She brought her eyes up even more, following the tracks of cowry shells and raffia. A blast of smoke from it almost caused her to lower her eyes again, but she continued raising her gaze higher.

There was no face. Only more cowry shells, raffia, and seeds. "Sunny Nwazue," it said.

"Danafojura," Sunny said.

"Woman show, bodyguard, warrior." It laughed throatily. "Juju has led you here. You are a fool."

"I'm not a fool. I have a purpose," she said. This time she

did turn to her friends. Orlu, Chichi, and Sasha were exactly where they'd been, utterly silent. "We have a purpose. We've come for—"

"I know what you seek. It is in the Power House. You may go in and find it, but you will not come out human."

Sunny felt her heart flip. It had not said she would not come out alive. It had said she would not come out human. What did that even *mean*?

"Let us pass," Anyanwu said. "It's not your concern. You're not here for any reason but show, so let us pass."

Sunny's eyes widened at Anyanwu's audacity. One doesn't just speak to a masquerade like that. This one had just stepped out of fire. It turned to Anyanwu, then turned right back to Sunny and said, "It is a place where they dump cultural garbage, store the greatest gifts, and place things to be forever lost. Are you sure you want to enter a negative space? Is obtaining what you seek worth who you will find?"

"We have come this far!" Sunny heard Chichi shout. "Let us pass, masquerade!"

Sunny could hear it look up. Toward her friends.

What seemed like an eternity passed before Danafojura spoke. "Only you and the princess will go."

It did not move or speak after that.

"Should we?" Chichi whispered.

Sunny turned around and shrugged.

Orlu nodded. "Go."

"Yeah . . . uh . . . go . . . I think," Sasha said.

Masquerades did not need to obey the laws of physics or the living. Chichi came up behind her. They looked at each other and then back at Orlu and Sasha. None of them said a thing. What was there to say? Entering this place as two instead of four was a bad omen; they all knew it. They were an *Oha* coven, their strength was as a four.

"But you can't argue with a masquerade," Chichi said as she walked toward the burned wall.

Sunny looked back one more time. The masquerade was still there, as were Orlu and Sasha. There was no way they would ever be able to sneak around it. "Are we sure about—"

"Shut up, Sunny," Chichi snapped. "Let's get this damn thing once and for all."

22

EVIL FOREST

"Where is Anyanwu?" Chichi asked.

"Right beside you," Sunny said.

They were steps away from the smoldering bushes. Sunny grasped Chichi's hand harder and stopped. "What is it?" Chichi asked, anxious.

"I have to . . . I have to . . ." Her eyes began to water. She turned away from Chichi and sneezed hard. "Uh," she said. "My God." She sneezed again and again and again. She let go of Chichi's hand and swung her backpack around. She had plenty of tissues. She blew her nose hard. "It's not just juju powder; it's the smoke, too," she said, wiping her eyes. "It's the smoke. How are you not coughing or sneezing?"

Chichi grinned. "My lungs are used to it, I guess."

"You mean too damaged to notice," Sunny said. "Smoking will always be nasty to me."

"Bangas don't contain nicotine or any other chemicals," Chichi said. "They're—"

Sunny blew her nose loudly. Chichi rolled her eyes. They continued. Getting through what was left of the wall was not difficult, albeit a little hot. Some parts still smoldered, but it was almost as if the Nsibidi cleared a safe path through. Where they stepped was mostly char and ash that puffed up beneath their sandals.

"I'll bet if we wiped our faces with a white washcloth, it would come away gray," Sunny said.

"The Himba women of Namibia take daily smoke baths to stay clean," Chichi said. "If you've ever seen how clear their skin is, you wouldn't be too worried about a little smoke in your face right now."

Once through, they stood gazing at what Danafojura called the Power House.

"It's in there," Chichi said.

"How do you know?"

Chichi looked at Sunny and smiled. "Come on, you know it is."

She did. "Yeah . . . I think I just want to feel like we're going to come out with it. Also, the way your mom described it creeps me out."

"We had *Udide's Book of Shadows*, remember? At least for a while. The thing has since mysteriously disappeared. Anything belonging to Udide is going to be creepy."

They crept closer. The path to the structure reminded Sunny of Sasha's mentor Kehinde's hut in that the jungle kept its distance—a perimeter of several yards, as if the jungle itself was afraid of this place. The ground they stepped on was dry dirt, and the breeze grew stronger as they approached, sending the dust and remaining smoke swirling around them.

It was a traditional house made of the bones of a massive beast. There were even sections of the outer wall that were crumbly and porous like ancient, exposed bone marrow. And it was skewed to the left like a fun house at a carnival. The doorway was covered by a faded blue cloth that looked a thousand years old. It fluttered in and out. Below, the white stone floor glowed from a dim orange-yellow light coming from inside.

"You ready?" Chichi asked, squeezing her hand.

"I wish Orlu were here," Sunny said.

"I hate to say it, but juju is the least of our worries right now," Chichi said, giving Sunny a sad look. They stared at each other.

Sunny thought of the day they had met. How Chichi had known exactly what Sunny was from the moment she'd set eyes on her. And from the moment she'd met Chichi, despite her impulsive ways, Sunny had felt comfortable going with her into the unknown. Sunny trusted Chichi completely. "Don't let go of my hand," Sunny said.

She pushed the cloth aside and they stepped into the Power House.

It was like stepping into outside. Expansive. How could Sunny have known it would not look as it did on the outside? Though in all her days of being a Leopard Person, she found this was more often the case than not. Udide's lair, the inside of the baobab tree in the Nimm Village, and now the Power House. The hallway was narrow, leaning to the left and winding to the left not far ahead. Where it turned was what looked like a thirty-story stack of flames. This was what was lighting the place, at least from here.

When she looked up, she could see so high above that she wasn't sure if it wasn't some sort of other sky, a dark sky. The walls were all made of the white stone . . . or bone, and drawn with black squiggles, circles, and dots that were so detailed, the walls had a reptilian look.

"No line or dot touches another," Chichi said, looking at the designs up close. "Whoever painted all this was some kind of artist who's learned to use their obsession with detail." She stood back and looked at it. "I find it oddly satisfying."

"Reminds me of Nsibidi," Sunny said as they crept forward.

"Do you still see the path?"

Sunny shook her head. "Stopped as soon as we stepped in."

There were moths fluttering around the strange stack of flames when they got to it. Some were quite large, most small. One of the large ones, a yellow moth with long tails on each of its hindwings, looked almost like a fairy. It swooped in on the flames, then dipped away at the last moment, seeming to flirt with death.

"Shoo!" Chichi said, slapping at an orange tawny moth with green vines on its wings. Sunny giggled as the moth landed right back on her head and then flew out of the way when Chichi slapped at it again. It zoomed at her one more time, slapping her on the cheek with a wing loudly enough that Sunny could hear it before it flew off. "Come at me again," Chichi shouted at it. "I will crush you to mush!"

Sunny took Chichi's hand and led her past the light. "Come on," she said. "No time to start wars with moths and butterflies."

The hallway led into a large white room that was stone from floor to wall to high ceiling. Sunny was glad to be out from under the weird sky-that-wasn't-a-sky. And here, the air smelled fresh. They'd walked into the center of the room, their eyes set on the seven doorways on the far side, when the music began. First the energetic beat of talking drums, then the haunting melody of a flute wound itself through the beats. The melody of another masquerade. Sunny moaned with dread. They brought out their juju knives. Sunny frantically eyed the seven doors, all carved into the stone and barely high enough for her to fit through from the looks of them.

"Any idea what this is?" Sunny asked.

"I don't even understand where we *are*," Chichi screeched.

A masquerade inside this place, this deep, deep mystical *obi* that harbored goodness knew what, was not good at all. This would be beyond anything either of them could do. "Anyanwu?" Sunny asked. "A little help."

Anyanwu's voice was right against her ear. "Behind you."

Sunny whirled around, and when she saw it, she gasped and dropped her juju knife. Chichi turned and screamed.

It was tall. Wide. Sloppy and rugged. Draped with rotted animal pelts and huge, hanging tufts of black raffia with a great crown of hundreds of thick black tassels tipped with brown cowry shells. Three large white feathers stuck out of the top as smoke billowed down the entire thing like lava. It shook to the music, hovering inches above the ground as it softly bounced toward them.

All the strength left Sunny's legs. Suddenly feeling very cold, she rubbed her hands as she sunk to the hard stone ground. To her knees. Tears filled her eyes as her nose was filled with the masquerade's acrid stench. Sunny called for Anyanwu, but she did not answer. She could hear Chichi beside her weeping. Sunny shut her eyes, pressed the heels of her hands to her ears, and waited for death to come. There was no fighting this thing. Its cowries clicked as it approached.

She heard Anyanwu in her mind say its name and this did not help her at all. *Ajofia*. Evil Forest. Sunny braced herself, the burning in her veins increasing. Something warm dribbled from her nose and she knew it was blood. There was a sting in her knee and the sharp pain got her attention. She opened her eyes. Her juju knife. She looked up and in that moment came face to face with Ajofia. There was a purse on its front, embroidered with cowry shells. She blinked. And then she did the thing she always did when she played soccer. She stopped thinking. She acted.

She glided at it, and for a moment, *everything* stopped. She was in outer space again. No sound here. No air. No weight. And Ajofia was vast. Stretched before her. Eyes blazing red. Thick, pursed lips of a spirit who gave forests to whole planets. Wide nostrils flaring, ready to suck her in. And in that moment, Sunny saw oblivion. And like a seed cracking open and tasting sunshine, she *understood*. She *knew*.

She *faced* Ajofia. Would doing so burn her essence away? Erase her breath? She still didn't turn away. This was the moment. She was here. Finally. And this was what she chose to do. She did not turn away. Afraid, but courageous. Because she *was*. Despite it all. Without it all. Beyond it all.

She felt a now-dead part of her shed away. And then . . .

She snatched its purse. It came off easily, as if not held

there by anything at all. She shot off as fast as she could, barely registering the sound of Chichi shouting her name. She glided into the first room she set her eyes on, the one in the middle. Would it come after her or go for Chichi? She was ready either way. She'd just looked into the truest face of a masquerade. She shuddered and flexed her warrior muscles. She saw Ajofia's face, the void around it, and she hadn't turned away. And here she stood, still in one piece. She giggled. Yet even as she smiled to herself at the new power she'd unlocked, she could feel it fading.

"What the hell did I just *do*?" she muttered. She touched the drying blood on her upper lip. "Ugh, gross," she said, and chuckled to herself. She wiped it with a tissue from her pocket. Feeling a bit better, she looked around. Her mind wanted to reel but she couldn't let that happen. "Focus, focus, focus. You're here for a reason."

The room was empty except for a large drum resting against the far wall. "That's not the ghazal," she said aloud. Her voice was shaky, *she* was shaky. "Wrong room. Of course it is." She looked around, listening hard. For Chichi. For Ajofia. What if the thing moved as she could? "My knife is still out there!" Though that wasn't what made her most uncomfortable. Forget her knife, *Ajofia* was still out there! She looked at the purse she'd taken. What would a masquerade carry in its purse?

It was the size of a football, rectangular, and embroidered

with the shiniest brown cowry shells she'd ever seen. She hesitated and then opened it. She smelled it before she saw it. Robust, green, and sharp, the herbs looked fresh. She reached in and took some of the leaves in her hands and her fingertips went numb. She put them back in the purse. Now her tongue was numb, too.

"Every child is a fool." Ajofia's voice was so low and rough that it could barely be called a voice. It made Sunny's ears itch.

When she looked up, she saw that it filled the doorway.

"Chichi?" Sunny called. No response. She wiped the tears from her eyes. If she had walked into this place in her human form, she'd have had to stoop forward to enter. The masquerade could not enter here . . . at least not in the physical way. But she was sure it had other ways. Something hit a cowbell and the flute played a sharp note that made her jump.

"Why have you come to this Power House?" it asked.

"I am a Nimm warrior," she said, trying to stand up straighter. She felt some of the strength she'd discovered surge through her. Her numb tongue made it difficult, but she was determined to not let this cause her to slur her words. "I am here to get Udide's scroll and return it to her . . . to right a wrong done by the people of Nimm."

After several moments, the masquerade responded. "To take from me is to prove you are a master of your craft," it said. "To take is easy. To have the nerve is not."

Sunny frowned. "I . . . I am no master," she said. "I am just here for—"

"It is not a choice once it is obtained. Those are yours now," it said.

Sunny looked down at the purse she carried. She looked up. "Let me pass," she said.

"No."

It was worth a try. "What of my friend?"

"She is out there," it said. "Why are you in the room of the Death Drum?"

Sunny glanced at the drum on the other side of the room. "I—"

"The stretched skin of men defeated in battle, the body made of the bone of women who died too young, one beat is all you need to win any war. An evil thing whose time has passed, for men do not fight wars as they used to and have no need for the Death Drum. No fire, stone, wind, water, abyss can destroy it. So it was thrown in my evil forest, where I guard it. And this is the room a new master rushes into."

Sunny looked at it again. "Not on purpose," she said.

"Have you eaten the herbs?"

Sunny wrinkled her nose. She couldn't help it. The thought of the herbs in the purse turned her stomach in a way that even her great fear in the moment couldn't surpass. "No. Never."

To her surprise and relief, it retreated from the entrance. As soon as it was far enough, she glided out. "Sunny!" Chichi shouted the moment she reappeared near the entrance they'd come in. Chichi was on the other side of the room near one of the other seven doors. They ran to each other and embraced. "I'm sorry," Sunny said, her chin on Chichi's head. Chichi's short Afro was both rough and soft. "I didn't mean to leave you! I was trying to get it to chase me . . . or something!"

Chichi was laughing and she squeezed Sunny harder. "I know!" She let go of Sunny, grinning. "You're *so reckless!*"

They glanced at Ajofia, who stood too close for comfort. Quiet. Watching them . . . though Sunny wasn't sure exactly how. It had no face or eyes.

"I am," Sunny said. She was still holding Ajofia's purse of herbs. "Are we going to die?"

Chichi's response didn't make her feel better, but at least she grinned as she said it. "Who knows!" She grabbed Sunny's arm. "Sunny!" Then she just stared into Sunny's eyes, still grinning. "Sunny! *Kai!* This girl, oooooo!" She stepped back and did a twirl. "Oh my *God,* I'm so lucky to be friends with you! You're amazing! Nimm warrior! Woman show! Most people will never see this in their life, but I just got to watch it happen right beside me. I am going to be bragging about this forever. And you're a free agent, at that?! Unheard of, ooooooo."

Sunny didn't know what to say. Or really what she was talking about. "Watch what happen?"

"You don't know what you did?"

"I mean, yeah." She glanced back at Ajofia. "Is it going to . . ." She lowered her voice. ". . . *kill* us?"

"I would have killed you by now if I wanted to," it said. Both of them stared at it.

Chichi reached up and took her shoulders. "Look at me," Chichi said. "You've just become a masquerade peer."

Sunny looked into Chichi's wide dark brown eyes as the phrase echoed in her mind. It was familiar. But not because of Anyanwu's memories. She'd read it in one of the books Anatov had them read, and he'd even talked about it. Masquerade peers were rare; Anatov had even said he'd never met one. She blinked, remembering part of the lesson. She remembered because she'd thought it was so strange that to gain something positive, you had to take from something negative. "'Only when the greatest witch has mastered witchery can she then go and extract roots from the evil forest,'" she recited. "So . . . that was literal? I always thought . . ."

"That masquerade peers were a metaphor? Of course it's literal. And you-just-did-that!" She pointed at the purse. "What do you think that is? You can now sit at their table! You can probably use it to pass the *Oku Akama*, if you ever try."

Sunny frowned and shook her head. The last level of Leopardom had only been passed by eight living people on

Earth. "Nah," she said. But she thought about how she'd faced Ajofia . . . and oh, how it *felt*. She'd felt . . . how she imagined Anyanwu felt. She paused at this, a question tumbling over her: What if Anyanwu wasn't meant to come *down* to Sunny, but it was Sunny who was meant to go *up* to Anyanwu? It would explain all that had happened since she'd become a Leopard Person—learning quickly and even gliding and stopping time as a brand-new free agent, facing Udide, stepping into being a Nimm warrior, unmasking Ekwensu, and now this. What if . . .

Sunny rubbed her temples as she understood so much. "Yeesh," she said. "Focus, focus, *focus*, Sunny." She smacked her forehead and glanced at Ajofia again and whispered to Chichi, "Evil forest. There's a reason it's called that."

Chichi shook her head. "Ajofia. Evil Forest. The masquerade who comes out to dance during dark times, it carries secrets and guards the darkest of those secrets until it is time." Chichi shook her head. "Much of this is true, but it's not the truth. It's colonialist rubbish. Evil forests have never been evil . . . just untouched. These places are so heavy with the spirit of the forest that people fear them. Lambs always fear what they don't understand. Most Leopards, too. You're here right now. See for yourself. A name can carry more than one story." She paused and then added, "But you have to be a great witch to face this masquerade. Ajofia is not 'evil,' but it has embraced the energy of its name. We have to be careful."

"Will it let us take the ghazal?"

"Before? No. Now? Maybe."

"It's in one of the rooms?"

Chichi nodded. "This place is like a museum of dangerous artifacts." She pointed at the door closest to them. "I looked in there. I know what the thing in there is," she gravely said. "I didn't touch it . . ." She stopped, remembering something. "Oh! Sunny, did you eat the herbs yet?"

"Uh . . . you mean the ones in the purse?"

"Yeah!"

"No."

"Eat some!"

"Why?"

She lowered her voice. "You're supposed to. It's polite." Chichi glanced at the waiting masquerade.

"I'm pretty sure it can hear you," Sunny said.

"Just eat some."

"Touching them made my—"

"Just eat some!"

Sunny opened the purse and looked at the herbs. She picked up one of the leaves, muttering, "Eating a masquerade's salad . . . What would my father say?" Her fingertips were already numb.

"Eat it!"

You better hope that's been washed, Anyanwu said. She was right beside Sunny now. Sunny glared at her and Anyanwu glared right back. Anyanwu could hold all of Sunny's memories far more easily than Sunny could hold even a fraction of hers. Anyanwu knew what she'd just experienced with Ajofia. Despite being pleased Anyanwu was back with her, Sunny felt an impulse to slap her. *Could* she slap her? Anyanwu had deserted her at a most crucial moment . . . *yet again.*

Instead, she popped the leaf into her mouth. She heard someone exhale. She saw a shiver fly through every piece of black raffia on Ajofia. Someone banged an *ogene*, a large metal bell. The spirited tune echoed throughout the room. Her nostrils filled with the smell of the leaves, and for a moment she wondered if she'd be able to talk, her lips and throat were so numb.

She coughed and hacked, terrified. But when nothing else happened after a few moments and the numbness wore off, she relaxed.

"*Iseeeeee*," Chichi said, holding her hand up, fingers spread and palm facing Ajofia. The Igbo expression that meant, "Let it be so." As if this acknowledgment was what it had been waiting for, Ajofia shivered again and then rose and began to dance to the *ogene's* toll. As it danced, smoke began to billow from its top, spilling over it like lava from a volcano. It danced around Sunny and Chichi, and soon Chichi threw caution to the wind and began dancing with Ajofia.

Sunny didn't move a muscle. "Chichi!" she said. "What are you doing?"

Chichi raised her hands in the air and shook her hips as she danced with the slowly twirling masquerade. "Living!" she said, laughing. "Who can say they have danced with a spirit? An Evil Forest, at that?! ME! *Gbese!*"

The smoke did not make Sunny cough or sneeze. It didn't sting her eyes. It filled the entire room. A breeze blew and soon the smoke was swirling around them. The *ogene* beat suddenly stopped and all the smoke was sucked out of the room. When it was all clear, it was only Sunny and Chichi standing there.

Ajofia was gone.

"Masquerades always know how to make an exit," Chichi said, breathing hard.

Sunny just stared at her.

"What?" Chichi asked, smirking.

They first went to the door of the room that housed a strange book. Sunny had been intrigued by the fact that Chichi was cautious about it. Plus, Chichi's live-life-to-the-fullest-and-see-what-you-can-see-while-you-can-see-it attitude was infectious. The book rested on a stone table in the center of the room.

"Do *not* touch it," Chichi said as Sunny bent close to it for a better look. The cover was so black that it looked three-dimensional. The sides of the pages were equally black.

"*The Black Pages*," Chichi said. "My mother and I always thought it was stolen in 2013 when Islamist insurgents set fire to a library in Timbuktu full of historic scripts. I'm re-lieved to see it here. Maybe one of the Leopard librarians managed to save it. This thing can *end* the world."

"So the pages themselves are . . . black?"

Chichi nodded. "And people with the skill to read it are very, very rare. It's like how you can read Nsibidi, but even rarer."

"Hurts my eyes to look at it."

"Because you're looking into a book that is also a black hole," she said, pulling Sunny away. "And we should prob-ably stop looking at it."

The next room they looked into had various items, includ-ing a pile of tiny glass bottles labeled FORMULA 86, a dusty but oddly futuristic-looking tablet, a pair of sandals, and a pile of black stones. There were so many potentially lethal things in this room, but nothing that looked like Udide's scroll.

They went into the fifth room, and Sunny knew it was in here the moment she walked in. The room was dark, lit only by a single candle in the corner. It smelled dank like soil. The air was cool. And there was a black wolf spider the size of a tennis ball standing at the entrance. Sunny stifled a shud-der. She was terrified of spiders, and though her thinking was illogical, she'd secretly hoped that if they finally found the ghazal, she wouldn't have to tolerate . . . any actual spiders. Chichi held up her juju knife. Sunny caught her wrist.

"No," she said.

"I know," Chichi said. "I'm not going to . . . but it never hurts to be ready."

The spider didn't move as they stepped up to it. "I am Sunny and this is Chichi. We are Nimm . . . women come to take Udide's property back to Udide."

When the spider spoke, its oily voice was accompanied by thunder and the beat of drums in the distance. "What is wrong with you?"

Sunny felt her heart drop. Even a spider in a Spirit Highway museum on the side of The Road could see that something was off about her. She opened her mouth to speak and nothing came out. Then she felt Anyanwu sweep into her, and she stood up straighter, stronger. "*Nothing* is wrong with me," Sunny said.

The spider scrambled back, and this gave Sunny great joy. "Step aside or I will crush you," Sunny said.

Anyanwu stepped away from Sunny now, stood beside her like a blazing sun, and said, "And then *I* will finish you off in the wilderness."

The spider skittered aside, and Sunny and Chichi entered the room. After a few steps, she heard Chichi yelp behind her, "Ouch! It bit me!" Chichi chased the spider around the room, trying to step on it, but it was too quick.

It ran up the wall, dodging Chichi's attack until it was too high to reach. "I had to make sure," the spider said. "I taste it in your blood. You speak true. You are Nimm and you have Udide's venom. I will not poison either of you as I was going to."

"What?!" Sunny exclaimed.

Chichi threw a juju at it, which it easily dodged; the spot where the juju hit blackened with flames.

"You cannot kill me," it said.

Chichi threw another juju at it, the spider zipping out of its way.

"Okay, Chichi," Sunny said. "That's enough."

"If this thing swells up," Chichi said, kneeling down to rub her aching heel, "I'll find a way to finish you off."

"Does it hurt?" Sunny asked.

"Not much, thank goodness."

Sunny looked slowly around the empty room. "It's in here," she muttered. "But where? Chichi, where would Nimm women hide something like that?"

Chichi was still rubbing her heel. "Well," she said, resting her chin on her knee. "They brought it all the way here for safekeeping because they no longer needed it, but they didn't want to give it back. It's a memoir told in jujus and recipes, written as a ghazal, a form of poetry that came out of the Arab world a long time ago. The thing is profoundly useful, to say the least. A Möbius band is like a . . ."

"A sort of infinity loop," Sunny said. "Where if you run a marble on it, it'll never be on the same surface . . . something like that."

"And it's made of that bug material your juju knife is made of."

"Oh!" Sunny suddenly said. "Maybe . . ." Sunny brought it out. "It's a long shot, but . . . it would make sense." She held her juju knife up and it glinted in the dim light. The green material was harder than any glass she'd ever seen, and perfectly clear like a piece of ice. But it was actually a piece of a beetle's exoskeleton, as the man at the market had said. She stepped to the wall and tapped her juju knife on it. She saw it immediately and grinned. She tapped it again. In the darkness of the room, the ghazal lit right up and then the green light slowly faded.

They rushed to it. "How?" Chichi said.

"Because nothing is a coincidence! It's made from the same bug's wing," Sunny said. "Remember that booth in Ginen where they were selling all those items made from this stuff? The guy said if it's from the same bug, it'll react to the vibration if it's close by." They stood over it and Sunny tapped her juju knife again. It lit up an even more brilliant green, lighting up the entire room.

"Wow," Sunny whispered, looking at her juju knife. "I never knew!"

The ghazal was about two feet long and a foot wide, graceful in its infinity-like Möbius shape . . . like freshly twisted glass. And every surface was etched with the most intricate Nsibidi Sunny had ever seen. Mesmerized, she knelt over it as the brilliant light gradually faded. The etchings were white, the Nsibidi so alive that it seemed to march about the glass, each individual symbol twirling, wiggling, vibrating, stretching, doing whatever it would do.

"Do you see it?" she asked.

Chichi shook her head. "I see something, but whenever I try to focus on it, it blurs up. I don't really know what I'm looking at besides a big, thick, green, glass Möbius loop."

"No," Sunny said vaguely. Anyanwu was kneeling beside her, and her shine illuminated the Nsibidi so that Sunny could see it even after the green light faded. "It's so much . . . more."

"You can read it?"

"I . . ." She stared at it, trying to process it. But no matter how much they moved and crept, Sunny could not concentrate long enough. She shuddered. "No," she said. She shook her head, shuddering again. "No way."

The presence of Udide was too strong. Drumbeats, the papery sound of the rough hairs on her many legs scraping against each other, the heat from her breath that smelled of burning houses. Who could read this under the weight of Udide's eight eyes? Under her scrutiny.

Sunny felt Anyanwu join with her as she reached for the ghazal. When she grasped it, an image of Udide flashed so strongly in her mind that she was sure the giant spider had materialized right there in the room. Sunny froze, looking around. Waiting. After a few moments, she relaxed. The ghazal was warm, like something alive, and heavy, like something that did not want to be moved. She strained and strained, and about halfway through, something let go and she was able to lift it. Not with ease, but not with all her strength, either. "Oof," she grunted.

She had it. She could do this. She paused, realizing . . . existing for the moment in the moment. Everything in the last half hour solidifying. *I am awesome*, she thought. She grinned. All of her grinned. Proud. Sure. Strong. Clear. In her mind, she stood with her spirit face shining. Anyanwu. Sunny.

Something fell from above her, landing at her feet. Sunny and Chichi both froze. The last thing Sunny needed was for the place to crumble while they were in here. There was no way she could run with this thing. Could she even glide with it? Not the time to find out. Chichi bent down and picked it up. It was the size of a thumbnail.

"A *chittim*!" Chichi said. The first one that had fallen since they'd left Earth. Not for the first or last time, Sunny wondered where *chittim* came from and who dropped them. Chichi held it to her eyes. "Made of crystal."

"Okay? But it's so small," Sunny said.

"You know who accepts these?" Chichi asked.

Sunny didn't want to hear the answer.

"Masquerades." She put it in Sunny's pocket, and they left the Power House as quickly as they could, Sunny carrying the ghazal like a baby.

23
SIGNS

"Sunny!" Orlu shouted.

Sasha jumped up and waved his hands, which were now wrapped with large leaves. Chichi broke into a run, laughing and shouting. "We got it!!"

Sunny grinned but kept walking at her steady pace. She was strong, but this thing was heavy. She grasped its loops, leaning it against her arms. She could feel the Nsibidi moving where it touched her skin, and she hoped it didn't have the capacity to absorb into her flesh. Anyanwu was walking close beside her. *You can't worry about everything,* Anyanwu said.

Chichi stopped at the burned bushes, Orlu and Sasha on the other side of them.

"Danafojura told us not to cross it," Orlu said. "Best not to challenge that."

"I'd have risked it if I had my juju knife."

"No, you wouldn't," Orlu said, annoyed.

Sasha chuckled sheepishly, looking at his wrapped hands. "He's right."

"Well, we can cross it now," Chichi said, stepping into the ashes and char. She paused and then kept going, and soon she was wrapped in a tight hug and then locking lips with Sasha.

"Is it heavy?" Orlu asked Sunny, ignoring them.

"Yeah, but . . ." She shrugged.

Orlu nodded. "Nimm warrior." He held up the arm without the *papa* and flexed a muscle.

Sunny crossed the charred demarcation and was relieved when nothing happened. Still, the moment she stepped onto the sand, her legs weakened and she sank to the ground. Anyanwu rushed into her. The three of them rushed to her. They hugged her, and for several moments they stayed like that. Quiet, holding on. Sunny shut her eyes, feeling strong but so tired. It was only in this moment that she realized how much she wanted this to be over. For everything to be okay.

She rested with her head on Orlu's shoulder, her lips to his neck. An idea came to her. "I think I know how we can get back quickly," Sunny said. She gave the ghazal to Sasha to hold. She didn't want to put it on the ground, Orlu couldn't hold it with his broken arm, and Sasha had insisted, despite his burned hands.

"The leaves numb most of the pain, anyway," he said. "Thank Orlu for finding them."

Orlu took a bow. "Forests are better than drugstores."

"True that," Sasha said, giving Orlu a fist bump.

When she gave the ghazal to Sasha, he gasped from the weight. "Hurry up," he said.

She went to the ashes and char and scooped some of it into the empty bag of groundnuts in her backpack. Then she ran to The Road. It was still quite empty there. This was not a place many liked to come to, for good reason. The strange vertigo hit when she stepped onto it, but with Anyanwu inside her and after everything that had happened, she took it in stride. And she used the ashes to draw. She didn't envision home, exactly. She drew her wasp artist Della, its lovely comb, and the tree she'd buried it beside.

The others stood on the side of The Road watching. The mix of ash and char sifted easily from her hand and fell and settled on The Road like a substance much heavier than it was. She saw Della and its comb clearly in her mind, and what she drew looked surprisingly accurate. The focused act of drawing it settled her nerves. When she stopped, she stood back and gazed at her work for a while. Something zoomed by on The Road, and she ignored it. When she smiled, Anyanwu smiled. "There," she said. She stepped off The Road and took the ghazal from Sasha.

"Oh! Take it! *Please*, take it," he said, groaning. He bent and stretched his arms and twisted his torso, this way and that way. "My *God*, it's like carrying a fifty-pound dumbbell! I'm not even going to front anymore, you're definitely stronger than me, Sunny."

"Yep," Sunny said, cradling the ghazal. "I know."

"I think I could carry it," Orlu said.

Sasha kissed his teeth. "Mmhm, you just happen to have the perfect excuse to not have to."

"Yep," Orlu said, holding up his arm with the *papa* on it. It snuggled and slightly shifted its position but seemed otherwise comfortable where it was, holding Orlu's arm in place.

"Come here," Chichi said to Sasha. "I haven't gotten to look. Let me see."

He bit his lip and went to her.

She took a peek under the leaves wrapped around Sasha's hands. She wrinkled her nose. "Looks nasty," she said. But by the way she said it, Sunny knew that it must not have looked that bad.

"Just the way you like it, baby," Sasha drawled.

Chichi giggled. "You know burns hurt like hell as they heal?"

"Yeah," he said with a shrug. "But I'm more worried about getting a new knife."

"What? Junk Man is still there," Orlu said. "I think my

father got his juju knife from him, too. Abuja isn't that far."

"It's silly of me, but . . ." Sunny put a hand over her face, embarrassed. "I kinda thought that you had your juju knife all your life. Like you only had one and that's it."

"Because knives can't get lost or . . . melted down by masquerades?" Sasha said. "A Leopard Person won't have a ton, but usually you have more than one over a lifetime." He looked at Orlu. "I got my juju knife in Tar Nation. It's in South Carolina."

"The States?" Orlu asked.

"Yeah. I'll get a new one there. There's this Gullah guy there named Blue who lives in a swamp. He will have my new knife. You coming with me, Chichi?"

"Nope. See you when you come back here."

"Fair enough," Sasha said.

"Hey! I see it!" Sunny said. She did a happy dance in a circle, even with the ghazal in her arms.

The *kabu kabu* that screeched to a stop in front of them looked like a futuristic SUV from Ginen. It was sleek, oily black, and the doors opened upward like wings. The driver was a dark-skinned black woman with shoulder-length salt-and-pepper locs. She smiled at them, raised her hands, and signed to them. Chichi pushed past Sunny, saying, "I got this."

"Hey, I know sign language, too," Sasha said. "Adam-orobe Sign Language in particular; it's Ghanaian."

Sunny and Orlu stood back while Sasha and Chichi con-
versed with the driver. Sunny turned to Orlu, hoisted the
ghazal up, and held out a pinkie. He smiled and immediately
grasped it. The *papa* on his arm chittered, curiously looking
at their clasped fingers.

"When we get home, I want to take you on a celebration
date. Where do you want to go? It's all my treat."

Sunny grinned. Before today, she'd have just kept this de-
sire to herself. But it was a new day. "How about somewhere
in the Dark Market? I heard there's a place that serves only
edible flowers and they're super nutritious. Pepper soup made
with flowers! Can you imagine?!"

Orlu laughed hard. "This is why I love you."

They both paused at this.

Then Sunny awkwardly leaned over the ghazal and gave
him a long kiss. "I love you, too, Orlu." She rested her forehead against his.

They turned to Sasha, Chichi, and the driver when the
three of them suddenly all burst out laughing.

"All right, she'll take us," Chichi said. "But you have to
hold on to the ghazal. Don't let it touch anything."

Sunny shrugged. "Okay. I can do that."

They all climbed into the back. Sunny perched the ghazal
on her lap. It wasn't comfortable, but she would be okay. She
looked out the window toward the burned bush wall and
wasn't surprised to see that the dried-out bush was back as

it had been when they'd first arrived. They started moving, and just before everything around them became a blur, Sunny saw Danafojura standing there in front of the dried bushes dancing in a circle. Sunny looked down at the ghazal in her lap; she looked hard at it. She felt Udide's powerful gaze once again. But instead of letting this deter her, for a little while she endured the burn of her gaze and looked harder.

The drive along The Road was quiet. No music. None of them talking. Just staring out the window. Sunny felt safe and after some time, her mind full, she began to really observe her surroundings.

She saw thousands of spirits of so many names, maybe some without a name. Some looked back at her, others were too focused. Something with a large suction cup for a mouth stuck to her window before tumbling into the quagmire of rushing spirits. It was like driving through an otherworldly tornado. For what felt like an hour, no one moved or said a thing.

When they finally left The Road and turned onto a path flanked by a forest of tall palm trees, Sunny realized her lap was aching from the weight of the ghazal. She stretched her shoulders. Then the driver signed to Sasha and Chichi and they turned to Orlu and Sunny. "We gotta pay up," Sasha said, reaching into her pocket. "We're nearly there."

"Aren't we going to wait until we—"

"Nah," Sasha said. "Three gold *chittim* each, the hand-sized ones."

"Orlu, can you get it out of my backpack?" Sunny said.

They fumbled their *chittim* together and handed it to the driver. She grinned at them, clearly pleased with their pay-ment. Then a black partition began to rise, separating them from her, and suddenly the inside of the vehicle felt so small.

"Wait," Sunny said. "Why—" Suddenly there was a green flash that lit up everything. She shut her eyes, "Ah! What was that?" When she opened her eyes, everything felt bright, crisp, clear, and when she spoke, it was with Anyanwu's low, husky voice. "Hold!" Without hesitating, Sunny did.

She turned to Orlu and was looking into the face of his spirit, the Nsibidi on his cheeks dancing. Chichi and Sasha also were wearing their spirit faces. And Sunny could see Anyanwu's sunrays with her peripheral vision. They were in the wilderness. The partition was for the driver's privacy and theirs.

A flicker outside caught her eye. The three fireflies were hovering outside the window. She touched the glass and the fireflies congregated where her finger was. She grinned. Now she understood.

"You remember where you left it, right?" Sasha asked.

"Yeah," Sunny said, watching the fireflies, which were now following the *kabu kabu*.

Outside had the glow of twilight, and the field of spirit grass they were driving through wavered as a breeze blew over it. They slowed down, coasting for a bit. Then Sunny saw it. The tree. She turned to look at Orlu, who was looking over her shoulder outside. She kissed him and his attention turned completely to her. It was so strange, his wooden spirit face felt like . . . his human face. They openly looked into each other's faces for a moment; Sunny giggled and kissed him again. She pulled back when she heard Sasha and Chichi both snickering.

"Damn, you two," Sasha said. "Spirit faces and all."

"That's hot," Chichi said.

When the *kabu kabu* stopped, they climbed out, and before they could say goodbye, it sped off down the field and disappeared. "You know she nearly refused to drive us," Chichi said. "She doesn't like driving in the wilderness . . . plus, she'd heard about what happened with that funky train driver."

"Man, we're going to be stuck explaining that situation to every driver we meet," Sasha said. "But she almost wouldn't drive you because of that ghazal."

Sunny frowned. "How would she know what it is?"

"She didn't. But she knew where we were coming *from*. Can you blame her?"

None of them could. Sunny turned to the tree and found the spot immediately. "Sasha," she said. "Can you give me a second? I need to . . . do something important."

He nodded, swallowing the question she knew he wanted to ask.

She handed the ghazal to him and stepped away.

She heard Chichi say, "What's she—"

"Shh," Sasha said. "Leave her."

Facing the field of spirit grass, Sunny held up a hand. They came immediately—the three fireflies, landing in the center of her palm. "I know who you are," she whispered.

"We've known you even longer," one of them said. The voice was childlike and joyous.

Sunny felt Anyanwu wanted to say something, but she told her not to. "I'm not returning here anytime soon," Sunny told them.

"It's fine," one of the others said. Its voice sounded like a grown man's. "We see you often enough."

And they were right. Sunny came to the wilderness far more than your average *ogbanje*.

"What are your names?" she asked.

"You don't remember?" the third one asked. This one sounded like a huge monster, its voice low and rumbly.

"No."

"That's all right," the monster-voiced one said. "You will get over this journey, and then we will see you." They flew around her head in a way that reminded her of her wasp artist, Della, and then they were tumbling along the breeze across the field. "We'll see yoooouuuuu."

When Sunny returned to her human friends, they didn't ask her anything about the exchange and she was glad. She bent down and started digging. She felt her zyzzyx, and the moment she grasped it, she let go. It was like the world shed its skin. The warm breeze stopped and became sweltering, heavy humidity.

Sunny stood up straight and put the comb in her hair. They were back in the driveway of Orlu's house. Chichi, Orlu, and Sasha all took an involuntary deep breath and started coughing. Sunny rushed to Sasha and caught the ghazal as Sasha's arms went slack. Tiny golden *chittim* showered around them, their shine glittering like a galaxy of stars over Ginen. Sunny watched it all, grasping their prize. *Ting, ting, ting, ting!* The tinkle of them was so sweet. These *chittim* were worth little, but what a beautiful spectacle they made! What a way to return home.

"Ouch!" she screeched when one of the *chittim* fell, hitting her right on the funny bone. She hissed as a horrible cocktail of numbness, pain, and pressure ran up her forearm. She struggled not to drop the ghazal.

"You guys all right?" Sunny asked as the three of them slowly stopped panting. She shook out and looked at her elbow. The bruise was already a deep red. Sugar Cream had said there was always a consequence for holding for an extended period of time, but Sunny would never have imagined the consequence would be so . . . *petty*.

"Felt like someone standing on my chest," Orlu said.

"Or someone sucking the breath from my lungs," Sasha said.

"Like I almost died," Chichi said.

"Never," Sunny said. "I was never going to let anything happen to any of you." And she really meant it.

"We know, Sunny," Chichi said.

"What day do you think it is?" Sasha asked.

Sunny sat down, resting the ghazal on her lap, and brought out her phone, her heart beating. They'd left days ago, and who knew how much time passed while in the wilderness and . . . beyond. Her father was going to go mad. She clicked the side of her phone and waited for it to turn on. She stretched her sore elbow; the pain had decreased, but the numbness remained.

"Looks like my parents are home," Orlu said. He looked at his arm, the *papa* still firmly affixed to it. "Not looking forward to all the explaining."

"Not-at-all," Sasha added.

"Sunny," Chichi said. "What day is it?"

Sunny stared at her phone. She looked at Chichi, startled. "It's the same day as when we left."

"What?" Sasha screeched so loudly his voice cracked.

"It's the exact same time as when we left. No time has passed."

And for a moment, they might as well have been frozen in time.

"The wilderness?" Orlu asked.

Sunny shook her head. "I've glided before and time had passed when I came back," Sunny said.

"It's The Road," Sasha said. "You called that *kabu kabu* and asked it to bring us right to where you put the comb; maybe the 'when' matters, too."

"Or maybe my phone is messed up," she said. She looked again, a sinking feeling in her belly. She hadn't checked the year. She went to calendar. She breathed a sigh of relief. Still, her phone could have been malfunctioning after all it had been through. "Let's all go home," she said. "We'll find out for sure that way. Plus . . ." She sighed. They all had to make things right at home in various ways.

"What about returning the ghazal?" Orlu said.

"Chichi and I will do it," Sunny said.

"Come home with me," Chichi said to Sunny.

"A'ight," Sasha said. "Let's meet up tomorrow night?"

Sunny gently put the ghazal on the driveway and stood up. She brought out her juju knife and turned to her friends. She held it up. "We did it," she said, feeling Anyanwu shining within her. Orlu brought out his knife, then Chichi. Sasha looked sheepish; his juju knife had melted back on the side of The Road. Chichi put an arm around his waist and pulled him to her.

"Here," she said, taking his hand and putting it to her knife. "Only this time."

"This is weird," Sasha muttered, but he held Chichi's knife with her.

When they touched the tips, it wasn't like last time when

she saw and felt through her friends; this time she felt the strength and love that existed between them shiver up her numb arm to her chest, to her temples. A thought came to her that was so strong and sure that she knew it would be true . . . They would each do great, great things. But just as she was sure, she was suddenly unsure of what the thought was.

Sunny hugged Sasha tightly and he kissed her on the cheek. She turned to Orlu and he took her hand. "We'll pick up all these *chittim*," he said.

"I know," she said, smiling.

"Be careful. Just give it to her and be done with it."

"That's the plan," she said.

"Plans are just plans," he said. He squeezed her hand. "Be careful."

Chichi's mother wasn't home, so Sunny left the ghazal with Chichi at her hut. The walk home was nice, as there were few cars on the road and people on the street. She was still deep in thought when she pushed open the gate. Not only were her parents' cars in the driveway, but so was her oldest brother's Jeep.

She used her key to open the front door, her heart feeling as if it would leap from her chest. *If he slaps me again,* she thought, *I won't leave. I have to face this.* But the thought of it made her hands shake. She could hear her parents in the living room, and Chukwu . . . and her middle brother, Ugonna? She frowned. All in the living room? She could hear the TV going. She looked in. They were all watching with wide eyes.

". . . announced a one-month lockdown to limit the spread of the coronavirus, banning all international flights and shutting land borders."

"Hi," Sunny said.

Her mother turned and a grin spread across her face, and Sunny wanted to weep with relief. This was all the answer she needed. "Oh, Sunny, I'm so relieved you're home! Have you heard the news?"

A brand-new virus was spreading around the world, and the Nigerian government had just put the country on lockdown. Sunny had heard fragments about it, but she'd been so focused on getting the ghazal. Udide could do a thousand times worse things than any virus, but Sunny didn't think such a focused assault on humanity was Udide's speed. Sunny was sure there would be meetings in Leopard Knocks over this. Leopard People could easily bring in the virus by other methods of travel. And they certainly would have people trying to cure it.

Sunny joined everyone in the living room and remained there with her family for the next several hours. Her brother had rushed home when the university closed. Everyone was going home. By the time Sunny got up to return to her room, she couldn't stop thinking about how her journey to being a

Leopard Person had started with an image of the end of the world, and now here was another threat of the end again. She was about to enter her room when she heard, "Sunny." Her father stood in the hallway.

"Yes, Dad," she said.

He slowly approached her. When he said nothing, she said, "Dad, I'm s—"

He pulled her to him and wrapped her in his arms. She was taller than he was now, but she still felt small, like his child. He squeezed her tightly and she hugged him back. She understood so much more now. Maybe he did, too. Now. "I'm sorry, Sunny," he said. "I'm so sorry."

"Dad," she said, holding on to him more tightly.

When he finally let her go, he touched her cheek. She looked deep into her father's eyes. She hoped he didn't notice the tiny red dot still in her eye from when he'd slapped her. It was slowly disappearing and probably would be gone in a few days.

"I will never understand," he said. "But I see you . . . all of you." He paused and then turned and went back to the living room.

Sunny stood there for a few moments. "I love you, Dad," she whispered. She entered her room. The moment she closed the door behind her, Della zipped around her head with joy and delight, landing on her comb, clearly pleased that she was still wearing it.

"Della, hi," she said, laughing. The large blue wasp flew at her face, bumping her cheek. It zoomed around the room and disappeared into its nest on the ceiling. She dumped her backpack on the floor, locked her door, fell onto her bed, and didn't wake up until it was deep into the night.

She looked out her window at the dead palm tree, then she went and took a long, hot shower, letting the water warm her elbow (it had gone from numb to painful, which Sunny assumed was better). She put on a pair of fresh jeans, shoving her juju knife in her pocket. She threw on a white T-shirt and sneakers. And without a second thought, she glided through the keyhole. Outside, the night was cool. The mosquitos were quiet. Her walk to Chichi's hut was swift. Chichi was waiting for her when she arrived, sitting outside, smoking a Banga. She put it out as Sunny picked up the ghazal beside Chichi.

Chichi didn't ask where Sunny was going as they walked. And when they arrived at the dead palm tree, Udide was there to meet them. The wind blew through the dried leaves of the dead tree, disturbing the calm of the night. A large leaf broke off and fell to the ground beside Udide. Sunny and Chichi stepped up to her, dead branches snapping under their feet. This was not a place people could easily walk through; it was full of lizards, snakes, and spiders. Especially tonight.

Sunny was glad she'd worn sneakers instead of sandals. Chichi couldn't say the same. They stopped in front of the

giant spider who wasn't really a spider, and Sunny was glad
when Chichi put an arm around her shoulder. She needed
both hands to hold the ghazal, otherwise she'd have grabbed
Chichi's hand.

"*Oga* Udide *Okwanka*, the Great Spider Artist," Chichi
said, lifting her chin. "We have brought you your work."

"My memories," Udide said.

Chichi nodded.

"Nimm women have read it and used some of my secrets
without asking me. What of that? Will you bring me those
women, too?"

Sunny's stomach dropped. *When will this be over?*

"No," Chichi said firmly. "I will not."

She saw Udide's forelegs come up and then start weaving.
Sunny had only a moment to decide to do it.

"You will anger her," she heard Anyanwu warn just before she did it anyway. Anyanwu was too surprised to stop
Sunny. Anyanwu had been with her for much of the drive
from the Power House, but not in the first part of it. Anyanwu had gone wherever she liked to go.

And in that way, Sunny had been left completely alone
with the ghazal in her lap. And she'd stared at it in the comfort of the car. And she'd *read* some of it. Because she knew
even back then that Udide was *not* going to make returning
what was stolen from her easy.

From the fraction that she'd been able to read, this was

what Sunny understood: Udide's ghazal was a memoir fueled
by, recipes inspired by, a weapon created from, a testament
to, a mystical command book centered on love. The journey
of it, the power of it, the healing of it, the price of it, the
weight of it, the *juju* of it. There were probably a thousand
recipes on that ghazal that could destroy, even erase, the universe. Sunny's eye had jumped around the ghazal, focusing on
the few words she could interpret, fighting the headache that
reading them caused . . . and she'd found what she needed.
And she used it now.

She slapped her hand to the soil just as Udide threw what
looked like a net of webbing at her and Chichi. She heard
Chichi screech and then Sunny felt the slap of water on all
sides. It squeezed at her. It took her breath away. And now, all
around Sunny was dark blueness. Less than a moment later,
she felt the rough scratch of what looked like one of Udide's
legs. If she'd had breath to spare, she would have screamed.
There was a wall of water wavering inches from her face. She
glanced down. The wall of water was inches from all around
her. She was in a bubble.

What have you done? she heard Anyanwu ask. For Anyanwu to say this was chilling, for she had seen lifetimes more
than Sunny. And Anyanwu sounded utterly alarmed.

"Don't leave," Sunny pleaded.

"*I won't*," Anyanwu said.

In the deep waters before her, Sunny saw a looming figure the size of Udide, and to its left, she could see what she was sure was Udide. The Nsibidi had worked. On the first try. Sunny had seen it on the ghazal and committed it to memory throughout the drive. Since arriving home, she'd spoken the symbols and the method to herself over and over, being careful not to accidently activate it. She'd told herself it was just a precaution, but just as she knew Udide would come for her and Chichi, in her heart, she knew she'd need this juju.

"Love rules all," Sunny croaked when she was finally able to take a breath.

"*Ah*," Anyanwu said. "*True love.*"

In the murk of the waters, the shape was as enormous as Udide and equally as intimidating. Sunny couldn't speak its name even if she'd wanted to. Its very *name* was juju. However, Sunny knew *of* it. Orlu had spoken of it back when they'd traveled to Lagos to seek out Udide. And then it had been mentioned again when Chichi told of her mother's theft of the ghazal; Udide had been visiting it and her absence at her lair had been the only reason Chichi's mother and her cousins had succeeded. This was the Great Crab, the love of Udide's life. They only saw each other once every millennia . . . until now.

Sunny had used one of Udide's juju instructions to spirit Udide to where Udide most desired. The juju was called "Over All Things," and it had been the easiest thing to read on the ghazal because it was so simple. But Sunny hadn't expected to be whisked along . . . or have her life saved by Udide when they reappeared underwater.

The hulking figure glowed a dim red as it lumbered toward Udide. Sunny took the moment to look around. She couldn't move. She was literally encased in a tight bubble. She looked up and only saw darkness. How deep in the ocean *was* she? The bubble was protecting her from more than drowning; it was protecting her from the weight of the water above, too. She still had her juju knife and powder, but moving about in here was impossible. She gently reached forward and touched the barrier of the bubble. Her finger passed right through it. The water was warm.

"Sunny," a voice said. The bubble around her vibrated from it.

"If you love Udide," Sunny blurted, "then make her do the right thing!"

That's your plan? Anyanwu asked in her mind.

"Sunny." The voice was louder as the giant red crab crept toward her, smooth and oily. "You bring Udide to me when I saw her so recently; you take such great risk coming to the bottom of the sea . . . You don't fear death?"

The bubble vibrated more intensely and Sunny was woozy with fear. And that made her even woozier. If she fell while in this bubble, would the air around her follow her or would she fall into the water and its terrible pressure? How would she ever get out of here? "I didn't know this would happen . . . I didn't know!" she said.

"You have pleased me," the crab said.

"I'm glad," she said.

"Why?"

Sunny felt woozier than ever and she swayed on her feet. She felt Anyanwu within her, helping her to stay up, stay focused. "Udide promised us something, my friend and me."

"Promises are made to be broken," Udide said, then Sunny's bubble vibrated as Udide laughed. It shrank even tighter around Sunny, making it harder for her to stand in such a tiny space. Sunny reached into her pocket for her juju knife. But what the hell could she even do?!

"Udide, will you then leave her to die? She has returned your book, I assume."

"She has."

"Then you have what you need."

"That is beside the point." Udide stamped a foot and the bubble pressed even closer to Sunny. Now the water was less than an inch from her face. One stumble and she was dead.

"My love," the crab said.

The bubble got smaller. It was touching Sunny's nose, the water warm like the water of a bath. How could this be at the bottom of the ocean? Sunny let out a terrified breath and it caused the water to splash in her face. "Please!" she screamed. She saw Anyanwu standing before her. Sunny felt both weak and strong. Anyanwu moved easily in the water, and now Sunny could see both Udide and the Great Crab clearly, even through the murk. The Great Crab had two huge, barnacle-encrusted foreclaws that looked as if they could crush whatever was brought before it, be it stones, lead, or diamonds. Then she realized why the Great Crab glowed—all over the rest of its body were large bio-luminescent sea anemones that wavered in the water like strange, squishy pom-poms.

"Udide, you do not see each other often. Sunny has brought you to your love for a second time in *years*. She has given you a great gift you two are too proud to give your-selves," Anyanwu said. She began to glow a bright sunshine yellow and Sunny smiled. If this was the last thing she'd see, she was fine with that. "*Let go* of what the Nimm women did so many years ago. *Honor your word today!*" Anyanwu shouted.

The bubble collapsed, and Sunny was squeezed so tightly that everything dimmed. She closed her mouth to keep the water out, but it seemed her lips were pried apart. Water pushed itself into her mouth, down her throat. She was yanked downward and then . . .

Udide crept closer. Sunny lifted her head up, feeling sore all over. As she sat up, she could feel sea water sloshing in her belly. The ghazal was in her lap; she pushed it off her. A cramp ached in her side. She looked around, her mouth tasting like seawater. She was back in the weeds with the dead palm tree. Chichi was stuck to its trunk, held there by spider webbing. "Sunny!" she screeched. "Are you all right? Udide! Please!"

Sunny slowly got up. Everything in her wanted to sob, but she held it in. She could barely stand up straight. But even hunched forward, she held her chin up.

"Fear," Udide said, drawing the word out. "I can feel her fear." She was close enough that the smoky scent of her breath actually evoked images in Sunny's mind of large homes in a suburb all on fire. Burning upholstery, plastic, wood, insulation, plaster, cement, clothes.

"So?" Sunny said, angry. She picked up the ghazal. "Why shouldn't she be afraid? They were her relatives and they tried to kill her. Then you . . . you're the Great Udide, and you play around with promises! You play with life!" She gingerly stepped closer to Udide. The sloshing in her belly made her feel nauseous. "We did what you asked. Brought what you asked. Please! Just *take* it!" The ghazal began to glow in her hands and the scratchy feeling of the Nsibidi against her skin intensified.

"Put it on the soil," Udide said, cool and even. Sunny did so, and the thing began to writhe like a coiled snake. It kept its infinity loop shape as it rolled, smooth like water, toward Udide. It wrapped around one of her legs and attached itself like a leg band. Its glow drained from it, returning to its usual crystal-white. "Tell the others to *never* speak my name again . . . unless they are ready for my answer."

"And you are satisfied?" Sunny pushed herself to ask. This needed to officially be over.

"I am satisfied, Sunny Anyanwu Nwazue."

Sunny cut Chichi free of the webbing with her juju knife. As Chichi scrambled back, she looked to Udide and asked, "Please, Udide *Okwanka*, will you bring the Nimm queen back?"

"That was . . . fake news. Mere incentive," Udide said, her hairs vibrating with mischief.

"Are you fucking kidding me?" Sunny heard Chichi mutter.

Sunny elbowed her to shut up. "Okay," Sunny said. She took a deep breath, closing her eyes. She slowly opened them. "Okay." The image of the Nimm queen being crushed in the baobab tree had never left Sunny. She was glad it was not real. "That is good," she said. She patted her chest as she belched; it tasted like seawater.

Udide wriggled her mighty mandibles as she looked at Sunny. "I will be watching," Udide said. She turned to Chichi. "Your Nimm warrior is a fast thinker. You are lucky." She paused. "Greet your mother for me."

She started to turn away from them when Sunny suddenly said, "W-wait! I have a request . . . well, a question . . . something."

"Sunny," Chichi said under her breath. "Let us just get out of here."

But Sunny shook her head. "You are the Great Weaver of Worlds. There is a virus out there. It's not bad yet, but they're saying it will be. Can you weave it away?" Sunny paused and then said what she'd been wondering. "Is that why you needed your ghazal back so soon?" She held her breath.

Udide stared at Sunny for several moments. "*That* is none of my business," she said. "Humanity will see this through, or it will not. Still . . . it's good that I now have all my tools." She retreated from them.

"You think the virus is as bad as they say?" Sunny asked, rubbing her belly as she watched Udide leave. She belched again and felt a little better.

"Yeah. My mom says some older Leopard People have already died from it in China and now Italy and Algeria. It's coming."

Udide scrambled to the dead palm tree and used one of her forelegs to scratch symbols into its trunk that looked something like: ⟨⟩⫰⫰⫰⫰⫰⫰⫰⫰⫰⫰⫰⫰⫰⫰

The moment she stopped, the dead tree began to fall. Sunny and Chichi made a run for it. Its crash into the cluster of trees was a quiet *crunch*. They were near Sunny's house when they turned back. When the dust settled, Udide was gone.

ﱞ ﱞ ﱞ ﱞ

In the early morning, Sunny got dressed and took her soccer ball with her. She slipped out the back of the house, and without a glance toward where the dead palm tree had fallen, she made for the road. It was eerily empty, but today it wasn't because of protests, it was because the country was on lockdown to help prevent the spread of the deadly virus. She'd even heard that the police were out patrolling, making sure people were . . . cooperating. As soon as she could, she took to the side road, then the path behind the school. She could have glided, but she wanted the fresh air. After all that had happened, being outside in the heat and sunshine and quiet was soothing.

When she stepped onto the soccer field, she relaxed. She walked to the center, her sandals crunching on the dry grass. As she walked, she let herself slip, and the dry grass mixed with the bright green wavery grasses of the wilderness. Anyanwu was draped in light with her tribal wooden spirit face of the sun. They sat down across from each other and Sunny rolled her soccer ball to Anyanwu. Anyanwu took it and rolled it back.

"I'm sorry," Sunny said after they'd rolled the ball back and forth for several minutes. Anyanwu said nothing. She rolled the ball to Sunny. She expected Sunny to do the talking, so Sunny did. "I've really thought it through. That's why

I'm sorry. I couldn't have known, but that doesn't matter. I can't imagine what it's been like for you."

Anyanwu rolled the ball to her harder than normal and Sunny caught it. She placed it in her lap. "We've all been treating you like . . . like a type of mother, a mother who is genius-level amazing and births a child . . . and then everyone expects her to step away from her genius . . . to come down and nurture her baby, to make herself less, so her baby can understand. But that's not right; amazing mothers should continue being amazing . . . and you're not my mother, you are *me*." She pressed her hand to her chest. "And I am you." She paused, looking hard at Anyanwu. "I would have been angry, and I would have kept walking away, too. But you also kept coming back. Thank you for that."

Anyanwu responded aloud and Sunny smiled at this acknowledgment. "Because I am you, Sunny," she said. "And you are right. You all—you, Sugar Cream, Sasha, Chichi, Orlu, Anatov, even the Mami Wata oracle Bola—you've all viewed me as the one who must come down to you. But it is YOU who must come UP to meet ME."

Sunny nodded. "I am a free agent, yet within a year, I had to face Ekwensu. Then again in Osisi. Udide knows me on a first-name basis. I am a Nimm warrior. Mami Wata herself has given me a gift. I have broken kola with Chukwu. Come to know the wilderness well, stopped time . . ."

"And you looked a masquerade in its eyes, its soul," Anyanwu said. "And you did not turn away; you stole its purse."

They gazed at each other. Sunny could feel it. In her mind, since leaving the Power House, she'd started referring to the feeling as "a glow-up." She'd done all those amazing things, sometimes by accident, in a panic, out of desperation, or while being courageous . . . but she'd done them. However, it was all aligned now. Solid. Clear. Strong.

"You have come up to meet me," Anyanwu said. "Ajo-fia helped you feel it, to understand." She glowed so brightly that Sunny could see nothing but light. Sunny shut her eyes, basking in her glow. They would be more comfortable now.

"I know we are called free agent and doubled," Sunny said. She pushed up her glasses. "But we will name ourselves now."

Anyanwu smiled.

24

THE ROAD

"That's quite a journey," Sugar Cream said, taking a sip of her creamy coffee. She scowled at it and then added yet another spoonful of sugar. She stirred it in. "You were lucky Udide didn't rewrite you into something awful when you said no to her. She's known for doing that."

Sunny pursed her lips. At the time, she hadn't really considered this possibility.

"The Road is a wild, wild place," Sugar Cream said. "And Ginen . . . that is a discussion for another day. You continue to surprise me, Sunny. I'm proud of you. Learning so much." She stood up, and Sunny stood up, too. "Are you ready to test for *Mbawkwa*, the second level of Leopardom?"

Sunny nodded. She was wearing old jeans, old sneakers,

no earrings, and Chichi's Joan Jett T-shirt for good luck.

"Many pass this, but many do not."

"I know."

"To fail can be painful."

"I know."

"I'm not sure if you are ready."

"I understand."

"Everyone meets someone, and you may not like who you meet."

"Okay."

Sugar Cream nodded, picking up her wooden cane. "Let's go then, my student."

It had only been days since they'd returned the ghazal to Udide. Already, several things had happened. Sasha had traveled by funky train with Orlu to Abuja to buy a new juju knife since Sasha couldn't travel to the United States due to the lockdown. They'd had to wear masks the entire way and Sasha had hated this intensely. Sunny had decided to stay home and be with her family more. Chichi also opted out to spend more time with her mother at the library. And the nationwide lockdown and concern over this deadly new virus was causing people to cancel meetings and stay away from each other. Things were getting *weird*. And so Sunny knew now was the best time.

"Where are we going?" Sunny asked as they left the Obi Library.

Sugar Cream walked fast but bent to the side and slightly

forward. Her pace matched Sunny's long-legged gait. "The Leopard Knocks Sacred Grove," she said.

The Sacred Grove ran along the river just south of the tree bridge into Leopard Knocks. Sunny had never gone to see it for two reasons: the first was that being close to the river beast in any way was something she avoided when she could, and the second was that if you were under the age of forty, you weren't allowed there . . . except for level tests apparently. They walked along the path beside the river, Sugar Cream on the side closest to it.

It rushed energetically beside them, the churning waters white with foam and bubbles. If the river beast was there, Sunny certainly wouldn't be able to see it before it attacked. The trees and bushes here grew wild and high. Even the mosquitos were more aggressive here. She brought out her juju knife to work the repelling juju, but Sugar Cream caught her arm. "Not here. In the Sacred Grove, if they want your blood, they will have it."

As if it had been waiting for permission, Sunny felt a mosquito bite her arm. They turned and stepped onto a narrow path.

"Many have left behind the beautiful paths of the village," Sugar Cream said. "They used to be graced with palm trees, cassava fields, and pink-tipped pineapple bushes. Most people forget. Leopard People do not. We remember. Those of us who climb levels, we have the strongest memories of all.

We preserve, we work, we create, we birth that which keeps the future alive."

The path ended at a tiny house in the middle of the forest. A shrine. It was made of rose-colored stone with a pointed thatch roof. Its walls were painted with white swirls and squiggles. "Why are you here, Sunny?" Sugar Cream said, turning to face her.

"To pass to the next level of Leopardom, *Mbawkwa*."

Sugar Cream motioned for Sunny to come closer. She was holding a small jar into which she dipped a finger. It came out red. "Camwood dye," she said as she used it to mark Sunny's forehead. It had an earthy, woody smell that wasn't unpleasant. "My best student," Sugar Cream said, stepping back, gazing at her. She touched Sunny's cheek, and Sunny, for the first time, felt totally unsure.

Stop it, Anyanwu said. But Sunny couldn't help it.

"First you will fight," Sugar Cream said. "Bring out your juju knife, Sunny."

Sunny did so, looking around. "Fight whom?"

She felt Anyanwu step out of her, but she didn't go anywhere. *Oh, Sunny*, Anyanwu said. *This place is full.* Sunny nodded and was relieved when Anyanwu joined back with her. Sugar Cream was stepping away from her now. Then a shadow moved in front of her. Sunny brought her juju knife up just as something came at her. She relaxed when she saw that it was a *tungwa*, and punched it instead. It exploded with a *PAFF!* Tufts of black hair bounced against her face, and what sounded like a thousand white teeth clattered to the stone all around her. She stumbled toward the entrance to the shrine.

"You are not ready," a woman's voice said.

Sunny did a fast flourish, grasped the cool juju bag that she caught. She was about to throw it at the shadow before her, but instead, she waited. The shadow was going to zip to the side. She knew this feeling of intuition. Here she was on the soccer field again. She threw it to the right just as the shadow moved into the spot.

PHOOM! FLASH!

"Goooooooal!" Sunny shouted, not knowing why.

"No." The words were spoken in a whisper like a knife. Then *THOOM!* She saw it just before it smashed into her head. It looked like a soccer ball, but it hit like a garbage bag full of hot water. Every part of her felt like it was scalding. And there were the drums she'd heard with Sasha, Chichi, and Orlu. They were low, the energetic beat of talking drums. Then there was the occasional *THOOM!* that shook everything, including her brain. She stumbled back and fell to the ground at the shrine's doorway, not knowing if she was wet or on fire.

THOOM! Something pulled her down, pinning her neck to the ground. She struggled, and suddenly her ankles, thighs, wrists, elbows, and chest were pinned. Someone was laughing. Someone was crying. And someone said, "Come on, then." All to the beat of the talking drums.

THOOM! The force was pulling her so roughly now that it hurt. The ground was hard and unyielding. Sunny screamed, but the pulling didn't let up. She was sinking, slowly.

THOOM! The ground was breaking up. Deeper she went. Into the sweet-smelling, churning earth. Her mouth filled with earth. She couldn't scream! The talking drums seemed to be right beside her ears, following her on her journey. The earth was pushing its way down her throat, pulling up her eyelids, scratching her eyeballs, grating her clothes away, and pressing at her skin.

THOOM! She broke through something and the falling grew faster, easier. Now the dirt was finer. She held her breath. Then she fell through and landed hard. The drumming stopped. Everything stopped. She lay there, curled tight. She could feel her clothes. Her jeans were in tatters around her legs, her Joan Jett T-shirt ripped, her sneakers gone. She still had her juju knife. She clutched it to her chest.

When nothing came to fight her, kill her, eat her, she uncurled herself. She heard only the wind. Slowly, she opened her eyes to near pitch blackness. She was inside. She knew this because the cave exit was not far from her, only a few yards that way. She pressed at her arms, sore and in some spots bruised. The elbow the *chittim* had hit was numb again. Her legs were also bruised. Her face felt raw. She stood up. She was okay.

She flexed her bicep. "How does the proverb go?" she asked herself. She remembered and said it in Igbo—her grandfather would have been proud of that. "*Oku a gunyere nwata n'aka anaghi ahu ya*," she said, brushing herself off. "The fire that is intentionally given to a child does not hurt him . . . her, me. You have sent me here, so here I am."

Sunny stepped out of the cave into the cool of the desert at night. The sky was bright with stars, even the filmy specter of the Milky Way. As far as her eye could see to the right, left, and beyond was black. But directly ahead of her was the bright light of a fire. When she saw the five figures who were gathered around the fire, she gasped. Two had smoke dribbling from their heads, one had four faces, all were over ten feet tall. She reached a sweaty hand into her pocket and brought out the tiny crystal *chittim* that had fallen for her back in the Power House.

She grasped it in her hand and confidently walked toward the fire.

ACKNOWLEDGMENTS

It was such a joy to jump back into this world with these characters, with all the spirits and creatures, this mystical part of Nigeria. Once I started writing *Akata Woman*, the story flowed like a river that knows it's also a road.

I'd like to thank my daughter, Anyaugo, for the title of this book, *Akata Woman*. Thank you to Taofik Yusuf for his insight into the deeper meaning of the Danafojura masquerade. Thanks to Igbo language expert Yvonne Chiọma Mbanefo for her help with the Igbo. I'd like to thank my editor Jenny Bak for her excellent insight. Thanks to the artist wizard known as Greg Ruth for yet another epic rendering of Sunny. Greg and I talk in-depth before each book cover illustration, so the results you see truly carry the essence of the character. Many thanks to my cat Periwinkle Chukwu for keeping me while I was writing this and also making sure I constantly felt like something creepy was in the room with us (cats truly do see things we humans cannot).

Lastly, I'd like to thank the terrible, no good, very bad virus known as COVID-19. Without all the *wahala* it caused, without the world going on lockdown, I would not have finished this novel this soon. Working on *Akata Woman* helped me through those scary months of 2020; I got to travel with Sunny, Chichi, Sasha, and Orlu into worlds within worlds when the world wasn't able to go anywhere.

NSIBIDI FOR "COVID"